A
SPOKE
IN THE
WHEEL

Amita Kanekar lives in Mumbai, where she teaches
architectural history and comparative mythology. This is her
first novel.

MBD / History

'The excellent young man, Devadinna... loved Sutanuka, the slave-girl of the god.'

— Inscription on the wall of a cave at Ramgarh in the Vindhya hills, dating to not long after Ashoka, according to Prof. A L Basham, and quoted by him in his book, *The Wonder that was India*, 1967.

A NOVEL ABOUT
THE BUDDHA

A
SPOKE
IN THE
WHEEL

AMITA KANEKAR

HarperCollins *Publishers* India
a joint venture with

New Delhi

First published in India in 2005 by
HarperCollins *Publishers* India
a joint venture with
The India Today Group

HarperCollins *Publishers*
1A Hamilton House Connaught Place, New Delhi 110001, India
77-85 Fulham Palace Road, London W6 8JB, United Kingdom
Hazelton Lanes, 55 Avenue Road, Suite 2900, Toronto, Ontario M5R 3L2
and 1995 Markham Road, Scarborough, Ontario M1B 5M8, Canada
25 Ryde Road, Pymble, Sydney, NSW 2073, Australia
31 View Road, Glenfield, Auckland 10, New Zealand
10 East 53rd Street, New York NY 10022, USA

Typeset in 10.5/13 Bembo
Atelier Typecraft

Printed and bound at
Thomson Press (India) Ltd.

Acknowledgements

The interpretation of the Buddha's enlightenment is completely owed to Iqbal Singh's *Gautama Buddha*; I read and reread this absolutely lyrical rendering of the Buddha's message in the course of this project, and warmly recommend it to all those interested in the Buddha as well as those who just love great writing. The sources for the Buddha legend include the writings of A.L. Basham, Joseph Campbell, Edward Conze, T.W. Rhys Davids, C.A.F. Rhys Davids, Noble Ross Reat, D.D. Kosambi and probably many others read much earlier. The politics, economics, society and administration of both the Buddha's and Ashoka's time would have been impossible to understand without the writings of Romila Thapar, A.L. Basham, R.S. Sharma, Uma Chakraborty, Suvira Jaiswal, Richard Lannoy, A.K. Warder, G.S.P. Mishra, Narendra Wagle, Debiprasad Chattopadhyaya and D.D. Kosambi. To the last indeed, I am indebted for opening my eyes to the endless fascination of Indian history. Needless to say, any errors in historicity are my own.

The sentence about mothers warning their children to be still or else, on page 337, is of course inspired by *Sholay*.

I have to thank Parul Kumtha, Chrissie D'Costa and Lancy Fernandes for lots of things in general but specifically here for ploughing through the book when it was still fairly raw and offering criticism and suggestions; Purnima and Yateen Joshi for invaluable support during the research and then the publishing stages; Prof. Kunal Chakraborty of JNU, Delhi, for advice on research, and JNU's Centre for Historical Studies and Library for allowing me to read there; Ritu Menon of *Women Unlimited* for taking the trouble to read and recommend the manuscript of a nobody; Anand Kumtha, Vilma Fernandes, J. Chitra and Jocelyn D'Mello for lots of encouragement always; my students, past and present, for helping me think; my three siblings, Shami, Cheryl and Nissim, for just being there; and, most of all, Medhamami.

KAPILAVASTU

566 BCE

'Dibha, bring my son here....Do you hear me?'
Dibha did not, for she was asleep, squatting on the floor at the foot of the bed.

'Dibha! I want my son!'

The whisper had become shrill. Dibha awoke and jumped up in the same movement: 'Will you eat something, Mistress? There is some sweet mango here – '

'Quiet, fool! Go get him. At once!'

The slave hesitated. The Chief's orders were clear – the child was not to be brought to the sickbed. Even so, defiance was not easy. 'Mistress, wait till you are better....'

Maya rose slightly – 'Are you arguing with me, girl?' – but losing her temper was a luxury she could not afford. She slumped back, eyes squeezed shut in pain, felt her face wiped with a cool cloth and wished for the strength to knock the wretch's hand away. Damn her to the worst of hells! She would have had her head off for such insolence only a few days ago. But now she was helpless.

Maya had just given birth to her first child but instead of the triumph that an Arya mother of a son should feel, the only thing she felt was blood, trickling out of her. The top-three physicians of Kapilavastu visited her morning and night, doing their best with a three-pronged attack of potions, ointments and melodious spells, to no effect. In fact, the trickle had distinctly increased that morning. One of the doctors' assistants, a youth who had trained at Shravasti, believed that the last prescription, a potent brew of milk, dung and dried skin heated up together by the first rays of the sun after a moonless night, was responsible. But the potion was an old and respected one while the assistant was young and full of new ideas; his opinion was undesired, indeed suspect.

The senior-most physician had conveyed a gloomy prognosis to the Chief, as also the interesting vision he had had, of the god of death actually hovering over the sickbed. The family astrologer had read the same forecast from the flight pattern of a flock of pigeons that morning. The household's reaction was stoic. After all, Maya was old, over forty years, too old for a first child.

'Call my husband.... Right now!'

Her husband was Shudodhan, Chief of the Shakyas and the son she yearned to hold would be famous in time as the Buddha. But Maya would not live to see the day. Later on, as the legend of the Buddha grew, people would say that she died in bliss, well-pleased with the treasure she had bequeathed the world. There would even be those who marvelled poetically at her smooth labour and delivery, at the perfect form, blue eyes and golden skin of the newborn, at how the heavens had opened above to send two streams of water, hot and cold, to wash mother and child. Such is the legend and it is a pretty one.

Dibha left the room to stand in the veranda outside though she knew that the Chief was awake. He had given express instructions not to be disturbed. She would have liked to go to the baby's apartment to find her friend, Tara, who was deputed to look after him. But there too the Chief's orders kept her out. Nobody, not even the doctors, were to go from mother to son without purification in between.

Neither house nor town slept that night. Small brushwood fires crackled all over, lighting up the figures of slaves as they swept the streets, sprinkled them with water and festooned them with garlands of marigold and jasmine. The fires seemed to add to the heat. It was the hottest time of the year, the eve of the rains, when the dust rose from the roads and hung still in the air.

It was a Golden Age, the bards would sing later, but those who lived it might have disagreed. Things were changing rapidly; things had never been too secure to begin with. Civilization had come to these lushly forested foothills only a few centuries before, a tenuous thread of cities and ploughed fields and chariot-borne arrogance that held the base of the mighty Himavat and slowly, grimly, battled to expand southwards. New and ambitious nations now straddled the plains all the way south to the Ganga; great new cities drank the water of the cold, fast-flowing, mother-of-all-rivers herself, and looked thoughtfully northwards. Kapilavastu, where Maya had come as a bride more than twenty years ago, was the capital of one of the earliest and most northern republics, or sanghas, as they called themselves. Small in territory, not as rich as the southerners, and constantly at war with their neighbours, the sanghas were independent and fiercely proud of their ancient lineage. But, like the woman raging helplessly on her deathbed, the bells had begun to toll for the land in which she lived.

The child, who would be called a Saviour in the future, could not save either his mother or his motherland.

He was to be named the next day.

Below, in the great reception hall of his ancestral mansion, lit by a wavering fire in the family altar, his father sat cross-checking the arrangements with his young friend Mahanaman and the family priest. The two Shakyarajas were somewhat similar in appearance – tall, muscular, battle-scarred, and unhappy at the moment. Mahanaman's sprawl on the mattress was bored and irritated. He had purchased a pretty new dancing girl the previous week and was eager to get home to her. But here he was, finalizing a ceremony that had been finalized at least five times in the last four days.

Shudodhan hunched heavily on the edge of a stool. 'We have four hundred and ten litres of milk. At dawn another hundred or so will come in from the market. That's enough, right, Kashyap?'

The priest squatting on the floor nodded. 'I think so, my lord. There is as much ghee, I hope?' He was thin, swarthy and blessed with five daughters – which was five more than he had really wanted.

'Nearly 400 litres.'

Kashyap was silent. His eldest had been rejected as a bride that morning, for the third time.

'Enough, isn't it?'

'Oh…yes…. And cattle?' Was there anyone else in Kapilavastu whose daughter had been rejected three times? No, the honour had been reserved for him.

'One prime stud bull, fifty horses, a hundred young bullocks. And two hundred goats. All of my own herd. That's enough, right?'

He would have to offer a bigger dowry, Kashyap thought sadly – 'It's never enough.'

Shudodhan was surprised. 'Well, I suppose I can increase it, but slightly….'

'I mean, it will do. Yes, my lord, I think as far as the sacrifice goes, things are fine.' The worst had been this last time – too dark, the astrologer Asita had explained smugly. When his own son had a misshapen foot, besides being dark enough to be tripped over at night.

The soldier standing at the door intervened hesitantly. 'Sir, about the milk. There was some unhappiness in the market this morning. Over the shortage of milk, I mean. Perhaps we should let tomorrow's be….'

'I can't believe people will grudge me this – ' began Shudodhan.

But Mahanaman scowled. 'I heard of complaints too. Many. Forget the extra milk.'

'Many?' Shudodhan could not afford many. The elections were less than a year away. 'Priest, is what we have enough?'

Kashyap shrugged. 'You said you wanted to make offerings to all the gods, my lord. But if you want to cut down – ?' He would show Asita. He would make him rue the day he refused his girl... but what about her? And the four that followed?

'No, of course not!' He was in his fourth term, Shudodhan reminded himself, he was sure to be elected again. And both his father and grandfather had been Chiefs before him, for many terms each. But both had been celebrated war-heroes, addicted to battle and contemptuous of peace. Shudodhan himself provided less material for the balladeers, for it was not as easy to panegyrize wealth as war, and it was with the former that he had triumphed. He had steered the republic into quieter but more prosperous times, with many former warriors now substantial landlords and entrepreneurs. The slaves were quiet, the peasants were quiet, and the borders were, if not quiet, then further away than they used to be.

But he had his critics.

'Believe me – there were a lot of complaints,' repeated Mahanaman. 'Besides, Gangadhar did all the sacrifices last year for his son, and used barely 200 litres!'

Shudodhan looked at the priest; the latter just looked grave. He would have to seek out some poor country families, he was thinking, they would be grateful for an alliance with the priest of the Chief.

'Mahanaman, the yagna has no formula – it reflects one's need.'

And it was all very well for Mahanaman to argue; he was already the comfortable father of three sons. Shudodhan glanced at Kashyap a second time, then glared, till the priest snapped to attention with a rather vague, 'The signs so far have been mixed.'

It was enough. Shudodhan plunged into gloom. So far almost everything had gone wrong. The child had not been born in Kapilavastu, not in any city nor even a house, but in the open, in a forest on the highway while Maya was on her way to her parents' home for her confinement. She'd travelled in comfort, in a cushioned palanquin carried by the eight best porters among the Chief's slaves, but she'd felt a little uneasy from the start. The party reached the forests outside Devadaha without incident and stopped there at the old temple of Lumbini, site of the consecration ceremonies of all Shakya. Women came rarely nowadays, but Maya was the Chief's wife. The priestesses attended her respectfully as she bathed in the cold green waters of the sacred tank and made the necessary offerings. But her prayers were apparently unheeded. Back on the road the palanquin had just begun moving when she called a halt.

'Put me down,' she insisted, though they were in the middle of the jungle. 'At once! See, this is a sal grove – it is quite safe.' They were indeed surrounded by dense walls of the tall, wavy Shakya totem. Her servants lifted her out of the palanquin and into the cool green gloom where her pains rapidly climaxed and the child was born – the much longed-for male child – but amidst immense confusion, pain and fear.

Maya's blood started to flow then and quite fast, until someone had the idea of staunching it with earth from near an altar in the grove. It did stop temporarily; mother and child were gathered up and rushed home, though after this disastrous beginning, the efforts of the city physicians were hardly needed to seal her fate.

Shudodhan had nearly collapsed when he heard the news. Would this son, for whom he and his wives had struggled so much, survive? The legend would glowingly remember an otherworldly conception, of how one night Maya dreamt of a white elephant who lifted her up and carried her through the heavens to a golden palace on a silver mountain, where, on a beautiful bed, white as milk, he pierced her womb with his tusk and she conceived the Buddha. So easy and beautiful, in a dream, no less. But nobody knew better than Shudodhan the nightmares he and Maya had undergone for this child. She of course had suffered more – even three traumatic miscarriages – but he too had done his bit. Fasting for two days before intercourse, bathing in the ice-cold river at dawn before intercourse, sacrificing continuously from his herds, flocks and slaves before the same, partaking of strange almost inedible foods and abstaining from many normal ones, all for this child. Had he come only to go? Worse, the grove of his birth was no ordinary grove, but a chaitya bhoomi where the heathen worshipped their goddess and her snake consorts – would he carry the curse of the she-devil? And what about his horoscope? Would the astrologers be able to read what the stars intended, after such a messy start? The future looked bleak to Shudodhan.

Mahanaman, meanwhile, went after the brahmin. 'Rubbish, man! Extra is all very well, but more than double?'

Mahanaman had a scar on his forehead that reddened when he lost his temper. Kashyap looked away as he spoke. 'I only advise....'

'And what do you mean by saying that the signs have been mixed? The auguries have been unanimous about the bright future of the child! The only thing that has gone wrong so far is the birth.'

Was anything more required? But all Kashyap said was, 'Whatever my lords decide.'

'No, I have to do all the rituals,' interrupted Shudodhan. 'Perhaps we could get the milk from Devadaha?'

Mahanaman emptied his tumbler of rice beer in one gulp and barked, 'Our enemies are already talking about the herds, Shudodhan! Twenty years ago Shakya lands were white with ranging herds, now they are hardly to be seen – that is what Hemant said at the jyotistoma sacrifice at Silavati. "What is an Arya without his herd?" – he asked in his loud ugly voice! A lack of milk would strengthen the point! And don't forget, the Sabha is meeting only three days hence!'

Shudodhan began to regret asking his friend over. Mahanaman belonged to a family of old Vedic priests and was nearly an atheist as a result. His family no longer presided over rituals themselves but at the same time considered the brahmins a very shoddy substitute. In fact they, like most Shakyas and Shudodhan too in calmer moments, believed that it was the kshatriyas who had taught the secrets of the yagna to the lowly brahmins when they themselves became busy with the responsibility of government. The brahmins laughed at the idea, but privately.

Mahanaman had not finished. 'In fact, Shudodhan, I wanted to tell you – you have to stop bunking the Sagiti. Hemant calls every absence of yours an insult to the republic!'

The Sagiti was the Shakya communal dining system, a once-in-a-fortnight ritual. Shudodhan was embarrassed. 'It's just that I have been fasting....' He knew Mahanaman considered fasting an un-Arya practice.

'Well – come and do it there!'

'All right, all right! Priest – can we find a substitute for the milk? Priest!'

Kashyap put his daughter hurriedly to one side. And hit upon a happy solution immediately. 'Gold, Aryaputra. Only gold can be the substitute, if any.'

'Into the fire?'

'No! To individual brahmins.'

'How much?'

The priest stared thoughtfully at the chunky yellow ropes resting on the Chief's chest. 'One coin for every five litres should do.'

It was Mahanaman's turn to forget his dancer; it was about a hundred times the market rate. But Shudodhan ignored his gasp. 'Fine. You select the brahmins. Have you checked the daana for the astrologer? Fifty cows and fifty gold coins.'

'Twenty's enough.' Asita was the astrologer.

'Only twenty? No, I'd rather stay with fifty. Well, that's all, I think.

The priest bowed and left and and Mahanaman exploded: 'Fifty cows for the astrologer, Shudodhan? And that jackal Kashyap will get double, as usual? Are you in your right mind?'

'Just cautious, that's all. I want the blessings of all the brahmins for my son. You know where he was born. The priests understand Naga magic and curses – '

'Pah! What's there to understand in that barbaric bullshit? The only thing those charlatans understand is how to use their so-called knowledge for the most foul ends, from selling divine salvation to sleeping with – '

'I know all that.'

'And they know you!' Mahanaman gave up and rose. 'Anyway, I'm a little tired… and there's not much time for the morning….'

Shudodhan knew his friend too. 'Exactly. So why don't you forget your plans for tonight?'

'Well….'

'I'm going out of my mind here, but all you can think about is some whore!'

'All right, all right!' Mahanaman flopped down heavily. 'But you have to show more spine with those rogues! Besides, you're not the Raja of Kosala to sacrifice 200 head of cattle on one day. You'll pauperize yourself!'

'Don't compare me to Kosala. He gives 500 at minor yagnas, haven't you heard? For a son he would give 10,000!'

Mahanaman grinned. 'His brahmins are running rings around him.'

Shakya sentiments about the southern kingdoms were very mixed. On the one hand, they held them in ritual contempt, as they did all non-Shakyas. The Shakyas considered themselves Arya kshatriyas and also Suryavanshis, tracing their bloodline all the way back to mighty Aditya, the sun of the midday sky, or rather to two eggs hatched by that great burning orb. The eggs comprised the blood and sperm of their ancestor Gautama, whose name then was taken by the chief gotra of the tribe. It was a bizarre origin by most standards, but they were proud of it and what's more, had gone to war many times to avenge slurs on it. Those kingdoms on the Ganga might be rich, said the Shakyas, but they were polluted places where people did not even know their own ancestors. Every Shakya bore the title of raja; each one could trace a pure lineage back at least ten generations. To what could the solitary raja who ruled Kosala trace himself? To nowhere and nothing – he was a mongrel cur, with perhaps some slight Arya blood (so he claimed) mixed with much low-caste and even Naga stock. Filthy, barbaric, outcaste, half-breeds, sneered the Shakyas.

But it was a contempt mixed with fear.

For Kosala was rich. And strong. And very ambitious. The Shakyas were warriors, born of the mighty arms of Brahma, born to rule. How could such a destiny, written in the stars and sanctioned by all scriptures, ever be challenged? Yet they expected a challenge. Many Shakyas were worried about the future. Some even accused Shudodhan of not being worried enough. With some justification. For Shudodhan, Kosala was one of many dangers.

'I wish the Sabha meeting could be put off. Hemant has really publicized this issue of Kosala. Did you hear – he wants to propose an emergency meeting of the whole Gana Samiti! A thing nobody has seen since my father's day!'

'He's just trying to rouse the rabble against you – the last thing he wants is to obey them!'

'Not so loud!' The rabble was the supposed ruler of the republic, making up most of the Gana Samiti, the Shakya assembly. But the real ruler was the Sabha, the elected council which tended to comprise the same rich, aristocratic and powerful families, respected and re-elected as much for their blue blood as for their ability to provide the army with horses, war-chariots and the odd elephant; the commoners provided the infantry. But now even the oligarchs of the Sabha were being sidelined – by the Chief – and some didn't like it.

'The milk would have been a good issue for those back-biting whiners.' Shudodhan was bitter. 'They just hate me. When the truth is that I've brought wealth and peace to the Sangha.'

His critics pointed out that he was among the wealthiest. Kapilavastu was now an important halt on the international highway connecting the port of Champa in the far east to Takshashila on the Sindhu to the northwest. Three years ago the leading guilds of Kosalan merchants had requested the Shakyas to allow through traffic in return for an annual payment. Shudodhan acceded, to the horror of the conservatives. Nor did he ask them for their opinion.

He just issued a proclamation in which he also warned all Shakyas situated near the highway who had always looked upon foreign merchants as legitimate prey, to back off. Vast numbers of caravans began to pass through the republic, halting to rest and replenish at Kapilavastu, and the Chief's popularity soared among the 'rabble' who invested in new lodging, boarding, brothels and game-houses for the moneyed visitors.

But his critics did not give up. The barbarians were taking over, they said, and were being invited to do so! If the Shakyas wished to save themselves, the only way was to rejuvenate the republic and all its ancient traditions. It was the last thing Shudodhan was interested in. Sabha meetings were thus often fractious affairs. Shudodhan's solution was to call fewer meetings.

'But listen, Mahanaman. About tomorrow. The Licchavis are likely to send an envoy for the function, to broach the confederation idea again. I'm really worried that if we let things slip, if they get a chance to confer with Hemant's lot, we might just be swept into this confederation, under the leadership of the Licchavis!'

'But let's not refuse too fast. Let's hear them out and talk delay.'

'You handle it.' Shudodhan walked to the windows and stared out.

Tomorrow was close. The eastern mountains were already outlined in the dull glow of the imminent day. Streams of greyness were trickling through the black, revealing the edges of the forested hills, then the river, then the figures of slaves heading home. They were hurrying – it was inauspicious for the Shakyas to set eyes on them early in the morning, and therefore inauspicious for themselves; all the more on such an auspicious day.

Thanks to their efforts the city looked festive. Kapilavastu, Kapila's residence, the capital of the republic, was a small place whose sole claim to fame before this baby grew to manhood was that about a hundred years ago it had been the home of the sage Kapila, he of the strange ideas of creation. According to him, or rather those who spoke about him nowadays, the universe and everything within was a simple duality, the product of the constant interaction of two categories – purusha, the principle or soul, which was male, and prakriti, the substratum or matter, which was female. Kapila's ideas were reviled by his fellow Shakyas and their brahmins, and not surprisingly, for he also ridiculed the exalted position of the one and the claim to represent the gods of the other. But he became famous, or infamous depending on your point of view, and his hometown came to be known after him.

His vastu was an elegant little township, nestled in a wide curve of the Rapti and looking inwards, as did its inhabitants. Shudodhan could just make out the shadowy bulk of the neighbouring Moat Hall, the venerated assembly hall and law-court of the republic; he bowed his head for a moment in respect. In front of it was the huge field of public rituals and army drills, around it all the patrician mansions. Immediately outside this walled centre was Kapilavastu's new hub, the market, closely packed about by hostelries, workshops and the homes of commoners.

He could see nothing beyond, nor was there anything worth seeing in the rough and smoky city-fringe, just workshops and the humble wattle-and-daub residences of foreign merchants and workers, among them the despised but invaluable Naga iron-makers – invaluable according to Shudodhan, that is. He believed that the black shiny metal was the weapon of the future, not least because Kosala was experimenting a lot with it. Most Shakyas disagreed. To even compare that Naga-metal to bronze, the gift of the sun, weapon of the Aryas since the beginning of time, was unthinkable. Shudodhan's interest was actually another weapon against himself in the conservative arsenal.

Beyond the workshops were the rings of wall and moat, and right outside, silhouetted against the dark jungle and watched hungrily by its denizens, the last and most offensive layer – of outcaste huts. 'Dung-hills' the Shakya called them.

Everything went off well the next day. The mistimed and misplaced birth seemed to take no toll on the child and the astrologer was ready at the crack of dawn, horoscope in hand. But there were offerings to be made first. A huge altar was waiting on the Moat Hall field. At dawn the fire was lit and a seemingly unending stream of animals rolled up to be slaughtered, garlands of red flowers around every neck. Among them was a great humped black bull with long angry horns, raised especially for such an occasion. Shudodhan had spent many pleasant moments exulting over this beast as it grew to magnificent adulthood on his estate, and he immediately recognized the confused terror in its bellow. His eyes misted suddenly; he could hardly see as it was tied to the stake. Then he felt ashamed and stared unflinchingly as the shining blade rose and fell, again and again, till the great neck gave way.

Earlier, just before dawn, another sacrifice, short but even richer, had taken place on the river bank. The offering was a slave boy, a worker in the city granaries, where he had been caught stealing twice. The first time he had got away with a whipping after he explained that his mother was ill. He could not use the excuse the second time for his mother was dead. He was asked whether he had wanted the grain to offer his gods – the Shakyas did not like to mess with the devilish Naga gods. But he said that he wanted to eat it himself, which was intolerable.

Many Shakyas did not subscribe to human sacrifice any more; in fact some called it a practice of the jungle-folk. But those wise in ancient lore said it was a powerful offering, one that no god could refuse, so a balance was maintained by treating every execution as sacrifice. Shudodhan however wanted the best for his son, and the best was obviously a personal offering. But he was uncomfortable, with the strange quiet, the stranger priest – an expert in these matters according to Kashyap – and his unintelligible mantras. He irritably refused the dagger offered by the expert and closed his eyes as it swept the boy's throat, just above the red garland.

'Take this offering, give me my heir,' he prayed, and opened his eyes straight into the boy's hate-filled gaze. His head lay on the stone pavement. Shudodhan shivered. The expert anointed his forehead with a mark of blood and he walked home feeling ill.

The last sacrifice was grander, longer, noisier and more conventional. It was the biggest ever for a private yagna and everybody began to wilt almost as soon as the ceremony began, the first being Shudodhan's second wife, Prajapati, Maya's younger sister, who was weighed down under all the jewellery she owned.

Columns of hot smoke curled languorously around the gathering; the sun beat down competitively; the priests scurried around making worried adjustments, advising last-minute changes, painfully prolonging every ritual. The lowing of the beasts and the mingled odours of blood, ghee, smoke and sweat were almost overpowering on the field, nauseating even in the town, where all the lowborn, from rich traders to slave sweepers, remained quietly indoors to prevent any ill-luck to the proceedings. Shudodhan was happy.

Until the arrival of two guests. The first was a Licchaviraja who had come with the secret proposal that was no longer secret – of building a confederation of republics against Kosala. He was warmly welcomed, especially by Mahanaman and Hemant, who retired to the edge of the field to hear him out. Hemant was enthusiastic, as was Mahanaman, but he cautioned against any rush. The people would have to be prepared, the terms carefully worked out. Where would the office-bearers meet? What would the security be? The Shakyas would find it difficult to trust the Koliyas or the Mallas, their neighbours and foes for longer than anyone could remember. Or the Licchavis, he added but silently. His caution could not be faulted. The republics all shared a bitter past of warfare over land, livestock and water that was not yet history.

If the reception for the Licchavi was secretly mixed though seemingly cordial, the other guest was greeted with open consternation. For he was Bundala Karayana, the general of the

Kosalan army. That Kosala should send an envoy was amazing, the choice was downright alarming. He had come to bless the child on behalf of his king, he explained; nobody believed him.

The Licchaviraja left in a huff almost immediately. The Shakyas expected Karayana to leave soon too, especially as most of them did not bother to greet him. But Karayana was unhurried. He sat through the sacrifice and the naming ceremony as well. He claimed to be fasting and thus avoided any insult to himself at the mid-day meal. The Shakyas for their part did not urge either guest to eat with them, for they never ate in the company of lowborn. The Licchavis also considered themselves kshatriyas, as did the Mallas and the Koliyas, but there are grades and sub-grades within the varna, obvious to anyone hunting for them. And there was nothing lower than the Kosalans. Except perhaps someone like Karayana. The general was a Malla who had heinously transferred his loyalty to Kosala, polluted himself beyond redemption, and received rich rewards for it.

With many subtle political messages, real and imaginary, shooting about over him, the newborn was forgotten. Only in the afternoon, when Shudodhan was seated in front of his family altar to hear the horoscope, did his mind come back to his son. 'Agni, younger brother of Aditya,' intoned Kashyap the priest to the fire with the customary gloom plus a little, for seated next to him was Asita, the astrologer. The fire did not respond noticeably to his grandiose address, and with good reason. Though the fire in the Chief's altar was always hailed as the same undying one brought by his ancestors all the way from the sun of the midday sky, it was Kashyap himself who had lit this one, as he always did whenever it chanced to die out.

The fire was impassive but the infant started howling, perhaps to remind everyone that he existed. Shudodhan recovered some of his cheer. Recent times had been hard on him, what with Kosala looming on the horizon and the conservatives constantly snapping at his heels at home. And it had begun to look as though he would go to his funeral pyre without a son to light it and ensure his salvation in the hereafter. But gazing down at the purple-faced howler on his lap, the future suddenly looked fabulous. He had a son! Two wives and several concubines later, Shudodhan had obtained his passage to the golden heaven of Varuna.

Then his gaze fell again on the large figure of Karayana. When was he going to ask for a few minutes aside, to say whatever he had come to say? Or perhaps there was no message, perhaps this was some kind of spying visit? But what could Karayana achieve in the open? Wait, wait... what of his charioteer? Where was he? Was he being watched? The fire cast a heavy sandal-scented haze over the hall, through which Shudodhan struggled to keep his eyes on the Kosalan conspiracy.

Asita had the child's horoscope ready but was waiting for the right moment, when the most favourable planets were in the most favourable position. When it came, he had to clear his throat with elephantine thoroughness to get his Chief's attention. He cleared it again to silence the room, poured some more libations into the fire, and having obtained the required decorum among flames and men, told them what the stars ordained. It was as expected. A great chief, an indomitable war-hero, nemesis of foes, epitome of dharma, multiplier of herds.

He was named Siddarth, the One who has Achieved his Ambitions. This name was for common use. His real one was whispered by the priest into his father's ear, and into his own by the latter. The Shakyas gave a lot of importance to the name, believing that the correctly chosen one nurtured the seeds of an individual's potential and made him flower. In fact, they gave the name so much importance that they wound up terrified of it, believing that to know a person's name was to have power over his life. As a result all Shakyas had two names, one for use, and the other, the real one, known to only the person himself, his parents and his priest, and never mentioned once the naming ceremony was done.

Shudodhan could have testified later to the absurdity of the whole scheme, for he was never able to control his son's life, despite knowledge of his real name, and not for want of trying.

The astrologer Asita received his gold and cattle and left happy. Karayana left soon after too, without saying anything at all, and Shudodhan decided to interpret the visit as a sign that Kosala wanted to be friends. It was, he announced, the first political triumph of his son, the future super-chief.

Luckily for Asita, he did not live to see his prediction repudiated. And the later legend either ignored his mistake or more frequently, with the wisdom of hindsight and the noble desire to protect the institution of astrology, corrected it. If not the greatest of chiefs, the child would be the greatest of sages, so saying which Asita is said to have wept – not, as might be assumed, for having forfeited his reward, the Shakyas not being fans of sagehood at all – but in the knowledge that he would not live to hear the sage himself.

Gold was also gifted to thirty other brahmins, all, coincidently, of humble background and the fathers of marriageable lads.

Shudodhan had his wish. The Sabha meeting was cancelled in deference to Maya who died two days after her child was named, without seeing either him or her husband. Despite the overpowering heat, all the great Shakya families were represented at her funeral ghat, for she had died a married woman and the mother of a chief. For a daughter of the Aryas, there was no greater fulfilment. Some rajas even blessed their own daughters that they might enjoy Maya's good fortune. The daughters kept their own counsel.

Her son did not notice her absence. In fact he had not noticed her presence once he had fought his way out of her womb; he had spent nearly all his time secure in the crook of his nurse's arm. But the nurse, Tara, was not oblivious to the tragedy of a mother's loss. She had lost her own when a child, after a failed slave-break from Kapilavastu. Tara could not remember her mother clearly. Nor her father, who had been executed with all the men in the group, all garlanded with the same pretty red flowers. Tara's memories were vague but painful, of ugly violence and sudden orphanhood. It was the ugliness that tormented her rather than the deaths, because her people saw death as part of life; their supreme divinity was the earth mother who controlled both in a continuous cycle. The dead were not cremated but buried, to sleep for a while in the womb of the earth and then return. In the case of important people like witches and chiefs, the graves were marked by sacred mounds called chaityas. There were many chaityas in the Shakya realm, but the most revered was the one at Lumbini where her charge had been born.

Now she took him up to the roof of his father's house, from where the cremation-ground could just be seen. The trees hid the goings-on, till the pyre was lit. Then a nervous little feather of smoke rose, thickened and swirled around before drifting away reluctantly, away from the town, away from the child. Tara joined his palms within hers in a final salute to the dead. He slept on comfortably.

MAHESHWAR

256 BCE

We don't know who first told the story of the Buddha's life, or rather the stories, for there are many. They range from simple accounts of a different kind of man, to wonderful sagas of a god who lived among men. There are no records either of those who first started putting the stories down in writing, nobody who remembers, for example, that the above version was begun by Upali, a monk at the small monastery of Maheshwar on the Narmada, during the rule of one of the strangest kings the world has ever seen. Ashoka, or the Beloved of the Gods as he styled himself, practically commissioned the story from Upali. By then the Buddha had been dead for nearly 250 years. But the accounts of his life and teachings had been memorized in verse by generations of his followers, which was why Upali's colleagues found it surprising, even appalling, that he did almost nothing for nearly a year after the royal command. He was mulling over it, he explained. Lazing is more accurate, said his colleagues among themselves. Let us hope he does not have to pay for his mulling, they added. Let us hope *we* do not have to pay for his mulling, they added further.

'Enough for today, Ananda. But just imagine – the mother never saw her child, for whom she had lived her life!'

His student rose and stretched. His hand ached from dipping the reed quill and scratching it against the sheet. The palm leaf was slightly rough; it required care to pull strokes across the grainy surface without breaking the nib. He would never admit his tiredness however, for he was one of the few novices in the monastery who had mastered the skill of writing. Upali had taught him.

'But she attained ever-lasting heaven, didn't she, Master? And besides, didn't the Buddha visit her many times in heaven later on?'

'Ananda – !' Upali had been feeling well pleased with his first finished chapter. It had, he felt, just the right mix of politics and pathos. Perhaps it was a little too long, as Thera Harsha had opined. Harsha had said other things as well, about disrespect and sarcasm and so on, which Upali preferred to forget. But it looked so final and presentable, copied out in black ink and Ananda's beautiful long-hand. In fact, he had been feeling very proud of his student that afternoon. But he forgot all that now. 'Where do you hear such things?'

'At the class conducted yesterday by Thera Mohan.'

'Do you know any person who has seen heaven, Ananda?' The boy knew many, he realized. 'Rather, have you? Then how do you know that it even exists, let alone that the Buddha visited it? The Buddha and his mother were ordinary people, like you and me!'

How do you know, Ananda's scowl asked silently. Just because *you* have not seen heaven? But they had discussed such issues many times before; he knew it was futile to try to change his stubborn teacher's mind.

Upali saw the look and found himself thinking similarly about his student. But he had a responsibility to Ananda and decided to give it another shot. 'Well, maybe not just like you and me. The Shakyamuni was an extraordinary man, but a man. You shouldn't believe everything people say. I don't know whether even the dead go to such a place as heaven. Nobody has come back from there and told us. Nobody reliable, at least. Some philosophers like the Lokayats held that nothing remains after death. Nothing.'

Ananda decided he could not give up on Upali either. 'Thera Harsha speaks of rebirth. Nirvana is freedom from rebirth, he says.'

Harsha was the head of the monastery. Upali sighed. 'All I'm saying is that there is no *proof*. All that we know for sure is that a dead person's body becomes nothing very fast.'

'What about Santosh? He's exactly like his dead uncle, isn't he? He looks like him, speaks like him, even likes the same food! He is even beginning to remember his past life.'

Remembering past lives and visiting heaven are two different things, thought Upali irritatedly, though he had no sympathy with the Santosh story either. He glared at his disciple who glared back, eyeball to eyeball. They were equal in height now, but, as Upali, thinner, darker and slightly hunched realized, he would soon be the shorter. 'That is also just a belief, and a superstitious one, according to me. And I think it's better to sit down while arguing – to maintain the decorum of debate, you know.' He wrapped his cotton shawl around his shoulders. It was late September and the evenings were cool and windy. 'Now go get a wet rag for that spilt ink.'

Ananda left. Upali blew on the finished sheets and began stringing them carefully on the earlier pile.

To Upali's colleagues, his task seemed enviably simple. The story and teachings of the Buddha had come down in the form of simple verses called the suttas, memorized and chanted by generations of monks. Upali himself had begun learning them at the age of eight and now could have easily recited the entire Sutta Pithaka, as the corpus was called, backwards – that is, if he wanted to indulge in what was a popular but highly frowned-upon challenge thrown by novices at one another.

When one knew the verses by heart, what was the problem in converting them into prose, asked his colleagues. Upali said that there were gaps and even contradictions in the account. The suttas had been developed to explain the Way, and while many contained incidents of the Buddha's life, they were not one coherent whole.

Also, they had been composed for the oral tradition, hence arranged along a metre and with a lot of repetition. The chanting could stir one's soul, especially when seated with eyes shut in the midst of disciplined rows of monks, with the hall, the earthen lamps and the world itself seeming to reverberate as they raised their voices together and dropped them in very slight but marvellous imprecision. But to write them down as an account was another matter. Some sounded like riddles, many were mystical, some absolutely childish. They had to be explained, even deciphered.

Not all of Upali's colleagues were impressed by his efforts. Most did not subscribe to the importance of the written word, though all had heard of the fabled cities on the Sindhu where writing had been well known. But those cities had vanished long ago – if they had really existed – and for a long time now, rote learning had been the way to preserve and transmit knowledge. The croaking of frogs, was how a Vedic poet had described a school of his day. Writing was considered a new fad, a jugglery with learning, an idiosyncrasy of the present Magadhe-Raja, an anti-scholarly and foreign practice.

Writing, said Upali's colleagues, was something you would expect from a person like Upali.

Meanwhile, he struggled. The palm leaves on which Ananda had been writing were expensive – brought all the way from Banaras, where they had been carefully selected from among hundreds collected in the forests south of the Ganga, pressed, cut to shape, dried and polished with sesame oil – but he had crumpled more than a few and fed them guiltily to the lamp while he thought, wrote, paused, changed his mind and wrote anew.

Upali had actually started this work three years previously, after his transfer to this monastery on the edge of the Vindhya jungles. He had started almost unthinkingly, unhurriedly, comparing the suttas written by students of his writing classes, getting them rewritten as prose, rewriting them himself whenever he felt like it. Then came the command from the Magadhe-Raja. The Beloved of the Gods was happy to hear of Upali's efforts and wanted the work completed soon. Upali was aghast. His personal pastime was now an imperial commission. One of many such, for the Magadhe-Raja launched the transcribing of all the suttas around the same time. He called for brahmins to write down the Vedas and Upanishads as well. But since no brahmin would admit to literacy, the job was taken up by a merchant school at Banaras. The brahmins were furious, but they could do nothing to stop the Raja from covering the land with the written word, immortalizing his times, his faith, his achievements, himself.

Upali continued to work slowly though the whole monastery was now quite paranoid about the pace and quality of his efforts.

He placed the sheets in their red cotton folder and was tying it shut, when he heard running feet. Ananda burst in. 'Master, Master!'

'What's wrong?' Another snake, probably. Ananda was always yelling about them, even the harmless ones, who for their part tended to flock to the monastery in the monsoons. Thankfully the jungles were drying up now.

'The Raja's coming!'

'What? Here, sit down first. And stop shouting!' Upali sounded normal but Ananda read something different in the quick brush of palm over upper lip.

'A soldier's come – he's talking to Thera Harsha. The Magadhe-Raja's coming to Sanchi and he wants you there!'

'Me?'

Agitated feet pounded up the veranda again and the short, stocky and excitable figure of the Head Thera panted in. He glanced at Ananda but the boy was already moving out, head bowed and palms joined in humble salutation, but only, Upali knew well, to stand just outside. He had warned Ananda that one day he would overhear something he didn't want to and then regret his habit. Ananda chose to take his chances.

'Upali – the Magadhe-Raja wants to meet you!' Thera Harsha's large eyes bulged. 'He's on his way back from the south, and wants to speak to you – the Magadhe-Raja himself!'

'About the story, I suppose?' asked Upali quietly. 'It's more than a year since his order.'

'Yes, and I wonder what he'll say about its meagreness. But is that all? Sanchi is hardly en route to Magadh! There must be something more. After all those conferences with the monasteries – perhaps he has taken some decision? I tell you, Upali, he's up to something – that's for sure!' Harsha's round face was shiny with sweat. He ran his fingers through his non-existent hair and realized that his audience was not with him. 'Upali?'

'Yes. Yes, of course.'

'Upali, what's wrong?'

'Nothing. I'm a little surprised, that's all.'

'So am I! Anyway, you better leave early tomorrow. He's expected in four or five days.'

'Perhaps it would be better if you went instead of me? You can read the story to him just as well. Actually – ' Upali remembered the eavesdropper and hesitated, but only for a moment, 'I haven't been feeling well. My stomach – must be something I ate yesterday.'

'You and your stomach! This is the Magadhe-Raja, Upali – it's not an invitation, it's an order! Ask Loka for some medicine. I'll find you a litter if necessary.'

Upali was silent.

'Upali, are you – scared?' Harsha's voice was hesitant; Upali was so prickly.

'Of course not!' His laugh rang false in all three pairs of ears. 'By the way, how did your visit to Bhima's village go?'

It was an effective diversion. Harsha's face fell further. 'What did you expect? A complete waste of time! After all the difficulty I had in persuading Ujjayani to consider my proposal – the Deputy Collector even accused us of visiting the new villages secretly! I had to swear that not one of us has been there in the last two years, that it's only because those people come here for medical help that we meet them.' He glared at Upali.

The new villages were of easterners deported after the war, and strictly off-limits to all visitors except officialdom. But nothing so far, not the law nor Harsha's warnings, nor even arrest and a week's imprisonment some time ago, could prevent Upali from sneaking visits to them.

'But I soon realized that the real problem was something else – the accounting we did for the highway village, where we discovered that they were overtaxed last season. It was the Deputy's mistake apparently, that's why he was so angry! I had to insist on meeting the Collector himself and he actually decided to come with me to Bhima's village. And then they refused to speak to us!'

Upali had expected this. But Harsha had refused to listen to him.

'Then I got a long lecture about the futility of interfering with the Kalingas. None of the other monasteries intervened in political issues, he said, it is best we concentrate on our teaching.'

Bhima's people were not Kalingas – they were Bhuiryas, and had fought the Kalingas – and Upali had corrected Harsha about this many times in the past, but he remained silent now.

'See, Upali, that's exactly it. It never mattered earlier whether you were doing what others did. Things are difficult enough as it is, without worrying about everybody else! And nobody ever bothered – though my grandfather used to say that not a blade of grass swayed in the land without Chandragupta's knowing the reason why! But this Raja's been after our lives with his continuous prying and probing. All to what end? What's he going to *do*? Something, that's for sure! Look at the way he's funding his beloved Sanchi – their recruits are growing in leaps and bounds, but don't ask about the quality! Anyway, I just want him to leave *us* alone. What if he decides to close down – ? Upali – I'm really worried!'

Upali continued staring out of the open door. Harsha gloomily pulled himself together. 'Anyway, try to be firm. And be careful too. The Court is said to be a dangerous place – full of antagonistic and bloodthirsty lobbies. Don't trust anybody. It is the Court of the Mauryas, Upali – be on your guard!'

He got a response at last. 'Will there be a lot of people, do you think?'

'Well, obviously. But don't worry, the Sanchi Thera will be there too. I don't know him well but he looks a capable man. Very intelligent, and he seems to know everybody. You can trust him to help you,' said Harsha, having a second ago warned Upali to trust nobody. 'Come now, time for meditation. We can discuss this later.'

The sound was of very light feet this time but Ananda made it all the way to the main vihara before they even came out of the room; they found him busy enlightening the group of goggle-eyed novices there.

The monk at the head of the assembly waited till all were seated cross-legged in padmasan, the lotus position, then started to beat a heavy brass plate with a wooden mallet. Very light and slow. The monks were expected to relax and listen to the fill and collapse of their lungs as breath moved slowly in and even slower out, timing it to the gentle boom. If you did it right then somehow tension and tiredness flowed off like water, to be replaced by a calmness that was strangely alert. Harsha believed that more could be achieved if one concentrated enough; he believed that if one was focused and committed enough, a meditator could develop tremendous insight about the world, as mentioned in the Samanaphala Sutta, the Discourse of the Fruits of the Contemplative Life – even the ultimate salvation, of freedom from rebirth. He believed this, but had never managed to achieve it himself and was honest enough to admit it. No one else in the monastery had either, though many were trying.

Upali found the meditation sessions at Maheshwar too long. Today he sat more hunched than usual, staring at the smooth mud floor, stomach churning. He was going to see the Murderer of Kalinga. In the first months after the war, he used to imagine himself striding up to the Magadhe-Raja and slaying him, stabbing a dagger through the royal chest, cutting off the royal head, in revenge for the sorrow inflicted on all the harmless little hamlets Upali had known. In revenge for the loss of Nayana. Upali had spent more than twenty years of his life on the wild beautiful coast south of Tosali, and all that was left now of those placid, palm-fringed villages were cinders, ashes, ruins. A civilization had been destroyed, consciously and cold-bloodedly. And for what? Self-aggrandizement. Megalomania. Greed. All typical of the Mauryas and Magadh. Upali had not thought actively of the war for many weeks, but now the old fear and hate came flooding back. He felt sick. Maybe Harsha would have to organize a litter after all.

Thinking of Harsha made him remember his panic. The Magadhe-Raja had held two Sangha conferences in the region since Upali's arrival. Upali had attended the second, at Sanchi, though not the special royal audience where the heads of monasteries had been invited separately to explain exactly how they functioned. There Thera Harsha had spoken about Upali and his personal writing project, eliciting an enthusiastic response. Upali must do a good job of this, the Magadhe-Raja had declared, it was vital for the entire Sangha.

Despite this news, Upali had quite enjoyed the conference. He had first hunted frantically for anybody familiar, for he had heard that the monks of Kalinga had been distributed among different monasteries. He found nobody, but was distracted from his disappointment by all the introductions and discussions. There were seven monasteries in the province of Avanti, he discovered, and one convent. It was at this gathering that the myriad interpretations of the Middle Way also became apparent. Let each be his own light, the Buddha had said; his disciples seemed to have taken to the idea with a vengeance.

Later they learnt that the Magadhe-Raja was holding conferences all over the realm. Wherever he went he called together monks and listened quietly while they nervously explained or confidently boasted of their beliefs and works, both devout and mundane. Some spoke of Nirvana, others of medical aid. Some preached withdrawal from society, others downright meddling. And every Thera at every conference pointed out how their particular practice had originated with the Buddha's own. The Raja listened. But, as Harsha feared, this Raja was a do-er.

That night Upali had one of his old dreams. He saw the fires of that hamlet near the sea, then the army marching across the black fields, scorched long back by the Kalingas. Victory had been won. The houses near the monastery were aflame, trees too, people were throwing water and mud at them. Some children huddled near Upali, their faces streaked by the leaping flames. Where were their parents? The monastery was spared, an inviolate memorial to the long-dead messenger of humanity while around it people were burnt, speared and bludgeoned out of memory. That is, till Narayan, a fellow-monk, went crazy. He rushed to the blaze next door, grabbed at a patch of burning thatch, and just managed to run with his burning load to the monastery and fling it in, before soldiers caught hold of him and tried to drag his burning robe off. He struggled with them, shrieking foul abuse that Upali had never heard him use before, but they stripped him safely and stamped out his pathetic little fire. When they turned, he fled back into the inferno next door.

Upali and Ananda left before dawn the next day, on Bhima's bullock-cart. The cart and oxen actually belonged to Bhima's village, or rather to the administration who had assigned them to the village, but Bhima was the only one who used them and he was in the habit of visiting the monastery when free, to meet Upali and sometimes offer the monks the services of the cart. Harsha rarely accepted, for Bhima was a deportee and the law banned deportees from stepping out of their villages in the first place, but Upali actually asked for this lift down to the highway since there were two others who could use it – a boy and his father, jungle-folk who had arrived three days ago, the boy suffering from a high fever. He was well now but a little weak.

The early morning jungle was cool and noisy. The squelches of the bullock's hooves mingled with the raucous screeching of parakeets and the chatter of langurs leaping around above their heads, dull brown shadows against the brilliant greens. Not as brilliant as Kalinga, thought Upali tiredly. Half the night had gone in finalizing the second chapter. He had met Harsha at night, and again just now, but except for repeating his advice about being careful, there was little that they had to discuss. Not only because there were about twenty other problems being discussed by the others. That was normal. The monastery of Maheshwar was small, with only six monks and five novices, but since Harsha believed that the Sangha's work was not just teaching Dhamma, but also farming, dairying, medical help, dispute resolving, marriage counselling and a host of other things, many of which were lumped together – by a sizeable number of officials, peasants and jungle-folk – as butting-in-where-not-required, monastery discussions were often impassioned ones about how the monks had got into trouble and out of it. But the truth was that, besides worrying, neither Upali nor Harsha knew what to do.

The monastery was a small patch of field and orchard surrounding a few shacks, the whole scooped doggedly out of forest one hour above the river. It was a tiny scar in the vast wooded blanket that stretched on both sides of the Narmada, and a highly resented scar at that – it was a daily struggle to stop the jungle from taking it back. Ananda kept a thick stick in hand and eyes peeled for any unfriendly creature. A leopard cub had wandered into the monastery the previous week, followed by its sleek mother, who glared at the populace staring down from the roofs before grabbing her offspring by the scruff of its fat neck and stalking off.

Ananda was excited. He had never travelled as far as Sanchi, and the possibility of actually seeing the Beloved of the Gods was thrilling. But he knew Upali was worried; he was even better at reading his face than his writing. He tried to lighten the atmosphere with song, but Upali's eyes were shut, Bhima seemed off-mood, while the remaining two were shy. Ananda valiantly performed solo, which provided the extra service of frightening off all with sensitive hearing. The only creature to cross their path was bereft of the faculty – a cobra, who reared a dark gold hood up at them nevertheless.

They met no one else till the cart trundled onto the highway junction on the river, when Upali startled everybody with a, 'Wait! There's a new message up!'

It was the end of the ride in any case. This was where they had to wait for a caravan. The father of the boy got off, saying something in a local dialect that Upali did not understand. Ananda did, however. 'Farewell, he says. And may the gods protect us.'

'And him. But tell him to wait, let's see what Magadh says.'

The man placed the child astride his shoulders, raised a hand in either refusal or farewell and departed westwards, like the highway, but abjuring it for the forest which swallowed him and his burden up in a second.

The monks were headed in the opposite direction. The highway was new and awesome, running all the way from the port of Bhrgukacha where the Narmada emptied into the great sea, to Pataliputra, a distance of more than eight hundred miles, and apparently paved all that way with timber logs, all of a size and laid crosswise. It was not so much a road, as a declaration of power, ambition and colossal resources. Upali hated it; Kalinga had moved on mud tracks.

He jumped off behind Ananda. 'Come, let's read the board!'

Bhima remained on the cart, grimly silent.

'What's wrong?' Upali knew what was wrong. His friendship with Bhima was three years old, more than enough to know of his allergy to strangers. 'All right, but they really needed a lift. I'm sorry if you're upset.'

The forest had dissolved into another patch of field here. The air smelt sweet. The rippling sheets of paddy would soon be ready for harvest. Some men working in the distance turned and waved; this was the highway village which had been overtaxed. On the other side of the road were water meadows, gaudy with blue and red lotuses, and beyond those the frothing brown expanse of the rain-swollen Narmada.

At the side of the junction was a stepped platform covered with a tiled roof. On it was a large polished ebony board held up by two thick posts. About half a man's height and double in width, it was placed a little higher than the average person, edged with brass and inscribed in white lime. The author of the inscription was unmistakable, for the royal insignia of a four-faced lion moulded in gleaming brass topped each timber post, while the royal standard of gold-edged blue flew from the roof.

'Bhima, please – ' began Ananda.

'All right!' snapped Bhima. He guided his oxen to a patch of grass and followed them to the platform where Upali tapped the bottom paragraph.

'This is new. Read it to us, Ananda.'

Ananda obediently started, *'Thus speaks… The Beloved of… of the Gods…'* but the language was unfamiliarly formal. So Upali took over and read loud and clear:

Thus speaks the Beloved of the Gods, the Magadhe-Raja Piyadassi: In the past, government work, including the receipt of reports and the quick completion of business was never very efficient, whether at the lowest or the highest levels. But I have now changed this. Public affairs are paramount. At all times, whether I am eating, or in my inner apartments, or in the women's apartments, or at the stables or cattle sheds, or in my carriage, or in my gardens – wherever I may be – my informants are to keep me in touch with public matters. Thus henceforth I will examine and decide upon public matters wherever I am. And whatever I may order even by word of mouth, if there is any dispute or deliberation about it among my officers or in the Council, it is to be reported to me immediately, at all places and at all times.

This I have commanded. It is not that I find great satisfaction in hard work and the dispatch of public matters themselves. But I believe that it is my duty to promote the welfare of the world, and hard work and the quick completion of public business are the means of doing so. And however great my achievements, I have done them in order to discharge my debt to all beings. I work for their happiness in this life, and so that in the next they may gain heaven. It is for this purpose that this inscription of Dhamma been engraved. May it endure long. May my sons, grandsons and great-grandsons strive for the welfare of the whole world. But this is difficult without great effort.

'Well! This must have been put up just this month. Can you read the other two, Ananda? Do it slowly and you'll manage fine.'

Inspired by the unabashed loudness of his teacher, Ananda stumbled through both. In the middle one, the Beloved of the Gods informed 'his children' how he had provided two kinds of medical services all over his empire, one for men and the other for animals; plantation of medicinal plants had been taken up on a great scale; wells had been dug along the roads and shady fruit trees planted for the use of men and beasts. The top one made Bhima frown again.

The Beloved of the Gods has had this inscription on Dhamma engraved to announce that henceforth no living thing is to be killed or sacrificed here; nor is the holding of a festival permitted. For the Beloved of the Gods sees much evil, waste and immorality in festivals, though there are a few of which the Beloved of the Gods approves.

Formerly in the kitchens of the Beloved of the Gods, the Magadhe-Raja Piyadassi, many hundreds of thousands of living animals were killed daily for meat. But now, at the time of writing this inscription on Dhamma, only three animals are killed, two peacocks and a deer, and the deer not always. Even these three will not be killed in the future…

Ananda triumphantly concluded and felt very pleased with himself. Then he noticed that both Upali and Bhima were lost in thought.

'What does he mean, Master?' he asked. 'And who will read this – when nobody can read?'

'They are read out aloud regularly by officials from the city. But these messages are not really looking for readers – their purpose is just to constantly remind you of Magadh. Of the Magadhe-Raja. Earlier, most people would not even know who their king was. They would name the local lord or their tribal chief, if asked.'

Ananda promptly turned to Bhima. 'Who is your Raja, Bhima?'

Bhima nodded at him.

'Who?'

Upali sighed. 'Bhima knows.'

'How does he know?'

Bhima unbent at last. 'They come to our village to read out pronouncements in the name of the Magadhe-Raja, Ananda. About how they are going to give us bullocks and seeds and tools. Then about the tax we have to give back. They always start by declaring that he is our father. They think we're fools.'

The others waited, for like most men of few words, Bhima was wont to speak at length once he got going. His fellow-villagers were in contrast very silent, angry and aloof. The monastery was not unused to such antagonism, from both peasants and jungle-folk, and Bhima's people had better reason than most. They had come to Maheshwar not long after Upali, but walking, all the way from the east, a long column of about 300 families, each adult tied to the one in front and the one behind. Nearly a third had not survived the walk.

It was an idea of Chandragupta's – the first Maurya – to shift groups of conquered people far away to new areas of cultivation, boosting production while dispersing revolt. Bhima's village took more than a year to clear their valley, after which they were provided ploughs, cattle, utensils and a bunch of officials in Ujjayani to monitor every aspect of their existence. The harvests were poor at first, the clan being new to agriculture and less than eager to learn, but they were picking up thanks to promises that they would be sold into slavery otherwise.

'But it is true, at home we only knew the name of our Chief. I must have travelled the most but even I hadn't heard of the Kalingas. Let alone Magadh. Till both passed our way – and slaughtered whoever they met.' He turned away and spat. 'But the officials and police here are always talking of the Magadhe-Raja. And of his Dhamma.'

'Yes,' said Upali. 'His, not the Buddha's.'

'But why is he telling us all this?' asked Ananda. 'Why is he telling us how he wants to be disturbed by his officials?'

'I suppose he's scared. After what he did in Kalinga, he must be frightened that people hate him.'

'Frightened – him?'

'What he did was terrible, Ananda. Grotesque. He must be having sleepless nights thinking of what might happen to him!'

'But what can happen to him?' Kings possessed huge supernatural powers, Ananda knew; this one even called himself the Beloved of the Gods. 'And others before did the same, didn't they?'

'He's done much worse,' Upali said stubbornly. The Magadhe-Raja quaking in terror was one of his pet fantasies.

Bhima was scowling. 'He's against killing animals – I suppose it doesn't matter if people like us starve to death! But why stop our festivals too?'

'A waste of time and wealth, he says. And since he now claims to admire the Buddha, he talks against the blood sacrifices at the festivals. Isn't that ironic – the Murderer of Kalinga against bloodshed!'

'He's trying to finish us,' said Bhima. 'It's difficult enough to worship as it is. In this foreign country, with our temples unconsecrated, not a single ritual can be performed properly! That's why I try to avoid strangers – they carry their own curses.

My cousin died last week, in the village across the river. Of a fever.'

'I'm sorry.' Upali did not ask how Bhima knew of the death; the scattered deportee villages managed to keep in touch very well despite the law and the jungle.

'And our stockade has been broken thrice in the last two months and we cannot catch the culprits. Because there are none – it's a divine warning!'

Probably jungle-folk, or animals. But Bhima's people were never happy with simple explanations. On the other hand, if they did accept them, they were likely to do something about it. It was probably better this way.

'Your Thera came over two days ago, with a proposal,' Bhima's proud face, burnt a rich ebony by generations of sun, was again pale with anger, 'that we work as elephant-capturers and trainers.'

Upali nodded glumly. Harsha had considered it a brainwave.

'We're of the elephant totem – the last thing we would do is trap elephants for Magadh! The Chief was very upset. Life has become a joke, he said. We're slaves, in a land of slaves, just like those peasants! Without our gods – completely unprotected!'

'Yes, but – ' Upali was cut off by a heavy clattering of hooves. A group of mounted men swung into view around a bend in the road. Twelve arrogant steeds carrying twelve men, all uniformed in black pants and bronze helmets, heavy iron swords hanging at their side. The monks were familiar with the grim-faced patrols that kept a watch on the highway and the settlements around, but they were none the less intimidating. And Bhima was not supposed to be so far from his village. The patrol stared straight ahead till abreast of the three at the signboard, then turned suddenly, drew their swords and swept them vertically with a startling flash of metal. The three threw up their arms defensively, but it was just a salute to the board. The patrol ignored them and rode on.

Upali smiled a little sheepishly. 'I think *they* are supposed to protect you, Bhima.'

'And who protects us from *them*?'

'I know. But, Bhima – you remember what happened back then....'

Bhima nodded. 'Back then' was a revolt soon after they arrived in Maheshwar. It had been put down quickly, efficiently, with minimum bloodshed. Bhima's brother had been one of the minimum. He seemed about to say something, but changed his mind.

'I'm hungry,' said Ananda.

'We can eat, I suppose, while we're waiting. Come – it looks dry under that tamarind.'

They crossed the road to the tree where Ananda unwrapped their food – a khichdi of rice and lentils – but not very enthusiastically, for the monks on kitchen duty were Upali and Mohan, both miserable cooks. Luckily, Bhima was carrying his usual packet of sattu, or boiled dry rice, accompanied by a deliciously peppery onion chutney, both of which he offered Ananda – he himself refused to eat anything cooked by anybody outside his clan. Some langurs swung hopefully into the tree overhead. A red-billed quail hopped up too, followed by two pigeons. Despite the presence of the villagers, and a couple of scarecrows as well – buffalo skeletons partly covered by the black hairy skins and positioned vertically – all kinds of birds were wheeling and diving over the ripe fields, the only real deterrent perhaps the bird-eating ones gliding slowly around high above.

'How is your youngest, Bhima? He had a fever too, didn't he?'

'It has gone,' Bhima closed his eyes and touched his hand to the ground in careful thanks. 'He is quite well now.'

'So Loka's medicine worked, that's good. If he had treated your cousin – '

'Actually he said that it would take a few days to have an effect, and I didn't want to wait. After Karu, you know....' Bhima's eldest child had died the previous year of snakebite.

'So?'

'So, the Chief allowed me to give a goat at our temple. I had to,' he added, for he knew Upali's ideas on such things. 'After a flock of peacocks showed up around our village last week – something had to be offered. I was not sure it would work – but it did.'

It would. Across the roaring expanse could be seen another small hamlet, huddled against the dark Satpuras, near it a wharf. Caravans from the south would start crossing after the river sank a bit; caravans armed to the teeth, for the chief southern commodity was gold from the great new mines annexed in the last Magadhan expansion. Annexed peaceably, so it was said. By the annexers.

He felt Bhima watching him. 'Is something wrong, Bhima?'

'No.' Bhima looked away.

'Why does the Magadhe-Raja want to see you, Master?' asked Ananda suddenly.

'For the story, I suppose.'

'Are you frightened?'

'No.'

'Is he really huge? Like a giant?' Upali just looked at him. 'Santosh said so. I told him not to be a fool.'

They were in luck. A caravan showed up about an hour later, of horses, more than a hundred walking single file, almost as many guards riding on either side, followed by a double line of porters. The porters looked strained under their head-loads, the horses looked worse though unburdened – natives of dry sands, they were probably appalled by the wet humid greens all around. The two merchants in their covered carriage looked appalled too, but at Bhima, whose muscular frame was arrayed in almost all his clan finery – red and black paint on chest, stomach and forehead, bone bracelets covering arms and ankles, bamboo cap with two wickedly-curved bison horns on head – everything except his spear, blowpipe and raw-hide shield, and that because his people had been warned on pain of death against carrying weapons. The merchants were relieved to hear that it was only the two monkish types who required an escort. Bhima nodded an austere farewell.

The little patch of civilization was soon left behind. The road climbed out of the valley and into wooded darkness, dappled at places, opaque at others, tracing the river at first but climbing steadily high above it into the Vindhyas – the hills of the hunter. They passed a troop of army road-repairers at work, then another – the empire clearly invested heavily to keep itself connected.

Upali and Ananda marched along with the porters and Upali's legs were aching by evening; he'd become soft, he thought, he used to tramp all over the Kalinga hills for days at a stretch without noticing. Ananda was fascinated by the long scabbards of the guards but could not sum up the nerve to ask to see the contents. They stayed unrevealed till the end, for the journey was uneventful. These forests used to be famous for dacoity, a guard informed them, in fact the people in these hills were said to survive by robbing caravans. Magadh had robbed their lands first, Upali replied, they were just returning the favour. The guard was surprised. Was he calling the Magadhe-Raja a robber? Upali tried to explain the parallels between conquest and dacoity, but the guard frowned and Ananda began to worry. The discussion was interrupted by a little village, or rather the remains of one – a sad mass of charred huts, not a living soul to be seen. The Raja was not patient with evil-doers, explained the guard smugly. Upali opened his mouth but Ananda pressed his hand hard, so he shut it for the moment. The porters were engrossed in singsong incantations propitiating forest spirits and ignored the exchange.

They passed a second hamlet, in slightly happier condition, but saw no people. Nor ahead. They saw cheetal, neelgai and barasingha; they heard boar, elephant and thousands more langurs; Ananda was sure he saw a leopard tail hanging out of a tree, but of humans there was not a sign. Perhaps it was the wicked looking scabbards. Or the patrols that crossed them at regular intervals. Or the burnt village. Or just that horse caravans were not the favourite target of dacoits. Few could take away the strong and temperamental Arabs and do anything constructive with them later.

They stopped for the night at a post-house inn, deep in the jungle but armed with every comfort, including a well, meals, private rooms, hot water on demand and a broad veranda for porters and sramana types to sleep on for free.

They did not meet the merchants again till the next noon at another inn, not far from Ujjayani and in a sunny landscape of wheat fields and bright ponds fringed by wild willows. Next to the inn was a toll booth – merchants had to pay for using the highways – and a big shed where many horses had gathered with their attendants.

Upali and Ananda arrived with the last of the porters, offered help as usual in unloading, were as usual refused – the porters had their own system and scorned amateurs – and walked to the shed where the horses were gathered. There they found two men cleaning the sores on their feet. The shelves on the walls behind were loaded with various pots and stacks of cloth. A porter came up with a blister on his foot; it was cleaned and bandaged as well.

'You're surely not walking all the way to Pataliputra with that blister?' asked Upali.

The porter was astounded by such stupidity. 'Of course not! Our beat is to Ujjayani. They'll get a new gang there – to Vidisha or Kosambi, not all the way to Pataliputra!'

Upali felt rebuked. He turned to the physician. 'How much do you charge, brother?'

'Nothing. This service is free.'

'Are there such hospices closer to Maheshwar? For the locals?'

There was supposed to be one with every alternate inn, said the physician, and invited the monks to lunch – if they did not mind simple food. They accepted, and Upali walked to the inn to wash up at the well. One of the merchants was standing near the porch chatting with a small plump official. Upali had almost reached them when he noticed a movement on the porch. Somebody was watching, hidden behind a timber post.

The merchant took a leather pouch out of his pocket, glanced around, saw Upali, and put it back. 'Later,' he said. The plump official nodded and crossed the compound to the toll booth.

The merchant beamed at Upali. He was middle-aged, with chubby cheeks and a prosperous paunch. 'Thera! I trust the journey has treated you well?' His name was Milindachanda and he was a Pataliputran by origin and residence. Was the Thera a native of Maheshwar?

'No, of Kalinga.' It was not the exact truth, but Upali had adopted Kalinga for his own, if not vice-versa, and anyway how was this merchant to know?

'Kalinga?'

'I was brought here after the war.'

'Well, well.... Come, let us go in.' He saw Upali glance at the toll booth. 'Magadh's taxes are very high, Thera.'

He hesitated, then invited Upali to lunch with him and his son. Upali explained that they had accepted an invitation to eat at the hospice but Milindachanda was welcome to join; the other thanked him and vanished hurriedly into the inn.

The porters sat down in one corner of the compound with their food; the guards in another. Upali and Ananda had alternated between the two groups so far and neither had looked very happy. The physician was friendlier. He spread a mat under a tree, laid out thick bajra rotis, curried beans and mango chutney, politely refused the food in their packet, and explained that he was a native of a village near Vidisha, where the Sanchi monks often preached. He had visited the monastery many times himself. To pray, to the stupa.

'To pray? What do you mean? What of your own temple? Your family deity? Village gods?'

'We worship them too, of course! But I am also a follower of the Buddha; I feel stronger and at peace after visiting Sanchi. Many people from my village go regularly.'

Upali ate in silence for a while. The man seemed genuine, and they were his guests. But still. 'Forgive me for sounding personal, brother, but you follow the Buddha and still refuse to touch another's food? When that was one of his most important teachings?'

'I meant no disrespect, Thera.' He immediately served himself from the monks' packet. It had not improved by being one day older, but he said nothing and actually took a second helping. Ananda felt like giving him a medal.

When the journey recommenced they found that the merchant Milindachanda wanted to be friendly. He insisted on their joining him in his plush carriage, his son silently moving out to ride one of the horses. They were on their way back to Pataliputra after nearly eight months. They had travelled by road while going to Takshashila, Bactra, Persepolis and finally great Susa where Milindachanda had done his main business. He had come across many people who knew of Magadh as the land of the Buddha.

'What do they know of the Buddha?'

'Oh, that he was a sage, that he spoke of Nirvana, the usual, you know.'

The usual? But the merchant was not interested in the Buddha. He took his turban off, revealing a smooth dome graced by a small tuft of hair, and fanned himself complacently while describing the horrors of his return journey by sea, and finally how impressed he had been with the port facilities at Bhrgukacha. Good organization, terrific security. And these new highway inns were an enormous boon. Trade was becoming safe and almost comfortable. And the demand abroad for the two great products of the empire – iron and spices – was unlimited. The more you gave them, the more they wanted. But he complained of the taxes.

'Of course, I'm not complaining! One knows of the great expenditures of the administration. To run the new facilities, to maintain the peace. And not to forget, to fund worthy monasteries like yours! In fact, I wanted to know, is there any way a merchant like me could assist there?'

Upali was not feeling very gracious. 'They don't fund us! And there's no need to bribe me. I'm not a friend of Magadh.'

The merchant relaxed. 'Profit is limited by law to ten per cent – low enough, but they never let you come near it! With all these tolls, taxes, fees, fines, interest, everywhere you turn, one can barely eat at the end!' He paused to sniff. The others also smelt something. 'So, one must manage as best one can – right, Thera?'

Upali remembered the person on the porch, but only for a second. They had reached a small breezy plateau above a gorge where a small river fell turbulently down a series of falls. It was blessedly cooler. There was spray in the air and a view over the valley, and in the immediate foreground, silently ridiculing the panorama behind, eleven tall makeshift gallows built of bamboo, from which swung the remains of eleven men. Their bodies had been weathered by the elements, animals too. But a smell lingered.

'Robbers,' said Milindachanda. 'Captured by the patrols.'

'We should stop,' said Upali, holding his nose, 'and bury them.'

The driver threw him a shocked look and gave his horses a slap to go faster. Milindachanda was equally aghast. 'You would actually touch them? Anyway, it's against the law.'

'But we can't leave them like this – '

'Thera, do you think they string them up so that the next passersby can bury them? They are tokens – you can't touch them!' Milindachanda produced a tiny gold-stoppered bottle from a pouch, opened it and waved it about briskly. A strong smell of jasmine combined rather sickeningly with the background one.

'Have you ever been robbed?' asked Ananda after recovering.

'No!' Milindachanda made various signs against the evil eye. 'The patrols are efficient – any robbery and they just hang a few suspects along the highway and burn some villages as well. Earlier, most of this road had gallows on the side – it was really irritating for brahmins like me, you can't imagine the purification we're obliged to undergo after seeing corpses after corpses! Now things are more peaceful – people don't dare approach.'

'Magadh relies on terror,' said Upali in disgust.

'Yes,' agreed Milindachanda. 'It works quite well!'

They reached Vidisha the next evening and parted, the caravan continuing north while the monks had to climb the hill just behind the city.

Another regal board stood guard at the city gates, but Upali was now in a hurry. It was nearly dark and drizzling, but he was not to be swayed. It was very close, he assured the horrified Ananda as lightning flashed overhead. And don't forget, the Buddha often spent his nights in the most haunted spots he could find. Often alone. And nothing happened to him.

I am not the Buddha, thought Ananda miserably as thunder followed. But instead of witches, wild beasts, spirits, or head hunters, they met something else – heavily armed soldiers all the way up. Outside the main gates was a vast army camp. Large tents stood profiled in the dull light of oil lamps, shadows scurried about within, invisible horses whinnied, elephants trumpeted. Vidisha was left behind, the camp went on and on. They were stopped thrice in close succession, questioned and searched. The drizzle became a downpour, the soldiers raised stoic parasols over their torches.

They were soaked to the skin and walking very slowly now thanks to the crashing sheets of water, but Ananda didn't mind for their passage was lit up all the way by the stern parasol-brandishers. At last they reached the monastery. Upali had not expected anyone to be waiting for them, and planned to spend the night outside if the gates were closed. But they were open, and flanked by at least a hundred soldiers. Some monks as well. Again they were searched, this time even patted down carefully.

'Go,' ordered the soldier finally. The rain promptly vanished and a monk squelched forward.

'Welcome, Master. The Thera is expecting you. Please – '

'Has the Magadhe-Raja arrived?' interrupted Upali.

' – follow me.'

'He's arrived, hasn't he?'

'Yes. Please come.'

He turned and headed in, while Ananda jerked at Upali's hand. 'Master, the monks – they're all wearing the same robe!'

So they were. All the same saffron-ochre colour, a uniform. They followed the monk through the gates, then Upali stopped in his tracks. A majestic hemisphere had loomed out of the darkness before them. It was lit by great torches placed in stone stands all around. The torches were protected from the rain by stone canopies, though not from the gusty breezes, which sent the light dancing wildly against the smooth brick rings of the base. The higher levels were dark, calm, unbothered.

'The stupa! It's huge!'

'Come on,' said their guide impatiently. 'Come on – the Thera is waiting.'

Two novices were waiting, in the same uniform, with warm water for washing, napkins and dry robes, but no Thera. There was a bamboo tray too, containing bananas and a pitcher of water. Ananda fell on the fruit, while Upali drank a little water and felt his stomach begin an uneasy ache. The novices withdrew, time passed. Things were quiet outside except for the busy movement of soldiers. Upali went out on the veranda and waited; finally a monk appeared. He approached reluctantly when hailed.

'Brother, where's the Head Thera?'

'He will come. He is very busy at the moment.'

'Where is he? I'll go and meet him.'

'No, please wait. He will come when he's free.'

Upali was mystified. 'Is something wrong?' The monk started to move off, but Upali grabbed his arm. 'What's wrong?'

'I don't know if I should speak....'

'Tell me!'

'There has been a death.... One of the monks. He was found just now.'

'Found?'

'He was killed.' The monk looked scared.

'Snakebite? Or was it a cat?' Cats were a problem once they tasted humans. The Maheshwar monastery had been haunted the previous year by a leopard who had nearly killed a monk.

'He was stabbed.'

'Stabbed? By a person, you mean?'

No, by a cat, answered Ananda but silently.

'Yes.'

'A *murder*? Of a monk? By whom?'

'We don't know. He was found in his cell just now.' He pulled his arm out of Upali's dumbfounded grip and hurried away.

Finally, the Thera arrived. He seemed unchanged from the conference more than a year ago, as tall, thin and chatty as ever. His eyes were large and innocent, his smile wide, his fingers painfully bony on both of Upali's arms. 'Salutations, Upali! It's been a long time.'

Only his garments were different – the robes were of silk! Upali had seen this amazing cloth from the lands of China only a few times before. The Thera's robes looked alive, for the same saffron-ochre colour shimmered like liquid in the lamp light, making dark gold and orange pools that continuously changed shape and direction. Both Upali and Ananda gaped and hardly noticed the yellow-haired man standing behind the Thera.

'Let me introduce our Greek guest, Xantes. He's an aide of Lord Dionysus, the Egyptian ambassador at the Court. He wants to learn about the Buddha. I said he was lucky – he'd soon be meeting the official biographer!'

The Greek bowed. He looked hot and overdressed in a woollen tunic soaked either with rain or sweat, a leather cloak and leather boots.

'Well, I must go,' said the Thera. 'I am at my wit's end, Upali – I've been up three nights in a row, getting everything ready – then, in the middle of all the confusion, *he* arrived. Early! But the worst thing is... have you heard? Something terrible has happened. Here in the monastery!'

'I know. I was shocked!'

'Right here! And now of all times!' Ananda felt like asking him when and where he preferred his murders. 'It must have happened two nights ago, the body had begun… you know. Nobody remembers seeing him yesterday – we were all so busy.'

'It's really shocking.'

'It's worse! He's a Sunga – you know the Sungas, don't you?' Upali didn't, adding to his horror. 'Rajas of Avanti – His great-uncle was the last Chief! I've sent word – they'll be here any moment. I don't what to do!' The Thera walked up and down the room as he spoke, massaging his palms against each other. He reminded Ananda of some actor in a village drama, except that they never dressed so opulently. 'Can you imagine the infamy? Must have been a thief, of course. What do you think?'

'I'm shocked,' Upali was truthful if not innovative.

'One of those jungle-folk, don't you think? The security is so lax!'

'Really?' Soldiers were marching around outside; the place looked more like an army camp than a monastery. 'But have you had any robberies before? And why would they choose him?'

'I don't know! Who else could it be?' The Thera was suddenly irritated. 'What do you mean?'

Upali was surprised. 'Nothing – I've never come across such a thing before.'

The Thera was silent.

Upali stared out at the soldiers. 'What's the Raja doing?'

'He wishes to meditate for a while in front of the stupa. We are all joining him. And in the morning, we will start with your story.'

'I have only two finished chapters. The rest is still in rough drafts. I've brought everything.'

'Two should be enough – I think he'll leave tomorrow itself, so he can't spend the entire day listening to you.'

'But he's just arrived – '

'It's the Maurya style – they're always on the move! Anyway, bring everything. Now rest. Or join us outside.'

The air was ticklish with wood smoke scented with frangipani. There was a small group of nuns walking ahead, and as Upali neared the saffron-robed figures, one seemed strangely familiar. The thin frame, the slight outward swing of the elbows and the left hip as she walked…. It was – could it be? But where was her braid? Oh yes, she had shaved her head just a few weeks before the war. She had delayed shaving it for ages, on some pretext or the other, and Upali had been tolerant about it. Tolerant, that is, about his own weakness, for he had secretly admired her thick silky braid.

Upali did not realize that he had stopped short, that Ananda, walking sleepily behind, had bumped into him. She was alive! He dashed forward, caught hold of her arm and swung her around. 'Nayana!' And found himself facing a surprised stranger.

Upali let go. 'I'm sorry… I thought…you looked familiar, sister, like an old friend….' All of them stared at him silently; the girl rubbed her arm as if it hurt. 'I'm really very sorry….' He turned and walked on.

They reached the stupa just behind the royal retinue, Upali thankful for the confusion, though he could feel Ananda's eyes still boring into him. A crowd surrounded the Magadhe-Raja but a monk nearby identified a tall plumed helmet gleaming dully in the darkness as the royal one. The congregation sat down in padmasan and some people right in front started a low chanting. '*Buddham saranam gachaami, dhammam saranam gachaami, sangham saranam gachaami….*' I take refuge in the Buddha, I take refuge in the Dhamma, I take refuge in the Sangha….

The old Magadhi words rolled gently out and over the hillside, around the dome and up into the sky. A drizzle began, cool and very light, a delicate sprinkle of other-worldly blessings. The monks seemed as one with the stupa, the earth, the skies, the entire universe. Ananda was enthralled, even Upali was not unmoved, though he did not think much of the chant. He had heard it first at the conference here. It was not known at Kalinga, nor at Maheshwar. And, as far as he knew, the Buddha had not wanted to be a refuge.

After a while, perhaps a hundred chants, the monks rose. In single file they walked around the stupa. The Thera offered flowers, then prostrated himself, flat on the ground. Others followed, all except the royal company, and Upali. The dome remained unmoved.

He compared it with the stupa at Maheshwar. That was much smaller, and slightly lopsided because it had sunk over time and was sinking further every monsoon. The monks meditated in front of it in dry weather, only meditated, nothing more, though if anything it was a holier structure than this. At least for the jungle-folk who had built it, long before the monks arrived in Maheshwar. The locals called it a dagaba; in the north they were known as chaityas, like that at Lumbini where the Buddha was born. The Buddha had preached respect for the common people's faiths, and so, after his time, when the monks stopped nomadic preaching and settled down, they often chose such spots. Partly out of respect, partly for alms from devotees, and partly because of his other injunction to stop the blood sacrifices that were the norm there. The Buddha himself had spent many nights at some of the most fearsome sites, where even the most devoted devotee would not loiter.

Such were the original stupas. But after this Magadhe-Raja announced his conversion to Dhamma, the number spiralled, for he unearthed the Buddha's ashes from all their resting places, redivided them and erected new stupas over them all over the country. Sanchi was one.

The Buddha had asked his disciples to respect the people's worship of the stupas; now they worshipped him in the stupas.

SHUDODHAN

The Purusa Sukta, or the Verse of the Cosmic Man, was for the Shakyas the most sacred in that most sacred collection of hymns called the Rgveda, for it explained creation, it explained the power of sacrifice, and it explained their own origin. The very first sacrifice was by the gods, said the Verse. It was a sacrifice to sacrifice itself, and the offering was the first man, the original Purusa, equated later with the all-knowing Prajapati. His body was cut up and from it was born everything. The sun from his eye, the moon from his mind, the earth from his feet, and so on, but most importantly the brahmin from his mouth, the kshatriya of his arms, of his thighs the vaisya, of his feet the sudra. The Shakyas, who considered themselves kshatriyas, were thus below only the sun, the moon and some of the great warrior gods. And the brahmin, but that was obviously a small error.

Thanks to such venerable authorities, everybody in Kapilavastu knew their place in the world. Siddarth's was drummed into every pore of his body from the moment he was born. Arya, kshatriya, Shakya, Gautamaputra, born to rule, born to be chief of those who rule. Yet he managed to forget. Perhaps because he hardly knew the time when the Shakyas were really rulers. His first memories were of defeat to Kosala; he remembered it much better than the Verse of the Cosmic Man. It was a blasphemous attitude by any Shakya standard, for they almost dedicated themselves to forgetting the defeat.

But Siddarth had witnessed much of the process of vassalage first-hand, thanks to his father's belief that that it was never too early to train a future Chief. Official schooling started at the age of five, but Shudodhan began to cart his son about with him almost as soon as he was unswaddled. Citizens got used to seeing him riding straight-backed in front of Shudodhan, or more casually draped on his shoulder when on foot, and the child got used to accepting smiles, waves, toys and other goodies from the world. Training was really only one reason for his ubiquity – Shudodhan believed his son's presence made people warm to him.

Which was useful, for the Shakya feuds were getting bitterer by the day. It was actually a time of unusual prosperity. The republic enjoyed a streak of victory in its chronic disputes with other neighbours. Labour was cheap thanks to several successful slave-catching expeditions. The local tiger population was down with some calamity, the cattle stock doing accordingly well. The paddy fields glistened a ridiculous fluoroscent green, the storehouses were stuffed full of grain, spice and oil, Kosala was busy elsewhere, the gods seemed happy. It was a time of peace and plenty in which the Shakyas were free to squabble among themselves, and they did so, very viciously.

The Gana Sabha was openly divided between the conservatives led by Hemantraja, and the merchant lobby with which Shudodhan was commonly clubbed. Shudodhan's strategy was to ignore the existence of the Sabha, take all decisions himself, announce them at the Common Table and drive his opponents crazy. They started referring to him as 'the Merchants' Whore' and they used the Table too – to warn that the Shakyas would soon be a minority in their own land, and subjects instead of rulers, while the Whore became monarch!

So time passed, till early one summer when, apropos of nothing at all, Kosala remembered them. A message arrived. 'We invite the Shakyas to become our vassals,' Kosala said. 'A relationship of allegiance, tribute and protection, to the benefit of all concerned.' It came at a most inopportune moment, when Shudodhan was on his way home from a campaign in the east. In great triumph. The Mallas had been taught a lesson they would not forget, so he declared, though actually they already had. Nobody remembered anything very long in the eternal border wars. Shudodhan himself had already forgotten that this particular victory was mostly thanks to a simultaneous Naga attack from the north. Crowds lined the roads as the victory cavalcade passed, offering flowers, incense, sweets and wine. Despite a leg wound, Shudodhan looked strong, handsome and sternly benign as always.

The sternness was not feigned. He had got the message. It was shocking. Insulting. The Kosalans really needed to be taught a lesson – if only someone else would do it! To add irritation to injury, people in Kapilavastu had already called for a Sabha meeting.

'I don't see why the Sabha has to be convened,' he said to Mahanaman yet again.

Mahanaman sighed. 'You would prefer to throw the messenger out, and wait for the Kosalans to attack?'

'Are you joking? We have to think of some way of avoiding war.'

'Exactly. But it's never been done before. You have to address the Sabha.'

Shudodhan's interest in the Naga-metal was undimmed by his countrymen's continuing scorn, fired in fact by reports of a battalion of Naga sorcerers at work in the Kosala army compound. He himself had found the metal unreliable so far, sometimes it could break a bronze at one blow, sometimes it snapped into two itself. It was clearly a matter of finding good sorcerers.

There was no option. The Sabha convened, and argued and argued. The merchants wanted diplomacy; the conservatives wanted the impalement of the Kosalan messenger at the gates. War with Kosala would destroy the republic, said the merchants. You mean it would destroy profits, accused the conservatives. And so on.

The resolution was postponed to the morrow. There was another issue on the agenda – the disappearance of a Kosalan merchant. The reception for Shudodhan's victory had ended abruptly with the conqueror being yanked right off his horse by an agitated Gangadhar, a Shakyaraja who was also the richest merchant in Kapilavastu. The missing Sethi was his partner. It was not the first such mishap but the biggest, the partnership being the richest trading outfit in the republic. Shudodhan himself had a heavy investment in it. The Sethi had been away in the Kosalan city of Shravasti and was expected back this month. But another caravan had reached before him and reported finding carts and bodies scattered in the marshy forests near Silavati. The Sethi had vanished.

It was the conservatives, declared Gangadhar baldly; he wanted a combing of all estates in the area. Most rajas were aghast – the army had never been used against Shakyas themselves. And for some *mlechcha*? Mlechcha was the Shakya term for foreigner and foreigner was another term for dirt. Out of the question, said some. Blasphemous, declared others. Did Gangadhar have any proof, asked a few.

'How do you know he's kidnapped? I'm more worried that this scum might be freely roaming our lands – up to who knows what mischief!' declared one, a friend of Hemant's. 'Incidentally, Gangadhar, where were you at the time?'

Shudodhan was distracted by Hemant's face. The leader of the conservatives was silent, but not relaxed. His large podgy mass was stiffly upright, his lips drawn.

Gangadhar rose, hand on dagger, and Shudodhan had to intervene, if only to protect his remaining investments. The arguments wore on; Hemant remained mum. Something was clearly wrong. He had been in great form at the last Common Table before Shudodhan left for the border – where he had accused

Shudodhan, or rather the Merchant's Whore, of driving Shakyas into destitution. Foreigners now owned some of the largest estates in the land, he had declared, besides mortgages on many others. Many Shakyas were in debt, a few had even been sold into slavery. But the Whore would not be happy till all were slaves!

So why had he not gone for the jugular today? Shudodhan's friend Anula agreed that it looked suspicious; they decided to call on Hemant in the evening. Gangadhar and Mahanaman were invited too but the former pleaded exhaustion. Siddarth went along as usual.

It was a brief and unsuccessful visit, but one with long consequences for the nation. All thanks to Mahanaman. His position as head of perhaps the most blue-blooded of Shakya families made him a respected intermediary on all such occasions. But he let Shudodhan down this time, by completely forgetting his lines. Hemant, meanwhile, seemed to have recovered; he welcomed them by congratulating Anula on the new Malla lands.

' – especially since you didn't even fight in the battles that won them!'

'I'm only the overseer,' said Anula stiffly. 'A lot of responsibility and hard work.'

Hemant grinned. 'Of course, very noble of you to take it on!' Everybody knew that conquered lands eventually wound up with their overseers. Hemant himself owned huge estates gained exactly the same way.

'Where's Vilas?' asked Shudodhan, settling down on a mattress irritably. Hemant's reception hall was bigger than his own, and elegantly strewn with gleaming oil lamps, embroidered bolsters and a few friends. 'He wasn't at the Moat Hall either, was he?'

Vilas was Hemant's younger brother. 'With friends at his estate. They're planning a hunting expedition.' Three women entered with wine and snacks and began to serve the visitors.

'The estate near Silavati? What was he planning to hunt? Not the Sethi, by any chance?' Shudodhan watched the whole room; his hand was near his dagger.

But Hemant just looked wary. 'What exactly do you mean?'

This was Mahanaman's cue, but he was distracted. By one of the slaves. He was staring at her as if in a daze and Shudodhan felt like hitting him, really hard. After all, Shudodhan was tempted too, by the wafting aroma of spiced meat – Hemant's cook was known for his finesse – but business came first.

He tried to glare a signal across but it was useless. Anula tried to step into the breach. 'Listen, Hemant, let's not waste time. Does Vilas have the Sethi?' Shudodhan gave up and bit into a mutton cutlet; it was as delicious as he had suspected. Cloves definitely, and a hint of something else.

'I think you should leave,' said Hemant.

Anula's voice remained friendly. 'We are prepared to forget this matter entirely, Hemant. Just return the merchant.' But it did not really make any difference. Anula was a merchant and on bad terms with the conservatives.

Hemant heaved himself upright. 'Out!'

Shudodhan rose, Siddarth in his arms. 'Remember, Hemant, the Sabha has taken action against its own members in the past, and will not hesitate to do so again!' Just cardamom, probably.

'Shudodhan, I always feared for the sangha, with a pusillanimous fool like you as Chief. Now I see that you are insane as well!'

'It's Vilas, no doubt about it,' said Anula as they mounted their horses outside. 'You must send a troop to search his estate, Shudodhan – immediately!'

'If the Sabha permits,' murmured Mahanaman. 'Not before.'

'It's all your fault, Mahanaman!' snapped Shudodhan. 'Hemant would have settled the matter. He was damn scared in the morning!'

But Mahanaman looked distracted again. And Shudodhan was surprised the next morning to see Hemant arrive at the Moat Hall looking almost jaunty. The debate on the Kosalan demand for vassalage ended with a message of sharp refusal being drafted and the messenger was sent home unimpaled. Then Shudodhan spoke of Vilas.

The assembly was stunned; Hemant was calm but aggressive. 'After this insult from Kosala, I personally would be grateful to anyone who finishes one of those barbarians. I would reward any Shakya who puts Kosala in its place! But our Chief prefers to attack Shakyas instead!'

'Let us wait a while, I think,' said Mahanaman. 'This is a time to remain united.' Shudodhan glared at him. What was the smarmy bastard up to?

'No, send troops after Vilas!' Hemant almost laughed. 'And let's hope Kosala sleeps the meanwhile!'

'Let us take a vote,' said Shudodhan quietly.

Mahanaman abstained, as did most on seeing his example. Nine of the eighty-odd present voted with Shudodhan. Nineteen voted against. Shudodhan stalked out at the end, and refused to receive Mahanaman later on.

A peasant boy arrived that night, with a message that he tried to leave with Gangadhar's gatemen – a hundred gold coins had to be placed below an old banyan tree near the highway on the north-west border, for the Sethi to return. The gatemen however did not let the messenger go. Hours later the broken and blinded boy only repeated what he had said at the start – he had received a silver coin from a slave and did not know anything more. His body was hung outside the city gates and Gangadhar got the money ready. He set out the next day to the border, where he found the banyan and left the funds. Soldiers kept a watch on the money day and night but it was not touched. Finally, Gangadhar asked them to stay away. The money vanished that night and was replaced by the Sethi, neatly stabbed in the heart.

Kosala announced horror at the murder of their citizen. The Shakyas rushed additional forces to the border, but nothing happened. They never found out the details but apparently treachery was suddenly discovered at the very heart of the Kosalan court –

and by the time all those involved had been hunted out, the rains had arrived. The next four months were non-fighting ones! The Shakyas celebrated the warm sheets of water by mocking the cowardice of the barbarian – blood had finally told – but everybody knew that the respite was likely to be short. The conservatives began to speak of the need to contact or even join the Licchavi confederation. The Licchavis were impossibly orthodox, argued the merchants privately, even vassalage to Kosala was preferable. Independence, Shudodhan announced publicly, was the Shakya tradition – we refuse to be under anybody.

But many traditions were under attack, never better illustrated than when Shudodhan was himself attacked, on the street in broad daylight. By a lone youth, who approached openly, with the usual respectful genuflection. The Chief paused, his friends around him, his son on his shoulder, all expecting an application, perhaps for a change of job or posting. There was an easy informality between the rajas, a casualness strengthened by the knowledge that they were always armed.

'Traitor!'

Shudodhan was just able to deflect the driving wrist, so that the blade of the dagger went into his shoulder. Siddarth toppled off to the ground and was lucky to be picked up by Mahanaman before getting trampled in the ensuing confusion. Shudodhan was lucky too; it was a new blade which left only a clean flesh wound that healed rapidly despite the city doctors. The would-be assassin turned out to be related to Hemant through his wife, another bit of luck. He should have faced the death penalty, but Shudodhan opted for banishment. A young misguided soul, said the Chief publicly, he added in private that it was better not to provide any martyrs to the conservative cause.

But the question of Kosala remained. There was no way the Shakyas could refuse to fight, if things reached that point. Because this was Kosala. Negotiation, settlements, even vassalage was acceptable between equals or near-equals. Not with dirt like the Kosalans. War was the kshatriya's dharma, that beautiful and infinitely rich word that meant righteousness, responsibility, duty, the divine order of things. War belonged to the kshatriyas, it was their vocation and glory, the spilling of warrior blood was the supreme sacrifice to the gods. The Kosalans had no business, no background, no right to challenge the Shakyas. The Shakyas had no way out.

They tried nonetheless. Hundreds of animals and quite a few slaves were sacrificed to win divine favour, including the more un-productive of Naga iron-workers. Which was difficult, for Nagas tended to be even more recalcitrant than their metal.

But it was the animal offerings that caused waves, thanks to the unprecedented reluctance of a few commoners to put in their share. It was the first time any Shakya had even criticized the sacrificial dues. It had to be a bad omen. The sacrifices were increased and the blasphemers warned, which seemed to work for the moment.

Military drills were beefed up too, the Moat Hall field reverberating with the clanging of bronze, the commands of instructors, and the panting of running, charging, jumping or wrestling soldiers. New chariots were built and the old ones repaired, all of them joining the army with long ceremonies invoking Indra, the Shatterer of Cities, the hard-fighting, hard-drinking god of war. Decorated with flowers and daubed with blood, their four-feet-high, eight-spoked wheels straining for the race, and the kill – for each axle was fitted with a long wicked blade that could mow down anything in its path – the new vehicles were good morale-boosters, for they recalled great victories and greater legends, of the first Arya warriors who had swept into these plains and smashed all before them.

But those days the chariot-borne Aryas had faced only the earth-cowering Nagas. Nowadays the chariot-borne faced other chariot-borne, and while each might call the other non-Arya scum, the chariots were not put off by such sneers.

'We can't fight Kosala,' said Shudodhan for the thousandth time, watching his soldiers break the consecrated chariots in.

'I know,' said Mahanaman. 'But we can't refuse to fight.'

'Even if we leave our borders open, we can manage only about twenty-thousand on the field – to Kosala's easy forty-thousand. That's all!'

'But we're better fighters.'

'How much better? Can we afford to find out?'

'I can't understand how they've become so strong!'

Nobody could. Was it the blessings of the sacred stream washing Kosala's south, said to have flowed for aeons from the matted locks of Shiva? But Shiva was not even of the Vedic pantheon, though the brahmins now advised that his name be included in yagna dedications. Or was it the heritage of the great Kuru warrior-king Ram, of Ayodhya which was now part of Kosala? Or was it the wealthy Kashi province, with her talented cotton weavers whose wares attracted buyers beyond the great seas? But Kashi had been a free republic herself many years ago, the richest and most powerful, before she was inexplicably conquered by the SisuNagas, a small and clearly non-Aryan clan on her east. And the legendary Ram's pure-blooded Arya descendants had been toppled, without much fanfare and by another lowborn character from god only knows where, who conquered the neighbouring Kosalas too, styled himself Raja of Kosala and made Shravasti his capital. He soon went to war with Kashi, defeated the SisuNagas and created one enormous kingdom out of the three old republics. The present Raja was his son.

It was bizarre and frightening, but Shudodhan did not give up. He even tried direct diplomacy, despite the near-hysteria this drummed up at home. Siddarth accompanied him on a trip to Shravasti, not long after the monsoon departed, when the Shakyas were suddenly invited to grace the opening ceremonies of an ashwamedha yagna. The Raja of Kosala had decided to announce his dominance to the world, and how better than by the yagna that proclaimed the yajman a king of kings? Shudodhan accepted the invitation, to the surprise of many of his own friends. The ashwamedha was essentially a ruler's signal to all his neighbours that he was interested in their lands. A stallion was released to wander where it willed for a year, followed by the yajman's troops. If it entered neighbouring lands, the neighbours had to either pay vassalage or fight. And with Kosalan domains edged by the Ganga on the south, the Himavat on the north, and dense tiger-infested jungle on the west, the best option for the stallion if it chose to travel abroad was east, to either the Videhas or the Shakyas. It made more sense for the Shakyas to stay home and sacrifice like mad.

Instead, Shudodhan travelled with a small delegation to the Kosalan capital, and sat amidst thousands of guests on a vast field, to watch the sacrifices that launched the yagna. Even young Siddarth found the scale humbling. Giant altars devoured rivers of butter, milk and grain, more than a hundred horses, hundreds more of bulls, goats and sheep, finally even monkeys, peacocks, river dolphins and three tigers. The stupefying display of wealth and its reduction to smoke was interrupted only once, and that by terrifying visitors. The audience turned to stone as towering figures of the Vedic gods suddenly appeared amongst them and pushed through to bless the king. Indra, Agni and Varuna were instantly recognizable, not least because they were more than double human height. Most people threw themselves on the ground in obeisance. Some fainted, at least two died. Later on, as the practice became common at grand ceremonies, audiences would become more sanguine and Siddarth too would learn that the gods were just two tall acrobats each, one standing on the other's shoulders, enveloped in long robes, masks and crowns.

Finally, a magnificent white stallion was led to the river and driven into a shallow part with a broom. A dog was ceremoniously clubbed to death in the water on the north side of the horse, and its body floated under the horse's belly southwards. Then the stallion was free – theoretically – to roam where it willed, followed at a respectful distance by the troops. Actually, any king knew how to guide the horse's feet, or at least discourage them, so that it went where *he* wanted his troops to go.

This first trip to Shravasti always remained vivid in Siddarth's mind, partly perhaps because of the commotion that followed. They went back to Kapilavastu one person short – Anula pleaded some urgent work in the Shravasti market. When Anula insisted on joining the trip, then brought along his family, and finally stayed back with them, suspicions should have arisen. But he and Shudodhan were friends. They had grown up together, they had worked, played, fought and plotted together, they knew everything about each other. So Shudodhan thought.

So it came as a shock when news arrived that Anula had accepted a high position at the Kosalan court. The Gana Sabha met immediately; Anula was sentenced to death, his estates confiscated. But the proposal to send someone to carry out the death sentence was rejected. Kosala might interpret it as an attack. It was the worst crisis in Shudodhan's career. How could Anula have betrayed his sangha, his tribe, his blood? And the Shakya overtures now looked foolish. Kosala had purported to receive them with honour and then bought one of their number! And now their blasted horse was probably half way to Kapilavastu.

Shudodhan felt shattered. He had no option but to talk war. Everyone did; the only question was when. The horse was seen heading their way, then it was seen turning back. There, rallied Shudodhan tiredly, how could that filth ever imagine he could pollute their land?

There was a lull, occupied by an epidemic of fever in Kapilavastu. Special yagnas were offered, to no effect. A cowherd worked out the reason – the river. People who used the river water were falling sick, those who had wells, like the patrician households, were fine. It was a curse on the republic, hypothesized Shudodhan sadly. It was a curse on the republic, agreed the priests happily, descending on the river banks with all their paraphernalia. Meanwhile, a couple of fishermen dived into the depths where they found dense clumps of reeds that they could neither penetrate nor hack apart. It was quite possible, they said, that something had got entangled and rotted in the depths. But nobody listened. It was a curse. It had to be the Koliyas downstream. The Mallas upstream would have made more sense, but fighting the Koliyas was easier. Besides, curses are hardly slave to geography.

Shudodhan did not want to fight on the south-east, not with Kosala looming so large on the west. He suggested 'paying the Koliyas back in their own dirty coin'. It was a new, even unacceptable, method of warfare, but the Koliyas were non-Aryas, he said, so that didn't count. The Kapilavastu physicians were dispatched in a body to where the Rapti emptied into the Rohini, which then flowed into Koliya lands. There all the poisons they had ever heard of were brewed and poured into the water.

The success of this attempt to poison an entire nation was difficult to judge, but Kapilavastu recovered almost immediately – perhaps due to the absence of the medicos. There was no time to rejoice though, for even as the Koliyas sent troops to investigate the strange activities to their north, the white stallion appeared in the western borderlands, and this time wandered steadily along the highway towards the Shakya town of Silavati. Shudodhan vacillated; the Koliyas attacked and captured some land and many physicians.

Extra troops were dispatched to Silavati. The rest of Kapilavastu rushed about putting finishing touches on the new defence systems. The second city wall was ready, twenty feet thick and separated from the first by a new moat. New wells were dug and tested on slaves, animals. New tunnels were ready; the old ones, which the swine Anula would certainly have informed about, were either filled up or renovated with inlets down which boiling oil could be poured on to visitors, and trapdoors to divert them smoothly into the moat. Auguries were commissioned; they were thick with ifs and buts, as is normal at such times.

Shudodhan managed to bolster his own popularity in the middle of everything by freeing all enslaved Shakyas and also cancelling all Shakya debts; it was probably just a coincidence that his friends got their debtors to pay up while a few even rushed to borrow large amounts of money just before the announcement.

But they were all actually deeply worried. They met one evening at Mahanaman's house, ostensibly for a banquet to celebrate a daughter's betrothal, but really to finalize a little ruse. The only way out, they felt, was to sue for an honourable peace, a vassalage that looked more like an alliance. Shudodhan and Gangadhar had met secretly with a group of the city's Sethis; the Sethis agreed to loan them five hundred gold coins as an initial offer for Kosala. But when Shudodhan announced this at Mahanaman's house, he was greeted by a barrage of doubts.

'It's too risky....'

'If it ever came out....'

'It won't come out,' insisted Gangadhar. 'And we'll deny it if it does. They will have no proof.'

'Gangadhar, the rains are only a month away....'

'The horse is outside Silavati!'

Gangadhar could not be budged. It was decided to send the money with a trusted foreign merchant.

The young chief-in-the-making Siddarth attended this meeting, but the only thing he remembered was the dance performance that accompanied the banquet, thanks to the central performer. Mahanaman owned the best dance-master in Kapilavastu, but this dark Naga girl moved with a grace that could not have been wholly taught. She was clearly special, for money had been spent like water to adorn her. She was draped with yards of gossamer-thin Kashi cloth, through which flawless coppery skin glowed darkly. Slender rings of gold hung from her ears and around her neck, more circled the high pile of her glossy hair. Her eyes were dead, but who noticed her eyes? Even Shudodhan couldn't ignore her, and the more he stared, the more familiar she seemed. The evening ended with not a few queries about her. Her name was Nagamunda, answered Mahanaman curtly; she was a slave in his household and she was going to stay there. That's when Shudodhan remembered.

'Good god! It's that wench from Hemant's! That's why you voted against me! For a whore!'

'Shudodhan, listen – ' began Mahanaman.

'To what? How you sell your vote – ?'

'That's enough!' Mahanaman started shouting too. 'Yes, Hemant did offer her for free! And he tried to convince me that your policies would destroy the sangha. I heard him out, but I paid for her. And I voted for what I believed in!'

'And you kept her, even after he tried to kill me!'

But Shudodhan could not afford to lose another friend. He recovered and dismissed the episode from his mind, as did the others. They would never think of the beautiful Nagamunda again, though she went on to become the mother of a queen, the queen of all deceptions and the saviour of the Shakyas. That was much later. And it did not last long.

The money was sent to Kosala, and received, but with a lot of fanfare. The Raja of Kosala appreciated the bribe, he announced, but the Shakyas had to be more open-handed. His statement reverberated through the republic, with Hemant's friends braving the summer heat to announce in every town and village that the Chief was selling the nation out. Shudodhan staunchly denied the whole thing and called it a Kosalan ploy to destroy Shakya unity, such as it was. Kosala could not take on a united Shakya nation, he declared. But when the chariots of Kosala travelled through the night at apparently the speed of their iron-tipped bamboo arrows, followed by thousands of foot-soldiers, to appear at dawn one day before the gates of Silavati, he knew they could.

Silavati did not wait for instructions – it was a conservative stronghold, which, though shocked by the size of the Kosalan host, took serious umbrage to its presence on Shakya land. They attacked and were defeated. Surrender was out of the question; they died heroically, many belatedly appreciating Naga-metal for the first time. Most still believed that bronze was the gift of the sun, an integral part of an Arya's godly strength; there were enough who spoke of how their sword tensed up eagerly before a battle, how it jumped into their hands when danger approached, how it was actually the sword that fought, not the man attached. Nobody could argue against such conviction, though the Naga-metal tried the hardest – many proud warriors spent their last moments seeing their beloved bronzes cut, twisted or simply shattered by the ringing, mirror-like blades which bent sometimes but only to spring amazingly back into shape.

At the end of the day more than three thousand were dead. It was the most comprehensive defeat the Shakyas had ever suffered.

The nation reeled in shock; the rains began, crashing down furiously amidst lightning and thunder like a troupe of manic dancers. In two days water was roaring down lanes, over the edge of moats, into poorer houses. Shudodhan was simply ecstatic, he could have danced like one of the peacocks on the river banks, except that the republic was in mourning for Silavati. Kosala was defeated, at least for the moment.

But Kosala did not withdraw. More troops arrived at the great camp outside Silavati, driving their chariots through the rivers of mud that were the recent roads.

Was Kosala actually going to fight in the rains?

For the first time since he became Chief, the entire Gana Samiti met to discuss a real issue, the entire assembly, thousands of men, without invitation, some travelling to Kapilavastu with families and as many possessions as possible.

They were followed by an advance regiment of Kosala. Through the rain – it was absolutely unheard of. A sea of men, horses, chariots, catapults for heaving stones and torches, and about a hundred elephants, arranged itself in front of the city gates. The great white stallion they were supposed to be following was nowhere to be seen.

Drink the river water and die, prayed the Shakyas. The Kosalans drank and survived, the rains having apparently cleared out the poison. The city had stocked up food and fuel, and started rationing it out, preparing for a long siege. But there was no need. The third day began with a fusillade of catapulted torches, which caused pandemonium on the streets and at length convinced many damp but drying roofs to catch fire. More than a hundred torches were sent and then the Kosalans paused.

Inside Kapilavastu, while soldiers stood in the mud calmly passing buckets of water from wells to the burning houses, and crowds milled around hysterically in between, the Samiti met. Shudodhan kept silent, but Gangadhar said, 'Let us agree to vassalage now. When we are ready for battle, we will declare independence.'

'I agree,' said one raja, a conservative but with estates near Silavati. 'We cannot defeat them now.'

'Your words appal me.' Hemant really sounded appalled. 'Why then did the rajas of Silavati die?'

'Our total foot-soldiers are the same in number as this advance force. And they have double the chariots. More than double the elephants. And the rest of their army may arrive any moment.' Gangadhar was stoic and businesslike.

'And who is responsible for this weakness?' Hemant was anything but. 'When it was suggested that emergency taxes be collected from the wealthiest merchants of Kapilavastu, our worthy Chief was not interested!'

'The main thing is that they use the Naga-metal!' shouted Mahanaman, 'while you still use bronze!'

An old man suddenly spoke up, a commoner, bony shoulders proudly straight under a patched shawl. 'Lords, brothers, I am a farmer and an ignorant one, but a Shakya all the same. My father campaigned under the old Chief all his life; I did too as a lad, in the infantry. But my sons have never seen the army, for they have no way of arming themselves, and now it is the law to arm oneself. They do not earn enough for one decent set of clothes in a year. I myself sold my old sword for the metal long ago.'

There was a pause. Then both Hemant and Shudodhan started speaking at the same time.

'I'm truly disturbed, brother,' said Shudodhan. 'For the moment however, we have to decide about Kosala.'

'Yes,' agreed Hemant. 'Let's not get distracted.'

The distraction pushed the meeting to a hasty adjournment. They would decide the next day, it was decided.

They never did. Kosala attacked without warning and simply pulverized their defences in the middle of the night – a dishonourable method and time according to all Arya war-rules. The moat in front of the gates had been filled in and covered with boards. An old mare was tied to the gates, so that the elephant battering ram did not turn away from the deadly spokes in the shutters. The batterer charged, leather-armoured on head and sides, natural aggressiveness increased ten-fold by quantities of rice wine. The mare was crushed, the gates burst open. The second gate took longer, because there was less charging space in front of it – it was staggered in the old Arya swastika pattern, developed for just such an eventuality but used now more out of reverence than for tradition. Battles had become highly formalized and no one was expected to be so rude as to break into a city at night.

As it turned out, neither the reverence nor the gate worked. Led by ten trumpeting elephants, all enraged by spear-stabs in the tender skin behind their ears, the Kosalans were in Kapilavastu. The beasts scattered the night patrol, ignored their flying javelins, pulped those unable to get away, and headed down the main road towards the inner city. Deep ditches had been dug along the way, hidden under light bamboo mesh, but amazingly only the first elephant fell victim, crashing in and breaking its front legs. The others detoured. Timber balconies of buildings on the street crumpled as they thundered closely past, roofs collapsing with a hellish clatter of tiles. Fire torches had been kept ready in these houses; they were lit and thrown quite accurately, but the drunk and blinkered animals simply didn't notice.

The infantry poured in behind, iron in hand. Shakya troops racing down the new tunnels for surprise rear attacks were surprised by Kosalans coming the other way. Five elephants of the city patrol stood shielding the inner city gates but the ear-splitting trumpeting and clanging bronze bells of the approaching Kosalan stampede unnerved them and the Shakya mahuts, like many who would rely on elephants in armies of the future, discovered too late that the animal was prone to panic and running amok. An army had to attack if it were not to be crushed under the prancing feet of its own high-strung, four-hundred-tonne-plus monsters. One of them now turned and bolted, the others followed. The Kosalan charge broke the gates without much ado and trampled over everything in turn till they reached the Moat Hall. But somehow some of the Shakyas made it there before the Hall was touched. Shudodhan spoke only one word: 'Peace.'

'Then, my lord,' said General Bundula Karayana from the top of an elephant, 'please ask your troops to retire. Only Kosalans will be on the roads tonight. Anyone else will be put to death.' He had already ordered a few such deaths. It created the correct atmosphere.

The deed of vassalage was signed in the morning below an overcast sky darkened further by smoking buildings and many pyres. It was a terrible moment for the Shakyas, though Karayana played host well, offering seats, sweets and goblets of wine in his regally-appointed tent, of which they coldly refused the last two. Karayana took the insult in the spirit it was offered and happily announced the terms of vassalage. An annual contribution of a thousand gold coins, two thousand carts of rice, four thousand heads of cattle. And, in due time, a bride.

'A bride?'

But of course. Vassalage was traditionally sealed by marriage among Aryas, a sign of the friendly relationship between conqueror and conquered, in which the latter were free to manage their internal affairs. But the conqueror and the conquered were normally equals. And the Kosalans had hardly held to Arya tradition so far.

A downpour began as the Shakyas tottered home, and continued for two months without pause. The heavens wept, said their brahmins. Shudodhan didn't believe it for a moment. Why hadn't the heavens sent a thunderstorm to drown the Kosalans? The heavens were with Kosala. And his problems were far from over. Marriage with Kosala! When the Gana Sabha met next, it was to warn the Chief that no raja would even consider it.

The great thing was that there was no rush. The Raja of Kosala was still engrossed in the year-long aswamedha yagna, which required him to remain celibate even while sleeping every night between the legs of his favourite queen. Abstinence was also mandatory for the stallion roaming the world nearby, and ensured by his armed escort. He didn't even have the consolation of becoming king of kings at the end; he was killed instead.

The year passed without any solution being found. But the new Raja of Rajas seemed to forget the marriage proposal. He was busy, pushing south of the Ganga to swallow the free town of Mathura, annexing the republic of the Mithilas, then the Videhans, the latter so violently that many Shakyas were glad of the stand they had taken. They decided to lie low, pay their tribute on time, and do exactly nothing to attract attention. Four years after their defeat, the Raja suddenly took ill and died. He was followed by his general, Bundula Karayana. It looked suspicious but the Shakyas were not about to question their good luck. The new king Pasenadi threw himself immediately into the same expansionist enterprise. He ignored the Shakyas so completely that they finally relaxed and began to recover.

It was not easy, though. Their new position in the world was difficult to swallow, incomprehensible really. Aryas, kshatriyas and warriors born, they had been reduced to a tribute-paying fief of the most upstart realm in the region. It should have made at least a few of them wonder whether their glorious identity was just a myth. But the truth was too painful to imagine, impossible to accept. It was easier to forget the whole business.

They did the same thing later, when Siddarth left. Why did he leave? Why did he, born of the purest blood that Bharatvarsha could boast, spurn his heritage and opt to become a nobody, at the mercy of the taunts of the dregs of the world? He would have become a Chief, but he chose to become a beggar. The questions haunted his family for years. They knew that in some way they had driven him away, yet had there ever been a son more cherished?

Then and now, they decided to forget. They pushed the questions away and clutched tighter to their past. They paid their tribute, tolerated the visits of Kosalan generals, even flew the flag of Kosala at their gates, all by convincing themselves that one day, very soon, they would regain their freedom. Their astrologers knew their need and declared the vassalage a momentary aberration, the result of the rise of malcontents like the planets Saturn and Mars. No need to worry, the will of the gods would finally prevail.

It was only a matter of time.

SANCHI

Upali lifted his head from the last sheet, saw a tumbler of water nearby and felt his throat dry and hurting. There was silence in the hall as he drank. The tumbler was of silver and he could taste the metal. Did silver dissolve in water? It was probably his imagination. The dead monk had used a silver tumbler too. He should not let his mind wander. He put the tumbler down. The silence continued. Everybody was waiting for the Magadhe-Raja to speak.

They were seated in the main hall of the Raja Vihara, the King's Abode. He was directly in front, on a dais – Upali had managed a quick glance from the doorway before a soldier's ungentle hand on his back helped him fall on the floor and begin crawling ahead on hands and knees. Past many men distributed equally on both sides, many aristocrat types and some monks, to a flat rosewood seat about halfway down, with a stand before it for his sheets.

It was a large room and magnificently furnished by Upali's standards, which is actually not saying much. The seats were covered in some kind of thick silk, as was the bolster placed behind him, though his back, taut as a bow string, had yet to touch it. An astoundingly soft rug patterned in red and black covered the floor.

Tall lamps shone like dull gold sentinels along the walls; the royal divan looked like ivory, but was that possible?

Upali tried to memorize everything he could see, to use in his story. But did they have the same kind of finery three hundred years ago? And was this proper court finery or just the amazing new Sanchi? After the Thera's silks, Upali inclined to the latter theory.

His eyes began to protest against facing downward while squinting forward. But Harsha had warned him to look down unless addressed. Then he peered sideways and was amazed to find all his neighbours gazing straight at the centre of the dais. He followed suit and discovered the reason – one eye was closed, the other invisible under a band of black silk that crossed his brow and was knotted behind his head. He was deep in thought, or dozing, and Upali stared and stared and felt a little giddy. There were others on the dais, two women, some young men, attendants at the back, but he saw only him. The Murderer of Kalinga. Self-proclaimed Beloved of the Gods. Grandson of Chandragupta, and master of an even greater realm, a realm that dwarfed the old Bharatvarsha of the Buddha's time. He was apparently blind in an eye – had he lost it in Kalinga? Upali felt a stab of triumph, but only for a moment. Mainly he felt awe.

He felt awe, though the Devanampiya hardly looked like a god or even beloved of them. While everybody in the room except Upali shimmered in gold brocade and silk, he was dressed almost like a soldier who had forgotten his armour and weapons. His chest was bare, adorned only by two long greyish-red scars on one side. There were more on his arms. The black pants looked like regulation army wear. No crown, no earrings, not a single necklace or ring, nothing but thick gold anklets, the prerogative of royalty. His hair was thick and jet-black, dyed no doubt, for he had completed more than four decades on this earth. His figure contrasted even more sharply with his guests. The Magadhe-Raja was a third generation monarch through direct descent, but one look was enough to know that the most powerful name in the land was not of the highest lineage. Upali could not discern his height, since the king had not seen fit to rise in his presence as yet, but the swarthy skin and thickly-muscled shoulders could have belonged to a physical worker in his prime. Or to a fighter. Upali had heard Ananda-like stories of how the king could fell an ox or stop a galloping horse-driven chariot with one hand, and he didn't completely disbelieve them now.

He felt a little tense. His throat still hurt and his stomach ached. He had not eaten anything since the day before and it was now past midday. He had spent the morning roaming around the monastery with Ananda, while the Raja was meeting delegations from Ujjayani and Vidisha. Ujjayani was the capital of Avanti, while Vidisha was a trade centre and more importantly the hometown of his beloved Devi. It was she who was said to have converted the Magadhe-Raja to the Middle Way – though the very idea that the Murderer could follow the Way was grotesque.

But Sanchi was clearly an advertisement of royal devotion. The undulating green slopes were studded with stupa-esque monuments, interspersed by grand viharas built in solid teak instead of the wattle-and-daub of Maheshwar. The smallest stupas were little stone sculptures half the height of a man; the largest towered over the double-storeyed viharas. Crowds of monks, soldiers and indeterminate others hurried along the broad stone paths, each tile cut to snuggle exactly against its neighbour. The atmosphere was busy, urbane, and rather wary – as befitted an elegant little township perched high above the wilderness. Somehow Upali felt uncomfortable.

They had automatically gravitated to the great brick ovoid of the main stupa. Around it was a high timber stockade, with swastika-shaped entrances at each of the cardinal points. The stockade was simply three plain broad rails held up by similar verticals, but the elaborately-carved and painted entrance portals more than made up for this. Scenes of city streets, marketplaces, river ports, armies at war, and all kinds of people – nobles, farmers, weavers, hunters, dancers, gods – the artists had tried to cram in the whole world. Despite the crowd, each figure was detailed lovingly, some perhaps a little more than others. Upali and Ananda were transfixed by a yakshini, a wood nymph, holding up the cantilevered end of a lintel. She was a bracket, but had there ever been such an enchanting bracket? Her pose seemed modelled on a liana vine, her ridiculously generous curves on fruit-laden trees, but her expression? The amused challenge in her eyes was so disturbing that Upali had to finally drag himself away, and Ananda too, both silently promising her that they would come back when alone.

The female figure was beloved of artists; almost every village Upali could remember had their own precious figurines and paintings. But usually as a creator, heavily pregnant and nursing, or a destroyer, with gigantic hips, pendulous breasts and hungry eyes, her image stained with blood and her tongue lolling out for more. She was woman at her most powerful, protector and eater of the tribes. The urbane world of Magadh saw women differently. Their goddesses, nymphs and dancers were benign and alluring, friends and comforters of mankind. He had seen a few like this before, in merchants' mansions at Tosali. But... in a monastery? On a stupa?

But then Sanchi was a different kind of monastery. The first set up not by monks, but by a king, and as a mark of affection for the city where he had found love many years before.

It had been one of the most difficult moments of his youth. He had just proved himself by putting down a rebellion in Takshashila, returning to the capital in triumph only to be sent away again. This time as Viceroy of Avanti. Some said the rivalry between him and his brothers was becoming impossible for the old king to handle. He had many sons, Ashoka being the third, and all of them tended to function as if they had never heard of the right of primogeniture. Some said that the father had begun to fear for his own life, Magadh having the unfortunate history of being ruled more often than not by parricides. So Ashoka had come to Ujjayani, angry and determined to return to Pataliputra at the earliest. But his anger had melted temporarily at the house of a wealthy Vidisha merchant, when he saw his nubile daughter. The Viceroy was smitten, but not enough to marry her – a low-born wife, that too from provincial Vidisha, was not a great asset for a man whose sights were firmly set on the imperial throne. But he wanted her badly and there was little way her family could refuse a Maurya.

So Devi became a royal concubine and Ashoka was said to have remained besotted for years and more, through many marriages, his viceroy-ship and then his terrible and successful fight for the throne. It was she who left him, nauseated by the same fight, it was said, and then the war. She returned to Vidisha, to the horror of her community who expected to be destroyed by royal rage. But Ashoka remained a munificent benefactor. The Sanchi monastery was his gift to Vidisha for giving him a son, Mahendra, his oldest son but not the crown prince; his mother raised him to be a monk.

It would be claimed at Ashoka's death that he had a total of 84,000 stupas built, which, since he ruled some thirty-seven years, averages 2,270 each year, or more than six a day, a feat clearly impossible for anyone not Beloved of the Gods.

Recently he had discovered a new passion – stambhas, or free-standing columns, in the style of the totem poles that once graced the gates of every free republic. Except that his were simply enormous, inscribed with his continuous missives to his subjects, and, remarkably for those timber times, built of stone. Not surprisingly, these stambhas had achieved some celebrity and Upali was thrilled to discover one being finished in Sanchi that very morning, in the open-air workshop that he and Ananda found on the eastern edge of the monastery. The sound of stone being chipped led them halfway down a wooded hill, to a secluded clearing where they found a few men and many blocks of stone. The blocks were being cut, shaped, ground and polished, most for new votive stupas. Uncut blocks stood around in anticipation. But Upali was drawn to the men working on a huge cylinder, the biggest piece in the workshop, different in colour and also in sheen – its lustre

was like sheet metal where the sun hit it. He sank down uninvited
next to it and stared at his own face in the shaft.

'But this is metal!' he said. 'Isn't it?'

The workers had risen, palms joined respectfully, and shook
their heads, smiling a little. It was stone, but transformed into a
solid cylindrical grey-brown mirror that looked exactly like steel.
It was a stone monument to steel!

The workers were still standing. Upali got up and joined his
palms. 'Salutations, brothers. Please forgive my rudeness. We'd
heard much of these pillars but never seen any.'

The stone-cutters sat down and those near the column went
back to polishing it with rough palm-twig scrapers dipped into a
grey paste. Rivulets of sweat ran continuously off their bare heads
and shoulders onto the stone and perhaps into it. It would be about
nine times human height when erected, Upali estimated. Just the
capital was the height of one man. And very strange too. Where
were the buxom goddesses, their consorts, attendants, goblins,
apsaras, yogis, rivers and foliage that always attended important
edifices? This was starkness personified. Four lions sat facing the
four directions, on an inverted lotus pedestal. The beasts were
regal, the lotus delicately moulded. Between lions and pedestal was
a disc, on whose sides was carved the four animals of royalty –
lion, bull, horse and elephant – and between each was a chariot
wheel.

The stambha had come from Chunnar in Kashi, explained
one worker, an old man with thick grey stone dust in his nails, a
thinner coat over the rest of him. The workers were from Chunnar
too. They had brought it here by river, up the Ganga, the Yamuna
and the Betwa, then up the Sanchi hill on a long specially-built
cart with twenty-five wheels on either side, drawn by five elephants.

'All that effort! But why one single block? Wouldn't building
it up with many smaller blocks be easier?'

'Much easier. But the joints would be visible. For an unsculpted
shaft this is better. The Magadhe-Raja expects perfection.'

'Did you sculpt the capital?'

'With my brothers here. But the design is by the Raja himself, so I heard. '

'Has he sent the inscription for the shaft?'

'The mantra? No, not as yet.'

'Mantra? I mean the "Here speaks the" – no, wait, I think it's "Thus speaks the Beloved – "'

'Lord!' The old man looked pained. 'It is a divine mantra. The words are powerful, not to be juggled around carelessly.'

The juggler of words scowled. 'What do you mean?'

'We put up a Dhamma Stambha just like this at Sarnath two years ago and when the rains were late last year, the villagers prayed to it. I heard that it was hardly a week before they found a new spring nearby. It is good magic.'

Dhamma Stambha? But the old man's hands didn't pause in their steady caress of the stone; it was somehow relaxing to watch him, Dhamma or not. But Upali had been instructed not to stray far.

'I hope I can see this erected,' he said. 'It will look magnificent!'

The sculptor beamed. 'Do you know, my lord, some people believe that the stambha is itself the work of the gods!'

They took their leave, started back uphill and had nearly reached the outlying viharas when a voice called, 'Hi, master! Please wait a moment.'

It was one of the sculptors, a young man whom Ananda had noticed staring intently at Upali a few times. 'Lord, if you can spare some time….'

'Yes, what is it?'

His name was Devadina, he said, and he was from Pataliputra. 'I have a problem. I wish your help to solve it.'

'Mine? I'm an outsider too. You should speak to the Thera.'

'I've been trying for days. I was hoping that you could speak to him for me. I wish to marry a girl from Ujjayani.' He was an attractive young man, tall and bronzed, with an open direct gaze.

'Well, tell me.'

They sat down under a palasa laden with red blossoms. Below them the forest tumbled downwards to the rooftops of Vidisha. The sculptor had a real problem – his love was a devadasi in an Ujjayani temple. A priestess-slave of the god.

'A devadasi?'

'Yes, my lord. I saw her at the market first, then I followed her to the temple. Then I went again, and once I got a chance to speak to her, and… and we became friends.'

'And?'

'And I wish to marry her. But I need someone to speak for me, to her temple. I hoped the Thera might.'

'What does she say?' In what world was this lad living? A devadasi – a temple prostitute!

'She has accepted my proposal. But the priests saw me with her and were really angry. She is frightened now; they are very harsh people.'

'And her family?'

She has a brother. But why would he object?'

Upali could think of many reasons but continued his questions. 'Hasn't she… served the gods… I mean, with her body, as yet?'

The sculptor looked suddenly stern. 'I don't care. I want to marry her.'

Upali felt ashamed of himself. This sculptor might be a simpleton but he was a noble one. 'Who runs the temple?'

'It belongs to the Sungas of Ujjayani. So I was told.'

'The Sungas?' The name was vaguely familiar. 'Did you meet them?'

'I tried. But I was not allowed into their mansion.'

'Wait a minute – that's the name of the dead monk, isn't it?'

The sculptor nodded. 'Yes. Sutanuka told me that one of the family was a monk here. The lord Pradyota. So I tried to meet him too, more than once. But he was always surrounded by people. Then I heard that he had died. It was very sudden, I believe.' He paused. 'Could you speak to the Thera? It is no life for a girl like

Sutanuka. I know it is a sacred position, but Sutanuka is different, she's delicate, she's like a flower, she's....'

'I'll do my best.'

They bade him farewell and walked up the slope, past large and small viharas, heading for the slightly isolated royal one, when a monk startled them by rising up from nowhere almost in their faces. He turned to hurry away, but Upali stopped him.

'Brother! Were you bowing just now?'

He nodded. 'Yes. That was Thera Pradyota's room.'

'Really? Why, was he – ' Upali paused but could not think of any reason for monks to bow before the room of a dead colleague.

The monk however rushed ahead in explanation. 'It is a terrible tragedy, Master. He was a great man, a genuine sage. We relied on him!'

'You relied on him?'

'He prayed for us, Master. He never thought of his own salvation, only of others – he said that that was the meaning of Dhamma. He was a holy man.' Ananda had to stop a grin at Upali's expression.

The monk however was oblivious. 'Would you like to see his room?'

Why not? They followed him in and up a polished timber staircase to a broad balcony off which many doorways opened. Their guide entered one after bowing again. Upali and Ananda followed, the first distinctly uneasy, the second muttering some quiet incantations against ghosts. It was not a dormitory but a large personal room, with a cot, shelves, and a low table with two silver tumblers and a lamp.

'Do all of you have individual cells?'

'Not all.' The monk flitted about the room lovingly polishing a glass here, wiping a shelf there. 'But he was used to privacy, from his years at Takshashila.'

Upali's stomach had begun to hurt so he sat down on the cot. 'Takshashila?'

'He joined us only four months ago. We were lucky that he decided to leave Takshashila.'

'Why did he?'

'Probably jealousy. He was very wise. Enlightened. He had attained Nirvana, you could see it.'

'What could you see?'

'Well, he could answer any question.'

'What kind of question?'

'Oh, I don't know – anything.'

Upali shifted uncomfortably. A monk murdered was bad enough, but also worshipped? It was bizarre. He had come across two killings of monks before, both in Kalinga before the war. Both were by people who thought that the monks were against their gods. They were violent affairs, but open, everybody knew what had happened. This quiet business was different. His stomach jabbed him and he shifted again. There was a slight rustle below him.

He rose and lifted the quilt. Below was a mattress, which seemed on investigation to be stuffed with cotton. He felt again, more carefully.

'There seems to be something here.'

The monk and Ananda were watching him in surprise.

'Inside the mattress. May I open it?'

'Wait….'

'Just a little... there!' Upali had turned up the edge of the mattress and pulled some stitches open. He put his hand in and groped around before emerging triumphantly with two small pieces of stiff, shiny white material. There was some writing on them. He put his hand back in and came out with one more.

'See!'

'What is it?' asked Ananda nervously.

'Some kind of silk. And this is a northern script, perhaps Kharosthi from Takshashila. Some money seems to be mentioned.' He felt around in the mattress one last time. 'I suppose I should give these to the Thera?'

'Upali.'
'Upali.'

Everyone was staring at him. He looked up, straight into the single eye. He felt numb, but still managed to rise and fall flat on his stomach, arms outstretched, palms locked. 'Sire, I...I – '

'Rise, Upali. Sit down. You seemed deep in thought. Your story is interesting, Upali, very interesting...' the Magadhe-Raja paused. He spoke in good Pali, instead of the Magadhi used in court circles right from the time of the Buddha. Upali was glad, for he could not speak Magadhi well. He sat back and looked down. Like everyone else, he waited for the But.

'But there isn't very much at the moment. And you seem to have deviated from the Shakyamuni's own experiences. In fact, you have completely ignored them so far.'

'Yes, my lord,' said Upali to the carpet. He wiped his wet face with trembling palms, urged his stomach to calm down, peeked sideways and discovered again that everybody else was staring straight ahead. He followed and met the single eye again; it was heavy lidded, matching the lower lip. In a hard sensual face. 'I – I will be writing them, sire. That will be the main part of the account. Only, I wanted to build the background first.'

'Yes, but see that it does not distract you from the real issues.' Another pause. Upali looked down at his hands. 'Your story so far seems to be leading up to the end of the Shakyas.'

'Sire, I think the decline of the Shakyas, of the republics in general, seriously affected the Shakyamuni's life and ideas.'

'And you are also spending a lot of time on this Naga-Arya issue. Which I found quite interesting actually – I didn't know that Kosala was once ruled by Nagas.'

'Naga was what the aristocratic republics called anybody who did not perform the Vedic rituals. Many so-called Nagas were very cultured – like the SisuNagas of Magadh – or those of the ancient cities on the Sindhu. It's really a question though whether anybody was actually pure in the blood sense.'

He felt sweat running down his back. He was lecturing the Murderer!

'Fascinating. But you are taking far longer than I had expected. What's causing the delay?'

'Sire, I found it impossible to put the story down exactly the way it is recited. It needs some changes – '

'Changes? You're changing the story?'

'Sire – changes is not the correct word. What I meant is that there are many inconsistencies in the account. Perhaps because the suttas were written at different times, by different people. Ideas changed over time. So I had to compare and select.' His palms were wet too.

The Magadhe-Raja suddenly raised his hand; Upali tensed. But it was for an attendant behind him, who raised a gold flagon high above his own mouth and let a trickle of what looked like water fall in. He swallowed and handed the flagon to the king who drank deeply and then turned towards an old monk seated close to the dais. 'What do you feel, Mogallana?'

So this was Mogalliputta Tissa, the renowned and powerful Thera of Pataliputra. He was tall and stooped, with a long gloomy face, and seemed to be in a state of extreme debilitation. He rose very slowly, bowed, then started lowering himself to the floor, but the dais cut off his shaky manoeuvrings with a wave. 'Sit down.'

Mogalliputta remained standing, palms joined. His voice was surprisingly loud and clear. 'Your Majesty, with your permission. I agree with you, sire. Thera Upali has painted a vivid picture of the Shakyamuni's time.' He paused and immediately contradicted himself. 'Though I do find the style a little drab compared to the older accounts. And I seriously dispute that part of human sacrifice – it is impossible, quite slanderous actually. The account so far seems to almost *target* the Shakyas, which is very disturbing. But really, the important question is – where is this heading? Surely the Thera is not trying to say that the situation created the Buddha?

Surely everybody knows that he would have shone his light over any darkness?' He bowed shakily and returned to his seat. Behind him was seated another old monk who looked vaguely familiar.

But Upali could not afford distractions now. 'With all respect, Thera,' he began. 'You make the Buddha sound almost a god, almost like the Mahasanghikas – '

Mogalliputta cut in without rising. 'Please do not attribute strange ideas to me, Thera! And there is nothing *maha* about those people, except for stupid arrogance! All I mean is that the evils which the Shakyamuni preached against – of lust, dishonesty, violence, greed – all exist today as well. His message is universal. Or do you feel that Dhamma, the Dhamma that you have sworn an oath to, is no longer relevant a mere 300 years later?'

A mere? How old was this relic? Upali struggled to marshal his thoughts. 'No, it is relevant. The essence of Dhamma is in fact indispensable. But it is still important to understand the society at the time of the Buddha, so that we understand how Dhamma was born and also the changes that have taken place since. After all, the Dhamma that we – any of us – follow today is not the exact one the Buddha preached.'

Mogalliputta was grim. 'What do you mean?'

'Well, how many monks live off alms today? How many move from place to place continuously? How many only travel by foot? We are all bald today, thanks to the sramana tradition I think, since I've never encountered any such injunction by the Buddha. I am not saying that all the changes are bad. After all, what were his last words? "Change is eternal." But it is important to know them as changes.'

'His words were a warning to remain true to Dhamma. Not an invitation to change! You are confusing issues, Thera. The examples you give were not elements of Dhamma. They were part of the Vinaya, the Sangha's code of conduct. The purpose of the Vinaya was to ensure that monks practise Dhamma and reach it to the public. The methods of achieving this will naturally change with new technology and living conditions.'

Accepting royal funds as at Sanchi, as opposed to begging as they had first done at Kalinga, was not a difference caused by technology, but the old monk had turned away to the dais. Upali was grateful. It would be stupid to mention the royal grants here, stupider to mention Kalinga. And it was a long time since he had held the alms-bowl himself. His had been iron, belonging to their first year of wandering, when as a lad of ten Upali had accompanied his teacher southwards from Kashi, a long trek over nearly a year, till they reached the great forests at the edge of Magadh. They stayed there for many months, begging in the mornings and preaching Dhamma the rest of the day to the jungle-folk. But some of the locals became hostile after two boys joined them and they had to move on, further south, across the hills, through vast swamps and tiger-infested jungle, to the republic of the Kalingas. They continued to walk, speaking to peasants, tribals, merchants, even the rajas on the rare occasions they encountered them, and at some point right in the south, at the edge of another vast swathe of forest that was reputed to be unending, Upali's teacher decided to halt. They had started planting, then ploughing, and somewhere along the way put aside their alms-bowls.

It was all a long time ago, the time before death, before this man arrived there.

Mogalliputta was still speaking. '...the suttas are being put down – surely that is enough? We are trying our best to solve all issues of contention. Thera Upali's work will add to them, it will cause confusion, even anger, for it almost mocks the suttas.'

Finally the Magadhe-Raja spoke, and addressed Upali. 'Mogallana has a point. Confusion is the last thing we need. Mogallana is in fact composing an answer to the many philosophical disputes within the Sangha. I want to put an end, once and for all, to such fruitless debate. I am a strong advocate of writing, Upali, you know that. Some say I am crazy in this regard.' He smiled. Who were these some, wondered Upali a little wildly, had they lived to tell the tale? 'But I don't want to encourage controversy.'

'Sacred Majesty,' Mogalliputta started off again, 'I had earlier opposed this project because of the lack of flexibility it will create in the work of the Sangha. Till now, there were different stories of the Buddha, catering to the need of the hour. After all, what is the point of expounding abstruse points of philosophy before sweepers or forest savages? That is why there are different versions – not because of changes! I strongly disagree with Thera Upali. All the suttas have been memorized, each word in connection to the next. You cannot change even one word without the danger of forgetting them all. That is the safety in rote learning! But this project will concretize one version and make lies of the rest. And now, after this reading, I feel that the dangers are even greater. We cannot have such attacks on the legend respected by all.'

Upali was impressed. The old man must have nerves of steel to argue so coherently in front of the king. And he was right – rote learning fixed things. But he had also affirmed Upali's point – there were different versions of the Buddha's life, so all could not be correct.

The Raja was nodding. 'Mogallana, I understand your fears. I even agree with you to an extent. Not about the value of the oral tradition, however. The practice of rote learning has serious limitations. It is not conducive to understanding, or to keeping an objective record. Nor to progress, for it confers an over-venerable status on knowledge, as something ancient and unchanged, and therefore sacred and unchangeable. It leads to superstition and stagnation. I want all knowledge, information, and records put down in writing, and dated, so that they get a historical and human touch, instead of the impersonal timelessness that has been the norm. Future generations should learn from the past, not worship it! And I actually like Upali's attempt so far – it is very revealing of the times. But we should be careful to avoid confusion.'

The Raja looked all around as he spoke, eliciting ponderous nods and other signs of affirmation, except from Mogalliputta who remained grim, and Upali himself.

'I am personally very keen to hear of the Buddha's own enlightenment. And I am also keen for the story to be published across the land, along with the suttas. If the brahmins wish to preserve their religious scriptures in rote learning, I will not object. But Dhamma is for the masses and for practise. The Shakyamuni himself preached in the Prakrits to reach the widest audience possible. I look forward to the day when my subjects will not require my edicts to be read to them, when they will read for themselves! So what if the tradition and veneration of rote learning go back hundreds of years? It belongs to the past.'

Mogalliputta maintained an icy reserve.

'So, Upali, I await your completed work. And I shall have more work waiting for you.' Another pause. It was an effective way of holding attention, thought Upali the teacher. It made your listeners hold their breath. But again, that would work best only when you had the power of life and death over your listeners. 'There is one more thing – I wish you to keep my nephew Nigrodha with you for some time. Teach him the skills of writing. I feel he will benefit under your guidance.'

A boy, tonsured and dressed in Sanchi's saffron robes, descended from the dais, approached Upali, bowed low, touched his feet and withdrew before the latter thought of responding.

'Finally, Upali – I am concerned about the differences within the Sangha. That's why I've asked Mogaliputta to clarify the doctrinal issues. And I've decided to host a congress of all monasteries, at Pataliputra. We will discuss these matters and come to some conclusion. I do not want these disputes, these many and varied rituals, all these different interpretations to continue. I trust you agree?'

'No – yes, I mean – but it all seems quite out of control, sire,' The eye was suddenly sharp and Upali rushed on nervously, 'I mean, I've heard recently that the Buddha is being ascribed superhuman status by some, in the manner of the Mahasanghikas. While they themselves have gone much further, and hold him as the last in a string of divine reincarnations. Some say he preached tolerance, compassion and non-violence, others say Nirvana and personal salvation, and still others Heaven and universal salvation! Some followers almost worship, with circumambulation, incense and flowers. There are some who live on alms, others who drink out of silver glasses – '

'But the suttas surely guide you?'

Even some who patronize war as well as monasteries, both generously. Upali nodded, grateful for being stopped.

'Well, then?'

'Sire, they are open to interpretation. And it hasn't ever mattered, I think, because the monasteries hardly interact. I myself….' He himself had lived for more than twenty years among the Kalingas, he had nearly said, and met outside monks only twice in that period.

'It has to stop.'

Upali said nothing.

'It has to stop. There are many spiritual teachers in my realm – the Jinas, the Ajivikas, the brahmins, among others. I respect all, but the Sangha is special. Not only because of my personal devotion to the Buddha but because I feel his teaching provides the simplest and most practical guidance for the masses in their daily lives. I have heard of the efforts of your monastery, Upali, and I think you are doing a good job.'

The eye was suddenly benevolent. Which monastery did he mean?

'I liked the proposal to employ the Kalinga deportees as elephant-trainers – a beautiful idea! That is exactly what the Sangha should be doing – trying to unite our society, educating people about the opportunities that exist today, helping them improve their lives. I want the Sangha to be the moral, spiritual and practical guide of my people. For that, there should be no controversies within.'

Upali pondered for a moment on the consequences of telling the room what he thought of the beautiful idea, but only for a moment.

'So, Upali, exactly three months from the full moon, I will hear you and all senior Theras at the Third Council of the Sangha. And we will listen to a reading of your story. I hope there will be more of it. And I may delay you in Pataliputra longer. You may go now. Nigrodha, go with your master. Study hard.'

The audience was over. Upali prostrated himself, rose to his knees, backed away to the door, reached it, and through it the anteroom. He was out and free! He would have beamed around, except that he was now being glared at by a posse of soldiers, almost as if he was a criminal. He composed himself and waited for his new student. What would the Buddha have thought of all this? His own encounters with royalty had been on a very different plane. He would not have approved. But he would probably have laughed first at Upali's struggle to recreate his life.

They walked in silence to his apartment. Upali was not sure how to treat the boy; he had never had a personal student before. All his students were students of the monastery. Ananda was the closest but he was the opposite of royal – he was another Upali, a foundling adopted by the Maheshwar monastery as the Sarnath one had adopted Upali many decades ago.

Ananda reacted to Upali's introduction of 'Ananda, this is Prince Nigrodha, your fellow-student' by falling flat at the prince's feet.

'Rise, Ananda.' Nigrodha was stern but gracious.

'Rise, Ananda!' Upali was rude and irritated. 'There will be no more formalities. You, Nigrodha, are a novice like all the others, and will be addressed by your name.'

'Yes, Master.' Nigrodha inclined his head respectfully, but in the months that followed Upali would discover that he was the only person who addressed Nigrodha thus.

It was late and Ananda looked ravenous, but he didn't complain as the whole of Sanchi thronged the road leading downhill to watch the Magadhe-Raja depart. On the back of a great armoured tusker, followed by many more, surrounded by hundreds of chariots, armed infantry, slogans, garlands, pennants, the cacophony of drums and cymbals, and soldiers lined up on both sides to keep the road clear. All of it surprisingly familiar to Upali, especially the javelins, long black ebony tipped with a steel knife, and the celebrated Magadhan long-bows, great laminated arcs of horn and wood taller than a man, to avoid encountering which the Greek Alexander was said to have given up his dream of empire and turned back from the Beas. The army of the Maurya, last seen four years ago – Upali would have given up more than an empire to never see it again.

The army of the Maurya, now pouring out of a monastery to the Buddha.

It was sunset when a monk came to invite them to lunch. They followed him out of their room to discover four armed soldiers waiting outside.

'What is it?' asked Upali.

'Sir, we are the bodyguards of His Highness.'

Upali scowled and marched ahead of them to the dining vihara, which was hot and crowded and chomping away silently except for a jovial crowd around the Sanchi Thera, who saw them enter and motioned Upali to his side. Ananda and Nigrodha squeezed in at the end of another row.

Among those eating with the Thera was the yellow-haired Xantes, who immediately made space for Upali next to him. A monk hurried up with a banana leaf, and almost simultaneously heaps of rice, dal, stewed tapioca, a spicy cucumber concoction and a spoonful of ghee appeared on it, with a bowl of curd on the side. Upali was famished but it was obvious that his neighbour wanted to talk, so after a few mouthfuls he paused and nodded at him.

It was like unplugging a dam. 'Thera, I must tell you, I was in the audience hall during your reading and I was very impressed. Your story is amazing. I am from Greece – '

Upali had already guessed as much, from the smell. He himself had come across foreign merchants only rarely, but the Maheshwar monks never tired of recalling the hard, encrusted hair and beard of the Greek merchant who had visited the monastery some years ago. The only time his hair had ever been washed was when he was caught in the rain without protection. And he'd claimed to be of royal blood!

'My family is from Samoa, the home of Pythagoras – he who spoke of the transmigration of souls. Later I learnt that his ideas probably came from here, India, as we call these lands beyond the Indus. I had already heard of India, of course – all young Greeks nowadays dream of honey-filled reeds, gold-digging ants and hills of gems! So when I was offered this position, I jumped at it. And I read the books of Lord Megasthenes – where first I heard of the Buddha, your spiritual leader.'

There were many questionable points in this tirade, but last came first. 'Spiritual leader?'

'Or god? As some say. But I discern a different approach in your reading.'

'My understanding is simple,' said Upali irritably. 'The Buddha was a very wise man, but a man.'

'When I was reading of him in Greece, I understood that the Buddhists treat the gods with a kind of friendly contempt, like the Athenians. People in Athens openly laugh at the – '

'Athens is the city of Socrates, right? The city that killed him for his questions?'

'You know of Socrates?'

'A little. My childhood was spent in the Sarnath monastery, where we had a lot of merchant visitors. My old master was very interested in such things. He had read some translations of another Greek – Aristotle – and spoke to us about them.'

'Yes, well, Socrates was killed and Aristotle had to flee or he might have been killed too. But they were exceptions; it is more normal for rulers to ignore philosophers – unlike things here! Your Emperor is actually trying to implement the Buddha's teachings. I still cannot believe that the divine sacrifices have been banned, even those before a battle – it is amazingly bold! It would have meant chaos in Greece!'

It took a moment for Upali to realize who was being referred by the title of the Macedonian Alexander. 'I suppose he realized that the blood spilt on his battlefields was enough for the most gluttonous of gods!'

The Greek was surprised enough to return to his food. But not for long. 'I wanted to ask you, Thera – do you believe that the Buddha was higher than the gods? That was the earlier Sangha belief, wasn't it? But I heard in Pataliputra that Buddha himself was a god!'

'All I know is the Buddha's message was to ignore the gods. I have nothing against the gods, but I am not interested in them.'

'A very Athenian statement!' It seemed to be a compliment. 'And yet the Emperor chose you to write the story. He recently financed the enlargement of an old stupa at Kosam, you know, said to be the grave of the Buddha in a previous incarnation. Will you be mentioning the incarnations in your story – perhaps the famous ones, when he was born as King Brahmadutta of Kashi, or as that clever merchant leader, or the wise old elephant, or the ancient banyan tree – ?'

'This is the first I'm hearing of them! I think this incarnation idea has been adopted from the Jinas. They say their Mahavira was the twenty-fourth in a long line of ford-makers – some of the Buddha's followers must be seeking a similar pedigree,' Upali felt the Sanchi Thera stiffen a little on his other side, 'and the Magadhe-Raja did not choose me. I was already writing it; he became interested.'

'But why were you writing it?'

Upali shrugged and began to eat.

'I mean, it's quite a big job, and tedious too, trying to read between the lines of things composed such a long time ago, almost like a hunt – '

He paused again but Upali ate on. It was a hunt, but hardly explainable. He would have to explain how he had lost himself first.

Xantes changed the topic. 'The Emperor is almost a preacher, don't you think? In our part of the world, it is unknown for conquerors to challenge the spiritual beliefs of their subjects. Quite the opposite. All the Persians, beginning with Cyrus, worshipped at Babylonian temples after conquering Babylon, and called themselves the heirs of the god Bel-Marduk; in Egypt they worshipped at Luxor and Thebes, as reincarnations of Ra! Alexander and his generals followed the practice. This is the first time I have heard of a monarch deliberately interfering in matters of religion.'

'The Buddha is hardly a matter of religion.'

'But banning the sacrifices surely is? Risky, some would say. Much easier to just collect your revenues and let your subjects worship whomever – '

'But then His Majesty is a follower of Dhamma, and a scholar as well!' The Sanchi Thera was beaming away as usual. 'And he has been striving steadfastly towards enlightenment for many years now – he would obviously have a better understanding of such matters.'

Upali immersed himself in a glass of water, but Xantes was in enthusiastic agreement. 'Yes, of course! The Magadhe-Raja is a ruler of awesome intellect. And piety.'

'I'm really excited at the thought of the Congress. It is a great honour for the Sangha, don't you agree, Upali?'

Upali drank more water. Xantes was now eating heartily.

On the other side of the Thera sat two Magadhan merchants, who were on their way to Aden via Bhrgukacha, and volubly agitated about the number and rigour of highway checks, and the increased tolls. 'Does the government want to discourage trade completely? We're almost treated like thieves!'

Kautilya's exact opinion, remembered Upali. The redoubtable Prime Minister of the first Maurya, Ashoka's grandfather Chandragupta, had held that merchants, beggars, performers and, rather surprisingly, artisans as well, were all thieves by other names. Kautilya would not have been surprised by Milindachanda's little transaction with the toll-keeper, for his opinion of officials was much the same. Stopping a government officer from robbing the exchequer is like stopping a fish from drinking water, he had said. Kautilya's world was a world of thieves.

'And the worst thing is, the government wants to have a monopoly in everything – spices, grain, minerals, cotton, gems, everything! What is left for us? If we had more freedom and less taxes, the scope would be tremendous!'

'But what of the advantages of the system?' asked the Sanchi Thera. 'Better organization, protection, facilities? Look at the south. Or at Kalinga, where our esteemed Upali lived. There too there was wealth. Jungles teeming with iron, elephants, sandalwood, good land for grain and the whole eastern sea trade, but you merchants were hardly flocking there, were you? Why? No facilities, and plenty of ferocious tribals! But now Magadh has brought roads, ferry systems, porter gangs, inns, wells, all patrolled by the best troops ever seen – and caravans are wearing out the road to Tosali!'

'We pay for everything, lord Thera, with taxes, duties, tolls, fines, hundreds of things!'

'The peasants pay as well, and very faithfully too. If they complained I could sympathize! With you merchants, one can't be sure. Isn't it true that the toll-collectors are convivial with the generous, so that many a smart merchant crosses the toll booths with a very mild lightening of his purse? Around Ujjayani especially, so I've heard?'

The merchant laughed and turned to his food.

Having successfully defended Magadh on both flanks, the Thera allowed his attention to wander. 'For heaven's sake, Upali, is that Prince Nigrodha? We must invite him here!'

They planned to leave Sanchi at dawn, so Upali decided to take leave of the Thera after evening meditation. He found him in his office with two visitors. One was a fat nobleman lounging against a heap of cotton bolsters. Sitting stiffly next to him was the old monk glimpsed behind Mogallana in the Raja Vihara that morning.

'Come, come, Upali,' welcomed the Sanchi Thera, though he looked less cheery than normal. But it was the old monk's smile, especially the sarcasm in it, which held Upali.

'So, Upali, forgotten me, have you?'

'Thera! Salutations.' It was Mahanta of Sarnath, whom he had last seen about thirty years ago. He had not been particularly close to him. How old was he? He had shrunk to almost half his size and there were wrinkles even on the top of his bald pate. But his speech was as sharp as Upali remembered.

'Well, your memory is not all gone, Upali. I'm glad.'

'How are you, Master?'

'Very well, considering that I should be dead. But you have become very adventurous in your adulthood, Upali. I speak of your writing.'

The Sanchi Thera interrupted. 'We must all congratulate you, Upali. The Magadhe-Raja seemed very impressed with your story.'

Upali shrugged. Mahanta's smile was a little mocking.

'By the way, have you met His Highness, the Viceroy of Avanti, Lord Vishnugupta?' asked the Thera. Upali bowed; the Viceroy ignored him. 'We were just discussing this sad business of Pradyota.' The Thera picked up a ceramic pitcher, measured something very carefully into a tumbler and held it out. Upali took it uncertainly; it turned out to be water.

But it seemed to prod his memory. 'I found something in his room this morning, Thera – some bits of silk in his mattress. There is some writing on them, in Kharosthi, I think.'

'In his mattress?' asked the Thera.

'Where are they?' asked the Viceroy. Light brown eyes glared at Upali out of a pudgy face. Magadh normally appointed generals as Viceroys, Upali had heard, but if this man had ever been a soldier, his body had decided to keep it a secret. His stomach bulged generously over a silk cummerbund and he had three chins to his credit.

'In my room. They seem to be commercial orders for some goods. Why they were hidden so carefully is a question.'

'But why were you there in the first place? The police instructed everybody to stay away from his room!'

'It was a monk who asked me in. He was prostrated outside, actually prostrated, Thera, outside, and offered a strange explanation – that Pradyota had been a protector of the monks!'

'Who was this monk?' asked the Thera but the Viceroy interrupted.

'Everyone knows that! He was completely enlightened – he could remember his entire past, every single life. He was brilliant as a youth too, much esteemed by all Ujjayani, but he chose to become a monk. A genuine monk.'

A genuine – ? 'What do you mean by – '

The Thera cut in. 'Let us go and see the chits. I understand a bit of Kharosthi.'

'There is no tearing hurry. Collect them later,' said the Viceroy. 'And pass them on to the Police Chief. He's searching the whole place again tomorrow.'

'Searching the monastery?' Mahanta's voice was heavy with disapproval.

'Only after you've had a murder in your monastery, lord! And that too of a nobleman,' said the Viceroy. 'Royalty, I should say. The Sungas were the original priest-kings of Avanti, before their defeat by our Sacred Majesty's late father. They are descended from the famed Pradyota of Avanti, the purest Arya blood in the land. They can trace their lineage back twenty generations.' He looked pointedly at his beautifully manicured fingernails. Unlike our Sacred Majesty, was left unsaid.

But his point was taken. 'Talking of lineage, I must tell you, Upali,' the Sanchi Thera was suddenly grinning like a monkey, 'such an amusing thing. Our Lord Viceroy here is directly descended from the royal family of Kosala. Isn't that true, my lord?'

'So it is said,' said the Viceroy shortly.

'Direct from the half-breed Pasenadi!' The Thera beamed from ear to ear. 'You must inform your relatives of this illustrious history, my lord. Though it will soon be common knowledge.'

'I'm sure we all have colourful things in our past....' Upali tried to avoid the Viceroy's gaze.

'We do not know about your past, Thera Upali. But I think you will find many learned people who seriously dispute your ideas, colourful though they might be. Bloodlines are not a matter for fanciful speculation! As the great Kautilya said....'

Upali was distracted from what the great Kautilya said by the six strands of pure white, perfectly matched pearls around the large Viceregal neck, also by the extreme elegance of the Viceregal language, especially the use of the royal 'we'. But he was not really impressed. He had been spoiled by the audience of the morning, he realized, when the Magadhe-Raja had referred to himself in the straightforward singular. It was of a piece with the austere dress and the strange self-identification, the Beloved of the Gods, rather than the 'Raja of Magadh, Anga, Kashi, Kosala, Kuru, Gandhara, Avanti....' Was it humility? No, it was the opposite. It was the arrogance of one who had no need to impress anybody.

Perhaps his thoughts showed on his face, for the Thera said, 'Upali's problem is that he's unfamiliar with high society, he's more used to savages! He lived in Kalinga for decades – you're practically a native of the place, right, Upali?'

This was too much. 'Kalinga was no more savage than Avanti. And definitely less than Magadh, not to mention the Court of the Mauryas! If you wanted to see real savagery, you should have seen – '

'Upali – please!' The Thera looked pained.

'This is definitely the worst I've heard – a murder in a monastery, that too of a personage like Pradyota,' the Viceroy shook his head. 'I sometimes felt he was the Buddha reborn.'

Upali gaped around, but the Thera was pondering into his tumbler while Mahanta's eyes were closed.

'You are unlucky, Upali,' continued the Viceroy. 'You missed the chance to meet a genuinely enlightened soul. He was absolutely at the point of Nirvana.'

'When somebody decided to help him along?'

'It is a terrible, terrible loss.' It was the Thera's turn to glare at Upali. 'But the killer will soon be found. A thief, no doubt.'

'Why, was any of his gold missing?' asked the Viceroy.

'So you know about his gold?' The Thera seemed surprised.

'No – I mean – he'd spoken of it once.'

'We had no idea he had so much gold! Twenty tolas – a fortune. I was shocked. Of course his family is extremely wealthy – the Sungas – '

The Viceroy got up. 'Well, we'll take your leave now, Thera.'

Something, probably the name of the monk's family, suddenly reminded Upali of the sculptor. But the Viceroy was addressing him, and very jovially. 'Any plans of visiting Ujjayani soon, Thera?'

'No, why?'

'Do come sometime. Your story is fascinating. And we would like to know how your monastery is doing.'

Upali was slightly surprised. 'Well, there's something you may be able to help in first.' He narrated Devadina's problem in brief.

It went big. 'Sutanuka!' exclaimed the Viceroy. 'Every man in Ujjayani with a coin in his pocket is thinking about her! Does this boy claim that she wants to leave the temple?'

'Yes, but she's scared. She may be in danger.'

'My dear fellow, hers is a revered position! This carpenter, no, sculptor, correct? of yours must be crazy – these devadasis have great magical powers. Besides, of course, she has opened her thighs to many.'

'He knows all that! Yet he wants to marry her. Don't you feel it is a matter that should be encouraged?'

The Viceroy did not. 'What he wants is hardly the issue, Thera. I may also want to do something else tomorrow, become a monk perhaps – such a pleasant life! But there is something called duty, you know!'

Upali turned to the Thera. 'He asked me to speak to you. Perhaps you could speak to the – Thera, are you unwell?' The man was quite pale. 'What's wrong?'

'Nothing, thank you! But I don't think love stories are really our business, Upali. Anyway, I must get back to work.'

The Viceroy stopped at the door. 'So this Devadina told you about the Sungas? Did he meet Pradyota?'

The light eyes were suddenly piercing.

'I – don't know.'

'If he approached you, he must have tried Pradyota! He may know something of this matter. I'll speak to him.'

Upali could have kicked himself.

TARA

Siddarth was initiated into adulthood as his forefathers had been, with a bath in the holy puskara outside Devadaha, near the grove of his birth. This great tank, still standing today amidst the rubble of its temple, was at the centre of Shakya identity. The Shakyas were consecrated here as rajas and men, and assisted in both passages by the priestesses of the temple. Nobody knew exactly how old the place was, but it was said to be ancient, built when the gods had made men and chosen the Shakyas to rule over this beautiful cusp of land at the foot of mighty Himavat.

So said the Shakyas. One of the priestesses, a gentle soul who led Siddarth through his sexual initiation in one of the small stuffy chambers that reeked of musk and overlooked the emerald depths of the tank, told him that the priestesses were really the original rulers, on behalf of the goddess of the temple. But they had bequeathed their dominion to the invaders – why she did not know, but that was why the Shakyas needed their blessings at every step. Siddarth asked his father who dismissed it as a witch's tale.

Siddarth's consecration was a long process involving many days and much sacrifices, a big moment in which was his betrothal to a cousin, Yashodara. Shakyas often married their first cousins, though not their own siblings as claimed by their neighbouring

Koliyas, who propagated this as damning proof that the Shakyas were not Aryas. The Shakyas denied it furiously, even went to war to avenge the slander, and won quite a lot of land. It didn't stop the rumours but compensated somewhat.

As a result of a final ceremony called the 'second birth', the fifteen-year-old was declared a full-fledged Arya kshatriya of the glorious Shakya jati. A thread made of three cords of hemp was hung from his left shoulder, passed across his chest and tied loosely against his right hip. He was now dvija or twice-born. He had already been lectured at length on the importance of the thread. It was a certificate of spiritual exaltedness; its loss implied pollution and social humiliation.

When Siddarth left the land of his fathers in the middle of the night, his first act was to take off the thread and fling it into the darkness.

That was much later. At the time of his consecration, nobody would have imagined that Siddarth was unhappy with his lot. In fact, his father wondered if he was a little too happy. He was now a man and a raja. His schooling continued – the theories and practice of warfare, the memorization of the Vedas, the history of his people, or the mixture of fact, myth and legend that passed for it – but he was now fit to be sent on a campaign. Fit, but not as fit as his father would have hoped. The essence of Siddarth's education was a celebration of war; despite it and to Shudodhan's secret horror, he remained somewhat unmotivated. Even the stories of his grandfather, a stout warrior remembered by his kinsmen in the same breath as Kuru legends like Ram and Arjun, failed to enthuse him. Later admirers would describe the Buddha as having been a perfect student, the best and strongest, diligent, intelligent and manly as well. The truth was that he was somewhat laid-back about his studies. 'Lazy' is what only one surprisingly frank account calls him, though it makes amends later by claiming that he once silenced all critics during a tournament by picking up an elephant, twirling it around by its tail and hurling it a distance of five miles over the ramparts. Other reports simply say that he learnt archery, fencing, wrestling, riding, chariot-racing and everything else, but in such a desultory manner that his teachers were disappointed. Some of his relations, worried about the family reputation, even complained to his father.

Elephant-twirling apparently did not count.

One who was a favourite with all teachers was Devdutta, his cousin. Devdutta went on to become a dedicated thorn in the side of the Buddha, in fact he seemed to have no other ambition in life but to murder his cousin. The methods he used were colourful and devious but somehow they always failed and he was always being caught and pardoned, to try again with the same steadfast commitment and the same miserable luck.

The animosity was probably born during their youth when the young Devdutta proved himself the best warrior in the class. His fluency with Shakya history is not mentioned anywhere but it is quite possible that he learnt it equally well and thus knew that a few generations earlier his prowess coupled with his high birth would have guaranteed him the Chief's amulet. But those days were past. Siddarth was the descendant of three chiefs and that counted for more than the fact that he did not always shoot straight. It must have rankled.

One popular part of the future legend told of how, once during an archery competition, Siddarth rescued a dove that Devdutta had shot. Devdutta was the best archer in Siddarth's class, the first to be able to lift the heavy laminated teak and horn war-bow, string it, hold it steady in one hand and bend its hard unyielding length in the opposite direction from its unstrung shape, all without falling over himself, and finally actually direct and shoot an arrow. The competition was the usual one – of hitting targets placed further and further away, the last one of which was the arrow hit by the preceding student. Devdutta succeeded with every single shot, ending in a brilliant display where he split the target into slivers. The round ended, everybody gathered around to congratulate the victor, and their one-armed, one-eyed, war-hero tutor Bharat began enumerating the mistakes made by the others, when a flock of doves scudded across the sky.

Devdutta lifted his bow and fitted his arrow. The v-shaped formation had nearly vanished over a thicket on the other side of the field when he lifted his gaze and loosed the arrow. Just one bird could be seen now, a plump, brownish-pink dawdler clearly enjoying the warm breeze. The arrow streaked after it and both had nearly vanished from the sight of their squinting audience, when they met, and fell.

Once again there was an uproar around Devdutta; most did not notice the bird flapping its wings as it fell. But somebody called, 'Siddarth, what's up?' and Devdutta discovered that his cousin was halfway across the field. He pushed his friends aside and charged after him. Siddarth managed to reach the dove first, and found it alive. He picked it up and pulled out the arrow, ignoring his angry cousin all the while. The rest of the somewhat confused class arrived to find Devdutta trying to wrest the bird away by force.

Bharat had to intervene. He believed Devdutta was entitled to the bird, but the Chief's son looked very stubborn. 'Let go of Siddarth. Take the matter to his father. Now disperse!'

Shudodhan and his friends heard Devdutta out sympathetically. But Siddarth is said to have impressed them much more by his question of, 'To whom does the bird belong – he who tried to take its life, or he who has given it life?' Devdutta's intense hatred for him is supposed to date from that moment. The only problem with the story is that the Shakya elders were not likely to have been pleased at this critique of bloodsport by the future Chief. It would seem only further proof of his addle-headedness, which they would have hardly encouraged.

If Siddarth's lack of military prowess worried his father, it was his interest in philosophy that made him implore, bribe and harangue the gods. Some put it down to that old astrologer's prediction, that Siddarth would become either a chief-among-chiefs or a sage. But Shudodhan's fear is understandable even without the prediction. For it was a time of sage-hood.

A veritable epidemic of doubt was raging over the plains of the Ganga. Nothing was too sacred to be above query and no query too profane to find a following. Questions were asked about the origin, meaning, intent and destiny of man, and that of the world and the gods as well. There were even questions about the holy yagnas, questions that were really complaints and getting louder by the day. The peasants were the ones complaining, foolish as they were, but the Shakyas were sure that others, specifically the foreign preachers who had become a common sight in recent times, had incited them. Some of the blasphemy was home-grown though – by Kapila, whose infuriating ideas still found admirers a century after his death. The Shakyas had little patience with such nonsense. Anybody preaching new ideas was exiled, anybody insulting the yagna was impaled. A few wondered whether the action was not too strong – some of the heretics claimed tremendous magical powers. Spates of yagnas were held to disperse the evil eye. They seemed to work. Possibly the peasants realized that the more they scared the Shakyas by criticizing the contributions they were forced to make, the more the yagnas to which they were forced to contribute.

But the seekers, as most called themselves, continued to show up, many quite prepared to be flung out immediately, and what was worse, the Shakyas suspected that some of the new ideas were being propagated right inside their own classrooms. They were not wrong. In between reciting hymns to the glory of the Vedic gods, some of the newer teachers were busy sowing seeds of doubt about these very same personages.

'What is the greatest divinity in the world? Our great and powerful devas, you might say. But there were others, wiser than us, who were not content with this answer, who pondered deeper and further, who wondered about the supremacy of gods who, though invincible heroes, are always brawling, always drinking, whose concern outside these two activities is only how to slip into other men's beds and wives. And these wise thinkers concluded that there has to be a higher divinity, something that is not obvious to the common eye.'

'Varuna?' asked a student.

'Yes, stern Varuna is there with his golden and final judgment of course. But perhaps there is something more? What is this divine universe? The sky, the sun, the mountains, you rajas as well?'

Another boy got up, bowed, and launched himself into a recital of the Purusa Sukta. The brahmin waited for him to finish, but he was clearly impatient.

'Yes, yes, no doubt. But what of the cycle of the world – birth and death and birth again, rains and dryness and rains again? The earth gives birth to life, joy and beauty, all of which dry up and die with time, but then the earth gives birth again. Whence has all this come? For that matter, from where have the gods come? Who has given them their courage, their power and lust?'

The students were puzzled. Siddarth too, though he felt he had heard these ideas before.

'There is something higher than the gods. It is not enough to worship the gods. We have to worship the higher, the highest, the allpowerful and allpresent – Brahman!'

'Brahman?'

The students knew of Brahman. Brahman was the magic of the sacred mantras, an omnipotent force that was the secret of the power of the words, metres and every syllable of the Vedas.

That was not all, said the brahmin. Brahman was the world, the ultimate reality which fills all space and all time. Brahman was the source of all forms, all life, all phenomena, even the gods. The beginning and the end. And so on. The Shakya elders did not hear all the details, but what they heard was enough for them to condemn the whole business as intellectual ruffianism, eel-wriggling and sophistry of the worst kind. Some would have liked to put a sharp end to it, but the accepted methods were unusable here. The offenders were of pious brahmin stock and claimed that they were still teaching the Vedas; it was only their method of teaching that was different – it was an Upanishad, they said, or a discussion, on the deeper meaning of the Vedas.

'But why go so deep? If students plunge so deep into these matters, will they be able to resurface? Stick to the Vedas – they're deep enough!'

The brahmins humbly acquiesced but continued as before, though quietly. Siddarth soon realized why he found new ideas familiar. According to another of his teachers, 'Every being contains a soul, the atman, which is the breath and the essence of the body. It does not die when the body dies, but escapes to be born again and again, through glory and riches as well as pain and torture. But this atman is also part of Brahman – Brahman is thus also the human soul, and when a man realizes this, he is free – '

'The soul is not born and does not die. Yes!' interrupted Siddarth excitedly. 'I have learnt of this earlier, from Tara. These are the ideas of her people.'

His teacher was interested. 'Who is Tara? A follower of Kapila? But a woman?' Women were very far from the higher life. Even Kapila's Sankya, which also spoke of a soul and its need to be free, called it the Purusha or male principle, which craved release from Prakriti, matter or the female substratum.

The brahmin was not very thrilled to learn that Tara was a slave as well as a woman. According to him, only the dvija were capable of understanding these matters.

But when Siddarth told Tara of his class, she elaborated on the theme. 'Who knows what I will be in my next life? A slave again? Or a free woman far away in our tribal homelands? It's all a cycle watched by the Goddess. Round and round goes the wheel, like the wheel of a cart on which one is just a spot. Once again the winter, once again the summer and then the rains, once again the night after the day, once again birth after death.'

'But what's the aim of life?'

'Our lives are part of the cycle, that's all. The world is a cycle over which one has no control.'

The next day Siddarth asked his teacher, 'Is the world a cycle over which one has no control?'

'Yes, indeed! A cycle of birth, death, rebirth, and so on, endlessly. A wheel watched over by Brahman. The gods have no control over it – far less mankind. Each has just to follow his dharma. Even the great heroes of the past – the Kurus, the Yadavas, the Panchalas – had to accept their destiny whatever the sadness and hardships it brought them. But, as a result of such fidelity, they developed the strength and the wisdom to break free of the cycle. To be free of the cycle, to achieve Moksha, the union of one's soul with Eternal Brahman – that is the aim of the wise. It was this wisdom that Vasudev explained to Arjun before the battle.'

It was? The story of the great war of Kurukshetra and the destruction of the clan of Kurus was an essential part of Shakya folklore. 'But – surely he advised him about his varna dharma. That, in the clash between his blood dharma and that of his varna, the latter was superior. He was not to think of his kin on the other side of the battlefield, he was to remember only his duty as a kshatriya, which was to fight, without question, without thinking of the consequences.' It was a choice that the northern republics did not favour, and their bards always concluded the epic as a tragedy caused by the terrible advice.

'Yes. But Vasudev also explained that the aim of dharma is Moksha. Only by living such a pure life can one become free of the cycle of rebirths.'

'So death is the aim of life?'

'No – ' – you fool, the brahmin almost added, before recognizing the Chief's son. 'Death will just give you another life! The only solution is Moksha, or freedom from all lives.'

'What of the Golden Heaven of Varuna?' Where, so they had always heard, all the great Arya heroes were supposed to reside after death?

'That is another term for Moksha, but it is not true that it is achieved after every life. Some never achieve it at all. They go on and on through thousands of lives without ever achieving it. Moksha transcends life and death. The free atman is pure, imperishable, unattached, unmoved. It is incomprehensible.'

'It sounds like… nothing.'

It was all a bit confusing, but also interesting, partly because these were new ideas about the world and not scriptures.

The Shakya elders would have been absolutely aghast to learn that the heretical Upanishads had such striking similarities to the faith of their slaves. The real problem though was that the new generation was a mess. It seemed to take very little to make them forget their own traditions and fall for the most bizarre of new ideas or even stranger old ones. Some families were even forced to have their misguided offspring medically treated. This happened once after an old foreign sage, Makkali Gosala by name, had preached a sermon on the outskirts of Kapilavastu. Siddarth also attended.

'…They say that you can become holy by following your dharma, by doing good, by not telling a lie, by venerating all the gods, by forgoing pleasure. Do all this and you will quickly achieve the divine state of Nirvana, of freedom, they say. But this is not true. It is completely false! The truth is that how you live this life makes no difference. Do you hear me? *What you do makes no difference!* The truth is simple, and yet, because it is so simple, it is very difficult. Each of us begins our life as an atom, a monad. Each of us, each of these monads, has to go through eighty-four hundred thousand lives, starting with the original living atom, proceeding through all the elements – air, fire, water, earth, and then into the far more complex cycles of life – of rocks, grasses, bushes, trees, then insects, worms, serpents, birds, fish, living creatures of each and every kind. Once this journey of eighty-four hundred thousand life cycles is completed, the life of the monad is over. It is blown out. It is released. It achieves Nirvana.

'Look at this!' The old man suddenly rose, and the crowd raised its faces with him. He took a ball of string from his belt and threw it vertically into the air, while holding on to one end. It rose unwinding, higher and higher, fast at first, then slower, then stopped suddenly with the length taut, standing for a fraction of a second like a slender white spear which the sage held delicately between finger and thumb. Then it collapsed at his feet.

Gosala was smiling. 'Did you see that? That is your life. This string. It is the story of your sojourn in this material world. And there,' he pointed at the string, 'there it ends. Each of us undertakes this journey, has no choice but to undertake it, to face every single of the many thousands of lives. Whether you are good and generous, or cruel and greedy, it makes no difference. The ball of string has to run out. Once the ball has run through its length, your existence is over. Not before.'

He paused, then added gently, 'You must accept that this journey is inevitable. You cannot shorten it. The gods cannot. Learn to accept.'

The monad sounded suspiciously like the Upanishadic soul, Nirvana like the Upanishadic Moksha. Except that no brahmin had ever spoken about being reborn a fish or a mosquito. A brahmin was reborn a brahmin. Tara agreed – she belonged to her tribe and she always would, through all her lives. Siddarth also wondered how the sage had reached the number of eighty-four hundred thousand. Why not one more or less? But he did not ask, and nobody else did either.

Gosala's words impressed many. One young raja whose older brother had just been killed at the border, was so impressed that he determined to join his following, but made the mistake of informing his family first. His father, a raja of the old school who expected his second son to live and die as impeccably as the first, had him locked up. Gosala was escorted without ceremony to the border. Behind him departed two young men who had been more discreet about their plans. The locked-up one meanwhile insisted that he could not live without Gosala; his father reluctantly agreed to medical treatment, in the course of which the patient died.

Anything was better than the heresies, felt Shudodhan. Anything or even nothing. A pleasure-seeking drone like many of his friends, that's what Siddarth could be, even that was viable. All he would have to do is sit on the Chief's seat; others could take the decisions. To think was to act for Shudodhan – once he had confirmed that the clay in his hands was neither warrior-material nor convincingly statesman-like, he actively urged his son towards the beautiful, the thrilling, the sensuous or the delicious.

The options for which were legion. The most popular was of course big game hunting, considered the worthiest pastime for kshatriyas. Every young raja was judged by the numbers of tigers, elephants or rhinos he had sent to the afterlife, or to their next birth depending on your point of view. For those not up to the perils of the jungle, where predator can suddenly become prey, there were vicarious bloodsports arranged in the city itself, various military tournaments as well as fights between beasts of all sizes, shapes and strengths, where aficionados thronged every day to watch either hard-earned coins or ancestral wealth disappear down the pockets of the stage-managers. Gambling in fact was a passion, whether across a board or over the results from the battlefield, hunt, tourney, stables, bedroom, anywhere.

There were other sports as well, to cater to other passions. After his consecration, Siddarth could avail of the charms of the priestesses on all ritual occasions, and obtain spiritual marks too in the bargain; there were city brothels where most rajas maintained their favourites; there were services available at home too, for courtesans were a part of every noble household. And, for those in-between times, there were games like chess and hopscotch, and performances by balladeers, artists, jugglers, poets, dramatists and riddle-makers.

The founts of pleasure were many. And yet life was more than a little ugly. The legend speaks of a protected youth, spent in fine palaces among sylvan gardens, a different palace for each different season; of how he sported day and night with beauteous maidens and athletic friends amidst music and dance, and thus was thrown into turmoil by his first sight of illness, old age and death. But the truth is that the inheritance that Siddarth was born to did not allow for such innocence. He probably led the most luxurious life possible, but it was not that of a lotus-eater. Otherwise Shudodhan could never have hoped to make his son Chief after him. It was a time of confusion, even chaos, and a Chief had to at least understand both the old and the new divides, to defend his own interests and also swing popular feeling behind him. It was a tall order, as Shudodhan knew only too well.

The defeat by Kosala brought the worst of the conflicts out on the streets for a while. The Gana Sabha was rarely convened but conservative hysteria over vassalage resulted in a series of riots, arson, and attacks on foreigners and merchants. Some of the latter followed the example of Anula and emigrated. Others created their own private militias. The situation improved slightly however with the death of Hemant. Of a very sudden stomach ailment. Rumours spread that Shudodhan had taken Kosala's help to get rid of his most persistent opponent. Then a couple of Hemant's friends died too, in various accidents. There were no more rumours.

Relationships outside the sangha remained unaffected. The borders remained volatile and every young raja was expected to do his bit in pushing them outward. The future Chief especially. Shudodhan decided to send him first to the south where the main problem was of Naga raiders, ferocious but crudely armed. He prepared him himself, tying into place the layered bamboo and leather armour, fixing the quiver of arrows across his back and the bronze helmet on his head, buckling on his sandals and anointing his forehead with a blood-mark from the morning sacrifice, before handing over the laminated war-bow, the heavy bronze mace and the iron sword in its embossed sheath. He then led him to the family altar where priests sat tiredly with a group of old weapons; they had chanted hymns over them for days, all for the success of the new warrior.

'Ask them for strength, son. My father's and grandfather's weapons have seen many battles.'

Siddarth had long admired the longest sword, a dented and stained old bronze. Now he picked it up and weighed it in his hands – it was heavier than his own iron. Then, instead of touching it to his forehead, he knelt on one knee, placed it across his thigh and bent hard. It resisted, then abruptly gave way.

'Siddarth!'

'These were amazingly weak, weren't they?'

'That's a holy relic – give it to me!'

Siddarth turned the blade around and bent hard again. It straightened but not fully. 'They work against the Nagas, I suppose. But against iron, this would snap into two!'

Shudodhan jerked the sword away, and examined its new bend and then his son with the same anguish. 'You must never speak like this before war, Siddarth. Please take the blessing.'

'It's a bit senseless, Father – to take the blessing of such a weak weapon. Or for that matter of any weapon at all!'

Shudodhan furiously touched the sword to his forehead, charged him with the 'valiance of Indra, the fierceness of Agni, the wisdom of Varuna', and decided on another sacrifice. At the earliest.

Siddarth joined the regiment of Prafularaja, an old friend of Shudodhan's. The raja was familiar with the boy's reputation and placed him first in the surveillance patrols where Siddarth met the peasant tenants, or saw them rather, for they were a fearful lot, whose tendency on sighting their high-born protectors was to disappear. The reason was soon obvious. The farming here was new, the fields constantly preyed upon by elephant and buffalo, and the soldiers' presence an added burden over and above the dues to the Shakya landlords and their yagnas. Siddarth was sent with other soldiers to enforce the contributions once, when he stopped his colleagues from also lifting the daughter of the house.

She was the only female they had seen in three hamlets – probably because she was lame.

'You're supposed to be here for a religious duty. Let her go!'

The two soldiers looked surprised, but released the girl and joined their colleagues, two of whom were wrestling with the peasant's calf, while the third was loading a sack of grain on a cart. The girl limped into the house, and her father, who had been knocked to the ground by a soldier's kick, came and knelt before Siddarth's horse.

'You are a noble man, lord, a true Arya!'

'Since when does dirt like you recognize true Aryas?' Siddarth's fellow officer laughed but he was irritated by the Chief's son. Self-righteous little pup.

'What is your name?' asked Siddarth of the peasant.

'I am nobody, lord. I lost a buffalo to the Nagas last month, a calf to a tiger six months back, and now this calf and all my grain. But your gift of my daughter has made up for everything.'

It was not normal for peasants to talk so much. Siddarth's colleague was astounded. 'Call the yagna offerings a loss, scum?' He kicked out hard; the man went sprawling again. 'Apologize or – '

'Come on, let's go!' Siddarth rode out and after a moment his colleague followed.

On the whole, Siddarth enjoyed the first few weeks of his appointment. The small farms were surrounded by primeval tiger forest – wild and beautiful wetlands and riverine marshes supporting great herds of swamp deer, who in turn supported the great cats. Slave gangs could be found working in the marshes, hacking away at the dense elephant grass, wrestling with the roots, cutting canals for the water to drain, always running a good chance of suddenly meeting a rhino, for the gigantic beasts hid silently in the tall grass till disturbed, when they turned into amazingly fast killing machines. The sal forests above the swamps were intersected by innumerable streams whose water was clear and so full of fish that there were always a few bears or cats lounging at the edge.

The idyll was short. His company was soon pulled into battle, but not against the Nagas. The Koliyas were occupied elsewhere and the Shakya commander decided to use the opportunity to annex a stretch of hamlets and farmland. Shudodhan was aghast when he heard the plan, but helpless.

But Siddarth did not do so badly, though the Koliyas recovered and put out a force only slightly smaller than the Shakyas. They were armed similarly too except for the colours. In fact, the whole fight felt like one of the mock-battles of Siddarth's recent student-hood. Before it started, that is.

They met at dawn on the bank of a stony stretch of the river, on land recently cleared, drained and ploughed for rice. Siddarth's charioteer was Gopal, a slave born on the Chief's estates, a quiet obedient youth with downcast eyes who did not respond to friendly overtures at all; Siddarth was just about ready to give up on him. He sat perched on the chariot shaft like the other drivers, where he was exposed to the enemy's arrows with only his leather chest armour for protection. The horses had been doped, as was the custom, with rice wine. Siddarth himself was wearing all his weaponry but his bow was in his hands, many quivers of arrows fastened to the inside of the chariot all around. When the battle closed, he was supposed to exchange his bow for his sword. His mouth was dry, his palms wet. His regiment had ridden hard over two days, forded the river and rested for only three hours of the night. Nobody had slept. They listened instead to the Koliyas massing on the other side of the field. The Koliyas followed Arya war rules, they would not attack without warning. The air felt cold but sweat was pouring down Siddarth's neck. Even with all the rules in place, this was war.

There was a long performance of conches, gongs and drums, then the Shakyas attacked. The foot-soldiers at the front were archers, behind them were swordsmen, on either side stretched two long arcs of chariots. The idea was to get the opponent in a pincer-grip. The archers moved first. They charged upon the Koliyas at a run, dropped to their knees halfway down and began shooting, silently it seemed, for nothing could be heard above the drums and slogans. The Koliyas started shooting too, both sides lurched closer and closer, the archers fell like dolls all over the place, till the swordsmen leapt over the fallen and began to cut and stab their way through the other side. All this while the chariots were racing inwards almost without Siddarth noticing. He was supposed to shoot but he just watched, till Gopal was hit through the neck just as they closed in.

Thick clouds of dust arose from under wheels and hooves, but nobody coughed; perhaps they weren't breathing. The slogans had become screams of rage and agony, but the drums continued their grim chant while Gopal toppled slowly over and off the shaft, his mouth open and calling someone, but silently. The reins slipped out of his hands and Siddarth's horses halted, rearing and pawing the air angrily – the smell of blood penetrated their alcoholic haze, they wanted to get away. Siddarth jumped off and raced around, trying to avoid the killer axles of the chariots racing past. He lifted Gopal and dumped him as gently as he could into the chariot. Then he jumped back in himself. There was no question of using the bow now. He grabbed his sword and jerked the reins frantically. It was crucial to get into motion – the secret of the low mortality rate of chariots was high mobility.

He was surrounded by the battle now. A mace came hurtling straight at his head but he turned at the last moment and it landed with numbing shock on his shoulder. It was the goad he need. His horses reached the sender of the mace in a single burst of motion; he heard an ugly guttural scream, the shout of a crazed brute, but did not recognize his own voice for his sword was flashing through the air in a savage arc that stretched his arm way beyond its normal length and ripped the man's chest open.

The next moments took hours to pass. He first noticed his opponent's face – he was young, probably teenaged, with a light sprinkling of acne on his cheeks and large eyes that were staring down at his own front in disbelief. The huge force driving the razor-sharp iron had cut open the leather, horn and bamboo shield and armour, and the tunic too; sliced skin and muscle below it, then turned within the body cavity to come out; in the process making a hole through which Siddarth glimpsed for a fraction of a second the pure whiteness of bone nestling in light pink before it was all covered in a red wash that swept out and down to the floor of the chariot, a generous sweep that reached the ground before the boy made a very small choking sound and sank first to his knees, then off his chariot, finally resting with his face in the mud and his wound hidden beneath him. One hand still clutched his sword, the other was flung out; another chariot went by in that instant, the axle-blade freed the arm and flung it from the body.

It was the pinnacle of achievement for a kshatriya.

Siddarth's paralysis lasted for only a second, for another mace caught him a blow on the back of his head. He was saved only by the fact that his chariot was moving ahead at that moment. His head sang but still he turned – and lurched into an automatic frenzy of swiping, sweeping, pointing, thrusting, hacking, all the manoeuvres he had been taught, feeling the crunch of bone, the squishy firmness of flesh, the suck as he yanked the blade out, but knowing only one thing – he wanted to stay alive.

The battle ended suddenly. All at once, the screams of hatred turned into shouts of victory, the Koliya locking swords with him paused, then backed, his charioteer swung his horses around and dashed away. It was Siddarth's own colleagues who were shouting, many thronged around their commander. Conches started blasting triumph. Siddarth stared around foolishly. Chariots were withdrawing in both directions. The wounded were picked by infantrymen who carried them off on their backs. The dead were left decorously untouched. It was once again a game.

But Gopal was really dead, and icy cold. Siddarth lifted him and started walking through the bodies, the victory slogans and the bloody churned-up mud, but when he reached the edge of the field he found two carts setting out for the Shakya dead. A slave ran up, took Gopal and placed him on the cart where there was already one dead raja. Then he saw the copper collar and turned to stare. Had the raja gone mad to pick up a slave? But Siddarth was heading back slowly, through the muck, back to his chariot where he untied his shivering steeds and took them to the river. The slave went back to picking and stacking the dead separately. Later two huge stacks of firewood would cremate them separately too.

It was a small scrap, by the standards of such things. And there was no particular reason for the victory – so it was simply put down to the gods and Prafularaja. The commander was not unhappy with the Chief's son, especially considering he'd lost his charioteer right at the start of the battle. Prafularaja sent a glowing report to Shudodhan, calling it a small but excellent beginning of what was no doubt going to be a glorious career. Shudodhan offered a sacrifice in thanks. How was he to imagine that the glorious career was already as good as over? Nobody could have known. Siddarth just looked a little quiet. He did not join in the revelries with the other officers, nor did he join them in their hunting expeditions for rhinos in the valleys or girls in the villages, nor did he loosen up in the quieter drinking sessions in Prafularaja's quarters. Prafularaja put him back in the patrols.

One day in the local market, he came across the peasant self-introduced as 'Nobody', in a line of slaves. The market was a rude one – a few peasants with baskets of produce; and a shed on the river bank, which was the slave bazaar. It mainly offered Nagas captured by the army, also the odd indebted peasant. A soldier might sometimes buy a woman. Nobody was being led out on to the road along with some twenty others, when Siddarth rode by, and halted.

'Hey!'

Nobody continued staring at the ground. But the merchant turned.

'Lord, are you speaking to me?' He got off his horse quickly and knelt before Siddarth's. The young rajas had to be dealt with carefully, for they tended to be arrogant hotheads eager to avenge imagined insults.

'No, to that man. Does he belong to you?'

'Yes. Has he offended you in any way, Aryaputra?'

'What does he cost?' asked Siddarth.

The merchant looked unhappy but named a price and Siddarth asked him to come to the barracks that night and collect the money. The merchant put a rope into Siddarth's hand – it was attached to a collar around the peasant's neck – and led the remaining slaves away. Siddarth got off his horse and held out the rope.

'Here.'

Nobody looked up blankly.

'Take this rope,' said Siddarth. 'Don't you remember me? I'd come to your farm for yagna contributions.'

The man smiled at the ground. 'The funny thing is that they call it contributions.'

'I passed that way two weeks ago, but your house seemed closed. How is your daughter?'

Nobody looked at Siddarth for the first time. 'I remember. You saved her. For what, I don't know.' His creditors had demanded payments on his mortgage, he could not pay, they had taken the farm. His wife, son and he himself had been sold. His lame daughter had vanished.

'I'm sorry,' said Siddarth. 'But you are free now.'

'Free?'

'Yes. Go in peace.'

'Go where?'

He accompanied Siddarth to the barracks and silently joined his household. Every day he combed the district in a futile search for his daughter, an activity that did not go unnoticed. Prafularaja felt obliged after a while to warn Siddarth that the wanderlust of his slave was causing comment. Siddarth replied it was nobody else's business.

He took part in just one more engagement, after a Naga attack on a hamlet that left all the residents dead. Their heads had been cut off and carried away, along with livestock and grain.

'The houses and fields were set alight,' Siddarth told Nobody, as he cleaned his sword, sitting on the floor of the rather spacious apartment assigned to him. 'The mutilated bodies were arranged in a pattern on the burning fields.'

Nobody was silent, a tired little pile of dhoti and shawl squatting in the doorway. He had spent the day in the jungle, propitiating the local tiger population with rabbits and flowers, for his people believed that the tiger-god knew everything. The tigers had stayed away from him so far; he was beginning to despair.

'Half of my company has been deputed to find the raiders,' Siddarth added. 'It all seems pointless. Either we attack those who rob the peasants, or we rob them ourselves. Even those Nagas who rob you are doing it because we robbed their jungle in the first place.'

Nobody just smiled. Early in the morning, two hours before sunrise, a hundred and twenty men set out on horseback into the forest, using their swords to hack paths for their mounts through the matted walls of bamboo clumps. They moved in three separate groups, to avoid being trapped together, and quite fast, but for more than five hours through dark misty thickets they came across nobody. Birds and small monkeys kept shrieking in the overhead gloom and it was raining slightly, a light cold drizzle that further deadened sound. At least to their ears.

As expected, the attack was a surprise. The first troop had just descended into a dense green valley, when they were greeted by a hail of arrows from the right. The arrows were half the size of the Shakyan ones, but they were probably poisoned and in any case they were coming hard and fast and were aimed largely at the horses. The troop immediately started shooting back. Their heavy bows would have soon made a difference but their horses were wounded on their flanks and panicked. Many dashed towards the left and found too late that the area was a bog. It was an old trick and like many old tricks it worked again. Those behind were driven in as well, either in attempts to save their comrades, or by the whooping Nagas, some of whom dashed up brandishing heavy stone razors. They lopped off a few heads and vanished just as the second troop appeared over the hill.

The second troop, of which Siddarth was a part, helped the survivors up, then charged after the Nagas. They searched and searched for two whole days without rest or success. Till they were on their way back. They were hacking their way through clumped bamboo thickets as before, only harder and thicker, when their swords suddenly went through cleanly and they found themselves inside a mini-fortress. It was a small village of a few large huts and many people and cattle. There was a fire blazing on one side and a strange looking pot perched on it. Look-outs had apparently sounded a warning, for women were herding children off somewhere and the men arranging their weapons, when the soldiers burst in on them.

It was a massacre that satisfied the most vengeful Shakya heart, all the more because the Nagas fought back viciously, the women as well as the men, with spears, iron hammers, catapults and their usual single-stave wooden bows. But nothing could stop the razor-sharp iron swords – except themselves actually, for they were too strong against unarmoured chests, capable of going right in and embedding themselves into bone, leaving their wielder stuck embarrassedly to his victim.

Siddarth managed to get hit by a stone early in the proceedings, on his helmet, but his horse was rearing up at the time and he lost his balance and fell off. He hit the ground and then was hit himself by a crushing weight containing something sharp. It was a Naga, shot through with an arrow. Siddarth twisted his head around and saw the brown falcon feathers of the arrow's plumage sticking up above them both. It had gone right through the Naga without breaking, a beautifully-crafted Shakya arrow, the end tipped with an oleander thorn whose sharpness Siddarth felt in his own back.

The chaos looked uglier from his new position. And it was clear that nobody missed him. Tears of agony mixed with mud, blood and other tastes in his mouth as he began to crawl his way out of the crush. It was difficult but he struggled on, inch by painful inch, towards the side where the fire was blazing under its strange clay pot. It was a pregnant woman, a narrow neck at the top, two lumps for breasts and then the great, big, swollen belly forming the main pot. At the bottom was a spout, below it a wide, flat dish containing clods of black stuff. Naga-metal. He crawled into the space between it and a heaped-up pile of something, and took a long relieved breath before turning his face away from the fire. To find himself face to face with a friend. It was Kapila, from the first troop, or rather it was his head, with others carefully stacked over him. The heap was all heads. Siddarth vomited, once, then again, then lay still in his own dirt.

The Nagas did not have a chance against the sword-wielding horsemen. Only the fire was left alive in that little clearing and on it the pot.

It was not long before he returned to Kapilavastu. Prafularaja let him go without regret, for they had a serious difference of opinion and in public. It was at the local market.

A group of officers was riding through, when their commander was suddenly hailed. It was a merchant with a group examining a crowd of squatting Nagas, wet and shivering on the river bank – they had just been dragged through the water. Few Shakyas would openly socialize with slave-traders; it was a demeaning commodity, on par with poisons and prostitutes. But Prafularaja barely hesitated before reining in his horse and getting off. His officers stopped too and waited. Siddarth was at their head and as he stared at the captives he noticed one who was staring in turn at the commander's back. He was young and well-built for a Naga and tied loosely to those on either side by ropes around his neck, wrists and ankles.

Even as Siddarth watched, he reached a hand behind himself; it returned gripping a rock. The next moment he had leapt, silently but with such force that he jerked three others up around him. Despite the huge drag, he managed to reach just behind Prafularaja and brought his stone up with a great yell. The merchants squealed, the market guards came running up, but it was Siddarth who jerked his mount ahead and used both hands to sweep his sword laterally, bringing the flat past hard against the Naga's side, knocking him off balance and sending him tumbling backwards.

The effort sent Siddarth off his own horse, and into the mud next to the Naga who jumped up again, again yanking others with him. It was a superhuman and utterly suicidal effort, but he loomed over Siddarth now; the latter hit out with his sword-side again, made contact again and heard cheering. The Naga slumped down in a heap.

The market guards reached them; Siddarth saw one raise a dagger.

'Stop!'

The guard stopped. Siddarth got up slowly. 'Don't kill him.'

'He's dangerous, lord,' said an older guard carefully. 'We would keep him for a yagna, but he's too dangerous....'

'How much does he cost?' Siddarth pulled out his pouch, but Prafularaja pulled him away. The crowd, which had been expecting the usual end of difficult slaves, watched puzzled.

'Don't be foolish, Siddarth! He's savage. You can't buy him.'

'I think I can, sir.'

'To sacrifice?'

'No!'

'What work will he do?'

'Whatever I set him.'

'I don't think so. You already have one slave who is a joke – that's quite enough! I will not allow this man into the barracks. Is that clear? Now come on!'

Prafularaja swung up on his horse and waited, glaring at Siddarth, who remained where he was, examining the ground. The commander was furiously conscious that everybody – traders, peasants, captives, especially the other officers – were watching keenly. Anybody else would have been arrested for insubordination. But this was the Chief's son. He kicked his horse and rode off in a cloud of angry dust. The others followed quietly. Siddarth waited till they were yards ahead before he turned back to the guard and repeated, 'How much?'

The guard's answer was a shriek; something flashed past Siddarth. It took him a second to realize that the Naga had been skewered where he sat, the heavy ebony spear going through him with such force that it stabbed a woman behind. She keeled over screaming. The crowd erupted in cheers again. It was a tremendous shot, made at an angle, at a target slumped on the ground, from a horse headed in the opposite direction. It had to be Devdutta.

Siddarth shut his gaping mouth. And charged after the officers, who had halted to congratulate the maestro.

'Siddarth! Stop! Control yourself – !' ordered Prafularaja, but he had leapt on to his cousin by then, sending him spinning off his horse. Prafularaja jumped down too, in time to break Siddarth's hold before it broke Devdutta's neck.

Siddarth returned to the barracks, packed and left, without a word to the commander. This was insubordination too, but Prafularaja was grateful. The man Nobody, who had recently revealed that his real name was Vali, went with him.

But he found little peace in Kapilavastu. Not that things were different. Everything was the same, except him. The first things he noticed were the new impalements on the city walls, the result of a slave-break. The city had responded as usual, with impalements, whippings, and shorter tempers than normal. Siddarth fitted in well with the last.

He came across a scrawny little sweeper being thrashed by a soldier one day, tore the whip away and flung it into the gutter.

'He's an outcaste, lord,' protested the soldier. 'On the road, in broad daylight! And on my windward side!'

'So? Are you a man or a worm, to be frightened of the wind off someone's body? Why are you people so stupid? I'm warning you, if I ever catch you – '

The sweeper disappeared; he was surprised to be alive. The soldier was surprised too, though he bowed low and apologized abjectly – so abjectly that Siddarth felt stupid. Shudodhan heard the story from his friends, and declared it the sign of a Chief who knew how to command. But he called Siddarth to him later. How handsome he looked, taller and straighter, with hard, muscular limbs and an open, straightforward gaze. He looked pure, yes, like one of the epic warriors of old – but then listen to him talk.

'Your stomach is too weak, son,' he replied finally. 'You are a kshatriya, and you pale at the sight of blood? Toughen yourself.'

'But I do not see, Father, why we cannot speak to the slaves, try and understand their problems for a moment. Have you tried it even once?'

'Whatever are you talking about?'

'They work for us, they live with us, they are a part of us – but we are more thoughtful of our animals! It's a crime to overwork an oxen pair but with slaves, there are no crimes!'

Shudodhan could hardly respond, he was so surprised. But he tried. 'Siddarth – Siddarth, they're not like you and me! You cannot reason with them. You deal with them like you deal with animals – wild animals!'

'That makes no sense – ' Everybody could see how some Nagas had become peaceable peasants, while cities like Shravasti ran on Naga labour. But his father would not listen.

'They are savages, didn't you see for yourself at the border? Naked savages who worship snakes and devils, and know only how to destroy! The fact is that we have civilized them by keeping them here!'

'But – '

'Try to think like a ruler, son! Do you know how many slaves were offered every year in your grandfather's time? The gods still demand blood, but we've become soft. We offer only animals, and criminals!'

'But why do the gods want so much blood?'

'Now you want to question the gods? Siddarth, what's wrong? What are those fool brahmins teaching you? Don't you understand the faith of your fathers? It's a matter of sharing your wealth with the gods!' Shudodhan began to feel helpless. 'The problem is that you youngsters have been born into prosperity. You ride the chariots but you understand nothing, not a scratch on the wheel of their divinity! If you had seen the struggles that built this republic, the life and death battles going on even in my own youth, you wouldn't whimper like a woman!'

It was actually a woman who had given these ideas to Siddarth, but without any whimper. And he went back to her, for conversations with his father no longer satisfied him, and his friends were at the border.

Tara was not surprised, for she had an abiding faith in the Lumbini Goddess, a faith that Siddarth was different. And he seemed to need her. She herself had no family that she knew of but many friends among the slaves, while he was becoming a loner. He was growing into manhood not as a confident and virile wielder of arms, but a bemused misfit. Whatever the reason, or perhaps for no reason at all, she grew to love him fiercely. They met at least once a week, normally late at night, after she had finished her day's work. They would sit outside the slave bunker behind the Chief's stables, a long single-roomed shed of wattle and daub.

Sometimes they sat in silence. Sometimes he ate the tidbits she produced, pieces of bajra bread, or a bit of jaggery. Most often they talked. He told her of his day in the city patrol, his quarrels and childishnesses. She too told him of her day, but she preferred to talk about her people, especially their past. Her eyes would light up when she described the jungle paradise that had been their home. No land was under the plough there, she said, nor were there any chariots or horses. People had lived off the abundant wild grains and fruit provided by nature. She would sit straight and dignified when speaking of her deities – many extremely strong-willed goddesses and their lissome dancer-consorts – but she relaxed when recounting festivals and celebrations that were always filled with song and dance. She taught him some dances, to the amusement of the other slaves, for the two made a comical dancing pair, the boy tall, broad and light-skinned, the woman short, thin, dark and snub-nosed.

But Tara preferred to talk. The life she described at length – without bondage, with enough food and a peaceful death for all – was not one she had seen, for she had been born a slave. It was the collective memory of her community, a memory partly wishful perhaps, but it thrilled her in the telling and sometimes her listener as well, though he hadn't noticed any such joy in the faces of the jungle-folk he had recently met. It was a past to contrast with the ugly present and the hopeless future.

He could not sympathize with all her beliefs – like her affection for snakes or for her rather terrifying Goddess. She seemed even more bloodthirsty than his own gods, her demand being only for human blood. Would you offer Shakya blood if you had the chance, he asked.

'Perhaps I would have, earlier,' she said. 'The truly devout offer their own. But now....'

'Now?'

'Now I see my mother's face in the eyes of every beast that awaits the priest's dagger. And I need every drop of my own blood to live. Life is precious, even this slave's life!'

About the punished slaves she was matter of fact. She told him of her parents and how they had died. Her people had no answer to the monstrous horse-driven Arya chariots, but they fought them nonetheless. What else could they do? The eight-spoked wheel had brought ruin, thousands cut to pieces by the ruthless axle-blades, thousands more dragged in chains behind, but they continued to fight. Slave revolts had always taken place, they were always put down harshly, they always continued, that was all. One day, the Goddess would tire of the game she was playing with her people.

Some of her ideas reminded Siddarth of the peasants in the borderlands, people like Nobody. 'They too worship snakes and goddesses, and jungle spirits, like you – but they plough the land like us.'

'They must be different – not Pukusa.' He hadn't even known that there were many separate peoples among in the jungle-folk; the Shakyas called all of them Nagas – snakes.

The incident that really rocked Siddarth's life and led him to fulfil the worst fears of his father came nearly six months after he returned from the border. It was a major slave-break, sparked by the death of eleven-year-old Mala, slave in the house of one of the rajas. She died after being raped by the son of the house and his drunken friends.

His troop was on a hunt for a marauding man-eater that day. Siddarth retired early as was his wont, crashing off his horse into some undergrowth that contained a sharp tree stump. His arm started to bleed and his officer gave him permission to return. He rode back leisurely, enjoying the dark silences of the early afternoon forest. Monkeys leaped above his head, parakeets dipped their beaks into the wild pomegranates hanging lusciously at his side. He passed a glen where the ground was torn, branches trampled, flower bunches crushed and reeking their perfume, mixed with something else – elephants had been there just before. The violently-rutted swirls of soft mud at another place spoke of wild boar. He reached the hill above Kapilavastu and stood for a moment enjoying the vista of the city nestled in the Rapti's embrace. There were bright flat stretches of colour near the water at one point where tiny women had spread washed clothes over the reeds to dry. Near the walls were orchards of banana, pomegranate and sugarcane; then came the rice-fields stretching till the foot of the hills, interrupted by random bits of sparkling mirror – the water meadows, the horned flies which were in the heads of the buffalos lolling in the cool mud. Thick swirls of smoke rose lazily from many points within the city, warning of the piety of its citizens.

Siddarth's mood dampened a little and then further when he spied a group making its way up the road from Devadaha, in single file with a soldier on a horse at the start and end of the line. He put his horse into a gallop down the hill, reaching the gates in time to confirm his guess – they were slaves, all tied along a single rope with its ends in the hands of the soldiers. One soldier saw him and barked an order; his charges cowered to the side of the moat bridge to make way for the raja. Only one turned and looked up at him. He saw a beautiful round face, with large wide-spaced eyes, a small nose and a tiny, trembling mouth. She was a child and even as she looked at him a tear stole out of an eye and ran down a dusty cheek. Her bare feet were bruised and swollen. Siddarth rode home, bandaged his arm and went to sleep. The next day he woke up early for an archery competition and later went to meet Tara.

He found her in the kitchen court, talking away while preparing ghee with the other servants. They were stirring butter in huge copper vessels placed on wood stoves, waiting for it to boil down and the liquid butter oil to separate from the semi-solid waste at the bottom. The oil would be cooled and poured into glazed earthen jars. It would last through the year, unaffected by the furious summer heat.

His appearance resulted in a strangely abrupt silence. He sat on the veranda steps while the women lifted each pan off the stove and into the shade where they were covered and left to cool. Then he showed Tara his arm. She took him to the bunker where he munched on a rice pancake while she opened the dressing, cleaned the wound and bound it up again.

'You should be more careful, lord,' she scolded mildly. 'Every week a new cut or bruise.' She smelt strongly of ghee. He tried to hold his breath discreetly, then realized that her mind was far away.

'What's up, Tara?' She hesitated. 'You were discussing something. What's happened?'

'It's a slave.'

'Well?'

'A girl, her name was Mala, she came to the city only yesterday.'

'A small girl? In the afternoon?'

'Yes, she belonged to the raja Vidyadhar. His son had a dinner party in the evening....'

She told him everything. Siddarth felt sick, then furious. 'My father will hear of this. Those animals will be punished.'

'Punished? Surely you're joking, lord? No Arya has ever been punished for killing a slave. No one will be.'

Siddarth crashed down to earth. She knew the world better than him. 'Never?'

'Never. And your father will be angry. At you, my lord.'

'I'll speak to him. I'm angry too. I can't believe that he won't do anything.'

Tara knew that he had never had a big fight with his father before. And she wanted him to. 'Yes, you are an adult now, Siddarth. And you are special. You are the son of the Goddess. Never forget that.'

He stared. This was new. 'What are you talking about, Tara?'

'You were born in the grove of Lumbini. Didn't you know that? You are a gift of the Goddess. I don't know why she put you in the Chief's household, but her blessings are with you, remember that. Because they say divine blessings can also be a curse.'

'I don't understand you, Tara, but we'll speak of it later. I'm going to my father now. Those pigs will not get away with this!'

But they did. And Siddarth never spoke to Tara again. He raised the issue of Mala at dinner. There were three guests at Shudodhan's house that night – Siddarth's uncle and his wife from Devadaha and their daughter, his betrothed, Yashodhara. But Siddarth was undeterred, and the three guests and his stepmother Prajapati stared at him in surprise, and then at Shudodhan for his answer. The latter remained silent while the servant served him rice and mutton, then he motioned to her and the others to leave the room. He picked up the silver tumbler of water, poured a trickle on the floor around his plate, then mixed his rice with the curry. Only after swallowing a mouthful did he reply.

'Siddarth, you have to learn where to speak about what.'

'But Father, everybody has heard of this – '

'That's not the point! And you're wrong. I had not heard of it. It's disgusting, of course. That boy is a shame to his family.'

Prajapati agreed. 'Those boys are becoming degenerate – ' Shudodhan glanced at her; she broke off and began to eat. He himself chewed slowly on a piece of roast meat before looking again at his son.

'You aren't eating, Siddarth. What's wrong? The curry is very good.'

It was redolent of ginger and cardamom, but it tasted like mud to Siddarth. He did not explain that he had already eaten Tara's pancakes, for his parents would probably not have survived the shock.

Shudodhan and his brother-in-law began discussing the recent controversy in Devadaha where three commoners had refused to give their customary due of cattle for the Jvotistoma sacrifice. They claimed they had only one animal each and could not afford to lose it. Even if the great yagna floundered as a result. It was not allowed to, of course. The bulls were taken forcibly and the three jailed as well.

Siddarth waited, but when the conversation moved off smoothly into the question of adjusting the legal system to cope with the increasing number of propertied non-Shakyas in Kapilavastu, a hot topic that he knew could go on forever, he interrupted.

'What will you do, Father?'

'Do? About what?'

'About that slave!'

Shudodhan raised his eyebrows. 'What do you expect me to do?'

'I don't know. Punish them. Banish them. Something. This was just a child!'

His stepmother looked at Shudodhan seriously. 'Perhaps you should speak to the boy.'

'Speak to him?' exclaimed Siddarth. 'He should be hanged!'

'Perhaps the incident could be condemned from the Sabha floor?' asked Yashodara suddenly. A tall and good-looking girl, she looked especially charming this evening thanks to the ministrations of the beauticians of Kapilavastu who were more in touch with the latest fashions than those of Devadaha. Her hair was dressed in a high pyramid studded with flowers, gold thread and ivory combs, making her easily the tallest person present. Like her mother and her aunt, her bosom was nearly bare, covered only by the transparent drapes of fine muslin that crossed it from her waist to her left shoulder. It was a nice, shapely bosom, adorned with three pearl necklaces and a flowering creeper sketched in yellow sandalwood paste that centred on the nipples, and she was shocked that Siddarth had not glanced at it even once.

'Yashodhara, don't speak of things you know nothing about,' her father glared at her.

'Whatever are you all talking about?' Shudodhan glared at everybody. 'It's a private matter. I can't interfere.'

'You're joking surely, Father? Just because she was a slave? It's a crime – '

'It's a household matter. We cannot interfere.' Shudodhan's tone was final. He paused to drink some wine, watching Siddarth over the rim of his glass. As Tara had expected, he was surprised at his son. But not that much. 'Where did you learn of it?'

Siddarth too paused just for a moment. 'At the market. They were speaking of it at the cobbler's where I had gone to purchase new sandals.'

'I heard of it from the beautician.' Yashodhara silently willed Siddarth to look at her face if not her breasts, but he just glared at his father. Was this really the best husband-material in the sangha?

'And it has made all the slaves very unhappy, Father! It could cause trouble.'

Shudodhan raised his eyebrows again. 'That is worrying. You learnt this also at the market?' He ate some more; Siddarth didn't answer. 'But enough talk of slaves, son. Tell us, how did your shooting match go today?'

The change of topic was not a happy one, for Siddarth had ranked last. But the discussion of Mala was closed. And Tara was shifted the very next day to Shudodhan's brother's household. Siddarth discovered this soon after and angrily questioned his father, who said that his uncle had a new grandchild. Surely Siddarth did not need a nurse? No, Siddarth did not. He said nothing more, not even when he heard that the rapist had been provided a personal bodyguard.

He suddenly realized that he had no one to talk to. He had soldiering companions, hunting companions, wining-and-dining companions, but no one who would understand what he felt. Not that he really understood it himself. But his friends would wonder, like his father, if he was crazy. He had relied on Tara, he realized, whenever he needed a sympathetic ear.

The days passed; bad angry days. Siddarth first thought it was his own gloom, then he realized it was also outside him. Everybody had heard of the incident but few spoke of it. That was normal, one did not discuss the travails of slaves – but this time the silence was eerily loud. Siddarth was nonplussed, and irritated. He could not visit the slave bunker in his uncle's house without exciting comment. But it is doubtful that Tara would have explained anything to him, even if she had still been in his house. For an escape was being planned. For over five weeks, she regularly took grain, flour, ghee, salt, oil and wicks from the kitchen of Siddarth's uncle. Every night half a fistful of food or less – the slaves of the household normally ate the left-overs, so she could not take too much. The laddoos became hard, the rice began to smell, but they might still be invaluable in the jungle. In any case, no slave stomach was fussy about food.

She herself had no intention of going with them.

'I'm too old,' she said. 'I'll slow you down.' But the truth was that she still remembered her parents and that ill-fated escape so many years before. She did not want to die.

It was vappa mangala, the ploughing festival of spring, the only day of the year when the rajas took the plough in their own hands. It was a holiday for workers, who were gifted new clothes, ornaments and small entertainments with games, dancing and music. The rajas meanwhile strode out to the broad stretch of rice fields just outside the city that was jointly owned by the sangha – the oldest fields, so it was said, in the republic. The ritual was carried out by only the hundred and eight Sabha members, who fitted the waiting oxen with the ornate ritual ploughs – the Chief's sheathed in gold leaf, the others' in silver – and struck ritual furrows to assert their connection to the land. The brahmins chanted the history of the tribe, going all the way back through hoary battles to their ancestor Gautama and his friend Aditya, sun of the midday sky.

Of all the rituals in the Shakya calendar, Siddarth enjoyed this the most. The heavy plough, the squelching of mud under his bare feet, the sun on his sweaty shoulders, the breezes that suddenly and deliciously rolled by, all made for a pleasant morning. There was a clean sharp smell of new leaves in the air. But the best thing was that the ritual involved no spilling of blood. While the brahmins were winding up with libations and floral offerings to the earth deities, Shudodhan happened to glance at his son and was moved by the quiet smile on his face. He motioned him closer.

'I'm glad to see you so happy, son. I feel the same. This day always makes me emotional – proud and deeply conscious of my people. It binds our nation together as one.'

Siddarth stared at the long-horned cattle grazing in the meadows beyond the fields. Swarms of insects followed the herds, followed in turn by flocks of sparrows. Watching over them were a few outcaste boys, armed, if it could be called that, with green bamboos cut from the forest.

He smiled back finally, but it was a slightly twisted smile. 'Why, Father? After all, you own much land yourself, more than all this. Some of it won in battle by the republic, others that you bought!'

'Siddarth!' The private estates were one of the few issues on which the rajas were united, but it was neither polite nor auspicious to talk of them today.

'Why the nostalgia? When you and your friends are in fact breaking up the sangha ties – '

'Enough. I will not hear such rubbish. They are yours as well, you know that. They are for your future.'

'Yes, our fields. Our wealth. Our future. Then why this ceremony?'

Shudodhan took a slow deep breath, paused, then released it as slowly. His priest advised this as a good means of calming the head. But he was blessed with five dutiful daughters, how could he ever understand the affliction of a wayward son?

'This ceremony is just hypocrisy – ' Siddarth was saying but his father cut him off.

'Listen to me, Siddarth. Things change. One cannot go back to the past. You are a man now, you should try to understand life.' He paused and then asked, 'When are you planning to rejoin your regiment?'

Siddarth stared at the ground silently. 'Siddarth? When are you going back to the border?'

And he was shocked to hear the scion of a celebrated line of warriors vow, 'I think I've seen enough blood spilled, Father, in war and in the name of the gods. I will never spill another drop, not a single drop, in my life.'

'Siddarth, you sound like a coward! Are you frightened of battle?' It was a frightening thought. 'What happened? Praful said that you came through your engagements fine.' This was not fully true, but both the commander and Shudodhan felt that the truth was not always the best option.

'It's stupid. So many lives lost, just for a few robbed cattle, and the same bits and pieces of land that keep flitting between us and the Koliyas! These issues can surely be settled more sensibly!'

He turned away leaving his father staring after him. What had he done to deserve this?

The slave-break was discovered on the morrow – nineteen men, eight women, three children. They had dug a tunnel through the floor of one of the slave bunkers, all the way below both city walls and the shallower of the two moats. It must have taken months. The deeper moat they crossed swimming, to be sighted as they reached the banks. A soldier shot at them; one man was hit, the others managed to get away. The soldiers checked the bunkers and to their horror discovered three soldiers, their heads crushed by stones. The city was stunned.

A troop of soldiers left at dawn to hunt for the escapees. All their colleagues as well as known relatives were rounded up, whipped and questioned; they revealed nothing. The dead man was impaled on the walls.

But worse was to come. The next evening, men on the ramparts saw a lone figure on the road approaching the city. It walked slowly, unsteady and stumbling like an inebriated peasant. But it turned out to be a woman, Aditi, the wife of the raja Nakul. She, her two daughters and her son had gone to Devadaha for a family function a week ago. They were on their way back that morning, when their carriage was stopped in the jungle by a group of eight men. At first they appeared to be jungle-folk. But then she saw the copper collars.

They blocked the road and asked the family to get off. Her son who was on horseback ordered them aside and when they refused, drew his sword and charged. He was an armed and experienced soldier against only eight pathetic slaves – hardly difficult, one would have thought. But the slaves seemed ablaze with some strange new power. He did kill two, she thought, before the others dragged him down and bludgeoned him with heavy stones. The scoundrels then tied up the women, threw them behind a thicket, and began to make off with the carriage. Then they stopped, there was some altercation among them, and a few men returned. To rape the girls. 'So you do not forget Mala!' they shouted. Finally they left. She had taken a while to undo the ropes. Her daughters were almost unconscious, her son looked dead. The cart-driver had vanished.

Two heavily armed carts, a grim Nakul in one, went to bring his children home. They found two bodies of the renegades too; they were dragged back behind two donkeys and hung on the city wall. A huge crowd of people followed the carts to Nakul's house. The girls were carried in. The city's leading doctors were waiting to tend to the physical injuries, brahmins to the spiritual ones. Their brother's body, which was discovered to be mutilated in the barbaric Naga fashion, was taken for cremation by the other rajas. Nobody could believe what had happened.

The girls were scrubbed with holy ash, bathed in cow-urine and milk. But could anything wash off such a stain? Nobody was surprised the next morning when the bodies of Nakul and his wife were found sprawled near the altar in their hall. The daughters were dead in their beds. All had apparently consumed poison. It was the only honourable course.

The crackdown had begun the previous evening itself. The driver's wife was questioned so severely that she died on the spot, just a few hours before his body was found further down the highway, quite dead and ritually mutilated too. But the Shakyas were not in the mood to apologize. More than a hundred slaves were impaled, among them Tara. One of her fellow slaves had noticed her stealing food but had assumed that it was for Tara herself. Now she understood, and told.

Siddarth was dazed through the whole episode until he heard of Tara. He heard only the next morning and he charged out of the house and ran through the streets wildly, to the gates. Crowds were passing through, either averting their gaze from the ramparts, or stopping to stare. A group of soldiers stood divided on either side of the gate as well; inspecting them was Prafularaja, on short leave from the front. He called out to Siddarth as he ran out of the gates, but he was not heeded. Prafularaja sympathized with Shudodhan over his son, and he wondered what the boy was up to now. He left the soldiers and followed Siddarth around the wall, past the bodies hung up at intervals, all the way to the river, back to the gates and in the opposite direction. This time they found her. She seemed to be floating; only the tips of the bamboo spears holding her in place were visible above her head. Blood had dried on her back and legs.

Siddarth ran back through the gates, up the stairs to the ramparts, past surprised soldiers. He ignored Prafularaja's 'What are you doing? Siddarth? Tell me first!', reached the pegs above Tara, untied the ropes holding the bamboos and pulled them and her up. Her face was a muddy, crumpled yellow. She did not respond to any of his entreaties and finally he just sat weeping, ignoring Prafularaja and the large crowd that collected below. Till his father came and took him home.

In the morning Shudodhan came to Siddarth and asked him if he would like to study a while in Banaras. Siddarth would have preferred Takshashila, a thousand miles away to the west, where the Raja of Kosala had studied and where all the cultures of the world were said to mingle. But the Shakyas abhorred it for the very same reasons. And Shudodhan did not want his son to go so far.

Perhaps he did not trust him to find his way back.

UJJAYANI

There was silence as Ananda finished reading the third chapter, except for the lapping of water against the boat. The silence was as respectful as when Upali was reading the first two, but some of the younger monks were staring at him oddly. He turned away, to the river where a mist seemed to be rising, grey and tenuous. As Ananda picked up his tumbler of water, preparatory to starting the fourth chapter, the far bank seemed to drift away in the greyness and Upali felt his own mind drifting away too. Back to the reading at Sanchi. How many things had happened since then – was it really only three months ago? First had been the trip to the temple at Ujjayani. By royal chariot no less, thanks to Nigrodha. The security of the prince did not permit hitch-hiking. Upali was irritated but then distracted by other irritations, among them the discovery that old Mahanta of Sarnath had not liked his story at all.

'You are mocking the suttas, Upali,' Mahanta had said. 'Which is inexcusable. And you are changing things, adding an entirely new reason for the Shakyamuni's awakening. A political one. At complete variance with his message. You've got carried away by your writing skills – and produced fiction!'

Upali tried to explain that his story was the result of a study of the suttas themselves. And the accepted cause for the

Shakyamuni's awakening was clearly mythical; it didn't stand serious examination at all.

The response was curt. 'Don't be a fool, Upali!'

Upali felt a little annoyed. Especially as the Sanchi Thera was present, and clearly tickled. But he persevered. 'With all respect, Thera, you have to agree that there is some imagination and subjectivity in the accounts. So, it is necessary to examine them critically.'

'I am sure many will agree, Upali, after *you* complete *this* commission.'

A knock on the door had ended the conversation. It was Ananda. A monk had come to their room to tell him that Upali wanted him immediately. But Upali had sent no such message. He bade farewell to Mahanta in some relief and walked back with Ananda, to find their room in as big a mess as a somewhat bare room could be. The bedclothes were dumped in a heap near the door, the shutters of the empty cupboard stood open. One jar of ink was on its side, the ink on the floor.

'Who could it be? A thief? Expecting something rob-worthy in our room of all places?' Then it struck him. 'The silk bits!' He started searching through the sheets and rugs. 'They've gone.'

'Who knew of them?' asked Ananda.

'The Thera, the Viceroy, old Mahanta. And that monk who took us to Pradyota's room. But why would any of them – ? It makes no sense.'

They started cleaning up the mess. The Sanchi Thera arrived in the middle and seemed irritated by the news. He took Ananda by the shoulder and led him through the monastery on an unsuccessful quest for the monk who had come with the false message, which Ananda did not enjoy because the Thera's bony hand really hurt.

As it turned out, Upali had to change his mind about Nigrodha's chariot. It proved very useful, for he decided to visit the Ujjayani temple en route. The Sanchi Thera was clearly uninterested in the sculptor's problem; Upali decided to at least make sure that the girl was safe.

It felt like they were flying. The four black horses were sleek and arrogant, yoked abreast and apparently competing with each other. Ahead and behind were two more chariots, carrying four soldiers each and, like their own, flying the royal pennant above an umbrella. It was discomfiting to find villagers and farm-hands running up to see the cavalcade and even prostrating themselves at the side of the road. But soon they were racing through the jungle and Upali could relax and join the conversation as he clung to the rails. The elegantly weary manner of Nigrodha intensified as he explained one thing after the other about the vehicle. The charioteer corrected him a few times in a matter-of-fact way, to Upali's amusement. His name was Chandra and he had been in the Magadhan army for eleven years.

'Always in Prince Nigrodha's guard?'

'Only for about six months now. I am actually with the cavalry corps, we don't use chariots in battle any more.'

Upali stared at him. 'Why not?' asked Ananda.

'Cavalry's much faster – with the new stirrups – faster, better controlled – '

Upali interrupted, 'Did you go to Kalinga?'

'Yes, I did.'

'With the Maurya army?'

'Who else?'

'So you are one of the victors. You should be congratulated. You have been, I suppose.'

'Many times. Medals, promotions too. But Kalinga was no one's victory. I agree with the Raja on that.'

He could hardly afford to disagree, with Nigrodha next to him. But still. 'What do you mean?'

'There – Ujjayani!'

Viewed from the crest of a hill, the city was a jewel on a gold riverine ribbon, the whole lit up by the ball of fire sinking into the forests behind. The cavalcade fell silent in admiration, till the ball darkened to saffron and reminded Upali of Sanchi and the lost chits.

'The question is how did whoever-it-was find them so fast? I don't remember myself where I had kept them. Do you, Ananda? I'd decided to leave them in the room.'

'But did you?' asked Ananda sharply. 'Check in your waistband where you had tucked them.'

They were there. Upali looked at them ruefully. 'Now how do I get these to the Thera?'

The city walls reared up dark and unfriendly as they neared the city, or perhaps it was his imagination. Ujjayani was the largest city of his acquaintance and he usually enjoyed the crowds, the dusty traffic-jammed roads, the variety of buildings, the great market square. Even the raucous noise, a medley of pushy hawkers, harassed animals, traffic snarls, short-tempered soldiers and discordant temple bells. If he lived here he'd go crazy, but it was fun to visit.

This evening however the city seemed enshrouded in darkness and quiet. They passed the outcaste settlement, sped over the moats and through the gates; everywhere soldiers snapped to attention on seeing the pennants. But the gates were draped in white, and a group seated in a pavilion inside was dolefully strumming an assortment of stringed instruments. Was something wrong? A soldier revealed that there had been a death in one of the big families. He also provided directions to the temple, down a maze of congested streets in the inner city, to a pair of closed gates in a high wall. Nobody in the narrow lane of flower and incense sellers gave them a second glance. Evidently, regal chariots were not so rare here. Upali got down a little shakily, and rang the brass bell.

One shutter opened a crack. Upali explained that he wished to meet the head of the temple.

'Who?'

'The chief priest of your temple – or is it a priestess?' It used to be priestesses where he had lived, and priests in Tosali.

'Come tomorrow morning,' said the crack.

'We cannot. And we won't take very long.'

'Wait.'

They waited. Other chariots rode up. Noblemen got out, swept silk shawls over handsome shoulders, rang the bell and vanished inside. They could hear music from within. Finally the shutter opened enough to reveal an old man. 'Come after half an hour.'

'May we wait within?'

'Well… all right. But only dvija may enter from this gate.'

'We are all twice-born,' lied Upali blithely. 'Also monks of the Buddha's order.'

The gatekeeper looked disbelieving about the first and unimpressed by the last, but decided that he had done his duty. The three, with Nigrodha's guards following, entered a large mud-floored compound, swept, watered and very clean, in contrast to the filthy little lane outside. Directly in front of them was the main shrine, a timber pavilion topped by a steeply pitched thatched roof that sheltered a square plinth with an altar at its centre. Around the plinth ran a little gutter stained dark red; on one corner was a brass platter containing the huge head of a buffalo; the eyes were open and unfriendly.

The music source was another pavilion, to the side and very crowded. Upali decided to head there, but was arrested by the sight of Nigrodha climbing up the altar plinth. A priest rushed up, Nigrodha murmured something, the priest's frown became worried but he still argued, till one of Nigrodha's soldiers pushed him aside. The prince stood for a few moments at the altar. But when he turned back, he was frowning as well.

The crowded pavilion turned out to be a natya mandap. Another square plinth, under another thatched roof, but beautiful because two sides of the square were enclosed by a timber grill with tiny brass lamps. Their light shimmered like the intricate gold zari borders of Upali's Banaras childhood. He and his wards joined the standees at the back of the throng; their focus was a group seated in the centre and rendering a song in the wordless temple style, a study and a celebration of pure sound.

Upali, who had almost no exposure to the arts of the upper castes, began to feel sleepy after a while. But the singing was followed by a dance performance that thoroughly woke him up. There were four dancers but he decided that Sutanuka must be the youngest, a slender girl, the main element of whose performance seemed to be speed and a certain dexterity, for though her face was never clearly visible thanks to her rapid whirling, the diamond stud twinkling in her navel remained secure and very prominent.

Everybody bowed low at the finish, heads touching the ground to humbly receive the blessings of the dancers – a feather-light caress. But then a vaguely-familiar voice spoke up, confirming Upali's guess. 'Lady Sutanuka, we would be honoured by another blessing.' Sutanuka paused, apparently in thought; the audience stayed bowed. The deliberation reminded Upali that in earlier times a priestess would have been akin to a ruler, an incarnation of the goddess – nobody could have dared to ask for an encore.

But now she was the slave of the god. Sutanuka began to dance, slow at first, then faster, stamping the ground furiously, ignoring the crowd which had raised its heads, which was entranced even when she whirled too close and forced them backwards. Jasmine darted off her heavily garlanded plait as it whipped about her; one flew into Ananda's mouth before he realized it was open. Upali was shoved off the plinth twice before he decided to stay down.

She finished and immediately retired. The audience began to leave. A few men converged upon the priests, clearly negotiating for private blessings. Among them was the supplicant of the familiar voice – the Viceroy Vishnugupta. He was talking to an old priest but broke off to hail Upali.

'Well, well, Thera! You should have told me you were a connoisseur of dance – we could have travelled together!' He smelled of wine but his gaze was sharp. 'By the way, where are those chits?'

Upali explained the attempted robbery and the subsequent discovery, and pulled them out of his waistband. 'Here.'

The Viceroy turned away to examine them and Upali looked at the old priest who was frowning quietly at the side.

'Sir, I'd like to speak to the head priest.'

The man motioned him to a seat built around a mango tree and called a younger priest over as well. Upali explained why he had come, suddenly wondering if he was making a mistake. His doubts were confirmed by the younger man.

'I cannot believe this – can anybody be such a lunatic? He wants to marry a priestess! Has he no sense at all? But then he is only a mason. No, I'm really shocked at you, Thera – '

'I would not have interfered,' said Upali. 'I would not have dreamt of doing this kind of thing normally. But the boy is sincere. It's an exceptional case.'

'It is sacrilege – an insult to the temple! Her position is holy and inviolate – she possesses enormous power, to bless as well as curse. I tell you – he is raving mad!'

'Her position may be sacred, but if she is happier otherwise? Perhaps – '

But the old priest interrupted, 'Thera, please try to understand. The girl may be happier, you say, but is that all that matters? What of the sacred laws before which we all are helpless? If she flouts the law, there will be calamity – on her, on her community, on this temple.'

He paused; his colleague took off again, 'That's what they want!' but was cut off by a glance.

'Our concern is not a selfish one, Thera. You seem to be a foreigner, so I must tell you that this is the original altar of the Avanti rajas, the most respected shrine in Ujjayani. And Ujjayani is today a huge and confused city. All kinds of strange people, even barbarians, have made their home here ever since we came under the rule of Magadh. The natives live in a state of fear, the old rajas have no power and no say. In this situation of tension, in which our monarch in distant Magadh takes no interest save for his hefty taxes, what maintains the peace? It is the fear of the Gods, Thera, the Gods as reside in shrines like this!'

Ananda was impressed by this speech but also by Upali's answer. 'Forgive me, priest, but how can a shrine that does not allow even one-tenth of the population through its gates, prevail against hooliganism? Every small group worships its own gods, regards all others as devils – many clashes in fact originate here!'

'You've made yourself quite clear, Thera!' shouted the younger priest. 'Your people are apparently no longer content with defaming the gods! You – '

Ananda suddenly asked, 'Master, may I speak?' and rushed on without waiting for permission. 'Sir, the Buddha never defamed the gods. All he taught was how to lead one's life, he never spoke about the heavens at all.' He looked at Upali for approval but he seemed lost in thought. Ananda was torn between joy at not being silenced and the onerous burden of carrying on the debate. 'In fact, there are many monks in the Sangh who still worship the old gods….'

'How do they worship, pray tell us,' glared the younger priest, 'when the rituals are being banned? First the temple was taxed so heavily we could barely survive, now your Raja has even forbidden the holy sacrifices!'

Ananda could not help a glance at the buffalo head; its mood did not seem to have improved. 'It has nothing to do with us – and he's your Raja too!' He glared at Upali. Was he asleep?

It worked. Upali rose. 'Thank you for speaking to me, sirs. I would like to meet the girl.'

'That is impossible.'

'Why, is she a prisoner here?'

'Of course not! This is her time for rest, that's all.'

'And if I order her to be brought out?' interrupted Nigrodha.

The priest bowed. 'Sire, you approached the sacred altar despite our request to refrain. Your guards have the strength to violate the sanctity of this shrine again if you so wish.'

Nigrodha was pale with rage and then surprise, when Upali gripped his arm, 'Come.'

The Viceroy was standing with his entourage at the gate. He broke away as they approached. 'Thera – '

'I'm sorry, my lord, but we're in a hurry.' Upali climbed into the chariot behind his wards. 'Listen, let us go to the back of the compound. I want to try and meet the girl.'

The chariot drove around the temple walls to the back where a muddy lane separated it from a row of hutments. They stopped near a small closed gate and waited. A woman soon came hurrying out, one clay pot balanced on her head and another in her hand. She looked taken aback by the chariot and still more surprised when an occupant hopped out and addressed her.

'Sister, please wait a moment. I have a message for the Lady Sutanuka.'

She began to back off. Upali added, 'Please, sister. It's important, and secret.'

'Secret?'

'Never mind, just tell her that it's a message from Devadina.' The lady was frowning and shaking her head. 'Sister, I am a monk, do you think I mean evil?'

She disappeared into the compound, after snorting at his 'you can leave your pots here', and was gone a long time. Upali half-expected the priests to come charging out. But the lady returned, genuflecting humbly and repeatedly, for with her, wrapped in a dark shawl, was Sutanaka.

Upali turned to tell his wards to wait, only to find that both had already jumped down and were hurrying past quite oblivious of him.

Sutanaka turned out to be very different from his first impression. Not a young girl, but a woman clearly older than her sculptor lover. Small and slender, with glowing coppery skin and long slightly slanted black eyes, her confident and quizzical expression made Upali hesitate, till he caught the still-suspicious eye of the lady with the pots.

'Sister, I am Upali, a Thera at the Maheshwar monastery. I met the sculptor Devadina at Sanchi yesterday, and he said you and he wished to be married. He was worried about you, about your safety.'

Sutanuka turned to the lady with the pots and flicked a finger gently; the lady backed away out of hearing distance. Then Sutanuka smiled and Ananda caught his breath. He felt feverish. His mouth was suddenly and painfully dry, his armpits wet, he thought he would fall down any moment. He was in love. He clutched Nigrodha's arm tightly but the prince didn't notice this time, for Sutanuka was speaking.

'Lord, you do me honour by your visit. Tell Devadina that I am in no danger at all. And please tell him also to give up this mad idea. I really mean this.'

Upali felt even more at a loss. 'But, sister – why? I told Devadina I would speak to the priests here about you both.'

'Did you?'

'Yes, just now. They were very negative. I hope they do not do anything....'

'To me? Don't worry,' she smiled again and shook her head. Her shawl slipped off a little, revealing a high pile of blue-black hair dressed with jasmine and what looked like ivory and silver combs. 'The whole thing was hopeless from the start. Anyway, I must go now.'

'Sister, wait, just tell me – you do want to marry Devadina, don't you?'

Suddenly she was almost angry. 'It is not a matter of what I want! This temple is holy, devotees flock here for my blessings, my advice, my body.... I know no other world. Unlike my mother – she was pledged by her village and when she came of age they left her here. When she remembered her childhood, she was happy, and miserable too. But I was born here, I have nothing else!' Upali glanced at the gate nervously. But she adjusted the shawl and lowered her voice. 'Devadina made me dream for a while, but it's wrong to fight fate, otherwise my next life may be worse. I should count my blessings instead – that people want my blessings! If I had been born to those poor creatures on the cremation-grounds, people would have spat at me!'

'You cannot forsake this life for the next, sister. Let us try.'

'Thank you, Thera, but I think it is better to let things be.'

She turned and vanished through the gate, leaving the monks frozen in a thick fragrance of jasmine. The lady with the pots also walked off before Upali thought of thanking her.

They headed for Maheshwar through the night, for the royal chariots considered themselves immune to ghosts, bandits and carnivores. As they turned southwards they passed a cremation-ground brightly lit by two burning pyres. The soldiers made signs against the evil eye. Two ragged human figures could be seen sitting between the pyres. Chandalas. Sutanuka was grateful to be a temple slave rather than one of them.

The journey was almost completely silent, for all were sunk in thought. They had to stop at one point for a herd of elephants crossing the highway, right in the middle of the night jungle, a thick blackness full of layered sound, many hoots, the odd crunch, the unmistakable and chilling howls of wild dogs.

Upali decided it was time to recover. 'Do you know that in Kalinga the elephant is called the Lord of the Tribes?'

His audience was not with him. Ananda turned and asked, 'Is there any difference between a devadasi and a courtesan, except that one is in a temple?'

I suppose I asked for this, thought Upali. 'Devadasis originated in the old fertility worship, where the diety was the goddess of fertility. The dasis were her priestesses and wielded enormous power. But wherever agriculture came in, men took the power, often after ritual marriages to the priestesses. Male gods appeared and devadasis fell from priestesses to oracles, dancers, servants, whatever. Courtesans are different, a relic of the old group marriage custom, I think. Women who could not put together a dowry, or were simply felt too beautiful and accomplished, were married to all the menfolk of the tribe in common. Like the Buddha's disciple, Amrapali. But over the years, their respectability fell.'

Nigrodha was more pragmatically informed. 'Also anyone can go to most courtesans, if they have the money. Here caste counts. Though they might make exceptions for enough money.'

'How much?' asked Ananda. Upali just looked at him while Nigrodha appeared engrossed in the backside of the last vanishing elephant. That was the end of the conversation but Upali was sure the prince would enlighten Ananda when they were alone.

Upali was surprised at the pleasure he felt the next morning when the forest opened suddenly to reveal the small clearing of rice and millet fields set around the familiar shabby shacks. There was a time when he used to hate this place; when he used to wake fearful and find all his fears justified. Three years and prison had become home.

The clatter of the horses brought everybody hurrying out, to gape at the pennanted chariots and Upali and Ananda in them. Harsha and Mohan had just arrived too, from a nearby village through which some elephants had passed the previous day – in blissful disregard as usual of the distinction between forest, field and hut. They looked exhausted and dirty after spending the entire night in repairs and rebuilding, but Harsha insisted on a full report immediately. The invitation for the Third Council was greeted with nervous hand-wringing, but he was relieved to hear that the story had been appreciated, and then very pleased indeed with the praise for his own proposal concerning Bhima's village. The others were impressed too; Upali stared around at the happy faces and checked for Nigrodha – he had gone to the well with Ananda to wash up – before ending with, 'So, the Magadhe-Raja is now instructing the Sangha. As though we are here to follow his bidding!'

Harsha's beam dimmed a little. 'Yes, it's a little worrying. But he is a different kind of Raja, Upali, a follower of Dhamma himself.'

'A follower? He is a Mur – ' Everybody turned towards the well. 'Anyway, he didn't sound like a follower to me!'

He was suddenly yearning to get back to his old routine, which meant his classes and his writing, but the fields were ripe and the nine boys would be out harvesting for most of the day. He felt irritated, though he was aware he enjoyed his classes more than his students, and he sometimes wondered whether he was becoming exactly the sort of complacent word-cruncher the Buddha had deplored. But the story was all-important now. He worked rapidly, concentrating on finishing rather than content, though he would have liked to spend more time on the part about Buddha's departure from his home. It was a crucial chapter, one that old Mahanta would definitely hate, yet he hardly paused. Harsha, who normally acted as a sounding board, was not given much time to do his customary pursing of the lips, furrowing of the brow and 'give me a few days to think about it'. He listened, he furrowed, but Upali rushed on without waiting.

He did pause though, a couple of times, to think about Devadina and his priestess. And he kept an eye open for an opportunity to talk to Chandra, though this was not very forthcoming, for the man was conscientious and hardly ever left the shadow of his charge. Nigrodha himself was more than a little enigmatic. Upali attempted a personal discussion with him only once, when he asked him how he was finding things.

'Pleasant, instructive, and above of all safe,' was the answer.

'Safe?'

'The Court is a very dangerous place. Especially for those of royal blood.'

Upali gave up – he was damned, he thought, if he was going to ask for an explanation for every royal monosyllable.

With Chandra he was slightly luckier. After keeping an eye on him for days, he finally bumped into him alone one morning at the well. Upali had come to fill water for cooking.

'Here, let me take it.' Chandra reached out for the pot, but Upali shook his head. The charioteer stepped back immediately. 'I thought you monks didn't keep caste taboos.'

'Of course we don't! But it's heavy – ' Muscles rippled all over Chandra's bull-like chest; he was nearly a head taller than Upali. 'Oh, go ahead.'

He followed Chandra and the pot to the kitchen, thanked him and added hurriedly, 'I have some cooking to do, but I'd like to talk with you if you have the time.'

'About what?' Chandra was looking about with interest. The kitchen was a thatched shed with an earth stove built into one corner and firewood stacked next to it.

Upali stoked the fire, put some water on to boil, and then settled down on the floor with a knife, a platter and a basket of onions, gourds, yam and beans. 'Kalinga. The war.'

'What are you making?'

'A curry of dal and vegetables. And rice. Do you cook?'

'Sometimes when on duty – not at home! Here, I'll peel them.'

'Who do you have at home?'

'Mother, wife, two sons.' Chandra's face softened. The line between his brows disappeared along with the secretive almost-smirk that was his normal smile. He suddenly looked a little vulnerable and quite handsome. Upali felt an old pang of envy for the never-known turmoils of family life, stamped it out ruthlessly and got up to make the curry. He poured sesame oil into a large earthen pot and emptied all the vegetables into it.

'Everything together? Why don't you fry the onions first?'

'Well,' Upali began scooping them out, 'generally I like to save time. I wanted to ask you, Chandra, what did you mean about regretting Kalinga?'

Chandra offered another question. 'I thought you monks weren't allowed to eat onions?'

'Where did you hear that?'

'I don't know. Pataliputra, perhaps.'

'Well, some people do believe that they heighten the passions. But Loka says onions and garlic are very healthy foods.'

'You do a lot of things in this monastery which others don't, don't you? Like all this farming. Not so fast,' as Upali picked up the other vegetables, 'let the onion become translucent. Don't you use any spices?'

'I'll put in turmeric later.'

'Shall I grind it?' He took the bright yellow pieces to the stone quern and pounded them to a smooth paste.

Upali waited, inhaling the heady fragrance impatiently, then repeated, 'About Kalinga, Chandra?'

'It was a nasty war, Thera. No war is beautiful, I admit. But Kalinga was worse.'

'Meaning?'

'The onion is burning!'

Upali started to scrape the stuck part off while Chandra added a little more oil. 'Here, let me. Where is the salt? You get the rice ready.'

He took the wooden ladle from Upali and began to stir. Upali placed the precious mud jar of salt near the heap of dal, opened the rice-bin and started to measure it out. Vilas, who was on kitchen duty too, came in and quietly took the cutting board and knives outside to wash. After a little while Chandra began to speak.

'Kalinga was very viciously fought – see now the onions are ready…. Actually the Magadhe-Raja too insists on remembering, I don't know why. Anyway. Their army was better than we had expected. They used chariots, not cavalry, but you could see that fighting was in their blood. But no efficiency – everything based on birth and family. And so much ritual! All our surprise attacks found them in the middle of some offering or the other! But they fought well. And refused to surrender even at the end. We had to massacre them – and they took many of us with them.'

He paused, stirring away, and looked at Upali. The latter nodded. 'And that was not all. There were hundreds of tribes too, yes, hundreds! With their crude weapons – stones and catapults and those pathetic iron hammers standing up against Magadha! But they had the jungle too. That horrible jungle! The place was so *solid*, the noon was as dark as night sometimes. And rife with every kind of wild beast and witch and ghoul. That thick stinking hellish mud – I can still feel it on me. I was one of the few who escaped after falling into a swamp. Purely because my poor horse was thrashing around frantically; he kicked me out, right into some branches overhead. The kick broke my hip, but I was alive. But even more men died from the curse of the jungle-folk – I saw it myself. I still dream of it.'

The curry was bubbling now, but the charioteer's face was set tight. A bee buzzed in and decided to take a breather on his head. He didn't notice it. Upali let it be.

'The jungle-folk were typical really – we fight them elsewhere, everywhere, even here. But here one just drives them away into the jungle – it's a matter of destroying their ability to attack and rob. But there we had to cross their jungles to reach Kalinga. And they had no concept of retreat, not even of fear, even less than the Kalingas. They did not even cover their chests. I saw one of our archers take three at once, the same arrow shot straight and hard through three chests one behind the other, like chickens in the bazaar. Yet they kept on coming. Like ants out of an ant-hill.'

Chandra's colleague appeared on the opposite veranda and waved, bringing to an end his animal metaphors. 'I must go. Sorry if I bored you.'

'Yes. No, I mean! I was in the Kalinga republic too, in the south, for some years.'

'Really? You must be very relieved to have left.'

Two weeks before they were to leave for Pataliputra, when the pre-winter festival of the new moon came around, Upali was tired but satisfied. Two more chapters were finished and copied out in duplicate, a third was nearly so, while two more, after going through many drafts, were ready in terms of content and argument. Ananda was showing signs of writer's elbow, probably the first ever in the land. So he was happy when Upali decided to take a break and go with the people of Bhima's village on a trek to a shrine nearly ten miles away.

Harsha was not happy – Bhima's people were prohibited from leaving their village; Upali shouldn't be encouraging them. He was further irritated to discover that Upali had accepted an invitation to dine at Bhima's village the night before. Actually Upali had invited himself and noted Bhima's reluctant acquiescence – he was clearly disturbed about something, and Upali was determined to find out what. It would mean more visits of the local constabulary, Harsha warned, if not worse. 'Don't come to me, if you find yourself imprisoned again!'

Luckily, Harsha was unaware of Upali's fellow-guest – Ananda. Upali was unaware of this himself, for Ananda merely asked Nigrodha to inform the others later and then shadowed Upali through the forest till he saw a leopard in a tree. Then he panicked and shouted, Upali came running back, and the leopard melted away into the foliage with a disgusted flash of yellow eyes. By then it was nearly sunset and Upali didn't want to send him back alone. But he was annoyed.

It was a pleasant evening. The forest was drying up and preparing for the cold, the undergrowth thick with fallen leaves. Ananda scared a large rat snake and was scared in turn when it reared up to more than half his height; Upali was unsympathetic. Bhima's village was a cluster of some twenty huts surrounded by fields in a quiet little valley bottom with little waterfalls tumbling down the sides and a stream running through. He was waiting for them with his Chief and other elders, all looking a little grim – could it still be Harsha's proposal?

Ananda was distracted by the rich smells wafting around the valley. At the centre of the village, not far from a little group of wooden idols under a thatched roof, was the source – cooking pots bubbling away in the ground. Mats had been laid down and set with leaf plates and pots, the latter brightly coloured and crude in shape. They were made by the women, Upali knew, on the traditional table, though the village had many modern wheels provided by the administration a year ago. The men worked the wheels and the little kiln, producing perfectly round and thin pots, all for the taxman. The village refused to use them.

The food was served immediately – roast meats of deer, porcupine and iguana, to be eaten with boiled rice or gruel. The gruel was familiar and delicious, a sweet-sour concoction of jackfruit seed flour and tamarind, but the meats were exotic, the porcupine especially for it was clearly very lightly cooked. Ananda imitated Upali in reducing the heap of meat on his plate to barely a taste and concentrating on the rice and gruel. The porcupine bled as he bit into it and he had to remove the piece from his mouth before he gagged. The iguana was stringy. Two bamboo-stem glasses stood before each guest, one containing rice toddy mixed with honey, the other buttermilk.

'The rice is from the fields here,' explained Bhima's wife, Kali. 'It does not taste as good as the wild rice at home.' Small, thin and probably less than twenty years of age, she looked much tougher than her husband, though somewhat softer today thanks to the wild jasmine woven into her hair. Thinner than the string worn by Sutanuka, but as fragrant. Nayana used to say that jasmine was too strong a smell for the hair; she had preferred spider-lilies....

During the meal the reason for Bhima's grimness was revealed – a new one. A cow and her calf had gone missing and the neighbouring village was suspected of the theft. One of Bhima's clans-women was a mystic and had seen the robbery in a dream. Upali wished, as he had many times before, that there were fewer mystics in the world. It was probably leopards, he argued. In any case, they should report the loss to the police. The villagers responded with silence. Upali and Ananda stayed the night.

The whole village was up before dawn the next morning. Some carried bamboo spears and wooden clubs, a few even bows and arrows. But it was not easy to break the law. A patrol arrived just as everybody was assembling – looking bluish and ghostly in the half-light.

Where were the villagers heading, asked the officer in charge. And wait a minute, were those weapons? Most cubs and bows had already been dumped and the spears turned upside-down to explain them away as walking aids, but the explanations were ignored, the spears confiscated. But one old man refused to give his up. The assault on their livestock was the last straw, he announced, he would not be unarmed henceforth. It was a brave stance. He was dragged to the side, beaten, even kicked in the stomach. Upali and Ananda had been dilly-dallying behind a hut and wondering how to avoid being caught when they heard the noise. Upali pushed Ananda into the hut and pushed his own way to the head of the crowd.

The officer was not pleased to see him. What was he doing there? Weren't monks banned from the resettled villages? And hadn't Upali himself been warned of this, time and again? Well, the time for warnings was past. He motioned Upali to the side, and no, he did not want any explanation of the need for a spear. Just wait there and shut up!

The officer turned back to the crowd. The offender was very lucky, he said. Till now, any peasant carrying a weapon faced the death sentence. But the law had changed – the punishment was now lighter for a first offence. The man would be jailed, the monk also.

The crowd took a collective breath of horror.

The soldiers watched them stony-eyed, hands still on swords. It was a long moment. Upali's stomach signalled complaint, but he ignored it and rose slightly on his haunches. From the helplessness of villages, he remembered, comes concentration of men on their fields, and hence increases of tax, labour supply, wealth and grain. It was another thesis of Chandragupta's mentor, Kautilya. It took a while to make people helpless, even for the Mauryas; many had to be killed before they gave up.

But somewhere somebody shook his head. The crowd seemed to deflate. The soldiers relaxed. Upali sat back. One of the soldiers came up and whispered something to the officer. The latter looked surprised and disbelieving. They murmured some more, then he turned to Upali. 'You can go.'

'Him too?' Upali indicated the villager.

He shrugged and nodded. 'But remember. You might pay with your life for breaking the law a next time.'

'Can they visit the shrine?'

Another nod. Upali was amazed. Bhima made a sign and the surprised crowd began to shuffle out of the village. Upali ran and released Ananda from his hut. Why had they changed their minds, asked Ananda, but Upali didn't know and had no intention of asking. A song started up from somewhere. The somewhat staccato beat sounded militant, or even military.

The shrine was popular. They were soon part of a hot sweaty stream apparently without beginning or end, for bits could be seen tramping the valleys below, others higher, in the neighbouring hills. Langurs chattered angrily above their heads, spotted antelope, squirrels and rabbits looked appalled by the invasion. The pilgrims included both peasants and jungle-folk, but Upali found it really strange that it also included foreigners like Bhima. Foreigners otherwise allergic to strangers. The peasants behind them were celebrating some victory of their goddess, while Bhima said it was a marriage of two gods; both added that it was the beginning of winter. Upali wondered whether Kautilya had something to do with it. The old brahmin had been cold-blooded about the benefit of worship – to the State. He had advised taxing shrines heavily, even starting new ones when the exchequer needed it!

Bhima looked relaxed, swinging a heavy basket of bananas, fingering the length of gold-coloured silk on his shoulder lovingly. Most of his clan sported something or the other in the beautiful rough-textured mugga, as they called it, woven long ago on home-made bamboo looms and reserved for special occasions – for the wild silkworms with their shining little cocoons were not to be found in the Vindhyas; Bhima insisted the new land was barren. But he was happy now. It was good to be celebrating one of their old festivals, good to be in the jungle, away from the village and those hated fields.

But, asked Upali, forget everything else for the moment, don't the fields provide security, eliminating the chanciness of the jungle? No, said Bhima, the jungle provided more, and without this back-breaking toil. The jungle was rich, vast, unlimited in wealth and nourishment. The fields were cruel unnaturalness, violence to man and god, slavery to Magadh!

Upali stared around at the familiar greenness, stretching away up hills and down dark wooded valleys, sparkling brilliantly now in the noon sun, rustling, chirping, calling to itself with millions of voices. Familiar yet distant, for there was not a single sign of man, not a single comforting whiff of smoke, no road, well, shack or field. He had spent most of his life near such forest, but he could understand Chandra's horror of it, as a power complete in itself and contemptuous of man. The jungle-folk felt this too. They accepted the duality, and their own subservience. Every pilgrim carried an offering – baskets of grain, fruit, vegetables, many animals. Just behind them was a group with a fat young sheep who struggled along the climb gamely – a poor fool who little knew his ghastly fate, pointed out Upali; a godly spirit eager to embrace his divine fortune, countered Bhima.

When they finally reached, the shrine could not be seen in the great throng. Upali forgot his exhausted legs and pushed through behind Bhima, to find a stupa set in a clearing. Its curved surface was dark brown and shining, just mud packed together and then polished by the thousands of hands that touched its holy surface for blessings. It was believed to be the breast of Yamai, the local mother goddess, said Bhima. Its twin stood on the hilltop across the valley till it was destroyed in a terrible thunderstorm many years ago.

A breast? Upali had seen many such mounds in his life but now he saw them as if for the first time. The devotees too; there was something distinctly sensual about the way they caressed the hemisphere with both hands, some trying to touch it with their entire bodies. Was it the proprietorial caress of the infant? Or the persuasive one of the lover? Perhaps both were one here. Bhima was clinging to the stupa, eyes closed, murmuring to himself. Upali followed and found it smooth, hard and cool to touch. Around him people were murmuring, swaying, faces agleam. There was a drum beating rhythmically somewhere. It was a little like the meditational beat at Maheshwar, but here it was the heart below a female breast. The goddess' breast. Upali closed his eyes and pressed his ear against the surface to hear better, and felt himself surrendering helplessly, deliciously, to the pull of the eternal mother. She was beautiful, seductive, milk-giving. He clung to the roundness like a vine, his fingers softly searching the surface, seeking the nipple. The ground slipped away. The world as well. She encircled him with her warmth. But then the oracles started their chanting.

There were about twenty men and women. Only a few were chanting, others were seated in yogic postures, some rolling on the ground, one waving her arms and leaping around. As their frenzy grew, so did that of the audience, which began to sway and hum along in sympathy. The oracles began to address the crowd, one by one, some by song, some weeping, some laughing hysterically. Among them was a boy from Bhima's village. Upali hoped he would keep quiet, for he had been orphaned by the war and was yet to recover – there was no way he could say anything positive. But he spoke, in Bhima's native dialect, identified himself as some goddess whose name Upali could not catch, blessed the gathering, and started to wail. Louder and louder, till he was shrieking out the goddess' anger in a shrilly painful falsetto – her sacred cattle had been robbed, eaten by the barbarians. It was sacrilege, she said, punish the robbers, she wanted to see the blood flow! He beat himself on his head, sobbed chokingly and fell down in a faint.

His performance made waves. Most of his clan clustered together in awed discussion, so long and so awed that Upali decided to speak to Bhima on the way back. Upali had come across oracles before, and often found them interesting and strangely wise. They offered solutions, warnings, blessings, often emotionally but always trying to solve problems – rarely did they create new ones. Even as Upali pondered this, he was surprised by another one, a woman this time, who laid a hard hand on his head and said something in a language he did not understand. Everybody around stared, some laughed.

It was embarrassing. He moved out of the crowd and away, past a naked girl seated before several vermilion-daubed human skulls, and further, till he reached a small pavilion where a queue of people and animals watched while various creatures were efficiently converted into holy prasad by two priestly types. The priests paused on seeing him and made signs against the evil eye. Upali went closer, intending to say something about the sadness of losing such beautiful beasts, point out how much better it was to offer vegetables or flowers, then take it from there. If they ignored him, he would sit down in meditation nearby. Meditation attracted curiosity; most audiences were unfamiliar with its introspectiveness – they tended to expect some spectacular explosion at the end, or at least some minor magic. The anticlimax could be funny, sometimes hostile. If they drove him off, he would not argue, he decided, he was not in the mood.

Then he laid a hand on the knobby head of a garlanded calf, whose huge liquid eyes gazed at him with the same bemusement as her owner's, and changed his mind. Not because of her, but because of a couple just behind – they had no animal, nor any basket of produce. Only a small wrapped bundle in the woman's arms. Upali could see just the top of a little head. And a colourful little garland.

He felt his chest constrict suddenly and did not know what he shouted. The couple looked threatened and many other heads turned too. But he did know that he stepped forward and tried to snatch the bundle. The woman jerked backwards, the man gave Upali a hard shove, so that he stepped back into the calf. Then they were all startled by a curt question. Curt, arrogant and very loud.

'Who breaks the law of the Magadhe-Raja here?'

It was another posse of soldiers. Twelve of them on horses, and glaring at the priests, who stared back horrified.

'In the name of His Sacred Majesty, the Beloved of the Gods! I order you to take heed of the law! Stop all bloodshed! At once!'

The people dispersed, hanging on to their animals as if they might be snatched any moment. The couple with the little bundle vanished even before Upali turned back, completely, as if they had never existed. The priests disappeared too. Only a heap of skins and heads remained, and Upali himself.

Upali finally collected himself and moved too, right to the edge of the plateau on the quietest side. He stood hunched for a few minutes, breathing long and slow, letting his rage out, absorbing the silence of the gloomy wooded hills, the clouds banking up. Then he heard a woman's low laugh. It was from somewhere below him, and from the sound – a combination of breathlessness, excitement and secrecy – he knew that it was a pair of lovers. He moved a little downhill and saw them, a couple seated on a rock. Their arms were around each other, their faces together, but then one head lifted slightly and the peeping Tom above was amazed to recognize Sutanuka and Devadina. In a moment he was bounding down, slithering a little on the moss and frightening both quite seriously.

'What a surprise! You've come together? You're looking very well!'

She looked enchanting, eyes a-sparkle, lips painted a rich red, the same colour as her sari. He could smell the sweetness of the string of bakul threaded through her hair.

'Thera!' beamed Devadina. 'No, she's with a group from the temple. I expected them to come here today.' He looked thinner but cheerful. 'I've been trying to convince her that the only way for us is to go away.'

'To run away. Like criminals,' Sutanuka explained, but she was smiling at Devadina.

'It's the best way, my dearest. I know a trader who will hide us in his caravan.' Devadina caught her hands in his. 'And once we're out of Avanti – '

'I need a little time to think, Devadina, that's all.'

'Listen, sister,' Upali interrupted. 'I have an idea – you can take shelter at the Ujjayani convent! I can speak to the nuns there. Then this marriage will not be difficult.' He actually knew very little about the convent; only that it was there. Had been there a year ago.

Sutanuka's smile was kind. 'Yes, my lord, perhaps I can do that. Now I must go.'

'Wait awhile,' Devadina begged. 'Just for – '

'Enough dreaming for today! They will start looking for me….' She freed her hands but did not go; Upali felt awkward and began his own farewells but Devadina cut him short.

'Lord, I was wondering – could you speak to the Sunga family who owns the temple? They might listen to you – '

'Devadina!' interrupted Sutanuka, 'It's a complete waste of time.'

He ignored her. 'Please, my lord, we would be very grateful – '

There was a shout from above. 'There she is! Lady Sutanuka, we were searching for you!'

Sutanuka shouted quickly, 'I'm coming! I was just resting for a moment…' and started to hurry up the slope, but it was too late.

'Look! Look at that boy! It's that foreigner, that scoundrel who follows her everywhere!'

She turned back. 'Run, Devadina, quick! Run!'

'Why should I? Am I doing something wrong?'

A crowd arrived before she could enlighten him. Upali saw someone catch hold of Sutanuka's hand to urge her away. He himself was pushed to the side by a group of men who set upon the sculptor with canes. Upali tried to elbow his way in between, then to grab at one of the flashing sticks; he felt numbing blows on his arm and shoulder before he was pulled away. By Ananda and Bhima. A crowd had gathered all around.

'Master, you cannot fight them!'

'Ananda – I warn you! Let me go!'

Devadina had fallen, one arm wrapped around his head against the blows and kicks. But he struggled up, pushed his way through the men and dashed away down the hill-side. He was limping and bleeding from one ear, but was soon hidden in the trees.

Upali was furious with Ananda. 'Don't you dare stop me like that ever again!'

He was still furious when they got back to the monastery, and did not notice Harsha's excitement at first. 'They beat him badly, Harsha! They might have killed him – '

'Listen, Upali – '

'Right there in the open, and nobody protested!'

'Except you,' Harsha said. He was sitting on the veranda with Loka, helping him sort a big bunch of new herbs, and now absent-mindedly lifted a twig of tulsi towards his mouth. Loka rescued it just in time. 'Anyway – '

'Well, what did you expect, if somebody is getting killed?'

Harsha looked slightly exasperated. 'Have you considered, Upali, that you might be getting a little too involved? It is not the Sangha's responsibility to see that all lovers are united in marriage. Or is this how you did things back east?'

Upali glared at him. The shrines in the south of Kalinga had been all-powerful, and controlled by their old priestesses with an iron hand. Anybody caught in such an affair would have probably lost her head before questions were asked. 'All right – I admit there was no need to get involved – I got a bit carried away by Devadina's worry! But I don't see how we can remain quiet now. They could hurt Sutanuka, even kill her!'

'You probably worsened the whole thing, with your visit to the tem – '

'I know that!'

'Anyway, I don't see what else you can do. Except complain to the police.'

'I have another idea. Devadina asked me to approach the Sunga family – they own her temple – '

'Upali – '

'The Sungas!' Loka suddenly came to life. 'You better not trust those scoundrels, Upali! They are the most – '

'All right, Loka, I won't! But I can threaten them, surely?' Loka belonged to a rich merchant family from Bhrgukacha, one of those who still remembered the days when they had been an independent mercantile city in perpetual and bitter warfare with

Avanti's rajas. Upali turned back to Harsha. 'I just want to warn them against any violence.'

Harsha chewed frowningly – he had slipped some tender tamarind into his mouth unnoticed. 'I doubt they'll listen to you. Tell the police instead.'

'The police! I have no faith in – '

'Listen, don't insult the police today! Didn't they stop the sacrifices at that shrine? But the best thing is – you haven't given me a chance to speak – villages like Bhima's are no longer off-limits! The District Chief was here last night, to inform us that the law has been changed. The Sangha is now to be actively involved in rehabilitating the deportees into civil society!'

So that was why the soldiers had released them in the morning. It was good news, and Upali should have made the most of it immediately, but he got back to his writing instead, worrying if at all only about Sutanuka and her sculptor. He should have known what would happen, he fumed later, he had seen all the signs.

Mohan discovered a hole in the kitchen's mud wall, and a krait within. Upali and he were collecting twigs to smoke the deathly tenant away, when Chandra appeared, heard of the problem and promptly unsheathed his sword.

'Wait – we're trying not to kill it,' said Upali.

'I'll try too.' He inserted the blade delicately into the hole, fished about a bit and pulled it out with the dull yellow and grey creature writhing unhappily at the end. 'Where shall I throw it?'

'Give it here,' said Upali and to his surprise, Chandra did. The sword was much heavier than Upali expected, with a wavy design on the blade like silvery water, and a rhino horn hilt that felt warm to the touch. He carried it a long distance away, into the trees, trailed by Ananda who was torn between envy at the sword and horror at its burden, and placed the snake in a dry little hollow, where hopefully it would remain.

Ananda carried the sword back, and watched with distress as Chandra used it to chop the twigs up. 'I thought soldiers only picked up their sword in battle.'

'Oh, it's useful for many things.'

'How old is it? Did it belong to your father before you? What would you feel if you lost it?'

'Bad, because the cost would come out of my salary! And I would be questioned, and black-marked. It can be quite unpleasant. It belongs to the army.'

'But it's really yours, isn't it? I mean – I've heard that each warrior has a bond – a magical relationship – with his sword. That it knows your mood, speaks to you – '

'Speaks?' Chandra was staring. 'I should hope not! It's just a sword, Ananda – which the army issues when we're on duty and takes back when we're off. I must have used a hundred different ones so far!'

You had to give credit to Magadh for taking the myth out of some things. For bashing the myth out actually. Ananda just looked disgusted.

The news came the next day, during uposatha, the once-in-a-fortnight reporting session when the monks sat together to report their work and personal life, especially their mistakes. Mohan was gloomily describing a raging argument with a village headman over some petty issue, and the others were listening as despondently for his temper was an old problem, when a group of women arrived from Bhima's village. Six of their men had been arrested that morning, including Bhima, on charges of attacking two men from a neighbouring village.

'My god! Which village?' asked Harsha.

'Why did they attack them?' asked Upali.

Kali just shook her head tiredly. The other women looked tired too but they all ignored the tumbler of water offered by Loka. Nor would they sit down. It was the first time any of them was visiting the monastery.

'It's because of that stupid oracle, isn't it? What happened? I told Bhima to inore him!'

Kali shook her head again, her usually polished black complexion a dull grey, and suddenly fell at his feet. 'Help us, Thera. You know the soldiers, go to them. Before they – '

Upali raised her with surprising ease – she weighed nothing, and the many bone, seed and stone chains around her throat and waist probably accounted for half of that.

'What's the use of crying now? Why didn't Bhima come here before? You know what Magadh does to – '

'We will try, sister,' intervened Harsha hurriedly. 'They must have taken them to Ujjayani. We will try. The situation is not hopeless.'

Upali wasn't so sure. The last incident had been a year ago, a refusal to pay taxes, which had sent two men to jail; despite all the monastery's efforts, one had died there. Would Kalinga never end?

First they had to check on the victims. Their village was one of the oldest in the area, of local Avanti-folk who had always been quite friendly to the monks and their ideas. But now there was silence and averted gazes as they approached across the fields. Nobody returned their greetings. Harsha finally asked a boy about the wounded men. The boy led them to a hut where two men were lying on a straw mat. One had knife wounds on his arms and chest. They had been hunting, the boy said, and had just bagged a deer when they were attacked.

Loka squatted down to examine the wounds but before he could do anything the chief of the village entered.

'We want you to leave – we don't need your help.'

'Brother, I understand – ' began Harsha.

'Keep your understanding for your murdering Naga friends!' said another villager. 'Don't touch our men!'

'Those wounds need to be stitched.' said Loka.

'We don't want your advice. Just leave – right now!'

Ujjayani was gloomy too, the next day. The doleful group of musical mourners was still seated in a pandal near the gates. And

Bhima was greyer than Kali. His fellow-villagers looked worse though, some were moaning in pain – clearly the side-effects of interrogation.

'Who did this, Bhima?' asked Upali. 'I know it wasn't you.'

'It's not important.'

'But why did they?' asked Harsha.

'Those men were lurking outside the village.'

'They were hunting!'

'They were on our land. Planning to rob our animals.'

'They were not on your land but in the jungle! You can't kill people for being near your village – you can't kill people at all! Even if it was your land, you should have complained!'

'A warrior does not complain, Thera.'

'But you're no longer a warrior, Bhima.'

There was no response and Harsha's voice became abruptly quieter. 'It was a sacrifice, wasn't it? It had nothing to do with any robbery.'

So he too had noticed the pattern of slashes on the man's chest. Bhima said nothing. But he had explained the business to Upali once. It was a very old custom, in moments of crisis especially, to give a man to their goddess.

'Why now?' asked Upali. 'What happened now?'

But Bhima turned away and Ananda gasped at the whip slashes on his back, red and swollen, one caked with blood. Upali said nothing more, just crunched up his stomach between spine and thighs and listened to it throb while Harsha spoke to the slashes, gently now, of how the monks would do their best to get them free; but Bhima should try to convince his friends that what they had done was WRONG. The cycle of violence had to stop somewhere. They had to follow the law; otherwise everybody would massacre everybody else!

Violence answered by violence, tit for tat; and the best thing was that it was called a cycle, as if no one had ever started it.

The Commandant of the Ujjayani garrison was an overweight and overwrought Magadhan with a clear distaste for Kalingan savages, as he called them. The sentence would be decided soon, he said. It would probably be the death penalty for the two suspected assailants, imprisonment for the rest. You will drive them to rebellion, shouted Upali; Harsha intervened peaceably, with a friendly hand on the Commandant's shoulder, to propose a more compassionate view. These were, after all, misguided jungle people; harsh punishment would compound the problem. Re-education was required, in which the Sangha could help. He could only go by the law, said the Commandant and shrugged the hand off.

'I know what – ' said Harsha as they got back into Nigrodha's chariots. Why Nigrodha had come on this trip was a mystery – Ananda had wanted to meet Bhima and somehow Nigrodha and his eminently useful vehicles had also joined in. ' – You could speak to the Viceroy. He's the highest authority.'

'It's worth trying, I suppose.' Upali's hand was against his stomach.

'Didn't you ask Loka about that ache?'

Upali let his hand drop. 'He gave me something.' Loka had palpated his abdomen a bit, prepared a course of medicine and advised rest and extra meditation. Why meditation? For calmness. Many problems solved themselves if you gave them a little calm. Upali had not been able to meditate much since then. 'I feel bad for Bhima – I spoke to him that day at the shrine about the oracle, and he agreed. But he can't go against the others.'

'These Kalingas – ' began Harsha.

'Stop calling them Kalingas! I've told you time and again that they are Bhuiryas – see, this is the problem! They have lost their self-respect, we don't even take the trouble to remember who they are, and we presume to understand their problems!'

Harsha was embarrassed. 'I'm sorry, I don't know how I forget. But their problem is obvious. They have to forget the past and – '

'Accept their fate?'

'What's the option? To kill their neighbours and get hanged themselves? I know they have suffered, but the fact is also that their old life was terribly backward. They have to change, you know that, Upali, that's what you were doing there!'

'Yes. But thanks to the war, and this great resettlement policy, everything is a mess. Now that they've lost their land, freedom – '

'Freedom? You call that freedom – the grip of superstition and bloodthirsty ritual? It's the freedom of animals. It's not freedom at all, but slavery to nature!'

'And are they masters now? Living at the dictat of Collectors and police? With all the memories of horror? Now what you call their backwardness is all the identity they have left!'

'We have to get them to change, for themselves. That, I think, is the job before the Sangha.'

'So now our job is to clean up after Magadh?'

Harsha sighed. 'Magadh is changing too. Things are being reshaped, according to Dhamma. You may smile, Upali, but the changes are real.'

Upali did not smile. The chariot had reached the crowded market district, and stopped in front of a small but well-appointed building. It was the office of the cloth merchants' guild where Harsha had been invited to talk on the Dhammachakkapavattana Sutta, the Sutta on Setting the Wheel of Dhamma in Motion.

Upali got off. 'I'll go to the Viceroy's.'

Harsha got off too and changed the topic abruptly. 'I wanted to ask you, Upali, since you've made quite an issue of the Aryan chariot wheel in your story – was the Buddha referring to it when he spoke of Dhamma as a Wheel? I mean, he was obviously referring to the Universal Unchanging Cycles – birth and death, the seasons, the four ages of mankind, the world itself. But do you think he intended to use both ideas – that Dhamma was both invincible, and of recurring importance?'

'No, I don't! I think the Buddha meant it as a symbol of progress. Of moving ahead. But the old symbolism was too strong – even his own followers saw the Wheel of Dhamma as something unchanging as well as invincible. But I don't know, Harsha, how you can talk of getting people to change, when you also believe in Universal Unchanging Cycles!'

'It's the larger picture. Within the smaller day-to-day situation, one has to strive for change.'

'It is not any larger or smaller – it's the myth clashing with reality! The cyclical picture of the world belongs to the jungle-folk whose life barely changes from year to year, who can only see their own subservience every year, every nine months, every day, to the same old cycles of nature! It's the belief and practice of a relatively passive existence. But we're living in a different time, where everything has been turned upside down, by your Magadh, among others – even the chariot is obsolete today! That's why people have to be innovative. If they are to survive!'

The Viceregal palace turned out to be near Sutanuka's temple, in the oldest aristocratic quarter and amidst many great walled compounds, all cloaked in a dignified bouquet of sandal, musk and old open gutters. But the Viceroy was away, one of the soldier-guards said; the Thera could wait within. Upali decided to visit the Sungas instead.

These were the former rulers of Avanti, he remembered, as he was admitted after a long wait into a walled estate not far away, and led through a park into a palatial building, where his name was announced to the accompaniment of a drum before he was ushered into the presence of His Highness, the ex-Raja Pururavas, a tall handsome man wearing flowing white silk and a brahminical tuft on a tonsured head.

He nodded at Upali without inviting him to sit though he himself was ensconced on a throne-like seat on a dais, the only piece of furniture in the austere teakwood-panelled room, except for a cushioned stool on which lay his feet. There were gold rings on all his toes and a bevy of servants surrounding him. It was a small court, with Upali the only courtier. He was reminded of his visits to the Kalinga rajas – the same heavy formalities, the same thin layer of grace that barely covered contempt. But at least those rajas had really been rajas.

The ex-Raja heard him out and replied firmly that, no, he could not intervene.

'But it's your temple. You have the power to free any priestess.'

'It is not our temple and they are not our priestesses, Thera. Both belong to the Gods. And the priestess knows her duty better than me – it is not for me to free her! But one thing must be said. We are becoming increasingly surprised at you monks. You should rectify your own affairs before interfering outside.'

'I fail to understand you, my lord.'

'Our cousin Pradyota was a monk, sir, against our wishes. But even we never expected that he would die in your monastery. It happened two months ago, but your Sangha has yet to offer an explanation!'

'You mean... the monk at Sanchi?'

'Our uncle's son, our dear cousin. Murdered in your monastery.'

'My sincere condolences, on your loss.'

Your condolences are useless, whether sincere or not!'

Upali felt a little irritated. 'My lord, the matter is now in the hands of the police. As indeed your temple officers will be, if anything untoward happens to anybody in the matter of the priestess!'

Upali began the trudge back to the Viceroy's when he heard the sound of heavy galloping. A grand four-horse chariot had turned into the narrow lane and was rushing towards him, followed by one more. The lane was edged by two high walls; the ex-Raja's gates were shut. Upali had barely gathered himself into a run when the thundering pounding was upon him.

But the horses reared to a stop, almost over his head. Upali was still staring at their iron-shod hooves when a large hand smote him on the back.

'Thera! What are you doing here?' It was the Viceroy.

Thanking god he was alive would have been the exact truth. 'This is very opportune, my lord. I had tried to meet you earlier, but – '

'…And I want to speak to you too. I am lunching with the Raja, please join us.'

The double chins were wobbling benevolently. Whatever did the man want? Upali followed him back in, to be led this time to another hall in the mansion, where they found the ex-Raja reclined on a divan, flanked by two other guests, an array of silver dishes, and an intricately carved ivory chess set laid out on a mattress nearby. The game of kings. Upali had never played it himself, but he had heard that it was good training in the tactics of war. The two guests were a short fat nobleman and a rather flamboyantly beautiful lady, both of whom barely acknowledged the Viceroy's introduction of Upali. The Viceroy lifted lids and introduced the food as well – roast and curried meats of quail, peacock, deer and wild boar, stuffed vegetables, saffron rice cooked with tiny meat balls, sticky pancakes of imported coconut, almonds and honey, covered with silver leaf. The ex-Raja did not look surprised at Upali's return, nor did he eat anything. Upali followed suit for his stomach had started aching again.

'Thera, this is too much. You have even spurned the favourite dish of the Magadhe-Raja!'

'Peacock, you mean?'

'Though he says he's given up meat. He's stopped hunting too – the lousy wimp! Can you imagine a king who does not hunt or eat meat? He's a complete disaster – it really is proof that we have reached Kalyug!'

'He's stopped hunting too?' asked Upali.

'Can you believe it? And he wants everybody else to follow! Anyway – ' The Viceroy waved a hand to dismiss the whole unsavoury business. 'Anyway, let us talk.'

He could not promise anything about Bhima's people. The law was clearly delineated; there was little scope for interference. And it was an attempted murder – a serious crime.

'Things will worsen if they are punished harshly,' argued Upali. 'They are already depressed – '

'Let us see.' He took a draught of wine, staring at Upali all the while. 'But tell me frankly, Upali, what did you think of Kalinga?'

'What do you mean?'

'The war, the conquest. Were you happy with it?'

Upali smiled. 'Happy? It was a war. That says it all, I think.'

'Tosali was said to be a very beautiful city.'

The capital of the Kalingas had been tiny but elegant, with many fine buildings, parks, and halls for music and dance. And it had been a functioning republic, with a full-fledged assembly that met regularly, voting on every issue and implementing the decisions very efficiently. Far too efficiently for its neighbours. Down south, where Upali had lived in a straggling little village on the casuarina *coast*, Tosali was famous for both its ancient warrior tradition and notoriously short temper. The villagers near the monastery were only recently out of the jungle and they still fled to it when the rajas visited, or sometimes they took their little canoes and paddled way out to sea. A bright blue sea – not grey like Bhrgukacha. Often stormy. Was it blue when he left, or red? He could not remember.

The Viceroy was leaning towards him, a goblet of silver in one hand. 'A terrible tragedy, Upali. And yet one that has happened before, so many times. At Gandhara, here in Avanti, so many places. The thing is, it should not happen again. Don't you agree?'

'Wholeheartedly, but I doubt if my opinion makes a difference.'

'It does, Thera! You are a man of principle and sensitivity, not like those that populate the monasteries today. You would be an ideal person to head a monastery.'

Their host suddenly spoke up. 'The other monks are minions of Magadh! Instead of spreading the Buddha's message, they are spreading the Magadhe-Raja's. Now they are even desecrating the scriptures, thanks to his godforsaken craze for writing!'

The Viceroy nodded, but a little embarrassedly.

'It's not surprising, of course,' conceded the ex-Raja. 'When he has even thrown the purohit out of the royal council! His father and grandfather were bad enough, chasing those Jains and Ajivikas, but they had some respect for the system. This man is dedicated to ungodliness!'

'Upali,' intervened the Viceroy, 'I think you agree that what is happening is not right. Magadh is too far gone to be repaired perhaps, though I have not lost hope even there. But these new conquests have to be freed, returned to their rightful heritage and traditions, instead of the half-baked bastard culture created by this dictatorship!'

Upali was still unable to answer. What was wrong with him? What was wrong with *them*? This was Magadh's top man in the province, the Magadhe-Raja's own representative, and what he was saying was....

'Come, Thera, I know you feel the same.'

The ex-Raja erupted again: 'On top of the injury, is the insolence! Insulting public edicts telling us what to eat and how to worship! That too from a family of Nagas! Four generations back these Mauryas were peacock trappers in the jungle, now they think they can teach the world how to behave!'

The Viceroy coughed. 'People are pining for their dignity, their old democratic traditions. Do you know, Upali, ever since my lord's cousin died so tragically last month, all of Avanti has been in mourning?'

Upali suddenly noticed that the lady was smiling. Very slightly. But she caught his glance and her smile vanished. 'Yes, Thera,' she said in a husky voice, 'no festivities, no celebrations. Everything has been cancelled.' It was not much, but her eyes were wide and glinting with tragedy, or was it gold dust sprinkled on the eyelids? Her lips exactly matched the dark red stones in her ears; Upali suddenly realized that he was goggling at her face and looked away hurriedly.

'Yes,' repeated the Viceroy. 'And where was this prince, beloved of all Avanti, killed? In the Magadhe-Raja's favourite monastery! Isn't it obvious whose hand is behind it?'

'But why? He was just a monk.' Upali was relieved to find that his tongue was working. But just-a-monk was probably inaccurate; this was the monk who had 'prayed for us'.

The ex-Raja agreed. 'He was not an ordinary monk. He was a kshatriya – in a time when kshatriyas have been nearly wiped out by Magadh – not a single drop of kshatriya blood will be left in the world if they have their way! And he never forgot his sacred dharma! So he was a danger.'

There was a pause. Everybody was staring at Upali.

'I am not a friend of Magadh.' Where had he heard the words before? But he knew how Magadh rewarded sedition – with summary trials, variegated torture and death. 'But what can be done now? The old Chief is dead. So are almost all the other rajas. What are you proposing?'

The Viceroy smiled. 'Nothing. We just feel happy to have found a friend. Let us seek more, and think about what can be done.'

'Just one thing, Thera,' said the ex-Raja. 'You are going to Pataliputra soon, we hear. A monk who was a dear friend of our late cousin will also be coming there – Vipul of Takshashila. Can you carry a message to him?'

'Yes?'

'Tell him everything is as it was here. As it was. And we look forward to hearing from him. Then let us know, Thera, what he says.'

Upali gazed at the patrician face, the noble brow, the regal benevolence, and recovered a bit. 'Yes, I can do that. But in return, I want you to free Sutanuka. Send her to the convent tonight. Ask the Therii there to confirm this in a note to me.'

The ex-Raja's brows were elevated. 'That is quite a separate matter.'

'Separate or not. I will help you only if you do this.'

The Raja paused for a moment, then nodded. Upali turned to the Viceroy. 'And you, my lord, you must free those prisoners.'

'I will try, Upali, honestly.'

Upali lifted his glass and took a sip. Again a silver glass. 'It must have been a real relief to get those silk chits of Pradyota's before anybody else saw them. What were the orders for?'

'Two consignments of Magadhan – ' The Viceroy stopped and shook his head. 'No, Thera. It is better if you do not know.'

But he probably knew too much already, thought Upali. The Viceroy was smiling almost in congratulations, the ex-Raja looked thoughtful, the lady expressionless, the fat lord comatose. Did any of them really play chess?

No, or the game was seriously over-hyped, he decided later, when, on their way home in Nigrodha's chariots, they passed soldiers hoisting up new bodies on the city stockade. The monks turned away from the sight, but Upali saw enough to recognize one body. A small plump man, the merchant Milindachanda's friend, the corrupt toll-keeper from the Ujjayani-Maheshwar highway.

YASHODHARA

There is no heaven, no final liberation, nor any soul in another world. Spells, incantations, rituals, even the duties of the four varnas – all these are nonsense, invented for the livelihood of those destitute of knowledge and manliness. If a beast slain in the Jvotistoma rite goes straight to heaven, why doesn't the sacrificer offer his father instead? If offerings to priests can feed ancestors in heaven, how is it that persons standing on top of a house cannot be gratified by food served inside? They cannot – because all such long-distance gratification is buffoonery!

Such was the philosophy of the minstrels who called themselves Lokayat – of the people. It was not clear which people they meant. Probably not well-bred and pious folk, for these considered the Lokayats the worst of devils. Siddarth had never heard of them in Kapilavastu, but now found himself attracted to opinions that clashed so completely with those of the Shakyas. He came across them time and again in the Banaras marketplace, presenting their rather rude compositions to appreciative crowds. It was clear that the people of Banaras had a more relaxed attitude towards the gods, which was itself a balm to Siddarth's tortured mind. The programme of study at the ashram of the brahmin Vasu, famed for his exposition of the Vedas and the Dharmasastras, failed to interest him, as did his co-students. He preferred to roam the city, its crowded streets, markets and ghats – the stone terraces that stepped down to the edge of the holy river – especially the cremation ghats. The brahmins and the Chandalas got used to the strange boy sitting alone and staring at the grey sheet of water streaming past, its flat surface interrupted by an occasional log. No, not a log, another corpse. Tara's corpse.

No. Tara's corpse was probably back on the stockade from where he had dragged it, what remained after the crows and vultures. But where was Tara herself? Was she really gone, as the Lokayats said? Or was her soul alive and reborn somewhere? According to Shakya orthodoxy, of course, she was in hell and suffering even more than before. But Siddarth knew that if she was anywhere, in any form, she would have come and forgiven him for not saving her, for being blind to the misery around him, for being useless, for being a Shakya. She had sent no word. Where was she? Was death really a passage, a pause, the beginning of a new life? Or was it the end?

The questions gnawed at him day and night; he felt at times that he was dying too. But somehow the visits to the ghats kept him sane. The Chandalas acknowledged his arrival with a nod or a smile, or even a morsel of food on a leaf left silently near him. These little kindnesses helped, his gaze became less lost, he started to come out of his numbness. He did not know that the Chandalas thought he was a ghost.

He was desperate for change, and he did find this in Banaras for a while. Banaras was huge and industrious, renowned for its cotton textiles, and now also for its temples strung like jewels along the north bank of the Ganga. Hidden behind them was the weavers' quarter, a misnomer for it took up nearly two-thirds of the city, a world of its own, meditating day and night to the stern mantra of hundreds of looms. One of Siddarth's classmates, Yasa, was the son of a Banaras Sethi who traded in the cloth and owned a few looms himself. He invited Siddarth one day to his father's workshop, and was pleased at his acceptance. Most of their classmates were northern aristocrats – like Siddarth – none of whom would dream of mixing with a merchant's son. Banaras was unused to such insularity, at least where the wealthy were concerned, and the cloth manufacturers were among the wealthiest in all Kosala. The creations of their weavers would bring the city fame and fortune, besides financing temples whose swelling grandeur would in time completely eclipse the looms and their workers.

The temples with their high wooden shikharas were not all to the Vedic gods, in fact they gave primary position to Shiva, the Great Yogi worshipped by the SisuNagas, the old rulers of Kashi. Siddarth was familiar with them, even up to their innermost altar and idol – a stone image of the divine phallus – for the thread crossing his chest was his passport of entry to even those most restricted places. And he discovered that there was little to relate between their haughty grace and the weavers' quarter. The latter was a crowded, noisy, filthy mess of narrow lanes lined by ramshackle wooden shacks, two or three tottering storeys high, either workshops or tenements. Yasa had organized a chariot for the visit, but there was really no place for it in the midst of innumerable hand-carts, many loaded higher than the men pulling them, also bullock-carts, horsemen and palanquins, and any number of bovines chewing the cud with that typical air of phlegmatic conviction that the roads had been made for them alone. If indeed they had been made at all, for a large part was just dirt and puddle.

The workshop turned out to be a great wooden shed divided into two halls. One was full of men and looms, warps of thread stretched out with the aid of wooden pegs, shuttles darting to and fro with amazing speed. Woven muslin lay in gentle translucent folds on the floor at the far end of the hall. Siddarth was fascinated. He had never been this close to any kind of manufacture before. The Sethi was pleased with his enthusiasm and, conscious that this was a future chief, generous in his time and explanation. There were now many strains of cotton available in Banaras, he said, but the old original Kashi plant was the best. Its fabric was in demand all over, famous for its transparent fineness that was yet dense enough to prevent oil from seeping through. There was a kingdom far away, on the banks of a mighty river, where the dead were not cremated but buried with their best clothes, foods, slaves, gold, jewels, everything, for the people believed that death was sleep and dead kings would wake after a while. Bodies were preserved thus in gigantic stone tombs amidst the greatest of splendour and, said the Sethi triumphantly, the cloth the kings chose to wear when dead – wound around them like a lady's sari, only more than double the length – was our Banarasi cotton!

Siddarth felt as if he had never noticed the clothes he had worn all his life. This was an exciting new world, of creation and colour, free of the ritualism, the pathetic power-play and continuous back-biting of the sangha. Definitely far from it. He breathed in deeply – the workshop seemed fragrant with starch and sweat and freedom – and interrupted, to ask the Sethi for a job. The request brought the cotton chronicle to an abrupt halt. The Sethi gaped. For so long that Siddarth finally looked away and into the curious gaze of one of the workers.

The Sethi recovered, rose with a, 'Well... we'll discuss these things some other time... my lord... I have to rush,' and vanished.

Siddarth turned to Yasa. 'Your father seemed upset.'

'What did you expect? You're a nobleman, Siddarth, a raja! What job could he give you?'

'I could be an accountant. I know some arithmetic....'

'What world do you live in, Siddarth? It's difficult enough for us merchants as it is – we can't afford any political trouble!'

The worker near them was clearly listening to this exchange though his gaze and hands were back on his loom. Siddarth suddenly touched him on the shoulder; he jumped. 'Greetings. My name is Gautama Siddarth.'

The man glanced at Yasa who said, 'Yes. This is Raja Siddarth, of Kapilavastu. Speak with him, he wants to become a weaver!'

The worker smiled uneasily and turned back to his loom in silence. None of the others would talk either. Women were at work in the other hall, some carding the pile of grey-white cotton balls onto wooden bows, others spinning it on a wheel. The fabric was washed, starched and perfumed in the workshop next door, said Yasa's foreman. Behind were the dyeing ghats, where wooden vats stood around filled with bright liquids. The black was revealed to be iron shavings soaked in vinegar, the red was lac, the dark green was pomegranate rind mixed with indigo. The foreman had noticed Siddarth's overtures to the workers. 'Many of them are runaway slaves, lord, from republics like your own. They don't trust you.'

He was right. The very next time Siddarth visited, a worker took him aside to whisper that he knew of an escaped slave from Kapilavastu and could expose him for a small compensation.

Siddarth was disgusted. 'You'd send a person back to slavery for money?'

The man shrugged and walked away, but the foreman again proved informative. 'Dagu has his own problems, lord. His son has a lump in his stomach that is growing. He needs money to take him to Rajgir to the great physician Jivaka. He approached doctors here, spent all his earnings, but no treatment has worked.'

'How much does he need?' The foreman mentioned a sum and Siddarth ran after the worker. 'Here, I accept your offer! Show me this slave from Kapilavastu.'

Dagu gaped at the handful of silver Siddarth poured into his palm. 'So much?'

'That's how much it's worth to me,' Siddarth said lightly and was shocked to see the man's eyes fill with tears.

Siddarth had travelled on horseback that day and his mount was tethered outside the workshop. How far were they headed? Just near by, said the old man. He led Siddarth down a maze of lanes, each one narrower and filthier than the last. In and out they walked, dodging people, carts, horses, cows, and heaps of dirt and dung, till Siddarth's embroidered leather shoes were soggy and his dhoti edged with mud. His companion was barefoot. On the way he explained that his son used to work at the port but now was at home with a tearing pain in his belly. It had happened to others before and it was usually fatal. 'This place breeds strange diseases, lord.'

'Are you a foreigner?'

'Yes. My family is from south of Anga but everything was lost after Magadh conquered our forests. They cut and burnt the forests, violated the sacred places, enslaved many people.'

'Why?' Magadh was the kingdom to the south of the Ganga, the source of most of the caravans passing through Kapilavastu of late. But it was unknown for a conqueror to interfere so much with the conquered.

'Who knows? A few of us got away. There is work here, and wealth, great wealth. But it's different. I once picked up some bananas off a roadside cart – there were heaps just sitting there and my children were hungry. I didn't have money, I didn't know of money! But I learnt fast in the police lock-up. I still have the marks on my back. That was five years ago. Now I understand the way things work here. You can starve right next to a pile of food! But at least one is rarely hunted and captured like an animal.'

Siddarth did not point out that he himself was conniving at just such a capture at the moment. Dagu was silent for a while.

'I have begun to believe in what that Kassapa says, that life cannot be understood.'

'Who?'

'A sage, Purana Kassapa. I do not know from where he comes. He says that our life is decided, already. He's in Kashi now and speaks at the deer park at Sarnath every evening. If you come to the workshop an hour before sunset, I'll take you there.'

The weaving quarter was long behind them now. Siddarth was wondering how he would find his way back, when Dagu stopped at the head of another lane that was just a gap of about human width between two rows of mud huts. Yet a man was pushing a hand-cart into it and others were hurrying in and out past him.

'Take the first left turn. The first house on the left. And thank you, lord. My heart is doubly light for I know you will not harm them.' He bent suddenly and touched the ground near Siddarth's feet, then vanished in the direction they had come.

Siddarth reached the house as directed. And found a shocked Mir, who recognized him immediately. Siddarth however did not recall ever seeing this small, dark, sharp-featured man before, and he started with introductions.

'Salutations. I am Gautama Siddarth, of Kapilavastu, son of – '

But his host had jumped up from basket he was weaving and pushed Siddarth aside, preparatory probably to running out and away. Then he realized that Siddarth was alone. He turned back and interrupted, 'I know who you are! Why are you here?'

'You know me? I'm sorry but I do not recall – '

'How did you find me? Are you planning to give me away?'

'No, of course not!'

Mir was not really surprised. All the slaves in Kapilavastu knew of the strange prince. They knew more of the disappointment of his father than he himself, and they knew also of his birth in the sacred grove of Lumbini.

'Someone spoke of a slave from Kapilavastu. I thought it would be good to meet someone from home.'

'Your home. My prison. I'm Mir, a Pukusa, a sudra to you!'

Siddarth surprised even himself by asking, 'Are you happy now, Mir?'

Mir laughed but a little grimly. 'Happier, Gautama Siddarth, definitely happier. When I'm down, I cheer myself up just by remembering that I will die a free man.' He paused a moment. 'I'm scared to ask, but – what happened afterwards?'

'The rapes, that was a mistake,' Siddarth said in a low voice.

'I could not control those boys. They left us soon after we reached the Kosala highway. They were wild, animal-like, full of revenge. No good will come of it.'

'No good came to those in Kapilavastu. They killed a hundred slaves,' Siddarth mumbled. Mir looked stunned. 'Tara too....'

Mir sank down on the ground. His voice sounded suddenly gruff. 'We knew it, I suppose. All escapes are followed by killings. We are responsible. I am responsible.'

'Don't be ridiculous! The Sabha ordered it. It is your right to want to escape, you had to. I felt the need myself.'

Mir got up and entered his hut. Siddarth followed, took the clay tumbler of water that Mir offered hesitantly and emptied it down his throat before wondering if that was all his host had.

They settled down on the bare mud-packed floor, which felt a little wet to Siddarth. Mir picked up his half-basket and started weaving, adding in long horizontal strips of bamboo bark, and tying them in place with vertical spokes from the star-shaped base. He continued talking as his fingers darted back and forth. 'You too wished to escape? I can understand. You are the son of the Goddess after all, how could you be happy there?'

He stared out of the hut for a moment. 'But I can't understand our fate. Why were the Shakyas given this power and why were we made their slaves? Are your gods superior to ours? What do you think? Or is it just one turn of the eternal wheel of time? With us on top, in the next turn?'

And after that, bottom again? It was a depressing thought.

Mir decided to accompany Siddarth to the sage's discourse. Siddarth felt that it would be awkward for Dagu to face the man he had betrayed, so he decided not to meet him at the workshop. Luckily, Mir knew the deer park too.

It was some distance away, on the Shravasti road and past acres of rice-land. It had been an old sacred grove, Mir said, but desecrated now by its use as a hunting park by the Raja of Kosala and his viceroys, who had had it fenced to keep the deer from escaping. Commoners were free to enter though. There was a crowd at the gates, which turned out to be part of a larger crowd jamming the clearing just inside. Siddarth and Mir could not enter. But they could hear someone speaking.

'Nothing a man does will change his fate. There is nothing such as merit or sin. He who performs any vile or miserable act or causes any such act to be performed, he who destroys life, he who is a thief, a house-breaker, a plunderer, a highway robber, an adulterer or a liar, none of these commit any sin. Even if a man should pick up a razor-sharp discus, and reduce all life on earth to a single heap of dead flesh, he will be committing no sin. If he comes down the south bank of the Ganga, slaying, maiming and torturing, and causing others to be slain, maimed or tortured, he commits no sin, neither does sin approach him. And, likewise, if a man go up the north bank of the Ganga, doing good deeds, giving generous alms and sacrificing even more generously to the gods, causing good to be done and sacrifices to be performed, he acquires no merit, neither does merit approach him.

'Understand this well. Merit does not result from liberality, self-control, abstinence, honesty and such-like; sin does not derive from dishonesty, cruelty, impiety, gluttony, or vice. Your deeds are unimportant. They do not change either your existence or the fruits that will come to you. Your existence is already fixed, you just have to accept it. Everything else is rubbish.'

There was a long pause, then the crowd began to shuffle around. Siddarth and Mir managed to push through to where people were jostling to touch the feet of an old man, naked except for a shawl and a staff. Siddarth saw Yasa's father in the crowd, then his worker Dagu. The first smiled nervously and disappeared. The second came up beaming, quite impervious to Mir's presence.

'Lord! I thought you had changed your mind. Did you find the lecture interesting?'

'We missed the start. But yes, it was interesting.'

They started the long walk back under an orange and purple sunset. Closed carriages overtook them continuously, many drawn by steeds with gold-embroidered saddles, their manes plaited with pearls strung on gold threads, their heads crowned by feathery plumes encrusted with semi-precious stones. The sage had some very worldly followers.

'He recounted his past lives at the start. He remembers each and every one of them.'

'I thought his ideas a bit bleak,' said Siddarth. 'Just accept – that's life?'

'It makes sense,' said Mir. 'It's no use worshipping the gods. The gods are useless – at least mine are, and yours are evil! Better to accept and hope for a better life next time.'

Dagu looked aghast. 'You can't speak that way about the gods – you will be cursed!'

'Who will curse me?' asked Mir coldly. 'And you invited us here in the first place!'

'Not to insult the gods.'

'And what have your gods brought you so far? As long as things are good, the gods accept all sacrifices happily, the gluttons! But as soon as there's trouble, they up and leave!'

'It's a time of confusion…' said Dagu unhappily.

'No, it's simple – the gods are helpless before fate!'

'But you are not. Both of you changed your lives,' said Siddarth. 'You took a decision to act…. You could have stayed in Kapilavastu, Mir. But you changed your life.'

'I was forced here,' corrected Dagu. 'I would never have left my homeland willingly.'

'But you could have gone to Champa, or Magadh. You weighed the options, and you chose to come here…. And surely it makes a difference whether you do right or wrong?'

'What is right or wrong?' Mir was almost angry. 'Your Shakyas killed Tara – it was right according to them!'

Siddarth stared at him.

'Right and wrong is different for everybody – that's why it makes no sense.'

'I didn't try to save her,' said Siddarth slowly. 'I didn't even know what was going on – '

'It's the same thing. It's fate.'

'Like my son's illness,' said Dagu. 'Back home, when there was a calamity, the forest cured us. The women went deep to the most secret places where the sweet water rises, and they did magic. But here they told us to sacrifice – and it is useless.'

'You offered what?' Mir asked. 'A child?'

Dagu nodded. 'But my son became sicker.'

'What?' In one swoop, Siddarth had him by the shoulders and started shaking him like a doll. 'You killed a child – for your son's life! You deserve it if he dies! You – '

'Stop it, Aryaputra!' Mir pushed them apart, Dagu crumpled to the ground. Passersby paused and stared.

'I'm sorry....' Siddarth mumbled as Mir helped the weaver up. 'It's just that I hate all this rotten sacrifice – it makes no sense at all! And I know that it is possible to change – without the help of the gods!'

'Have you ever tried?' Mir sounded sarcastic.

'I could have saved Tara, if I had kept my eyes open! Now I can't bear to think of her, and I can't not think of her. It's a sickness inside, it hurts when I wake up, all through the day I can feel the pain....' He looked at Mir, 'Don't you think of Tara?'

'And others. It's not your fault. And she is not dead – she lives, I can feel her.'

Siddarth looked at him and spoke very slow and clear: 'She is dead.'

It was dark when they reached the city. The air was hot and smoky; the people in the huts outside the city walls were lighting their cooking fires. Mir pointed to them. 'We stayed there for more than a month, then I was lucky enough to be chosen for a building job, then doubly lucky to discover that the owner needed a charioteer. That is why I live inside the city. Others stay outside for years.'

'I'm hungry,' Siddarth said suddenly. 'Come, let's find a place to eat.' Both his companions stared at him in surprise. 'What's wrong?'

'You are dvija, lord,' said Dagu. 'I am Nisada, what you call Naga. And Mir – '

'So?'

'So? So you will lose your caste, as we did, when we ate your left-overs!' snapped Mir. 'Don't you know that much, Aryaputra?'

'Yes, I know – that food bears the caste of its cook and can defile you – I know it as a fairytale, like thousands more! Because I've eaten food from even the lowest of the low and seen for myself that nothing happens!' Dagu stared in horror; even Mir looked surprised. 'Sometimes I think that people spend most of their time hunting for things to be scared of and for ways to hate others! Surely you don't believe all this, Dagu – your sage himself said that nothing you do makes a difference!'

'But I can't break the sacred law.'

'But it doesn't make any difference!'

Dagu shook his head firmly. 'It's not that. I really can't – I wouldn't be able to, that's the truth. I'd be sick. I must leave.'

'I'm sorry for what I did earlier....' Siddarth felt worse for the weaver bent again to his feet.

Dagu turned away and then back. 'Your horse is at the workshop, lord. The foreman had it fed and watered before he left.'

Siddarth had forgotten all about the horse. Mir said a little sternly, 'Don't worry, horses are used to such behaviour. Men too. I have often waited at a door with horses and chariot, for a lord who chooses to turn up the next day. The stomach learns to adjust.'

Siddarth looked at the ground. 'I've never even thought of hunger, Mir. Food was always there. I've only thought of myself.'

Mir was surprised to find his companion suddenly sunk in misery. 'Lord, you just forgot – it happens. Let's get the horse.'

They walked on, seeing their way by the oil lamps of workshops where work continued. The horse was waiting outside Yasa's workshop. They found a stall selling dried grass and a public house not far beyond. The manager soon had the horse secured outside with its grass, the two young men settled inside on a mat with bolsters to lean against, and their order for rice, curried quail and fried river fish promptly served. Siddarth suddenly felt better than he had in months. The food was delicious, the atmosphere lively. Two or three languages could be heard at once. Then he noticed that a great deal of the chatter was coming from an inner room. Some customers went directly inside after a word to the manager; many who came out looked of high birth. One group had two beautiful and heavily-jewelled women with them, their faces unveiled, either aristocrats or prostitutes.

Siddarth called the manager. 'Is there a dining area inside?'

'Yes, my lord.'

'Then why did you serve us here?'

'I'm sorry, my lord, you did not ask.... But you are free to move there, if you wish. The price is double, that's all.'

'Let it be for now.' Siddarth went back to his fish, but found Mir looking a little quizzical. 'I just wanted to know if there was any barrier for going in. I'm glad there isn't.'

'But there is, lord,' Mir said gently. 'It's money, as is usual hereabouts.'

Siddarth had not even thought of money. 'Oh. But at least not birth. And there seem to be many ways to earn money here.'

'It's not easy,' was all Mir said. He didn't want to plunge his host into another bout of gloom.

Siddarth did not meet Mir again for many days for he was kept busy with his half-yearly examinations. The only break he had in the month was when the Raja of Kosala visited Banaras and all were summoned to attend his procession. The streets were swept and watered, hutments hidden behind screens, all kinds of banners, standards and floral festoons hoisted on gates, rooftops, and trees. Heaps of sandalwood and aloe were positioned along the procession route and ignited just before the Raja arrived, so that the he would smell their aromatic smouldering instead of the normal gutter fragrances. Not that he showed any appreciation. From where Siddarth stood, he looked like a solid silver statue crowned in gold. He was seated on a silver throne on top of a white elephant in the middle of a cavalcade that took more than an hour to pass by.

Siddarth was impressed. Yasa was not.

'You've never been to Rajgir, have you? You should see the procession of the Magadhe-Raja – that is real magnificence! And Rajgir is the most impressive city I have seen.'

'But Kosala is bigger than Magadh, isn't it?'

'Much bigger, but not that strong. The lords have too much power here, my father says. And look at the dacoits. Magadh is stronger and richer, much richer. You should see the houses there. I have two uncles in Rajgir; both live in palaces, looking out over lakes – their own! And the elder has an island on the lake, where he throws parties!' Siddarth had never seen Yasa so animated.

'Do your uncles belong to the royal family?'

'No! They're merchants. The Raja is much richer!'

'How are they so rich?'

'Well, they do much sacrifice there, huge ones to the Goddess. But my uncle says it is the Naga-metal. Black gold, he calls it, and Magadh has the best in the world! They have armies of Nagas at work extracting and purifying the ore, but it is already very pure and close to the surface, so the profits are fantastic.'

They started walking back to the ashram. Their colleagues walked ahead, the kshatriyas together, the brahmins likewise. Yasa's father was the richest of all their parents and paid much more, which was the only reason why Yasa and two other merchant sons were allowed into the school. The merchant boys sat separately, the furthest from the teacher.

'I saw your father at a meeting the other day... of one Kassapa.'

'Oh, you'll find him at all such. He broke with the brahmins many years ago – they used to demand herds of cattle whenever he signed a deal. He was not the first to refuse – many merchants follow the new sages nowadays – but he was in a depression for months. He's recovered now. He respects Kassapa especially, though I feel the Jinas make more sense. The Jinas are not so impious – Kassapa scorns all rituals! The Jinas believe that Moksha will be attained faster if one is devout.'

'What do you mean by Moksha?'

'What everybody means! Freedom from rebirth. Becoming a part of the Eternal, and so on.'

The Upanishadic ideas were apparently well-known here. Siddarth scraped through his examinations at the bottom of his class and remained unaffected by the reproaches of his guru.

'What difference does it make whether I know one hymn or a thousand? This kind of education is superficial; it offers no answers to any of the real questions of life,' he told Yasa, who rather surprisingly did not ask him what he meant by the real questions of life. Mir would have asked; he had a lot of answers as well, he was amazingly clear in his opinions on many issues. He was the most alive person Siddarth knew. Or maybe he was not unique, maybe it was just that Siddarth had never really spoken to any slave before, except Tara and that was different. Siddarth found himself thinking often about Mir, almost every day something reminded him of him.

Like the folk living outside the city gates. The children were always playing in the dust not far from the road, normally naked and unbathed. And the sound of approaching horses always brought a few women running out of the huts, yelling to the children to come away. The horsemen were not to be trusted.

He was not the only person who noticed them. 'Look at these animals!' exclaimed a fellow student, Aniruddha, also from Kapilavastu, one day. 'They're dirty, half-starved, they get kicked everyday. And remember our slaves, how well they are kept – enough food, clothes, even holidays – yet they try to escape! They should be sent here, then they'll learn gratitude!'

'They escape to come here,' retorted Siddarth. 'They prefer this.' But it puzzled him too. Not just these outsiders, even the workers within the city, like those at Yasa's workshop, looked really quite badly off. The next time he met Mir he asked him, 'Mir, is this an easier life than you were living in Kapilavastu?'

They were seated on the floor of his hut, eating rice gruel served by Mir's wife. She sat with them, a thin girl who had reacted with terror at the first sight of Siddarth, falling to the ground and begging forgiveness. Mir had lifted her up and explained, but it was a while before she stopped trembling.

'It is about the same, in my case. It is different for others. It depends on your luck. And your confidence and willingness to learn. Not on your tribe. You have to think for yourself, you can't just follow others. There are thousands of jobs here, but thousands more who want them. But it is worth it, I think. For the self-respect.'

'Is it respect, or just anonymity?'

'It's the same thing.'

'But the workers look so badly off. Those outside the walls especially. And they're treated horribly. I've seen the soldiers whipping them back from the walls. Some nobles even shoot at the children for sport as they ride past....'

'But they're still better than what we were,' insisted Mir. 'They're free, they were not dragged here! I don't think you'll understand, Siddarth, your background is too different.' He ate some rice; Siddarth waited. 'Anyway, there is no option to the cities. The jungle-folk are being wiped out. Your sanghas, for all their fancy culture, are killing themselves. I only wish I could free the others at Kapilavastu – all my people.'

'But do they want to be free?' asked Siddarth softly.

'They're frightened, that's all!' shouted Mir and his wife jumped. She was a frightened person. 'Being a slave does that. And there was no place to escape to, all these years. People were hunted down in the other republics, or starved in the jungle. Now there are these cities, with jobs for any strong back, any ready pair of hands. But this is strange territory. People need time to realize that the city is freedom!'

'Freedom?' The weaver Dagu of Yasa's workshop laughed grimly. He was not the laughing type, thought Siddarth. Workers were standing around the workshop waiting for their dues. His father was closing down the workshop, Yasa had told Siddarth, and expanding his trading outfit. 'Do I look free? We've not come here to be free. We've been goaded here by the fire in our bellies. When your child's stomach balloons above spindly legs, then you have to turn to the city!'

Yet Mir was not wrong, Siddarth felt. There was that tiny element of choice in Dagu's tormented life. Slaves were denied choice and they knew it and struggled continuously to get it, as a result they had to be held by the whip, the ropes, the guarded bunker – and they tried all the harder to escape. The lords of the cities seemed to have realized that slaves were expensive compared to the free labourer. Freedom from everything but hunger, that was enough.

The city was indeed a strange place. And no one could love it as much as Mir. He was enthralled by it, like one with a new love, constantly admiring, stroking, smelling, seeking to know more, completely blind to all its faults, to the dirt, violence, lewdness, noise, the large and small skulduggery, the all-pervading hunger. He remained cheerful even after he lost his job, as a result of driving too slow for his master's son's liking. He took his wife and Siddarth to the fair ground one day, where they listened to bards singing the love of Rama and Sita, the tragedy of Shakuntala, other old and ever-popular stories. There they also came across the Lokayat minstrels, a few ragged men, with ektaras made out of half a pumpkin shell crossed by a sheep-gut string and played with a bamboo twig.

'What is man?' asked one of them, an old man wrapped in a rough blanket. 'Tell me, what is man? A god? A devil? A part of a god – the head, or the shoulders or the stomach or the feet? A soul? Tell me, what is man?'

The crowd remained silent. 'Ajita of the Hair-Blanket,' whispered Mir in an awed voice.

'I'll tell you. Man is none of what they say. Man is made of four elements. The four elements of nature. Earth, water, air, senses.

When he dies, four men take up the corpse on its bier, they forget him and gossip above his head as far as the burning-ground, and there his bones turn the colour of a dove's wing and all his sacrifices are gone, finished, forgotten in his ashes. The earth in him returns to the earth, the water to water, the air to air, the senses into space. Everything ends for him. Those who preach alms-giving to brahmins for the dead are fools. Those who talk of things like heaven or an immortal soul, speak nonsense. When the body dies, whether fool or sage, beggar or king, all are cut off and perish. Nobody survives death.'

His audience absorbed this silently and after a pause the minstrels began their songs again. The crowd was clearly divided over the discourse; some looked uneasy, a few walked off in a huff, others laughed and clapped. Mir enjoyed it hugely. 'The Lokayats are the only ones who make sense of this senseless world.'

'Yes,' said Siddarth slowly. 'They mock the brahmins well. But is that enough?'

'Enough for what?'

Siddarth found it difficult to explain. 'Well, the world is such a mess – the false rituals are one part, but there's also the unhappiness, the lack of justice, the lack of sense even.'

After leaving the fair ground, they escorted Mir's wife home and then walked to the portside of the city. The gates to the jetties were closed, but Mir knew where there was a hole in the wall. They climbed through it, met a friend of his who worked on the port and went with him to a supervisor to speak about a job for Mir, loading cloth bales on boats. The supervisor looked him up and down and told him to return in a few days. Then the three of them sat on one of the jetties, after joining their palms in obeisance to the inky blackness in front that was the holy river. And they talked and talked, late into the night, of many things that Siddarth could not even remember later. But mainly of the cloth and the boats, and of change, and hope. And the city. That talk, while staring at the small pools of lapping light in the blackness, listening

to the invisible chimes from the temple bells, was the last time
Siddarth saw Mir.

The next month Kosala was at war with Magadh over Kashi.
The Raja of Magadh had suddenly decided that as he was
partly descended from the old SisuNagas of Kashi, the province
was rightfully his. His army, led by the aggressive crown prince
Bimbisara, crossed the river to the east of Banaras. The city erupted
in confusion. There were only three army divisions in town and
the citizenry was terrified that the Magadhans would reach before
reinforcements did. Attempts to strengthen the fortifications were
at first chaotic for the roads were choked with people trying to get
out – mainly merchants and manufacturers desperate to get their
goods away. Their laid-off workers roamed the streets desperate for
work. Riots erupted out of hunger, but targeted against anything
with Magadhan connections. The big Magadhan merchants, like
Yasa's family, lived in the inner city, where the mobs could not enter.
Poorer people were less lucky. Like Dagu, who belonged to south
Anga, now in Magadh. Dagu's life had been first wrecked by
Magadh, but now, as Magadhans, he and his family, including his
recuperating son, were barricaded in their hut and burnt alive.

Work appeared – all able-bodied men were asked to join the
infantry. Anybody, of any background. The jobless rushed to join;
the next casualties of the war were at the enrolment site where
soldiers had to use whips and swords to control the pandemonium.
Training began. Every day huge companies marched through the
streets, parading their new arms, testing the unfamiliar weights,
moving very awkwardly as compared to the beautiful rhythm and
harmony of the Shakya ranks. But then those had been almost
born in armed formation and weaned on battle-talk. And, as they
had learnt, beauty was not always enough. But there was little
doubt that Kashi's new infantry regiment was too raw for any
opponent. The new recruits marched out to battle, fought valiantly,
and were massacred. Mir was among the dead.

Reinforcements arrived. But instead of hammering Magadh to a pulp as expected, a halt was called. Two weeks of negotiations followed, which in a deafening blare of trumpets and drums, were declared successful. Pasenadi's sister was married to Prince Bimbisara and the villages that Bimbisara had captured were declared her dowry.

The whole drama played itself out in a couple of months and the city recovered immediately, as if nothing had really happened. The burnt houses and workshops were cleared and rapidly rebuilt. Merchants and their enterprises returned; markets were once again crowded and lively. The fair grounds were overfull and even more so the brothels, though there supply exceeded demand. Siddarth went to meet Mir's wife but their house was empty and the neighbours would not speak to him.

The city had become a monster and he fled again. He gave up his studies and returned home. To his family's joy. His studies were well over, they said, for he was a man – ready for grihastya ashrama, the third phase of dvija manhood, of adult responsibility, marriage and child rearing. He was immediately dragged into all the activities of the Gana Sabha, even and upto the meetings of the inner circle. But the elation on his return died down fast, for instead of responding with enthusiasm, he was lethargic and diffident. Shudodhan said nothing at first. Then the annual archery contest came around, in which all the younger rajas presented their skills on the Moat Hall ground to the pompous clamour of the army band. Many displayed amazing prowess. But not Siddarth. His shots were mostly off-target; to everybody's horror, he ranked last. Shudodhan was left with little choice. He called his son to him the next morning.

'Siddarth, what's wrong with you? Your behaviour yesterday was a mockery, of me and the whole nation.'

'I did not see any point in the exercise, that's all.'

'And I hear that you have still not sat for purification after returning from the south? You know those places are defiling!'

'That's rubbish. Nobody can defile another. You can only defile yourself.'

'Siddarth, please! You're not a child any more. Listen, I am leaving tomorrow for the east – the Mallas are trying their tricks again. I want you to come with me.' He saw Siddarth's expression. 'No, listen to me, son, be positive! Fight this melancholy. You are a great warrior, you are brave and strong, you have proved yourself many times – that's what you should tell yourself every morning! There is nothing wrong with you at all. I would have made you second in command – if it wasn't for yesterday – '

'I'm a great warrior? I'm brave and strong – at killing others? Father, you make me ashamed. If I told myself that every day, I would soon slit my throat.'

Shudodhan took a deep breath. 'Siddarth. This kind of talk insults your dharma.'

'And where was your dharma, Father, when you gave in to Kosala without fighting?'

'Is that the problem, son?' Shudodhan was relieved. He had given many successful pep talks on the issue over the years. 'I understand. But you must realize that it was not really a defeat. The idea of the supreme sacrifice is a beautiful one, especially for young people like you. Death before dishonour. But I have to think of the future of our people. And we will be free soon. The oracles agree.'

'I have no problem with vassalage, Father. But if we are going to pick and choose our battles – to war with the weak and bow before the strong; if real-politic rules our decisions, why talk of dharma at all?' He paused but Shudodhan was silent. 'In any case, I do not believe in war. It is evil. Those who talk of bravery and heroism and glory in war are fools. And I, for one, refuse to be a fool.'

'Siddarth, stop it! You are going too far. It is not for you and me to question the world. Your dharma is that of a kshatriya – '

'It was. It was, Father. Dharma used to be about fate. And faith. In your birth. The great heroes of the past had no answer to this idea, they accepted that their fate was ordained by their birth, and lived their lives according to it, even when times were bitter and they hated what they were doing. Like Dharmaraj. But the times have changed! We are not slaves to such myths any longer. You proved that against Kosala. You refused to die, though that was the kshatriya dharma. And I – I will not fight henceforth, Father.'

'Siddarth – '

'And I do not think I will be Chief.'

'Siddarth!'

'I have nothing to offer the sangha. And I personally feel suffocated here.'

'You seem... you almost seem to hate your people....'

Siddarth stared out of the window for a moment, at the river and the tamarind orchards that rimmed it, before he spoke. 'The truth is that I love many of our ideals. But I don't see them practised. And I'm exhausted by the rituals. All the killing, all the wealth poured into the fire – it's senseless. And primitive. How better are we than the forest-folk abjectly prostrating before every beast and tree?'

'I can't believe that a son of mine can be so.... You seem to hate me as well.'

'I don't hate you.'

'But you have no love for me.'

'You don't love me either, Father. You love your son, that's all. Because he's yours. If another were your son, you would love him. If I was another's son, you would hate me!'

'Siddarth, stop this childish – '

'Our nation is dying, Father, and do you know what is killing it? Not the vassalage to Kosala. Our problem is that the leaders of our republic hate republicanism the most!'

'Are you calling me a traitor?'

'It is at least hypocrisy – to sing paeans to unity and equality and brotherhood, while destroying them!'

He was suddenly tired, and Shudodhan seemed speechless, so he turned and left. The courtyard garden was full of mango trees in bloom. The sprays of tiny greenish-white blossoms hung heavy on the drooping branches, filling the air with a cloyingly sweet scent. Their lush splendour, surrounded by the carved and polished teakwood balconies of the elegant house, with fretted railings painted in muted colours and hung with delicate bronze lamps, all suddenly seemed false, garish. Unlike Banaras. That was a real city, with its ugly muddy roads, hovels, puddles and pushy crowds. Like Mir. Mir had belonged to Banaras, how had he ever lived in Kapilavastu? He had not lived, he had just survived.

Siddarth remembered something Mir had said. 'I left a part of me behind. My mother and my brother. She was ill, he stayed to look after her. He is a charioteer at the house of Shakuntaraja.'

Shakunta had many charioteers and it was the third who looked like Mir. His name was Channa. His mother was dead. Now he learnt that his brother was as well. Siddarth met him again a few days later and offered him a job; Channa accepted. Siddarth met Shakunta, a raja of a faction opposed to Shudodhan, who asked for double the normal price. Siddarth did not haggle. Channa arrived at Shudhodan's house that night, and became Siddarth's constant companion through his remaining years with his sangha. Unlike Mir, he was a quiet man who spoke little and dreamed less.

Shudodhan began planning Siddarth's nuptials. Yashodhara's family was pressing for an early date and he himself felt that marriage might be the answer to Siddarth's irresponsibility. He called him one day to discuss the matter and discovered that he had just returned from a visit to the family estates. How were things there? He did not really know, replied Siddarth, he had gone there to meet the ex-peasant Vali. He had found him missing from the household when he returned, and was informed by the other servants that Vali had been transferred to the farm.

'You went all the way to meet a field-hand?'

'A friend.' Siddarth was curt; and actually hurt, for Vali had said little to him though he seemed deeply unhappy. And it was not true that Siddarth had not seen anything on the estates. He had noticed the godowns brimming with grain, lush orchards, land being prepared for sowing. And oxen, pricked with iron goads and wounded by the plough-shares too; behind them slaves, exhausted and dirty with sweat and mud. Vali had become a thin shadow, but he made no complaint. He only spoke, in fact, to refuse Siddarth's offer of freedom. With a smile. He could go to the southern cities, Siddarth had said, and find a job.

'What difference will it make? People get tossed around there like bits of rubbish, I've heard. Nobody knows you, nobody cares. When you die, there is nobody even to weep.'

Who would weep for Vali on Shudodhan's estates? But there was little else that Siddarth could offer, so he just gave a few orders to the overseers and returned to Kapilavastu.

'I ordered the slave rations doubled, Father. And forbade the goad on the bullocks.'

Shudodhan looked at him, then shook his head. 'Siddarth, we'll go bankrupt – '

'That's rubbish, and you know it.'

'There are big yagnas coming up and I'm expected to offer the most. You seem to think only of slaves!'

'I can see only slaves – those working for us, and we ourselves with our ridiculous yagnas!'

'That's enough, Siddarth! You are unhappy, yes, I can see that you still grieve over Tara. But there has to be a limit to sentimentality.'

'Tara was my mother.'

His father was livid. He stepped forth abruptly and Siddarth thought he was going to hit him. But Shudodhan embraced him instead, very tight and very long, as if to control himself. And when he stepped back, there was sadness in his voice. 'Don't say that. I know Tara cared for you and I am eternally obliged to her for that, but don't forget your own mother.'

'I mean no insult to her. But I remember only Tara... and how she died.'

'It's the law, son. Those who break the law must face the consequences.'

'It was not her law! Or mine. The truth is that I find this place suffocating, Father, and not only because of Tara. Because of many things, but mainly because of the continuous hypocrisy. The south is at least honest.'

'You prefer those cities? Those rough, vulgar – '

'Yes, they are ugly, but still alive. They look ahead. Our land is gracious and beautiful in many ways, but rotten inside. We have a sickness, Father, and we have to cure it, or it will finish us.'

He really needs marriage, thought Shudodhan nervously. Marriage would settle him down. All Shudodhan's friends agreed. At the earliest, they advised. It was not that they had examined Siddarth's specific malaise. There was really no need. In Siddarth's native land, then and later, family would always be the answer to all problems, social and individual. If an individual looked thoughtful, the solution was marriage; if a couple was unhappy, the solution was a child; if that child was a problem, the solution was another; and so on. So that finally every person had so many people surrounding him or her, to care for and worry about, that they had no time to think, let alone be dissatisfied. But in Siddarth's time, marriage was more than suffocation; it was an essence of dharma. Every man required a legitimate son to preside over his rites of death. There was no other route to heaven.

So he married. His betrothed, Yashodhara, had been waiting for him these many years. Long ago, the reader will remember, she had begun to doubt the wisdom of her parents' choice for her, and time had multiplied the doubts. Why she did not break the betrothal and find someone else is a mystery, for it was definitely within the limits of acceptable behaviour for a noblewoman of her time. And she had already reached well past marriageable age while waiting for Siddarth to grow up to Shakya responsibility.

The only explanation was that he remained the future Chief. This definitely made all the difference to her father, who remained unmoved by all criticism of his daughter's age. It was a brave stance. An unmarried daughter was later considered a burden and even a curse, but in Siddarth's time she was worse – an insult of heinous proportions to one's ancestors and gods. People still remembered the times when a tribesman's most important duty lay in increasing the population of the tribe. They remembered even better the many old maledictions that attached themselves to shirkers. Whenever a ripe virgin had her courses, so the ancient sages had declared, her parents were the monstrous killers of the unborn child. If an unwedded maiden exceeded twelve years of age, they added for good measure, her anscestors in heaven were eternally condemned to drinking the blood she shed every month.

But the Shakyarajas were not slaves to these ideas. It would be silly to follow old sayings blindly in these changing times. Yashodhara's father was willing to let his daughter wait, for he believed that it was of greater import to net the future Chief as his son-in-law, than a grandchild every nine months from the moment her womb came of age. He was wrong, of course. He should have heeded the sayings.

Yashodhara may not have been in the first flush of youth but she was beautiful by Shakya standards of such things – tall, well-built, light-complexioned – and accomplished in many though not all of the so-called 'sixty-four arts of femininity'. Only prostitutes were expected to know all. And when she appeared at the wedding robed in gold-edged tussore, the bulk of it arranged in a fantastic spray of nearly a hundred tiny pleats – the very latest fashion – and tucked into the front of a cotton underskirt, the rest then draped lightly around her naked torso and shoulders and left to trail down her back in pleats to the floor, her long hair swept high in a shimmering pyramid, and intricate gold-dusted sandalwood patterns of peacocks and leafy vines trailing all over her forehead, palms, wrists, throat and between her breasts all the way down to her navel, Siddarth was quite envied. She was sexually accomplished as well, for the Shakyas still went by the ancient traditions which set little store by bridal virginity. And she was confident – she belonged to her society, community, class and caste without any misgivings. Indeed her only misgiving in life seems to have been about her betrothed and that was to prove fully justified in time. For he was full of misgivings in general, and the couple appears to have never found a meeting ground.

Siddarth instead drew closer to Channa. It was not that Channa understood – Siddarth was himself still unclear of the nature of his problem – but his job was to stay at all times with Siddarth, which included running behind his horse while he was riding. Siddarth asked him more than once to climb up behind him, at least when they were out of sight of his father, but Channa had little faith in his master's ability to protect him. As a result, since Siddarth would not have Channa running while hanging on to the tail of his galloping horse, they spent hours commuting where others spent minutes. And Channa became the recipient of most of Siddarth's confused confidences. Which made him grow to regard Siddarth with great affection, tempered, unsurprisingly, with concern. Kanthaka, Siddarth's horse, a white Arab bought in the horse-market of Shravasti, was another recipient, though we do not know what he made of them.

'What's the point of life, Channa?' Siddarth asked once. 'To have a family? To beget a son? Even animals mate and produce children and raise them. Is that all life is?' They were sitting in Channa's small room in the slave bunker. Channa had stepped on a thorn the previous day and Siddarth had ordered him to rest.

Channa was silent.

'What do you think, Channa?'

'Every man wants a wife and children, sire. You have the luxury to dream of more. Perhaps to achieve it. I do not know....'

'You have children, don't you? Do they make you happy?'

'Yes, they do. Children are joy and laughter. Worry and sorrow too sometimes, but much joy. Children are the future. How can you live without the future?'

'But what of their future, Channa? Will it be better than your life, or worse?'

Channa shrugged. 'It will be as She wills.'

'What of your will?'

Just then a child came running into the room. Tall and light-coloured like a Shakya, she had the sharp features, full lips and huge long-lashed eyes of the Nagas. Siddarth stared at her and she stared back boldly from within the safety of Channa's embrace.

'What a pretty little girl! Who is she?' Siddarth reached out; she came to him quite readily, attracted clearly by the thick gold ropes about his chest.

'The daughter of a friend. Her name is Vassabha.' A slave-woman appeared at the door, and Siddarth stared again, at heart-wrenching beauty that was strangely familiar. She herself was aghast at the child.

'Vassabha!' she hissed, but the girl was engrossed in the shining links of Siddarth's necklaces. The lady reached forward, plucked her out of his lap and carried her out wailing lustily. Siddarth gazed after them.

'I've seen her before,' he said. Channa said nothing. 'Where does she work, Channa?'

'In the household of Raja Mahanaman.'

'Oh, yes! She used to dance, didn't she? She was an amazingly beautiful dancer, I remember.'

'She works in the kitchen,' said Channa shortly.

'Yes, she's aged. Her skin has lost that glow. I'm sure her bosom had a sag – while our refined Shakyan tastes demand perfection in everything. We have a passion for beauty, Channa, of all kinds; we lust for it, drown in it, show it off without realizing how ugly we look next to it!'

Channa was silent. Siddarth changed the topic. 'Do you know, Channa, that Tara regarded me as a child of your Goddess?'

'Who does not know, lord? We are all children of the Goddess, but you were born in Lumbini. That was a divine sign. Every slave in Kapilavastu and beyond knows you as the child of Lumbini.'

'And? What do they say? Do they expect something from me?'

'I am not sure, lord. But I know that you can expect nothing but great respect and affection from them.'

'They don't speak to me. I can't understand if they wish to.'

'The man on a horse looks down on the man on foot. The man on foot has to look up – it doesn't make for easy conversation.'

So time passed. Shudodhan remained nervous for a while about the proclaimed admiration for the southern cities, but Siddarth seemed to have decided to stay put. He was clearly unhappy though. He had an exalted position, a beautiful wife, a palatial home, the best sport and recreations his nation and era could offer. All of which he seemed to quietly hate, preferring to spend his free time wandering around in a cloak of silent melancholy.

What did he want? Shudodhan was afraid to ask. Instead he fed the fires, questioned doctors, pleaded with priests, donated to brahmins, tried his best to interest his son in something, anything. But it was futile. Siddarth took part in Sabha activities mechanically. He participated in war games like a clown. He rarely attended the yagnas, and then always with a sacrilegious sneer on his face. ('I am not ruled by your so-called gods,' was what he actually said to Shudodhan who kept it to himself.) And he was uninterested in women. The most gorgeous of Kapilavastu's dancers and musicians performed outside his apartments every evening, all of them available to the handsome Chief-to-be in every possible way. But, except for the requirements of politeness, he ignored them.

He spent his free time with Channa, or any ascetic who chanced to pass through Kapilavastu. And he began to wonder whether these world-renouncers had the answers he sought. They seemed untouched by the madness around them, content in their own personal quests. Was their life itself the answer – the rejection of society, the withdrawal to nature? Or was it the way to answers?

While he wondered, others acted. One day, Channa informed Siddarth that a field-hand on the Chief's estates wanted to speak to him. Siddarth went over the very next day and discovered that

Vali had been impressed by the ideas of Purana Kassapa when the sage visited the area some months previously. Now Vali had decided to follow him.

Siddarth remembered Kassapa well, and his talk about the futility of doing good or evil. 'Vali, you know that you're free to go whenever you wish. You don't have to ask me.'

Vali nodded patiently. 'But you must tell the foreman, lord. Or they'll chase and kill me.'

'Oh!' Siddarth got up and walked to the foreman's hut. He explained the situation; the latter looked uneasy but did not object.

Siddarth returned. 'You're free, Vali. But tell me, why do you want to join Kassapa?'

'Because he understands the world.'

'But what does his understanding offer?'

'Acceptance. What else can he offer? You can't change your life.'

'I don't think that's true. Man is not so helpless. That's how it looks perhaps....'

'What can people do besides worshipping the gods? And that makes no difference. I've seen the devout treated worse than dogs. My wife – she was the most pious woman I knew – she was being dragged in the mud of the road when I last saw her. I could do nothing. The gods did nothing. It was her fate.'

Siddarth was silent.

'It's difficult to accept, I know. Most people can't give up the gods. They worship frantically, all for nothing.'

Vali left. Siddarth pondered some more. The years passed and he seemed content to live like a shadow of a man, listening to others while his own life changed hardly at all. In fact, so many years passed without any change that colourful rumours began to proliferate about his and his wife's failure to produce an heir. The truth was that Siddarth was not very energetic at his connubial duties and more often than not skipped the pleasures of his marriage bed to spend his time walking through the city, or sitting on the banks of the river with his strange friends, or sleeping alone in his own chambers. It had nothing to do with his wife, as the many courtesans enlisted by Shudodhan for his son's edification could testify. Nor did it have anything to do with Channa, though there was enough gossip about that as well.

The fact was that Siddarth had somewhere lost faith in passion of any kind; he had begun to see love and physical ardour as forms of selfishness, indulgence, even bondage and exploitation, especially as practised among his Shakya fraternity. His view was misunderstood – his distrust of passion would be interpreted as a passionate aversion for sex and the female body, for this fell in with the popular belief that the seed of human – i.e. male – greatness is the male seed itself. So that a man who does not waste this most precious resource in sexual activity, but preserves and nurtures it within himself, is possessed of tremendous powers. Many tried this brahmacharya path to glory and achieved nothing more than immense public esteem, yet the myth survived and with it the Buddha's representation as its epitome.

The legend can be quite graphic on this issue. It recounts that Siddarth once came across his beautiful dancers asleep outside his room, their bodies abandoned in tired flaccidity, their clothes and make-up a mess, one snoring, another drooling, a third with limbs lankly askew. All repelled him equally, and he realized that the human body was a disgusting object, a repository of potential rot, its various orifices all leaking the most repulsive of products. So the legend claims, and it fits in well with the most popular explanation for his departure – his horror at sickness, old age and death, at the ugliness of decay. But the story probably originated in the strictly celibate imagination of his later followers, who could only suppress their very natural urges of the non-celibate kind by painting the focus of their wet dreams in the most repulsive and yet highly sensuous of lights.

Matters however came to a head in Siddarth's own household when Yashodhara, plagued by the snide whispers of her maids and friends, determined that she would not be blamed for failing to produce an heir when she had not been provided the bare essentials. She confided in Siddarth's foster mother, who confided in his father, who called his son and harangued him on the usual topic of duty to family, clan and sangha. We do not really know what transpired. It is possible that Siddarth accepted the criticism and applied himself to the task. Or perhaps some other source was found to 'plough the field', as was not uncommon among the aristocracy of that time and later. But in due course, and some ten years after their marriage, Yashodhara became pregnant and then a mother.

To everybody's joy, it was a son. The child would convince Siddarth of his responsibilities, exulted his father. He was right, but the responsibilities were not those he had envisaged.

'A child is born,' repeated Siddarth, when a slave came with the news to the banks of the river where he sat. 'A bond is born.'

Rahul, or bond, would be the name of the child, decided the rajas who followed to offer congratulations. Shudodhan heard of the name as he sat planning another biggest-ever yagna, and liked it as well – yes, a bond, Siddarth's bond, to us, to his land and people, to his heritage. To our future. Yes, this child would be Rahul.

But bond is kin to bondage. And that is what Siddarth meant. One more link in the chains that bound him... to what? Surrounded by wild celebrations, as he was escorted back to his father's mansion, he felt lost, out of place. But to the people celebrating, he merely looked thoughtful, as befitted one embarking on the responsibility of fatherhood, as befitted a future Chief. One of them, a pretty young thing named Kisa Gautami, not of aristocratic stock but as bold and confident as any other, was especially charmed by his demeanour.

'Happy is the mother, happy the father, happy especially the wife, who has such a husband,' she called out. At that moment came a pause in both slogans and drumming; Siddarth heard her words clearly. And something snapped. Yes, this was a happy moment and he should have been the happiest. But he was not. He knew right then that he had to leave. Immediately. If he waited, more bonds would be born. His life was a fraud, on his people, his family, himself as well, because it disgusted him and he was doing exactly nothing about it. He could go on like this, watching time slip like water through his fingers, or he could leave and do something positive. What and where? A job in Banaras? No, Banaras held no answers. An ascetic's life? Perhaps. The future was a question mark. All he knew was that this was his past. There was no point waiting. He suddenly felt genuinely happy.

He turned, pulled off the strand of pearls around his neck and threw it towards Kisa. She caught it, and was thrilled in turn. For she read something quite different in his excitement and his gift. It had to be love at first sight. Perhaps he realized that Rahul's birth freed him from husbandly duties towards Yashodhara? Would the pearls be the first of many more gifts, the first of many tender moments stolen from the rigorous princely schedule? She clutched the strand to her bosom and dreamt on ecstatically.

Siddarth left that night. He paid a last visit to his wife's bed-chamber without waking either her or his son, and set off on Kanthaka through the jungle. Channa ran behind him, holding Kanthaka's tail and weeping, 'Don't do this, lord! Please!'

Siddarth brought Kanthaka to a halt. 'Channa, for the last time, climb up behind me! I have to get away tonight.'

'Aryaputra, please inform your father of your plan.'

'I'm sorry, I know I'm leaving you to face his wrath. But do you think he'd let me leave? He'd lock me up and suffer no criticism for restraining a madman.'

Channa climbed up unhappily and Kanthaka started galloping through the trees, heading eastwards to the Malla. Above the rush of the wind in their ears, Siddarth continued talking. 'They may beat you, Channa. They may even accuse you of killing me for my jewels. So take my jewellery back to them. And tell them that if they harm you, they will never see me again. Never. Tell them that.'

Channa continued weeping. He knew that the Shakyas were not so reasonable.

'Otherwise they can find me at the hermitage of Bhargava.'

It was nearly dawn when they reached the banks of the river Anoma, where they parted. Siddarth hugged Channa and the horse too. 'Now I'm an ordinary man, Kanthaka, and ordinary men don't travel on white steeds with fancy trappings.'

He gave Channa all his ornaments, most of his clothes, his sword, dagger, even his thick top-knot of hair. Kanthaka is supposed to have died on the spot from grief. Channa however made it back to Kapilavastu with Siddarth's gear and message, and, as he had expected, was berated, whipped till he bled, and imprisoned. A choleric Shudodhan sent his priest to Bhargava's hermitage, whence he returned with the happy confirmation that Siddarth was alive and the less satisfying news that he refused to return. He wanted, he said, to find enlightenment. His family retired for a spell of hysterics, at the end of which Channa was remembered and released.

GANGA

A shrill elephantine proclamation blared out from the thickets on the north bank as Ananda put the last sheet down and happily accepted both the approving nod and the tumbler of water that his teacher offered. Upali began to collect the sheets. Once in a while a heavy gust of wind would rise up from the water and he did not want to see the rather meagre results of three years' effort vanishing over the rail. He tied up the red folder and waited for reactions.

There were about forty monks seated on mats around them, under an awning of wooden poles and cotton cloth, bald pates gleaming in the noon glare – the only thing that identified them as one Sangha. Their robes did not, the colours being very mixed except for the strict saffron of Sanchi, while the cloth ranged from fine linen and rich Gandharan wool to old, unfinished and even experimental materials – like the one Harsha was wearing. Of cotton grown in the monastery fields, it was grey, rough and a little lumpy in places, woven on the monastery's version of the latest Kashi loom.

There were four nuns too, sitting together right at the back, as bald as the monks. And a few novices, who made do outside the awning, the sun beating down directly on their heads. It was the month of Paush, with winter just around the corner, but while there was already an icy bite to the nights, the midday sun remained fierce.

Everybody was silent, so Upali turned to look over the rail. Oarsmen were at work below deck, churning up waves that faded away slowly into the glassy distance. Nearly three weeks had passed since they had left Maheshwar. Nigrodha's carriages had carried them through the Vindhyas and across the Malwa plateau, through hundreds of miles of rolling woodland, then down to the plains and on, till they reached the sparkling blue Yamuna at Kosambi, where a great many monks were already assembled. Two days later this boat had arrived and carried them to the Ganga. Now Banaras' teetering skyline was behind them and there were just two days for Pataliputra.

Three weeks of travelling half-way across the realm and at a ridiculous speed. It would have thrilled Upali ordinarily, for it was a journey to the heartland of Dhamma, also to the best possibility of locating his old comrades, perhaps meeting them, perhaps even Nayana. But he was not sure of the meaning of Dhamma any more. And his friends were probably dead. As Bhima might be soon…. No – stop it! Calm down, he told himself. Plan something instead of waiting for the worst. After all, they were now in the land of Siddarth's awakening and work. This was where he had struggled, alone and confused; this was where he had made a few precious friends, and lost them too. Yet he had survived. He had survived despite being a misfit. Like Upali. When had Upali become a misfit? He had never felt one in Kalinga. And unlike in the Buddha's youth, there was little reason now to not fit, if what Harsha said was true, if the world was indeed being reshaped according to Dhamma.

Except that the reshaping was being done by an all-powerful hand, one that could easily crush those who would not fit.

Like Bhima.

Upali had finally discovered what was worrying him. He had learnt it actually from Loka, quite carelessly, the afternoon before they left for Pataliputra, outside a village where Loka had been summoned to a difficult childbirth.

The girl's brother had come to call them, but when Loka and Upali reached the village they found no welcome from the others. They were not even allowed to enter the girl's hut, though they could hear her screams. Loka pleaded that he had handled many such cases; the baby could be oddly placed, needing to be cut out. The villagers almost pushed the two away and scolded the brother too. The monks gave up finally, but Loka suggested that they wait nearby in case the girl's worsening state brought about a change of mind. So they stopped just outside the edge of the millet fields, out of the deceptive sunlight of the village, to sit on the rocks at the edge of a little stream.

'Sometimes I feel that the more you try to help people, the more they fear you,' muttered Upali. 'This girl will die – and her baby, and many more too – but they'll still thank god they didn't let you touch her!'

Loka smiled. He was a very calm person, except when the topic of Avanti came up. 'But you have to remember the boy who called us. He won't forget if his sister dies.'

They sat in silence for a while. The forest edge was a deep rich enveloping greenness, the darkness shining here and there like randomly scattered emeralds. Upali's feet dangled in the water, he could feel the nibbles of inquisitive fish.

'Upali,' said Loka suddenly, 'I saw a strange thing yesterday. I was hunting for my favourite chaulmogra tree, you know – '

'And?' Upali could not help but look at Loka's feet, at the stumps of his toes, nibbled away long ago. Chaulmogra seeds were what Loka used to treat leprosy and leprosy was what had brought him to the Sangha. His brother had heard Harsha speak of modern medicine in Ujjayani once, and told him about his sick brother. Harsha had taken Loka to a Magadhan doctor practising in Vidisha who treated his affliction with medicines instead of spells. The cure had transformed Loka; he had studied under the doctor, then joined the monastery.

' – and I lost my way a bit, because I met an old tusker who was in a bad mood, rushing around and breaking trees, perhaps in heat. Anyway, the trees and undergrowth were very thick at one point, so thick that I didn't notice an abrupt drop into a small valley. I slipped and rolled down, and when I got up I saw smoke. I pushed towards it and there, in a cave-like space under the cliff, were two furnaces, with two strange earthen pots on them, and a lot of mud heaped nearby. There was a man standing guard and a woman stoking the fire, I think she was Bhima's wife. A soft banging sound was in the air. There was a little altar too with some black lumps, like stone, near it.'

Upali's face was like stone too. 'What kind of pots?' A shadowy black streak shot through the water towards his feet; he jerked them out.

'Couldn't see clearly, but big, and with an outlet near the base, from which something black was dripping out.'

'You didn't speak to them?'

'No, they've never spoken to me, so…. What do you think they were doing?'

'Some ritual, what else? It's good that you didn't speak to them – they might have been upset at your presence.'

They would have definitely been upset. Loka was probably lucky to have escaped with his life. What was Upali to do? Harsha would rush to the authorities. To save lives, he would say. Then the clan would be in trouble. Big trouble. But if this went on to its logical conclusion, the clan would be dead. The cycle was going stronger than he had imagined.

There was a single shrill scream, then many wails, spontaneous and random at first, joining together in a familiar, depressing cadence. Upali and Loka got up and began to walk through the forest silently, away from the village and its dead. Upali felt the darkness reaching out to him, triumphant in victory, taunting him quietly, gleefully, unbearably; till he decided to confront Bhima's Chief then and there. And he had thought that they were beginning to settle down! What a fool he had been.

Again the welcome was cold. Kali was nowhere to be seen; the Chief looked tense. Upali himself was very tense by then, but managed to take the old man aside. Stop it, he said, at once. This was serious, really serious, not like carrying a bamboo spear. It was the end. The Chief just nodded grimly.

The next day the Pataliputra-bound travellers had set off, all greatly excited except for Upali.

'Cheer up,' Harsha urged. 'The story's not over, I know, but don't forget – the Magadhe-Raja liked it. You're going to be a star at Court! And remember, we must stop in Ujjayani to meet Bhima and those poor fellows.'

'Yes. That we must.'

They were fortunate to meet Bhima, fortunate that he was unwell, for the others were away with either the highway repair gangs or the forest clearing ones. The sentences had been handed out. All were to be jailed for a year. It was barbaric, said Harsha disgustedly, though he had expected beheading. It was ridiculously mild, said the Commandant disapprovingly, but that was the new dispensation.

Upali didn't comment but hurried to Bhima, to find him feverish and dull, so dull that Upali panicked and tried to scold him to life and anger. Jungle people could not take imprisonment; many of Bhima's clansmen had been imprisoned in the violent first months of their arrival in Maheshwar, two had wasted away to death, one more had died similarly last year.

But Bhima would not respond. Upali finally gave up, switched to a Kalingan dialect which Harsha and Ananda would not understand, and spoke of even more grim things, of what happened when a tiny village, or even two or ten villages, took up arms against an empire. Of the need to convince his clan before it was too late.

Making iron was death.

Bhima just sat and stared at the cold mud floor for so long that Upali wearied of his own monologue and was on the point of giving up again, when he spoke.

'I know it's hopeless. You don't have to tell me that – I've seen the dead! But there is no future anyway.'

'There is, Bhima! Your children will grow up to be peasants, or they can come to the monastery and learn the skills of the cities – '

'You're right. The future is slavery, many different slaveries, but we have to accept it. The problem, Upali, is that the others still have hope. They still dream of the past, even though it is the most dead of all. That's how they live.'

He looked at Upali for the first time and smiled. But his face was thin, his skin greyer than before; Upali could not smile. Bhima turned away and continued speaking, 'I thought of something else, actually. Sitting here staring at this wall, I thought of another option.'

He was talking to the wall now. 'It's a dream actually. Unreal, but the more I think of it, and I have a lot of time to think of it, I feel it could be real. A real option. Not like iron.' His voice was soft, persuasive, but Upali felt tense, his stomach began to knot. 'I was thinking of how it would be to leave. Quietly. Without fighting. Vanish into the jungle in the middle of the night. Nobody would be able to find us if we go far enough…. It won't be easy, of course – this is not our jungle. But we might succeed. We might even reach…. Anyway.'

The wall made no comment. Nor did Upali, for a few moments. We might even reach? But he couldn't discourage Bhima, not now at least. 'I don't know, Bhima. It seems a little…' crazy? suicidal? '…risky. I need to think about it. But you must speak to your Chief. About the iron. The cycle of violence must stop somewhere.'

They had to leave then, the chariots were waiting outside. They stood up murmuring farewells and Upali realized suddenly that he should be happy. Bhima was against the furnaces! He squatted and hugged him hard, to Ananda's surprise; he couldn't remember Upali ever hugging anybody. Bhima just nodded, but that was all right. He was against the furnaces. He would argue, plead, scold and convince the others to dump their plans. He would try, at least. What if he failed? What if they ignored him? What if he offered his own so-called option and they laughed at him? For it was bizarre. Crazy. Plus, and worst of all, he was behind bars. How much convincing could he achieve from there? Suppose nobody came to visit? Suppose they weren't allowed? Things were hopeless as long as he was behind bars. What was Upali to do?

He would probably have just worried himself sick, all through the journey, if it wasn't for Harsha. Harsha was upset, convinced that Upali had been firing Bhima up with some radical nostalgic pro-Kalinga talk, when what was needed was some very down-to-earth pointing out of the facts. So it was not long before he had dragged him back into their old argument, about the relative criminal stupidity of, on the one hand, a system that enslaved people, treated them like dirt, and expected them to dump their native culture overnight or die again if they did not; and on the other, certain monks who, instead of accepting a situation which could not be corrected and doing their best to ameliorate it, wilfully encouraged the sense of loss, hatred and privation, not to mention atavistic xenophobia, till people were finally pushed over the brink. They barely noticed when Ananda and Nigrodha left them for the other chariot. Chandra remained, but silently.

Upali was brought back to the present by a tiger, peering out from the tall clumps of grass on the near bank, before slipping smoothly into the river. It trod water for a few moments, then struck out upstream. He was surprised. It was broad daylight and the river was crowded. Little fishing catamarans bobbed up and down busily between merchant vessels of all sizes and a few police boats flying the royal blue. That tiger could find itself in trouble quite easily, unlike in Maheshwar where it was the villages that were isolated in a leopard-infested wilderness, or even more in the east – almost uninterrupted tiger country.

It was beginning to look as if Ananda's audience had taken a secret vow of silence. Upali stared about and noticed the Sanchi Thera. He had hardly spoken to Upali so far, though he made it a point to introduce him in glowing terms all around whenever they bumped into each other. It was after one such introduction that the Venerable Jeevana, the old and distinguished Thera of Takshashila, had requested a reading of Upali's story. Upali suddenly wondered whether the Sanchi Thera could help with Bhima – he had an informed air about him, an air of knowing all the strings worth pulling. It was worth trying.

At last the Venerable Jeevana spoke. 'You must be tired, Thera. Perhaps we can continue the reading after the meal?'

Sitting behind Jeevana was another monk who had also been introduced to Upali. As Vipul. Vipul of Takshashila. For whom Upali had a message from the ex-Raja Pururavas. Vipul was young, in his early twenties probably, and looked glum. Suddenly Upali realized what Jeevana had said. 'Oh! I'm sorry, but this is all we have at the moment. I am working on the final draft of the fifth and sixth chapters. The fifth should be ready by the time we reach.'

It was another monk, one Chinu of Topra, who responded and sharply: 'This is all? I mean no offence, Thera, but you have not even reached the Shakyamuni's enlightenment! I understood that this has been your main duty for the past year?'

His bluntness seemed to inspire Jeevana. 'I must say, Thera Upali, I'm disappointed too. I had hoped to make a copy of the volume to take back.'

One Nagarjuna Upagupta, of Mathura, now joined in. 'I was very impressed, Thera, with the details. How do you know so much about Shakya life – politics, technology, military manners and so on?'

Upali was rather relieved by the change of focus. 'Mostly from the suttas themselves. But a little, I suppose, from my experience with today's republics, like the Kalingas. Their political organization was probably similar.' Not their technology though. The furnaces of the Shakyas would have been more like Bhima's secret forest ones. Iron, not steel. The Kalingas had made steel and used much better ore and technology for the purpose, as well as spies to inform them of Magadh's methods. The last months of the republic had been almost devoted to a desperate creation of steel. He could still smell the iron and ore burning together with green sal leaves to alloy them with carbon, creating a cloud of thick black smoke that hung over the city gloomily. Black smoke hung over the forests too where people like Bhima's clan, who had made iron for generations for utensils and hammers, now made desperate and futile battle-axes. Everywhere the furnaces and the smell, and the red slag. Which looked like blood.

'I didn't know you were at Kalinga!' Nagarjuna was saying. 'That's interesting. But I have a question about the Shakyamuni's departure. Why do you interpret it as the result of disgust with his sangha, rather than with the sorrow of life, as commonly held?'

Upali looked at Jeevana. 'Perhaps we can have this discussion after the meal?'

He had to first speak to the Sanchi Thera.

Everybody rose. Upali shoved the folder at Ananda and hurried forward. 'Thera, I wanted to speak to you, if you are free.'

'Of course, come. Let us stretch our legs.' The Sanchi Thera flung his shawl – an elegant quilt of fine cotton, like his robe – over his head. He had apparently put aside his silks for after the journey. He was in a good mood and a couple of monks standing nearby laughed, quite immoderately too Upali thought, when he asked, 'So, Upali, which are you, an eel-wriggler, a sophist, or some other kind of intellectual ruffian?'

'That, Thera, I will leave to you to decide. But I need your advice first....'

It was not long before the Thera's smile vanished. He was shocked, he said at the end of Upali's story, really quite appalled – at the Maheshwar monastery. 'Why are you people involved in police cases? I knew that Harsha was a bit overactive, but this is really too much! And in the resettled villages of all places, when everybody knows how volatile they are!'

You don't know the half of it, thought Upali. He had not mentioned the furnaces. 'Yes, Thera, but what should we do now?'

'Nothing! Or rather, preach Dhamma as you are supposed to do and practise a little worldly detachment, especially when it comes to criminal matters! We should know our limits first – '

'Yes, but do you know somebody who might help?'

It took a while, but the Thera did at last offer some options. 'The police headquarters at Pataliputra, I suppose. And there is the Magadhe-Raja's Court of Grievances – where he, or the crown prince, or a minister, listens to public grievances every fifteen days. Though let me warn you – you yourself are likely to get censured!'

'A public court? For anybody?'

'Yes. It's one of his big passions. But I really think – '

'Thanks a lot, Thera.'

'I would strongly advise – '

'I'll see you later,' Upali turned away, then back. 'By the way, have you heard anything from Devadina?'

'I don't recall the name.'

'The sculptor. Who wants to marry the priestess.'

'Oh, yes. No, he seems to have left Sanchi.'

'What do you mean?'

'They can't find him anywhere.'

'Who's they?'

'The police. They're looking for him – in connection with the murder of Pradyota.'

'What!'

'I don't see why you're surprised – you told them about him yourself!' The Thera suddenly sounded irritated. 'They discovered that he was away from his dormitory that night. He said he was just walking around and thinking of his priestess. But now he's vanished. He's probably gone to see her, but they won't listen to such simple – '

'But – I met the Viceroy just the other day and he never said a word of all this!'

'You met the Viceroy?' The large eyes glared at him.

Upali felt a frog taking up lodgings in his throat.

'Why did you meet him, Upali?'

'I – I chanced upon him at the Sungas. I'd gone about that priestess.'

'I see. He and that ex-Raja seem to be good friends, don't they?'

'Well, I must go....'

But his inquisitor was undeterred. 'Wait a moment – what did the ex-Raja say?'

'Uh – he agreed. To release the priestess.'

'What! I can't believe it! How? What charm did you use?'

'He was quite reasonable.'

'Oh?' The Thera looked disbelieving. 'He's in heavy mourning now, I heard. You know that they are the old rulers, don't you? The family now swears allegiance to Magadh, but....'

'The others will be waiting for me – '

'All this mourning for Pradyota – almost of royal proportions, don't you think? And I still can't believe this business of the girl. What else did he say to you?'

'About what?'

'Anything. By the way, Upali, I must warn you, be careful about Nagarjuna Upagupta of Mathura. I noticed you talking to him earlier. He is a rather strange person.'

'I found Chinu much stranger. He's been staring at me fixedly.'

'Oh, him! Don't worry about him. He's just a spy.'

'A spy? A *spy*? Of whom? Magadh?'

'Who else?' The Thera was amused, as if Magadh had sole proprietorship.

'How do you know?'

The Thera shrugged, and Upali, though more than glad to seize a topic as distant from Ujjayani as possible, was genuinely annoyed. 'A Thera a spy! This is surely the limit?'

'Why are you so shocked? Spies are a part of government. An essential part.'

'When they spy on enemies, perhaps. When you need them to watch your own people, it becomes crazy, twisted, Kautilyan!'

The Thera looked shocked. 'Upali! Lord Kautilya was one of the greatest statesmen ever – and I thought you were a man of the world! Do you think this empire was possible without Kautilya? So huge, so enormously diverse, all kinds of people with all kinds of backgrounds, ruled by so many different kings not so long ago. Kings whose families are still alive. It's difficult to kill *every*body.' He sounded as if he had tried. 'How do you hold such a vast empire? No army is big enough!'

'And why are they paying fat salaries to all those thousands of bureaucrats and police – you trip over them wherever you turn – if they cannot keep an eye on things? And why monks? It's not our problem whether empires are held or not! As it is, people are calling us the minions of Magadh!'

'Who said that?' asked the Thera sharply.

'I don't remember now.'

'It is true that Magadh rules primarily through its bureaucrats. But how do you ensure that they work well? How do you ensure that they do not laze, loot, misuse their powers, commit treason? That's why you need spies. Just honest and patriotic citizens who know the importance of strong government. Who speak to people on the road, in the market, in the tavern and brothel even, and report on their problems and how they are being addressed. Who seek out sedition. Who continuously test the loyalty of officer, minister, general, viceroy and prince. It is amazing when you think of all the work, responsibilities and dangers that face the humble, loyal, very meagrely-paid spy!'

The Thera mopped his brow passionately with a large linen handkerchief.

Upali wiped his own with both hands. 'I've never heard such rubbish in my life, Thera. Don't you ever ask yourself about the need for an empire maintained by violence, where the rulers neither know nor trust their subjects?'

'It is in the nature of kings to seek kingdoms and then to expand them. Even the Shakyamuni had noted this. If we were not ruled by Magadh, it would be somebody else.'

'Anyway – '

'But perhaps you preferred the Kalinga republic? A beautiful system, but old-fashioned, surely? And they don't really work, do they? The day of the republic is over.'

'Thanks to Magadh,' retorted Upali. And its many more furnaces. Better furnaces, better ore, better magic too, according to the Kalingas, who had spent a fortune trying to find out and emulate everything. The basic elements were known – furnaces, hand-operated bellows, anvils, hammers, tongs, blocks of wrought iron, cast iron and steel, clay, rice ashes, leaves, charcoal, phosphorous, polishing stones. The rajas of Tosali experimented desperately with everything and with quenching methods too – they heard that Magadhan steel was quenched in secret – so they tried water, milk, curds, wax, blood, oil, brine, and even, so Upali had heard, living slaves. As the war progressed and defeat became a certainty, many of them still blamed their steel, but Upali disagreed – he had seen village smiths putting together steel out of just local earths, sal leaves, a hammer and a strong arm, and he had seen the ridiculous prices that merchants were willing to pay for it. Kalingan metal was clearly second to none. It was not the quality of Magadhan steel that won the war, but the quantity.

But the Thera was shaking his head. 'No, no, Upali – thanks to themselves *and* Magadh. All republics fall first from within. As your own story shows. And if it was not Magadh it would be Kosala or Avanti or whatever, so many possibilities! The Kalingas have suffered terribly, I know. Terribly. But their grandchildren will thank Magadh, mark my words!'

'For the death of their grandparents? That would be very generous of them. In any case, neither you nor I will be there to check it out.' Upali stopped at the stairs that went below the deck, 'I'll see you later.'

'Remember, Upali, be careful. Especially of Nagarjuna. And the monks from Kashi, though I don't know the details. But one can expect something from Kashi. That country has an affinity for the bizarre.'

'I'm from Kashi myself,' said Upali.

'Really? You don't look like a Kashi brahmin.'

'I'm a monk, not a brahmin.'

He washed up still wondering where Devadina was, and joined the others for lunch, sitting as usual next to the nuns of the Ujjayani convent, for Harsha was an old acquaintance of the head, one Therii Vrinda, who had confirmed Sutanuka's presence at the convent. But worriedly: 'It's a little awkward, for her and us. She has a powerful position at her temple, but public respect for her will collapse if it gets out that she has left. We will try our best to protect her, of course. But women come to us normally with the sanction of their family.'

Both the Therii and her colleague were tall, light-coloured, clearly high-born. Probably daughters or daughters-in-law of wealthy merchants or the rare liberal-minded aristocrat. Probably widows as well. Nayana had looked so different in the same robes. Short, dark, sharp-featured. Beautiful. A widow too, whose husband died of snakebite on the fifth day of marriage, but who shrank from the primary duty of kshatriya widowhood which entailed burning alive on his funeral pyre. She had run away instead. And turned up one day at the monastery. There were only men there at the time but she refused to accept refusal and argued at length about the need for nuns – so articulately that Upali had begun to feel only the Buddha himself could have kept her out, and that too on one of his good days. Seeing her, two more women joined that year. It turned out to be very good for the monastery, though not for Upali's peace of mind.

'Upali?' Nagarjuna had finished his meal and had come to sit next to him, clearly with a purpose. 'I was amazed to learn that you worked in the Kalinga republic. I would be grateful if you could tell us something of what happened.'

'What happened?'

'Of the war. I know that many lives were lost, and obviously that Magadh won. But nothing of the details.'

'Surely we've all heard enough of the war?' It was the old Thera Jeevana.

Nagarjuna ignored him. 'Did you actually see a battle, Upali?'

Upali looked down and made little circles with his finger on his banana leaf plate. 'I'd come to Tosali to meet the Chief. It was – '

'A long time ago,' interrupted the Sanchi Thera. 'I'm sure Upali has forgotten much of it. And perhaps it is best forgot.'

'Best for whom?' asked Upali.

There was a pause, broken by the Therii Vrinda. 'Do tell us, Upali. I'm absolutely ignorant about the whole business.'

But Jeevana suddenly snapped: 'Not now, Therii! Let us eat in silence!'

He was obeyed, nobody uttered another syllable through the meal, but the silence was heavy, embarrassed, painful. Perhaps they were right. Kalinga was best forgot, till another Kalinga, which would also be best forgot.

But Upali could see himself clearly, standing on that hillock outside Tosali above the last battle, his eyes smarting a little in the pall of smoke, though the furnaces were at last cold. He had reached Tosali in time for the Chief's last public audience. Magadh already had nearly half the nation. And more than half the Kalinga army was gone. The land had been laid waste by both sides, villages pillaged, fields turned into ash. The war moved southwards and before it fled thousands of people, a great, sad, ramshackle tide, dragging children and belongings with them, losing them little by little; the forests were too thick, the swamps too frequent, the river rafts too tremulous. Many were overtaken by the Magadhans, herded into temporary fenced camps, the men chain-ganged into portage or road-making, the women to the kitchens or army brothels.

But some outstripped the imperial cavalry and reached Tosali, to find the city gates barricaded against them. They filled the fields, orchards, villages and beaches all around, a dazed, hungry and weeping mob unable to forget what they had seen and what they had lost. Then, as the Maurya swept closer and closer, they began to flee south again. Not the Kalingas though. The rajas met in the palace of the Chief and decided to fight to the finish. Upali had hoped they would sue for peace, but it was too late when hundreds of thousands were already dead. But earlier, when the fighting had begun far to the north, it had been too early.

Patrols were sent out to confiscate all foodstocks and set fire to villages, so that the Magadhans found nothing to sustain them. Some peasants began wailing and fighting, and had to be beaten unconscious before the soldiers' work was done. Then Tosali closed her gates and the army took position outside, at the entrance to the valley. To wait for death.

Death took its time. A look-out was posted on the hill where Upali and a few others stood, and it was more than an hour before he shouted. Nobody else could see anything, but he started to bang his drum and raced slitheringly down the dew-wet slopes. It was the blue-grey hour, when the earth was fresh, cool, at its most beautiful, but Upali was hot and feverish. The Kalingas in contrast looked relaxed; the humiliating retreats were over, they would not retreat any more. The archers were at the forefront and ready. The bow and arrow they used was Magadhan in origin, and the style as well – the arcs of laminated layers of horn were huge, nearly seven feet in height, held in place by one outstretched foot of the archer who amazingly balanced himself like a dancer on the other, while drawing back the taut and heavy string with both arms. The arrow was known to go completely through two armoured soldiers at once. So Upali had heard. He waited on his hill, peering into the distance with his fellows, beyond the grassy plain, still damp after the torrential rains of the previous month, till at last they made out a flowing grey stream in the hills far away. Then, even as he squinted, it flowed evenly out onto the plain, and rapidly widened into a sea, closer and closer, till he could see thousands of marching, almost running, foot-soldiers. Behind them was a long double line of elephants, then rows and rows of cavalry, all racing towards Tosali.

Now he could hear Magadh. The boom of giant war drums kept time with shouts from thousands of throats, and the resultant sound was monstrous, hungry and hate-filled. Another roar went up and he realized it was the war cry of the Kalingas below – this was hate too, but mixed with defiance and paeans to the gods. Both were ugly, though, because just below the bravado was fear, the terror of men who were lost now, who had to kill to live, who knew these could be the last moments of their lives. Were they wondering at the futility of it all? Or did they still believe in their nations, their gods, the rule of their rulers?

By now Upali could see the faces of the Magadhans, for the front ranks had stopped only some hundreds of metres away. Suddenly, without any fuss or warning, torches began to fly from the backs of their elephants, trailing thick black smoke and landing squarely in the middle of the Kalingas. Then the archers began to perform, and here the Kalingas followed suit. Bronze shields crumpled like dried leaves on both sides. Then the ranks closed and the swordsmen took over.

The choreographed part of the battle was soon over. All decorum vanished and it became many beasts, rampaging wildly on their own, converging and convulsing all over the plain and beyond. Yet within the chaos could be seen superhuman strength and commitment; warriors spinning heavy maces around as if they were straws, except that the heads knocked to the ground stayed there; the nearly-dead spending their last breath on a last kill. Blinkered elephants trumpeted unhappily but did not resist the gentle urging to mash people to pulp; horses reared and trampled agilely over the dead and the wounded. But the viewers above were not connoisseurs of war-play. What they saw was a vision of hell, a ghoulish mockery of everything that was good and sensible about the world. Most, like Upali, could not move a muscle.

He did not remember the day passing. Every single Kalinga had to be killed, so it took a while, late into the night, or perhaps it was the next day, for the sky was black with smoke and the ground lit up by many fires. Finally it was done. From somewhere drums took over, beating a heavy tattoo of victory over the groans and the screams.

Upali's gaze was drawn to a great armoured tusker halfway across the plain, exactly like the others except that it was the centre of a growing concentricity of soldiers, horses and other elephants, as cry after cry rose into the air. Victory to Magadh! Victory to His Sacred Majesty, the Magadhe-Raja, conqueror of Kalinga! Victory! A man on the elephant stood up and raised a hand in acknowledgement. The uproar swelled, a magnificent effort of drums, dry throats and colossal relief, deafening but still unable to drown the silence of thousands of corpses, heaped up here and there like dolls poured down from some height, others half buried under the bloody slush, but everywhere torn, mangled, undignified and inhuman.

Carts trundled up to lift the wounded and sort the dead. Sorting away furiously were also hundreds of Magadhan soldiers, tottering in exhaustion, yet frantically tearing off rings, earrings, every bit of gold on each corpse before someone else got there....

Upali breathed deeply, to flush the smoke from his lungs, stirred the congealed rice and lentils on his plate and began to eat. Was he really wiser after seeing the war? Or was he just afraid? Or were both the same?

Most of the others were assembled and waiting when he finished. He headed towards them reluctantly, to be hailed first by the Sanchi Thera and motioned to his side.

'Upali – those silk chits you found in Pradyota's room and then lost – do you remember what they said?'

'Actually they were with me all the while, tucked into my waistband. I met the Viceroy in Ujjayani, in Sutanuka's temple, and gave them to him. I couldn't understand them.'

The Thera looked annoyed. 'You seem to spend a lot of time with the Viceroy!'

'Thera,' intervened a low voice. It was the monk Vipul. Upali stared at him, but he was looking at the Thera. 'Thera, I am Vipul of Takshashila. I wanted to offer my condolences on the death of Thera Pradyota – '

'Thank you.' The Sanchi Thera sounded curt.

'How has his family taken it?'

'His family? Do you know them?'

'No, but he had spoken of them. He left Takshashila to be nearer them.'

'Really? Well, Upali here has just met them. He knows their condition better.'

Vipul turned to Upali. 'Do you, Thera?' There were dark circles under his grey-green eyes. It was a sensitive, even beautiful, face. And head. Without a single blemish, without the awesome ridges, dents and stains that marked most bald pates.

The Sanchi Thera abruptly ended the conversation. 'Everybody is waiting for you, Upali.'

Jeevana started the proceedings, and very formally: 'Bhiksus, I would like to express our great gratitude to Thera Upali and his young student, for doing us the honour of presenting this valuable composition. It was a great delight.' Ananda scowled at the flowery language, convinced he was sneering at them, but Upali nodded. 'Some of us would like to ask questions, if it is permitted?'

Upali nodded again and Nagarjuna raised his hand. 'My question was already asked. About why the Shakyamuni left his home.' .

'Yes,' interposed Jeevana, who had apparently appointed himself master of ceremonies, 'according to you, Thera Upali, the Buddha left in confusion. And with some antipathy to his family. But that is not what the suttas say. Most say that he was disturbed by the sight of an ill man, an old man, a dead man and an ascetic, and so struck by the sorrow and transitory nature of life evident in the first three, that he decided that the fourth was the answer.'

'I have mentioned that it was impossible that the Buddha could have been so protected,' said Upali. 'And the fact is that he left his sangha. If he felt they were acting nobly and true, why would he have left them? His first disillusionment was with his people. These are later and simplistic interpretations of his sorrow. After all, two hundred and fifty years have passed, misunderstanding is very possible.'

'Two hundred and fifty years of misunderstanding, but now you can see through all the simplistic interpretations, Upali? Don't you feel you have insulted the legend?' Rice and lentils had not softened Chinu.

Upali glared at the spy. 'The legend is not something sacred – to be insulted. It is an account extracted from the suttas. And the suttas contradict one another at times – anybody can see that – for example, even in the names of people, like his wife, who is given four different names in different places. The suttas are inter-pretations of the Buddha's life and message, and open to error both because they were mostly composed after the Shakyamuni's death, and also because of the subjective beliefs of the monks. My story is, of course, in the same situation.'

Jeevana was stern. 'It is really very critical of the legend, Upali. And this is the first such record. Don't you think it should be the one which all of us are familiar with – an account, in prose form, of the suttas?'

'Then what is the need for it at all? The suttas are being put down as they are.'

'The purpose should be simply to remove the music and the poetic licence, so that the reader thinks seriously about what he may have been thoughtlessly singing.'

Nagarjuna raised a polite hand. 'Where did you find reference to these Tara and Mir, Thera? I've never heard of them. And to his military experience, and his stay in Banaras?'

'The suttas say that Siddarth was raised by a servant, that there were major slave escapes in his youth, also a rape by escaped slaves of some Shakya noblewomen. And being raised as a raja must have meant some experience of warfare. And he was very familiar with Banaras. I have tried to bring all of it to life.'

'So the details are all fiction then? I thought so!' Chinu was pleased. 'The suttas don't mention any unhappiness during his youth either, do they?'

'Look – you can believe, if you like, that Siddarth was blissful till he saw the four "signs" and then suddenly struck by sorrow. I myself cannot accept that he could get disgusted with his whole life in a moment, and dream up his ideas of reason, tolerance and non-violence from the air! He must have started to think about these things even earlier.... I've filled the gaps, that's all.'

Chinu was silent, the others looked perplexed. Except for Vipul. The young monk's eyes were clouded and unseeing. Vipul, Upali suddenly realized, was in mourning.

A young monk at the back raised his hand. 'I am Prashant of Mathura. Thera, you say you have only filled in the gaps. But what of your omissions? On what basis do you ignore all the miraculous episodes in the life of the Shakyamuni? His unique birth? The heights of meditation he achieved as a toddler? Are you also going to ignore his defeat of Mara? The intervention of – '

'I've mentioned the miracles.'

'Only to mock them. Perhaps because you have never witnessed a miracle yourself? But we all know that the Buddha was an exceptional being – is it not natural that the gods realized this, even before he himself? That they saw his pureness, enhanced through each and every one of his lives, and showered him with their blessings at every step?'

'I can only say, brother,' Upali spoke slowly, 'that I try to follow the Buddha's own example in my work. He ignored both miracles and gods.'

A familiar voice said, 'In which process, Upali, you are turning the monks who carefully documented his life and work, long before you were even born, into liars or fools. And degenerate ones – with your outrageous talk of wet dreams!'

Upali's heart sank. The sun was behind the speaker and his face could not be seen clearly, but... yes, it was old Mahanta of Sarnath. Luckily, Jeevana interrupted to address Prashant. 'Brother,

I am surprised at you. What do you mean by the Buddha's pureness, enhanced through every life? It sounds like the brahminical soul! The Buddha's own teaching was of anaatmavad – the absence of soul. The suttas mention this many times. You agree, I hope?'

The young monk looked uncomfortable, then glanced at Nagarjuna who asked softly, 'If I may speak, Thera? Is it really possible that each one of us can go through so many lives without retaining something, something individual, something unique? It is the eternal essence of the person, which in Nirvana becomes conscious, enlightened and completely free.'

Jeevana was even softer. 'Thera, the Buddha's Nirvana is freedom from rebirth. You are bringing in the soul by the backdoor – you are speaking of Moksha, the union of atman with Brahman! The Buddha's message was simple. Life is sorrow, and living it in ignorance only brings more sorrow in every succeeding life. One can escape sorrow only through the Middle Path, and through the Eight Fold actions. With this comes awakening and finally freedom! All this eternal essence business belongs to the brahmins, not the Buddha!'

'Awakening of what? Freedom for what? Not for the body, obviously, for you are liberated from all bodies. It is freedom for something else. I do not think there is a great difference between what you said and what I did,' said Nagarjuna. He was really a brave man, for Jeevana was furious and getting furiouser by the minute. 'All I have added is that when you achieve Nirvana, the release from the sorrows of rebirth, you are also simultaneously achieving a consciousness and a unity with the ultimate essence of the world – a freedom from distraction, a seeing of the world as it is. Seeing through the maya-jal – the web of illusion – to the real truth, instead of getting engrossed in the surface manifestations – whether sorrow, joy, greed, anything. This world around us is an illusion, a pond whose surface is ruffled by continuous winds. The disturbed surface is where you see beautiful, sad or strange visions one after the other. Nirvana is "no wind". To see the reality within.

Nirvana is freedom, the realization of truth, the truth which is within and without, which is the essence of man and of creation. Upali has mentioned how the Upanishads influenced the Shakyamuni. The fact is that the Shakyamuni took the wisdom of the Upanishads ahead.'

The Sanchi Thera seemed to want to make peace. 'Nagarjuna, you're going too far – '

But Jeevana was shouting, 'I've never heard such appalling lies! Thera Nagarjuna, now I believe the rumours that you are also worshipping your Cowherd God as the Buddha!'

'The Black One was a leader of the old Mathura-folk; he led them through many trials, showed them the good pasture lands, helped them live in peace with their neighbours – if you hear his stories, monks, you will see for yourself how similar his aims were to those of Shakyamuni – his methods were a little different, of course.'

'Thera, please calm down,' said the Sanchi Thera for Jeevana was looking a little purple. 'Nagarjuna, let us leave this topic for the moment – '

'I would like to say something, if I may,' said a new voice. It belonged to a tall old man of autocratic mien who had not been introduced to Upali. Jeevana looked, if possible, even more upset. 'I am Keshav Seshadri, Thera of Nalanda.' That was the reason – Nalanda, the headquarters of the Mahasanghikas. What was their Thera doing so far from home?

'I want to tell you of one of our monks, Ramu. A quiet boy, who displayed no special promise when he joined us many years ago. Then one day, about two years ago, something happened to him. A meditation session was over, we all rose, but he stayed in padmasan, eyes closed, murmuring something. We waited, finally someone called him, then touched him, he was hot with fever. But he was far away; he came out of it nearly an hour later, smiling quietly, speaking of a wonderful experience. That was all he would say – it was wonderful. He began to meditate longer every day, he reduced his food to nothing on most days. He became thin, but he said he felt better than ever before. And he helped people. Continuously. It was a girl first, the daughter of one of our servants – she was ill, but he visited her and the next day she was fine. People began to flock to the monastery to meet him, he would stay up nights to attend to their problems – a true monk was not interested in his own salvation, he said, but that of the world. Then one morning recently he said he had to go. A few days later he developed a fever and passed away.'

Like the Sanchi monk Pradyota, only less violently. And they had servants in Nalanda.

'On the last day, I heard voices in his room. I went in, but Ramu was alone and smiling, radiantly happy. "See there!" he pointed to the window. I turned and saw a bright light, though it was very early, just before dawn. Like a milky sun, it looked so pure. The light faded as we watched and Ramu spoke. "It was the Buddha," he said. "The Lokottara himself! My body was burning, and then suddenly I felt this cool hand on my brow. He was there! He embraced me and said he waited for me to join him. He awaits me!"'

The audience seemed spellbound; a few even bent their heads over clasped hands.

'When we went to him the next morning, he was smiling still, but dead. It was a terrible loss, as if the Buddha himself had left us.' He looked all around. 'And the light. I saw it with my own eyes. It was... different.'

Ananda was impressed too, though he could not see how all this had thrown any light on the earlier dispute. But Jeevana did not wait for even a second. 'Thank you for that touching but rather exaggerated account. We would not have expected anything less from you. But for the moment we would rather stay with the Buddha's own explanation of true monk-hood.'

'I only speak of what I saw.'

'But what you see is obviously what you believe, my dear fellow. Your poor monk was delirious, I do not blame him. But you yourself? I can appreciate the beauty of a sunrise and go about my work. Or

I can take the name of the Buddha and then imagine that what I see is unusual, inexplicable, miraculous, or in your words, Lokottara!'

'You are insulting me, Thera.'

This was becoming impossible, thought Upali. Soon everybody will be rolling on the floor at one another's throats. Or at least at Jeevana's. The old man was now glowering at him. 'Thera Upali. You should correct that part about the Buddha being impressed by the Upanishads.'

Upali was stumped for a second, long enough for Jeevana to lose his temper again. 'Thera Upali! Do you disagree?'

'Actually Thera... what I said was that his was a time of many new ideas, among which was also this idea of souls being reborn repeatedly and seeking union with an eternal Brahma. He was in a sense influenced by all – '

'Influenced by all!' said Mahanta. 'Upali's Buddha is a confused fool parroting whatever was said around him!'

'That's not true – ' protested Upali.

'Perhaps it is not deliberate,' conceded Mahanta. 'Perhaps it is only your stupidity.' He turned to the others. 'But just imagine, brothers, if everybody started this kind of imaginative interpretation, what will happen to the legacy so carefully protected this far? It will be torn apart – destroyed! We'll be left with only interpretations – each one more adventurous than the last!'

A blue-green burst of feathers took off from the bank, followed by another, distracting Upali. He was grateful. Take a deep breath, he told himself. There was no point getting angry; also, he tended to get confused when angry.

'Who will respect the Buddha if he really was, as this account would have it, a meek, almost confused and spineless personality through his youth? Upali seems to think the Buddha had no original ideas of his own!'

The Sanchi Thera opened his mouth but Upali spoke first. 'It was the Buddha himself who said that everything has a cause, that you can understand and even change things if you understand their cause. And the fact that his ideas were born of his time does not lessen his own wisdom. People live whole lives in much simpler situations without understanding anything around them. But his was a unique time and he was a unique man.'

He paused. But Mahanta had closed his eyes, as if he had done his best and now it was up to the others to save the Buddha. The Sanchi Thera looked embarrassed. Nagarjuna was watching the river, Jeevana was watching Nagarjuna. Ananda was just wondering whether he should oblige his teacher, when the young Prashant saved him the trouble. 'What was so unique about the time?'

'It sounds mundane now, but I think it was iron. And before that, rice. Jungle became rice land, cattle-herders became peasants or landed gentry, hunters became slaves. "What is an Arya without his cow?" was one of the great rhetorical questions of the day but the truth was the Arya was probably no longer an Arya, if he had ever been one, but he was living longer, and denser. For the new rice-based diet allowed mothers to wean children faster and conceive again. Conversely, the herds were shrinking, thanks to the lack of pasture, the cat-infested jungles and the gigantic sacrifices. Cities were rising and expanding carelessly, and within them, cheek by explosive jowl, were colossal differences in incomes and culture. Individualism was growing. Sanghas were torn apart by private wealth and interests; by each other too. Weapons were improving, thanks to iron. Aggression became more profitable.'

Or more desperate, like Bhima's furnaces in the Maheshwar jungle. Perhaps they had been found by now. And the villagers arrested. Or perhaps the work was still on. Heating, melting, hammering, heating again, hammering again, into the shapes admired and worshipped since before the Buddha.

Upali looked away, back at the kingfishers' bank. 'The changes made some people think, gave them the courage to think, to look everything in the face. Ritual looked irrelevant, whether Vedic sacrifice or the old fertility cults. And once the questioning began there was no stopping it. As a result you have all these new ideas, including both the Upanishads and the many anti-brahminical philosophies. Philosophizing became such a passion that it still continues today, as we all know, but in a withered way, more an intellectual pastime, a form of erudite exhibitionism, rather than the genuine search that it was in the Buddha's life.'

Jeevana simply ignored the entire speech. 'So then, Upali, you actually agree with Nagarjuna's nonsense, that the Buddha's enlightenment was the Upanishadic Moksha?'

'No. Not at all, but – '

But the Sanchi Thera suddenly murmured, 'Of course, Upali's account does make *sense*. As the Magadhe-Raja himself thought. He liked it.'

The silence that greeted this was complete, almost stunned. It was as if his words were a giant mace, swinging around and sending every head crashing into mute shock one after the other. Mahanta, whose mouth was open, closed it abruptly; the others just stared at Upali. Ananda was pleased with the rather confused awe in their eyes, but wished Upali could rise to the occasion with more dignity.

He almost spluttered instead. 'What the Magadhe-Raja thinks is not the issue! The fact is that there's hardly any difference between your Nirvana and Nagarjuna's – except that he talks of enlightenment as a freed essence. The Buddha himself probably did not take a stand on such metaphysical issues. When he was asked about the soul, he said he saw it as the sum of the feelings, emotions, opinions, and other mental activities of a person. He said nothing about its eternal character. Nor did he speak of rebirth or heaven. He was not interested in eternalities!'

Prashant was smiling slightly. 'You seem to have no fundamental beliefs yourself, Thera. Everything was born here, or there, or from something or another – you seem to know nothing eternal, universal, nothing that is the truth. You don't even uphold Nirvana! What are you striving for then? Why are you a monk?'

Ananda scowled at him. Upali himself looked taken aback. 'It's just a matter of trying to understand, of trying to maintain a rational and historical approach to life....'

'Of being an intellectual, in an ivory tower existence! Which Kalinga fostered, I suppose, by being so backward that any

Magadhan was automatically a great thinker, however fanciful his ideas!' Mahanta had recovered.

'Thera, my ideas are based on the hard facts we have. The differences between the stories of the suttas and my own are actually few, much fewer, for example, than the differences between the practice of the Sangha today, and that in the Shakyamuni's own day – according to the suttas!'

'There is no change in practice among true followers,' returned Mahanta. 'The problem is that there are many who call themselves followers but are not so. Like the monks who are really prosperous agriculturists, as at Maheshwar. Or the ones who consume flesh!'

Harsha opened a shocked mouth but Upali was quicker. 'Where did the Buddha preach against eating flesh? He was against killing, yes, but he accepted whatever was put in the alms-bowl, whether flesh or stale or nothing. In fact, the suttas say that the Buddha's last meal was a dish of pork, offered by the woodcutter Chunda.'

'That I do believe is a lie, made up by those who crave flesh.'

'Really? So some of the sutta composers were liars? Isn't this your personal interpretation, Thera? What some might even call fanciful?' Mahanta remained silent. Upali looked at the others. 'And what of the fear of the truth that you see in the Sangha today? Do you remember the Buddha ever being as scared? He spoke against war all his life, but here we are scared to even remember Kalinga, leave aside condemning it! Tell me – how many of the Sangha condemned the war?'

There was a long pause. Mahanta looked at Jeevana, but he was engrossed in the river. Mahanta finally had to say very coldly, 'You know very well that nobody here is for war.'

'But nobody is against war either, correct? It's not our business, correct? But it was the Buddha's, that's all I'm saying.' It was mine too, he added silently, and what did I do? Upali turned away to the river himself, and saw dark suffocating clouds of smoke and his old friend Narayan for the hundredth time, vanishing into the inferno. And the shocked faces of the soldiers.

Nobody argued with him any more, perhaps because he was now the royal protégé. Jeevana instead went back to his old foe. 'Nagarjuna, as far as I can make out, you are following precisely in the path of the so-called Mahasanghikas, which resulted in their expulsion from the Sangha in the Second Council many years ago!' This with a glare at the Nalanda Thera.

'I believe, Thera,' said Nagarjuna, 'that the expulsion took place because of their indiscipline and worldliness. They were accused of accepting money instead of alms-food, of eating more than once a day, and of following improper procedures at meetings. The first two things, I may mention, are the open practice of many monasteries today. Do you accuse them too of being with the Mahasanghikas?'

Upali wondered how many of the monks were waiting, like him, for the discussion to end.

Not all apparently, for another joined in at this moment, a smiling middle-aged man of shabby attire. 'Brothers, I am Deepak of Kushinara, and I have been listening to all this with interest. And dismay. For the more I hear, the more I see diversion from Dhamma and Vinaya. We of the Kushinara monastery live exactly as laid down in the Vinaya. We beg for all our meals in the town, a practice that I believe most others have discarded. And we move around through the year, preaching the Way, returning only in the four months of the rains, when we meditate.'

'But where does your Way lead?' It was a blunt question and the face that asked it was also rather blunt and forthright. It was the Therii Vrinda and she was smiling a little. 'To Thera Nagarjuna's liberation of the essence, or Thera Jeevana's freedom from rebirth, or the miraculous public salvation that Thera Keshav spoke of?'

But Jeevan cut her off. 'Enough! There is one Middle Way. Obviously its practise does not include the production of wealth, in the style of the Maheshwar monks. Nor, of course, do its ideas include those of Nalanda or Mathura or any others like them!'

Harsha burst out, 'I am tired of this accusation, Thera Jeevana! We are not producing wealth – at least not for ourselves! We have taken up agricultural work as an education for the people.'

'But it is definitely moving away from the Buddha's teachings,' said Jeevana. 'He directed the Sangha to live off alms. The monks were to be aloof from economic activity, their task was solely to seek Nirvana for themselves and preach Dhamma to others.'

'That is not our understanding. Living off alms was a way of inculcating humility and also of breaking varna barriers and food taboos. And it was not economic activity that the Buddha condemned, but the ownership of wealth,' Harsha's eyes bulged dangerously, 'but his Dhamma was first about changing society. People in Maheshwar need agricultural education for their survival. Taking it up also helps them to move away from barbarian beliefs and practices. That is why we are involved in it. And our own monastery production, though small, regularly helps those in distress. And let me say finally that I see no crime in production. No, I see virtue!'

The boat heaved a little and Harsha rocked substantially as he finished. But it was well-spoken, Upali had to admit, very well going by the expressions of Jeevana and Mahanta. Deepak of Kushinara took the chance to continue his self-introduction. 'We at Kushinara also do not subscribe to the Magadhan practice of funding monasteries. The Buddha had specifically said that the Sangha was not to be involved in money.'

'Practice has changed, Deepak,' said Jeevana. 'Because the conditions have changed, the cities have changed, the responsibilities on the shoulders of the Sangha have expanded – and, in some cases, due to confusion. But ideas are constant, they have to be!' He glared at Nagarjuna, 'There is no choice in the matter. Otherwise the Sangha is doomed!'

It was a good apocalyptical one on which to close, and Upali was grateful that Nagarjuna remained silent. But Keshav Seshadri of Nalanda jumped back in. 'My understanding of the Second Council is different. It was called by the Thera Mahadeva to criticize those who dominated the Sangha at the time. They were accused of not fully having conquered passion, of even having wet dreams. They were also accused of not being omniscient, of being still subject to doubts, and of having gained their knowledge through others rather than through their own experience. I do not know how true these accusations were. But the result was the expulsion of Mahadeva and his disciples.'

Jeevana was icy. 'That is a version proffered by the blasphemers themselves. Do not forget that my own teacher Thera Nagesha of Takshashila was taught by the Thera Yasa, one of the most respected Theras present at the – '

Upali felt like clutching his head. Luckily Harsha interrupted here. 'Theras, I can't understand why we are arguing like this. These differences have been around for a very long time, and not surprisingly, for the Buddha himself said that Vinaya and Dhamma were to be our guides. Obviously then, everybody has been trying to interpret them to the best of their ability. I think we should respect each other's efforts, even if we do not agree with them. After all, this is a vast land and we may never see each other again – I don't think we need attempt to unify our practice, because it really isn't possible!'

'And yet impossible things do happen!' beamed the Sanchi Thera. 'Who knows what amazement awaits us in Pataliputra? We are fortunate to have a Magadhe-Raja immense in both faith and courage, who sees himself as a proponent of Dhamma, a Turner of the Wheel. A Chakravartin, as the Buddha himself had acclaimed.'

This was too much. 'I don't think the Buddha ever spoke of a Raja as a Chakravartin,' said Upali. 'He was very critical of kingship – in his quiet manner. His idea of the first king was of a Mahasamatta, a Supreme Elect.'

The Thera still smiled, benevolence incarnate. 'And perhaps you feel that it makes no difference for the Sangha if the king is a believer of Dhamma, or a non-believer – like the former Kalinga Chief?'

Upali was silent. The late Chief had not actively opposed the Sangha but he had not been particularly amenable either.

The Thera looked smug. 'I think we are fortunate. Especially because the Magadhe-Raja has committed himself to strengthening the Sangha.'

Deepak smiled too. 'Is that what he is doing?'

'Why else do you think he's called this Congress?' glared Jeevana.

They all stared at him. Upali suddenly saw how long his shadow was; the day was nearly over. He got up, bowed and made his way out of the throng and down to the lower deck. Ananda followed. The others watched them go silently, and as Upali settled down before his writing board, he realized that it was not just him. Everybody was worried – why had the Magadhe-Raja called this Congress?

Two fishermen were bobbing up and down in a tiny catamaran, holding up a giant mahseer that gleamed like gold in the setting sun; a crew member on the deck below was waxing horrified at the price. Upali and Ananda, who had come up to stretch their legs after a day of furious non-stop work, watched the excited exchange for a while, then walked to the back where dolphins were leaping out of the water in the wash.

'Who are the Mahasanghikas, Master?' asked Ananda. A big brown dolphin leapt up almost level with him; it turned and smiled. It knew the answer and even found it funny.

Upali was staring at the sunset. 'Monks who were expelled many years ago, long before I was born, from the Sarnath monastery. They were accused of preaching that the Buddha was a god. They also believed in an immortal soul – quite similar to what that monk Nagarjuna spoke of. And they were unrepentant, insisted on calling themselves the Mahasangha – the *great* Sangha – and set up base elsewhere, some at Nalanda. But the really interesting thing is how many others have veered around to their views today, in different ways, almost without realizing it.'

'But what's wrong with it? So what if people do think he was a god?'

'Well, I'm sure the people on this boat can argue this for days, Ananda, but I think it destroys the very core of the Buddha's teaching. Some people say that core is non-violence, others say compassion, others freedom from rebirth. I think it is humanity. Man as the measure of the world. The realization that there are no gods, no supernatural forces taking responsibility for everything, no magical formulae. We have to deal with the world ourselves, and we have to do it standing straight, not prostrate in front of an altar.' Ananda was staring at him. 'It's a frightening idea. You, Ananda, who are so conscious of gods, ghosts, goblins and all kinds of spirits, have no idea how frightening the world is without them.'

They jerked back to avoid a splash by another dolphin and almost stepped into Vipul. Upali had forgotten all about the message from ex-Raja Pururavas. And he wished he hadn't remembered it now. But he had promised.

'Greetings, Thera.' Vipul's voice rasped as if he had a sore throat.

'Greetings.' Upali turned to Ananda, 'Will you go ahead? I'm just coming.'

He waited for Ananda to vanish; Vipul just stared downwards, his shoulders sagging, apparently comparing his own sandalled feet with the bare toes before him. 'I have a message for you, Vipul. From the ex-Raja of Avanti.'

'Yes?'

'Just that things are fine. Things are as before. And he looks forward to hearing from you.'

'As before. Yes.'

Upali suddenly realized that the young monk was close to tears. 'Vipul – are you ill?'

'No, no.'

'What's wrong then?' Upali placed a hand on the other's shoulder. It was trembling slightly. 'Is it Pradyota? Was he a friend of yours?'

'He was... everything. Everything.' He looked up almost defiantly, then sagged again. 'I still can't believe it. I never thought it would reach this point....'

'What do you mean?'

'The jealousy…. It was terrible.'

Upali suddenly noticed the Sanchi Thera watching them from near the staircase. 'Pradyota was transacting some business for his cousin, wasn't he? Was it about some weapons?'

There was a long pause. Upali regretted his big mouth and stared out at the shimmering light on the water, wondering how to take back his question. The river was at its broadest ever, thanks to tributaries that had joined on either side, and very crowded. Some of the bigger boats sported the lofty masts and sails of sea-travellers and many were manned by light-haired foreigners quite like Xantes at Sanchi. Their presence in such large numbers was startling, the result perhaps of Chandragupta's war and peace with the Greeks. Chandragupta had obtained a bride in that treaty, Governor Seleucus Nikator's daughter; there were rumours that she was the grandmother to the present Raja. Unconfirmed rumours, of course. The palace would hardly admit to mlechcha blood on the throne – sudra was bad enough.

'What do you mean?' Vipul's thin voice was cold.

'Nothing, nothing.' The Thera had disappeared. 'I must go – Ananda will be waiting.'

It was late at night when they rowed into the port of Pataliputra. They had to wait for permission to dock. And the passengers had to wait till morning to see the capital.

The morning session of meditation ended just before the sun began to reveal its aura. At that moment, standing on the deck, Upali forgot Bhima for a few minutes. And the furnaces, and everything else. The first revelation was that the painfully cold wetness of the world was the work of a mist just beginning to clear. It withdrew faster as the sun rose and they found themselves still far from the jetty, mid-river almost. But it seemed as though you could walk to it over all the vessels jammed in between. Beyond was the city, floating nearer every minute.

Upali was not sure what he had expected. Buildings of solid gold, perhaps, and streets paved with silver. Well, nothing like that was visible as yet. Only a very tall yellow wall, with a battlemented top interrupted by numerous watchtowers and stretching in both directions as far as the eye could see. There was a chariot and horses waiting on it at one point. The tallest structure on the skyline was a cluster of silver-painted barrel-vaults, which soared at least two storeys above all else. Was it the palace?

The brightening light revealed a great expanse of docklands between river and wall, many sheds, weighing machines and towering stacks of sacks, crates and bales, swarming with hundreds of loin-cloth-clad workers. The river water lost its sheen and looked murky. Perhaps with the ore. Most of the vessels nearby were iron barges, loaded with hills of red dust, except for one carrying horses, many sneezing unhappily. You could smell the iron. Or was it just his imagination? No, there was a fine red haze in the air.

'Well, Upali!' The Sanchi Thera seemed to pop up from nowhere.

'Well, Thera?'

'How do you feel?' A bony finger jabbed Ananda in the shoulder. 'Do you realize where you are, boy? All the way from icy Bactra, up to the borders of Chin, to the swamps of Assam in the east, and far down to those burning plateaus of southern rock – this is the centre of it all. Pataliputra. The richest city in the world! Why are you so silent, boy?'

'It's so... red.' Ananda shifted uncomfortably.

Yes, with blood. This, a little riverside village in the Buddha's time, was the centre of it all, where the spiders sat, controlling a vast web of violence, power and avarice, a web made of iron hammered into ugly swords. Begun by Bimbisara, spun further by Ajatashatru, the Nandas, Chandragupta, Kautilya, many others – and greased with the blood of the Shakyas, Lichhavis, Mallas, Kalingas, Bhuiryas and how many more?

They stood waiting out at anchor for a long time, nearly the whole day. Nigrodha and his charioteer Chandra joined them on the deck in the afternoon. The prince had spent most of the trip in their cabin, doing copying exercises more rigorously than Upali required.

'Nigrodha! How do you feel to be back home?'

Nigrodha held the rail with both hands and stared out silently.

'You are not enthusiastic?'

The prince-monk smiled. 'Well, considering that my dearest uncle is also the murderer of my father, I am always unsure about the welcome I will receive in his glorious Court.'

Upali was silent, engrossed in a flock of terns passing overhead, golden-yellow bills ablaze, heading apparently for a great sand-bar on the opposite bank. Then he felt a coward. 'Your father was his brother, wasn't he? And the crown prince. You would have been his heir.'

'I'm just grateful that I survived the Four Dead Years.' Nigrodha turned away. 'I have some work remaining.'

Upali felt worse now but was still unable to leave. Chandra returned alone later and was surprised to find him still there.

'I'm rather impressed with the view. But you must have seen this sight many times?'

'Many times, lord. But I never tire of it. This is my native land after all! And Pataliputra is the most beautiful of cities. See those silver vaulted roofs, the highest of them all? That is the palace and the flag flying above shows that the Raja is in residence. They say that he watches everybody at all times. He may be watching us at this very moment.'

Upali somehow managed to dismiss the idea.

But at the huge Pataliputra monastery late that night, he was reminded of it. Meditation over, he was sitting with Harsha on the broad veranda outside their dormitory, wrapped up in two shawls apiece against the chill. They could hear chatter and laughing from the dormitories. The monks had been informed that the Congress would begin two days hence, so they had time for rest and recovery – and writing, for Upali and Ananda. They had also learnt that the royal Public Grievances Court had been held that very day; the next one was a fortnight away. They would have to go to the police headquarters to get help for Bhima. But Upali did not have much hope from there. They should try to speak to somebody higher.

'We could try to speak to Thera Mogalliputta. If we get a chance,' suggested Harsha.

'Mogalliputta? He was more alarming than the king. And less friendly.'

'Well, would you prefer to try to walk into the palace, over those walls and through the army? To the Magadhe-Raja himself? You'll reach prison first! Mogalliputta is powerful. The Raja is said to be his disciple.'

'And he hated the story, and probably me too.'

'Well then, I'll speak to him,' But Harsha was frowning now: 'Most of the Theras on the boat didn't like it either, did they? Especially Jeevana and Mahanta, who are said to be the senior-most nowadays after Mogalliputta.'

'They were not exactly cheering your monastery either,' pointed out Upali. Harsha's face fell further. 'Anyway, forget it. They're not worth bothering about. But suppose Mogalliputta does not come? Suppose he refuses? Suppose – '

'Suppose we try first, and then worry?' asked Harsha gloomily.

Upali sighed, taking a deep breath of cold jasmine-and-frangipani-laden air. He found it hard to believe that the Magadhe-Raja was anybody's disciple. The Buddha's perhaps, but only because the Buddha was dead and unable to disown any disciple.

'Tell me, Upali, why is that monk Vipul staring at you so strangely?' Upali had noticed it too. Vipul had taken to almost following him around, and Upali was getting tired of it. He had no intention of getting involved in the Viceroy's plot. Pradyota must have been murdered because of his role in it – and not for any jealousy. Who had the most reason but the Magadhe-Raja? But who had actually done the job? As if in answer, the Sanchi Thera appeared around the corner.

'Upali, two soldiers have come, asking for you.'

'Me? For what?'

'I don't know. Come and see.'

Upali and Harsha followed him out of the courtyard and past other viharas, most of them vividly painted with scenes from the suttas. By a variety of painters apparently, for the Buddha was variable, sometimes tall, pale and gloomy, sometimes shorter and dark like a Kalinga, somewhere haughty, elsewhere beatific, always bald.

It must be Chandra, Upali thought. In fact, Chandra might be able to suggest a solution. There had to be faster ways of reaching the powers-that-be.

He was right about the latter, as it turned out; the fastest way was treason. The soldiers were strangers, from the Prime Minister's office. The Lord Prime Minister wished to speak to Thera Upali.

'The Prime Minister? What about?'

They did not know.

'But so late at night? Can't it wait for the morning?'

It could not.

'I'll come with you,' said Harsha, but the soldier shook his head.

'Am I being arrested?' asked Upali. 'What if I refuse?'

'We've orders to escort you to the Prime Minister's office.'

All his fears fortified, Upali climbed into the chariot, which started immediately. At least Harsha knew where he was headed. But what could he do? Suppose they hit Upali on the head and dumped him in the moat? What could Harsha do, save hold a dignified but puzzled memorial ceremony later in Maheshwar? Upali's stomach began to ache. Luckily he had not eaten anything at all that day or it would have stabbed him to death before anybody else.

The chariot raced through crowded and brightly lit streets, then over a bridge, through tall gates and past rows of soldiers. On and on, till they reached a small court within a large building complex. Upali was hurried indoors and down a confusing series of corridors to an anteroom facing a doorway. One of his escorts

vanished within for a second, returned and snapped his fingers.
'Come on.'

He was almost pushed into a thankfully warm office. There
were three men there, two of them young and seated behind desks
and scratching away on palm sheets. They ignored Upali but the
old man reclining on a divan nodded. 'Apologies, Thera Upali, for
disturbing you at this late hour. Pray sit. May I offer you some
wine? Water? Milk?'

Radhagupta, Prime Minister of Magadh for longer than most
people could remember, and said to be the critical factor in the
bloody somersault of the late king's third son to the throne, was
a fat old man who sagged all over. Even his round bald head hung
in bags and folds of pale, almost translucent, flesh; a shawl slumped
off his shoulder as he spoke, revealing breasts that drooped to his
waist. A gentle smile lit his face and gave him a soft, rather
grandfatherly look. Except for his eyes which were unpleasantly
cold. Upali sat down on a satiny carpet, drank a little water from
a glass made apparently of gold, and felt no better.

'The thing is, Thera, we know of your meeting with the
Viceroy of Avanti and the ex-Raja. Why didn't you report it?
Perhaps you suspected the loyalty of the administration there?'

Upali could not even nod. But the Prime Minister hardly
paused.

'Would you like to make a statement?'

'About what?' Upali felt sweat roll down his chest.

'Don't take us for fools, Thera. We deeply respect the members
of our Raja's Sangha.' It's not the Raja's, interrupted Upali silently.
'But we know exactly what was discussed at that luncheon. Your
role may have been innocent but – '

'I'm sorry, Lord Minister, I was a bit distracted. We have a
serious problem at Maheshwar....'

In one burst, Upali poured out the whole story of Bhima's
village, except for the furnaces. As well as that of Devadina, including
the visit to the ex-Raja – where he and the Viceroy had sympathized
profusely over Kalinga – and finally Upali's discovery that Devadina

was suspected of murder. He was not interrupted. The young men scratched away at their sheets; the old man apparently went off to sleep, his head drooping lower and lower on his baggy chest so that Upali was finally addressing three white hairs on the centre of his pate. But he had hardly closed his mouth, when the head snapped up. 'Why did you give those chits to the Viceroy?'

Upali coughed, once and then again. Now he understood the Sanchi Thera's panegyric to the royal spy. What had seemed like a speech from the heart had actually been one from the pocket. 'Because he is the Viceroy. But I need your help, lord, in the matter of the deportees – '

'What did the chits say?'

'I could not make out fully, but they seemed to be an order for something.' He wiped his upper lip and his forehead, then his throat too, but decided against his chest.

'And the ex-Raja agreed to release Sutanuka?'

'Yes.'

'In exchange for?'

'Exchange? Nothing – what could I give him?' What, in fact, had he agreed to do? Say 'as before' to Vipul – it had sounded ridiculous then and now.

'Perhaps your support to the little plot they seem to be hatching?'

'Actually, my lord, I did not fully understand their talk.'

'And that was the last you heard of them, and Pradyota?'

'Yes.'

'You didn't speak to the monk Vipul, of Takshashila?'

'Oh, yes.' Damn that Sanchi Thera! 'Yes, I forgot. He came up and spoke to the Sanchi Thera, to offer condolences. I don't really remember what he said.'

'You didn't speak to him again?'

'No – yes, once, when he passed by looking ill, but nothing much again – '

'So, who murdered Pradyota?'

Upali was caught off-guard. 'I – I....'

'Come on, you must have your suspicions!'

'Perhaps some thief?'

'Pah! The ex-Raja told you what he believes, didn't he? Is that your guess as well?'

The stream of patter dried up and Upali stared down at the dragon pattern on the carpet.

'I am amazed at you, Thera. Do you actually believe that the Magadhe-Raja's government would commit murder?' Upali believed much worse but silently. 'And why would the Viceroy search for Devadina if they think Magadh is behind this?'

'Perhaps he thinks Devadina is Magadh's man?'

'Well, he's wrong. Magadh does not commit murder.' Radhagupta drummed fat gold-ringed fingers on the ivory-legged desk before him; a large square bright green stone adorned the ring in the centre. Then he turned to one of the scribes. 'Finished?'

'Almost, Highness.'

The old man rose. 'Take his signature. Upali, you will not leave the city without permission.' The Prime Minister tripped out with a sprightly gait, silk shawl trailing at least six feet behind, and was gone before Upali realized that he had made no promises about Bhima.

BUDDHA

The Purusa Sukta, or the Verse of the Cosmic Man, was not the only one of the 1800 songs of the Rgveda that tried to explain creation – it was just the one most exalted by those who called themselves Aryas. There were other songs along more or less the same lines, and one that was very different.

This last, the Nasadiya Sukta, declared that the beginning must have been nothing, neither what is, nor what is not. There could have been no death, hence nothing immortal. There must have been no difference between night and day. Perhaps there was water. And, perhaps in that water was something, something that breathed, but without breath as we know it. How was it born? Perhaps by the power of water, then heat, then other powers? Could this have been the first creation – a seed in a husk, maybe with seed-bearers to help, with power within and without, quite like a human birth in some ways? The Sukta hypothesizes to this point, only to be overcome by doubt. How could anybody really know, it asks. The gods came later, so how would even they know?

The Nasadiya Sukta was not half as respected as the Purusa Sukta, indeed some considered it a bit blasphemous. But it was a verse that expresses well the state of Siddarth's mind when he left his people. He had no answers, only doubts, questions and blasphemy. He had no goal but to get away. But there was a germ of something growing in him, he could feel it. He needed time to think and for that he first sought refuge at the hermitage of his friend, Bhargav.

Bhargav welcomed him but with some concern; he was the opposite of a doubter. An extremely respected brahmin, he presided with his wife over a traditional brahmin ashram deep in the forests to the east of the Shakya republic. It was a large and busy establishment thanks to the many brahmin boys who arrived following their thread ceremony and stayed on for at least twelve years, imbibing the essence of brahminhood at the feet of the guru. Bhargav was actually a very rich man, but he had tired of material comforts early, opting instead to earn spiritual merit in forest austerities and teaching. Siddarth respected him.

Bhargav however was horrified at Siddarth. He questioned him many times, especially to find out why he would be leaving soon even though he was not sure of his destination, but they seemed to converse at cross-purposes. Bhargav wanted him to leave too but not to wander any further. He wanted him to go right back home and shoulder his responsibilities, as he put it. It was not for us to choose our path in life. Everybody had a duty in the world and Siddarth's was that of a Shakyaraja and a householder. That was his dharma, and morality lay in being faithful to it come what may – one could seek within it for the life that best suited one, for the system was not rigid.

This Bhargav sincerely believed and that was how he ran his ashram. The curriculum was both traditional and modern; it included the Vedas, the Brahmanas and Aryanakas of orthodoxy – the last two being practical instructions for rituals and certain extremely secret and powerful spells – as well the newer Upanishads and the much older Yoga. He described the Upanishads as Siddarth's old teachers had, as a deeper insight into the Vedas – the jnana-kand, or the knowledge part, as opposed to the karma-kand or ritual part. Siddarth however could see little in common between the simple incantations asking for food, health, cattle, soma, offspring, good weather and so on that comprised the Vedas, and the much more complex dissertations on the soul, its immortality, transmigrations, release and unity with almighty Brahman, of the Upanishads. The only meeting point was the yagna.

He disagreed with Bhargav's view of dharma too. 'Dharma is not to be blindly inherited, Bhargav, and definitely not to be compromised with. One is after all a man, not a mindless lump of mud who actually believes in the priests' talk!'

'Siddarth! You reject dharma?'

'Their dharma. I don't accept what the world calls my dharma. I think each person has to find his own. I don't know what mine is as yet. But it wasn't in my life in Kapilavastu.'

'Well, you can stay here for some time, if you like....'

The ashram was a carefully protected community; outsiders were strictly prohibited. Siddarth was an outsider but a friend of Bhargav. Also a Shakyaraja whose people ruled over the land on which they sat. So he was even invited to attend the classes, where the students sat ramrod straight in a forest glade and recited hymns for hours, thousands of them, each one again and again, in a sing-song tune. Eighteen hundred in the Rgveda alone. And then listened to the elucidation of each. The main thing however was committing everything to memory. Twelve years did not seem sufficient for the task. It was hardly surprising, at the end of this rigorous and isolated training period, to find that the brahmins nurtured within them a strong community-consciousness and solidarity, or even parochialism, nor that many of them distrusted the cities, nor that brahmin knowledge – such as it was – was the most jealously guarded secret of all time.

Siddarth was not interested in becoming privy to it. 'All this finally leads back to the yagna. My father calls my aversion cowardice but he has no answer to the opposition of the commoners. Except force. Everytime a yagna comes around, the peasants have to be threatened, their so-called contribution taken away by force, and punishments meted out.'

Bhargav was disturbed as well. 'It's really shocking. And the attitude affects the rituals too, you know. How can they succeed amidst coercion and half-heartedness?'

'It was different earlier, I understand. Then all the sangha cattle were herded together, so the decision to sacrifice affected all equally. But now some rajas own five hundred cattle and some only two – how can they contribute equally?'

'In fact the poorer should be more generous, if they want to prosper....'

'And the sacrifices are becoming bigger. When I was consecrated, the ceremony was four days long and about two hundred animals were offered. Now it goes on for more than ten days, and more than a hundred are slaughtered each day! This time there were not enough people to eat the sacrificed meat. Peasants and brahmins had to be rounded up and herded in from the nearby villages to carry away the prasad – among them were also the ones whose animals were taken away forcibly. The waste has to be seen to be believed!'

'The thing is, Siddarth, your people are much richer today than they used to be. And the gods have to be given their share. So the sacrifices have to be bigger. You can't haggle with the gods.'

'Some are richer, not all. And who knows what the gods really want? We only have the priests' word for it. And they are definitely more demanding by the day – some even claim that the gods are two – those in heaven and those on earth, meaning themselves!'

Bhargav dabbed his forehead with his shawl and sighed.

'The rituals are a wasteful sham,' continued Siddarth. 'They make no difference to the poverty, the cruelty, the indebtedness, anything. They do not even provide prasad to all! There are so many poor and hungry people in the outcaste settlements, but no – '

'Siddarth, you surely cannot be thinking of offering holy prasad to low-born – '

'Anyway, I've made up my mind to study under a teacher. Someone not slave to these dead rituals, nor to the ambitions and avarice of modern life. Someone seeking freedom, and with the courage to be critical. Someone enlightened, as they say.' There were actually many such, even more than in his youth, though they were still shunned in the conservative republics. But most were able to build some kind of a following in the south.

'Siddarth, you don't have to follow anybody for enlightenment – just your own dharma. If you are dedicated to your dharma – in the process you will naturally abjure ambition and avarice – Nirvana will be yours.'

'I find it difficult to accept those Upanishadic ideas – they wander far in their musings but finally place their heads back on the edge of the altar. I will never return there.'

Bhargav frowned. 'Who are you going to follow then – the fatalist Ajivikas, like that Kassapa whom everybody is talking about?'

'No. Somehow I can't agree with the helplessness they preach. I prefer the mockery of the Lokayats – who say enlightenment is realizing that there is nothing beyond what can be sensed with one's own faculties. But mocking the gods only scares people. I'm not sure. I'll have to see for myself.'

'And what of your family?'

'What of them? The wealthy have diversions, normally at the cost of others. They may miss me a while, but that can't be helped.'

He sought a brave teacher and an innovative one, who had dispensed with the prevailing rituals but not for want of hope. After much thought, he selected one Alara Kalama, said to be a follower of Kapila's Sankhya. Kapila had rejected both gods and brahmins, holding that the world was simply the unity of a male principle, the purusha, and a female substratum, the prakriti. Enlightenment was freedom of the purusha from the prakriti. Alara was said to have developed the idea, by preaching a road to enlightenment that comprised of seven steps of samadhi, or intense concentration and thought control. He lived with his disciples in the hills above Rajgir, the capital of Magadh.

Once he had decided, Siddarth hurriedly bid farewell to Bhargav, hardly hearing his friend's exhortations about not wandering too long, and not forgetting his dharma, nor his family who was, Bhargav was sure, worried sick about him. Siddarth just thanked him warmly.

He took the uttarapatha, the northern trade route, which travelled all the way from Takshashila in the northwest through Kapilavastu, Kushinara, and Vaishali, crossing the Ganga to divide and go either east to Champa or south to Rajgir. 'The man on the horse always looks down on the man on foot,' Channa had said. Well, now Siddarth was the man on foot. His embroidered leather sandals soon wore out but he repaired them somehow and hung on to them because his soles protested furiously when he tried to walk barefoot.

It was a difficult trip, this first of many cross-country treks, and unforgettable. It was really the beginning of a new education, not in any lofty or esoteric philosophy, but in ordinary, even familiar things. Like the heat of the sun. He had never noticed how it built up from a mild lighter of the path at dawn to a ferocious torch by midday, pulling out all the water from his body, burning his uncovered head, burning the top and then the bottom of his feet, drying the skin of his eyes, tearing the skin in his nose and throat. The Shakyas worshipped the sun in every form, from Ushas, gentle goddess of dawn, to burning Aditya of the noon sky, and not surprisingly, for they too were rulers – arrogant, uncaring, robbing the earth and all who walked on it of their juices. Nobody dared look the sun in the eye. How sharply different was the moon. Yes, now he could understand why so many of the low-caste worshipped that gentle lantern of cool white light. Anybody who had to expend sweat and energy through the day unprotected by even the flimsiest of shades would. The moon was a reinvigorating friend, so that even the tiredest could think of poetry and love in the night, or sleep well and find the strength to rise and face the sun again.

He was struck too by the richness of the land – farmlands bursting with rice, lentils, beans, peas and sesamum, interrupted by tall stands of sugarcane and gardens fragrant with spices, fruit and flowers – and even more by the poorness of its labourers. Most were busy transplanting rice seedlings now, bent double, sickle in hand, feet swollen from standing hours in the flooded fields. They fell at his feet at first, in fear, when he spoke to them. The lash-marks on their burnt backs reminded him of Vali. They were kindly people but very ignorant.

'Whose fields are these?' he asked them in Magadhi, the local Prakrit or commoner's tongue. It seemed ridiculous to even try Sanskrit.

'Lord, the Sethi's.'

'Who is the Sethi?' They did not know his name, he lived in some town while his overseer lived here in the village. 'Who is your ruler?'

They did not know. Strangely, they were more concerned about Siddarth instead, sympathizing with his bruised feet, hesitantly offering him food. They were amazed when he accepted, served him sour gruel with raw mango and salt, smiled with pleasure when he wolfed it down – only to bring it up not long afterwards – and advised him not to walk the roads too late. There were many man-eating witches on this stretch.

The small peasants were friendly, and also a little fearful of this sramana whose high birth was evident in the big build and the pale skin that was now angry and sunburnt. His clothes were simple – he had exchanged his robes with those of a surprised peasant the morning after he left Kapilavastu – but he was clearly new to the life. He did not enter the villages unless invited, normally spending the night just outside the gates. The cowherds going to the meadows woke him up before dawn, the best time to walk.

He noticed the women bathing next to wells and on the banks of rivers early in the morning, and how most of them did not bother to cover their bodies from the sramana. On the contrary – a few seemed to flaunt themselves. Did they trust him, or was it some devil goading them to tempt the declared celibate? Again and again he saw this, for the rivers were too many and too full, and he learned to wait patiently through the night on their banks, for the morning and the tirthankars – the boatmen on whose rickety craft everybody dared the swells with admirable and foolhardy confidence.

Even away from the fields the world remained absurdly bountiful. The jungles were laden with fruit and nuts, and generous in offering them, dangling litchis, amlas and pomegranates within easy reach of sight and hand, piercing through the gentle stink of swamp and rank undergrowth with the tang of tamarind or mango, or the overwhelmingly over-ripe richness of a burst jackfruit, dropped from the heights by some simian in a hurry. Nature was sramana-friendly. It would not be very difficult, if one trained one's stomach a bit, to subsist solely off the wild, as sramanas did. It was just a thought for the moment; his own stomach was not easily trained and often upset, but he hoped that things would improve.

Especially because, somewhere along the way, he had decided to beg food from passers-by and householders. It was another rejection of his past, like throwing away his sacred thread, but difficult to do, more difficult than living off nature. The response was normally shock, disgust, even revulsion. Many shuddered and hurried away, a few threw food at him from a distance, often leftovers and rubbish. It was not easy to ask and even more difficult to eat the alms obtained. His stomach protested strongly. But he persevered.

He was not bothered by robbers, though the jungles were said to abound in them. But it was quite possible that some passersby were robbers who did not bother to introduce themselves to one who had clearly nothing to offer. They may also have been wary of him, for it was not normal at all for anybody to travel anywhere without protection or company, the forests being well-known as the home of every kind of demon, ghost, man-eating animal and head-hunting tribe, besides those who had become bandits from among them. Siddarth himself could not help commending body and soul to the protection of all the gods he knew as he strode into the rapidly darkening greenness of the first stretch between Bhargav's ashram and the Malla republic. This was primeval jungle, opaque, untamed, linked to civilization only by the soft tenuous mud of the road, while he was alone, on foot and unarmed. Odd screams, rumbles, barks and trumpets filled the air, great fronds of entwined bamboo gazed down from overhead, clumps of vines reached out into his face, blocking both sun and wind, and driving rivulets of sweat and tension down his body. He encountered what could have been the ruins of a caravan, just pieces of wheels, planks and a few yellowed sticks which could have been bones; it was his imagination, he told himself, probably just the remains of a repair and overhaul job. He was nonetheless pleased to meet another and very healthy-looking caravan halfway through, at least a hundred bullock-carts with as many mounted guards. The pleasure was clearly not mutual though, for both guards and merchants unsheathed their swords, whipped their animals into a trot, and made signs against the evil eye – for who could say whether he was man or well-disguised ogre?

He passed through small farming valleys, more forests, reached the Malla capital of Kushinara, and decided to spend the night just within the main gates. The soldiers on guard stared at the tall young man, of aristocratic and military bearing yet wearing peasant rags, but said nothing. Siddarth entered and settled down in the intermediate grazing stretch between the two city walls. Citizens hurried past on foot, chariot or horseback, among them some young noblemen he had known at Banaras. Nobody spoke to the sramana at all, in contrast to the friendly slaves and curious village folk, so it was not long before he dozed off. But the soldiers were genuinely intrigued; one went and reported the odd sage to his officer, who came back with him, woke Siddarth and asked his name.

'Gautama Siddarth.'

'What – a Shakyaraja?'

'Yes.'

'What is the name of your father?'

'Gautama Shudodhan.'

The officer was aghast. The Chief's son? He invited, begged and finally ordered Siddarth to his estate. There he was served dinner, while receiving the greetings of many Malla rajas, including the Chief. They were not just shocked but downright suspicious. What were the Shakyas up to? Siddarth was unable to disperse their fears and finally left early in the morning having decided not to enter any city, nor to use his full name. At the Licchavi capital of Vaishali, he did not approach the main gate at all but put his cloth down near the ragged settlement of outcastes outside.

It was between the lands of the Mallas and the Licchavis that he met jungle-folk for the first time. Once again the forest was dark, silent and dense, but now Siddarth was quite relaxed, able to enjoy the shade and almost ignore the humidity, walking briskly for a good many hours before he saw life other than that in various animals and birds. The first was another caravan, which responded to him like the first. Then another three hours passed without any encounter and after chattering back at some friendly langurs, admiring a large herd of grazing neelgai, and ignoring some elephantine crashing from somewhere in the green depths, he was just beginning to wonder how jungle dangers got to be so exaggerated, when he saw a face poking out from behind a tree. The face immediately let out a whoop and leapt out onto the road. The whoop brought out eleven companions hidden on both sides of the road. They were all naked but for a covering over the crotch. Vivid streaks of yellow and red decorated their short wiry bodies, bone ornaments pierced their ears and nose. In their hands were stone hammers and bright green bamboo blowpipes.

Siddarth was tense. Spirits did not cast shadows, he remembered, but the shade was too dense to make out shadows in any case. He had heard of cannibals too in these parts. Get a grip on yourself, he thought. He decided not to run. What was the point? And he was not sure if his legs would obey him. He waited as they approached, talking among themselves in a tongue he did not understand, and then was most surprised when one came near and touched his chest and his own in some kind of communion. Perhaps they recognized him as a holy man. Definitely they recognized him as a man of no wealth.

'Greetings,' he said in Magadhi. Now that they were close he found that they smelled rather strongly. Perhaps of the skin caps on their heads, on which most of the heads of the original owners were still to be seen. Jackals, they looked like.

'Greetings,' said the first one, who seemed to be their leader.

'You speak Magadhi?' he asked. What a relief! His fear evaporated. Language was the simple solution. If people could speak the same language, would they ever fight? Yes, they would. Look at us and the Koliyas, the Mallas, Kosala…. The men introduced themselves as Khattis, a tribe that Siddarth had not heard of. Their home was a long way deeper into the jungle, more than two days away, they came here only for the caravans. It was the occupation of their entire clan for the past many years but they faced serious competition nowadays. Somehow they managed.

They asked Siddarth to come home with them, for a meal they said. It was an invitation difficult to interpret; Siddarth declined warily. Some other time, he hoped. They smiled back and walked around him, touching his peasant robes, squatting down in the dust and fingering his torn sandals. They talked a little to each other in their own tongue, argued a little even, and then pulled him off the road and through the undergrowth till they reached a clearing. Siddarth had no real choice in the matter. In the clearing one lit a fire, while another started digging a hole nearby, to reveal a cache of dead rabbits, five in all, that they had clearly kept for carrying home. The man took out two and deftly skinned and cut them with a stone knife. Siddarth was not hungry but they were so enthused by their own invitation that he could not refuse. It was a cheerful meal, though he did not understand much of the conversation, followed by a cheerful parting, in which they bowed repeatedly and even hugged him, as if it was he who had been the host.

Siddarth crossed the sacred mother-of-all-rivers, a great expanse of wind-tossed water much huger than what he remembered from Banaras, in the boat of a very gnarled old ferryman who charged him a blessing since he had no coin and somehow managed to chart a course against the frighteningly strong current to an invisible jetty on the horizon. And thus he arrived in Magadh, the most powerful kingdom of the day, smaller than Kosala but richer thanks to its huge mines of iron, copper and other minerals, and to its early control of riverine shipping on the lower Ganga. The recent conquest of Anga had extended this control of the river right up to the sea.

This land south of the river was different. The jungle was the same densely overgrown swamp and sal thickets as on the north, opaque green walls on both sides of the road. But away from the river the flat plains of grain were richer, and the villages bigger than in the north. Sometimes he had to wade through shallow canals of water, either irrigation streams cut from the river, he was told by villagers, or drains from the marshes. He also passed large tanks, square in outline and quite deep, with bathing ghats on one side and canals to water the fields cut from the other.

But he was tired now and slower, and irritably surprised at the position of the capital, far south of both the river and the most fertile grain lands. Later he realized that Rajgir was located for a purpose – it straddled the access to the mines and controlled it literally with an iron fist.

He did not visit Rajgir then. Passersby showed him a route that bypassed the city and climbed the hills, higher and higher, till the road wore out and he was stumbling through the undergrowth in his ragged sandals. It was hot here, steaming hot, hotter than Banaras, much hotter than Kapilavastu. But he finally reached Alara Kalama's ashram – some half-dozen thatch huts in the woodland, home to the small community of sage and disciples who lived and meditated together, seeking the Ultimate Truth while subsisting frugally off the jungle. Alara accepted him as his student without much ado and for the first time in his life Siddarth applied himself to studies with some dedication.

All existence, or samsara, was sorrow, said Alara, and the only way to escape sorrow was by freedom from the cycle of birth and death. That was his Truth. He had renamed Kapila's old male Purusha and female Prakriti as the 'evolvent' and the 'evolute', or the 'manifested' and the 'unmanifested'. The evolute held the evolvent in bondage, but the evolute, which is the whole world around us, was also really Nothingness in an endless cycle of birth and death. And escape from the cycle was only possible for the evolvent, or the manifested, by appreciation of the Nothingness – by reaching a state where you felt neither pain, nor craving, nor disappointment, nor happiness; where you were conscious of no emotion at all. This was Moksha or true freedom. It was to be sought through meditative absorption or jnana, by developing tranquillity and concentration. The method was to sit in various yogic postures and concentrate on one's own consciousness, just concentrate deeper and deeper, till one left the material world and was absorbed into the realm of pure consciousness. There were degrees of such absorption and Alara was admired because he knew and taught his students how to rise through as many as seven.

It all sounded suspiciously close to the Upanishadic soul trying to escape the body, but Siddarth put aside his doubts and determined to achieve all seven degrees. It was not easy for him, it was probably not easy for anybody, especially because below and visible from certain vantage points was Rajgir – huge, colourful, rich and noisy. The noise wafted up at times through the jungle to the meditating community, a medley of military parades, markets, music and other cacophony. Alara was wont to say that they should shift further south, though he never actually initiated any such action, perhaps because he received many visitors from the city, quite a few of them rich and influential. Siddarth rarely took time off his studies, but when he did it was to examine the vista below, in some fascination, for this was a different city. Huge and superbly located within a high bowl of hills, its perimeter was fortified by three walls, the outermost of which were great Cyclopean ramparts filling the gaps in the hills. It was unconquerable, so he heard, for it had an excellent water supply within from both hot and cold springs, also rich grazing lands. The amazing grid layout of the streets impressed too. At night the place was even more disturbing, sparkling like a heap of diamonds, as if to gently lure them to its wealth and pleasures. But there were familiar things as well, like the vast settlement of shabby hutments outside the ramparts. Bigger than that outside Kapilavastu, bigger even than Banaras.

Siddarth did his best and even achieved success according to Alara. But he himself was not satisfied. Meditation to the seventh degree had not told him anything about the sorrows of the world. All it did was develop a certain mental calm and alertness, an improved ability to focus and remember. Which was useful, no doubt, as were the other skills he learnt at Alara's, a critical one being the ability to live as a property-less and homeless ascetic. He learnt to walk barefoot, to make do with minimum food, clothes and utensils, with the open air for all ablutions and natural calls, without many things that his past life had considered essentials. And he began to practise yoga, that old science of mind and body discipline. He had learned yoga at school too, but never so rigorously.

He left Alara after a year, to join the following of another teacher, Uddaka Ramaputta, who was said to have mastered an eighth degree of jnana. He studied under him and mastered that as well. He had now reached the uppermost levels of meditational consciousness. He valued his learning for he discovered that his body and mind were under his control as never before. He discovered within himself unknown resources of stamina, alertness, patience and concentration. He felt leaner, stronger, fitter. No longer did his body crave food, water, rest or companionship the way it had. Not that it did not need and want them, but he could handle such needs in a much more frugal and disciplined manner. He could fast for one week, even two and three weeks at a stretch. He could meditate while sitting in the lotus position, or while standing in the hot sun, or the rain, or even on his head. The last too was different – his mind felt sharp and clear, yet more relaxed. The only thing that stubbornly refused to change was his stomach, which was often upset.

The meditational exercises were truly strength-creating, he concluded. But they were both personal and mundane. He was aware of the mystical experiences that people claimed to have during meditation, the visions of heaven and hell, of gods and demons, of loved ones long departed, of their own past lives, of becoming Nothingness itself. They did not impress him, though almost everybody he knew considered them a sign of impending or successful enlightenment. Such experiences were only hallucinations, he argued, delusions caused by excessive solitude and inward contemplation, even certain foods.

So he left Uddaka as well. He approached other teachers and other schools of thought and spent much time learning whatever they had to offer, but nowhere did he find anything that went beyond meditation and yoga. What he found were very minor differences in practice but awesome differences in theory, with the proponents of the One, the Many and the Nothingness, the theists, monotheists, polytheists, atheists, agnostics, the Vedists and anti-Vedists, the materialists, fatalists, existentialists, nihilists and many many others all at continuous and verbose loggerheads with everybody else. They enjoyed these disputes so hugely that they even had fixed days set aside for argument – the 8th, 14th, and 15th day of each fortnight were the days for 'religious discourse', fixed at specific sites in different regions. Sramanas walked miles to attend these meetings, berate each other and attract followers, for lay people were also welcome. Philosophical debate was a mad addiction, he found, and a substitute for useful action.

So, after much thought, he set out to find enlightenment on his own. He was not the first such. There were others before and later who had also concluded that society held no answers at all – not even sramana society – the only way was to get away from everybody and seek alone. Complete solitude was not easy, not even for sramanas accustomed to long vows of silence, or brahmins who believed that the last quarter of life was for solitary wandering. It could be terrifying, which was why some saw it as a last barrier to freedom.

Siddarth took up the challenge. He would commit himself totally, he decided, to the most complete penance. He would seek within, in solitude, undisturbed by the world, an immovable rock in the cycles of chaos. For a while he moved from place to place, avoiding settlements and the busier roads, meditating for longer hours, eating little and less frequently, and that too only river water and the fruits of the jungle. He found himself heading southwards again, bypassing Rajgir and Alara's ashram, further south to the secret of Magadh's strength – the iron deposits which occurred here as amazing and generous surface encrustations, which could be scraped off the rocks and hammered out at white heat into tools, weapons, utensils or bars. Slave teams of local jungle-folk slogged away through day and night, watched over by a well-armed unit of Bimbisara's army – not even a single meditating sramana was allowed to go near. He kept at a distance, not too difficult because the jungle was vaster and settlements few. But even at a distance the woodland rang with the deafening hammering, the abuse of the supervisors, the complaints, hatred and curses of the workers. Further south was the large military town of Gaya; beyond that eastwards, through primeval forest, were the richest deposits of copper and iron, just beginning to be exploited.

He walked and walked. And, despite his efforts, not alone. Very early in his wanderings, he managed to collect a small band of followers, five in number. They were also in search of the ultimate truth and chanced to come across Siddarth meditating in the forest one day. They were struck by his determination, independence and youth, and decided that he would be a good guru to follow. They approached him and were rejected politely, which impressed them the more. He must be very near enlightenment, they felt, and were jealous of his success. They had to have him as their teacher. So, for the next few weeks, then months and years, they became his students – but unknown to him. They were his shadows, trailing faithfully but at a distance, always out of his sight.

Time passed, till one day when the strange sextet chanced to pass through the jungle near Uruvela, a small army township in the region of Gaya. They were making their way slowly through the wild tangle of thorny shrub and abrupt bits of overgrown bog, when Siddarth stumbled across a pleasant spot – a grassy patch of trees, more open than the jungle around, on the banks of a sparkling river whose water was clear and deep, yet easily fordable. The wild dense surroundings isolated the grove; it was absolutely still, except for birds and a herd of chital grazing relaxedly. Siddarth decided that travelling was becoming distracting. His companions waited and waited, and finally realized that their guru had put down roots; they settled obediently just outside his grove and continued to surreptitiously mirror his behaviour. Siddarth began his penance.

It was a long one, many years long, and comprised all kinds of austerities and contortions including self-mortification and starvation, not uncommon among seekers of the time. The idea was to overpower the mortal body and liberate the immortal soul. Siddarth reduced his food, at first eating only what fitted into the palm of one hand per day, then less, and less. He set his teeth, pressed his tongue to his palate and tried to crush and burn out his mind with his mind, with such force that sweat flowed painfully from his armpits. He tried to enter a trance-like state without breathing at all, till it felt as though someone was trying to impale his head with the point of a sword. He held his breath for longer and longer each time he tried, and the pain was varied, according to the legend – once it was like a strap being twisted around his head, then as if a butcher were cutting up parts of his body, even as if he was being held over a fire of live coals.

Not content with slow starvation, he tried to benumb his sensations further by eating all kinds of foul substances, including his own waste. He cut his body and drank his blood. He wore cloth made of hair, at times he went naked. He stood meditating waist-deep in the cold river for days on end while his feet became numb and little creatures nibbled on them without let. He spent nights in the town cemetery in the company of half burnt pyres, old bones and all the ghouls normally resident in such places; they did not disturb him, though the converse may not be true.

He spent more than three years like this. The legend quotes him recalling, 'I was unclothed, indecent, licking my hands... I took food only once a day, or only once in seven days. I ate rice only at fortnightly intervals, if that... I subsisted on the roots and fruits of the forest, eating only those that fell of their own accord. I wore rags from a rubbish heap nearby, or clothes of grass and of bark... I made my bed on thorns... I became one who always stands... I did not bathe at all, and the dust and dirt of years accumulated on my body... I subsisted on the dung of suckling calves... so long as my own dung and urine held out, I subsisted on that... because I ate so little, my limbs became like the knotted joints of withered creepers, my buttocks like a bullock's hoof, my protruding backbone like a string of beads, my gaunt ribs like the crazy rafters of a tumbledown shed... when I touched my stomach, I actually held my spine; when I thought to touch my spine, I felt my stomach... my eyes were sunken deep in their sockets... my scalp was shrivelled... my body hair rotted at the roots, and fell out if I stroked my skin with my hand.'

The universe continued in its familiar and primeval cycles while he tortured himself. Blazing hot days gave way to blessedly cool nights. Saplings became trees, scattered their seeds and withered around him. Ant-hills reared up nearby, sheltered generations of ants, crumbled under passing hooves or falling trees or their own internal tensions, only to rise again. The sun, the clouds and the winds lashed at him, exhausted themselves and rolled on, to return again and then again, to find him as agonizedly determined as before. He tried to notice nothing, to become a lump of stone on the exterior, while searching deeper and deeper within. And he seemed to be successful for the first part. His disciples at least thought so, for they watched him avidly and copied him fervently, and the more they watched and copied the more were they convinced that both he and they were at the very brink of enlightenment.

But he disappointed them. He horrified them by simply changing his mind. After nearly four years of penance he began to doubt, and finally concluded that he was on the wrong path. His disciples couldn't believe his weakness. What were five years in the life of a sramana? What were four years in the pursuit of the ultimate truth? There were sages who had spent multiple lives in the quest and yet not tired. They had not expected Siddarth to be thinking of the rightness or wrongness of the path at this moment. This was not the time for doubt, but for complete whole-hearted commitment, even if it took another thirty lives to show results.

But Siddarth did not have the time for such pursuits. He had changed his mind. All these self-tortures lead nowhere, he felt. In fact, they made one less than a man. To deliberately give up the elementary decencies that made human society, the decencies and abilities and faculties that people had struggled for centuries to achieve, which had transformed their lives all for the better, to reject all of them, was as bad as living only for them. In his eagerness to reject the soft over-indulgent life of his past, he had gone to the other extreme. One tried to become more and more a lump of stone, but how enlightened was a lump of stone? Enlightenment could not be in this direction. He broke his fast, supposedly with a bowl of rice porridge offered to him by Sujatha, a woodcutter's daughter, and resolved to lead a more natural and reasonable existence, a moderate middle between the crass self-indulgence of the aristocracy and the self-mortification of the ascetic. His five followers decided to be frank with him as a last resort and for his own good, and accused him sternly of backsliding and even betrayal. But he remained so unmoved by their pleas, remonstrations and accusations, indeed exactly like a lump of stone now, that they finally abandoned him in disgust.

It was a critical moment in Siddarth's life. He was thirty-five years old and alone in the world. It was six years since he had left Kapilavastu and a life of comfort and power, six years in which he had studied every discipline that promised salvation from sorrow, tried the most difficult yogic penances in search of the ultimate truth about existence. All without finding anything. But he didn't feel defeated. The opposite, really.

He realized that he had always had his doubts about the promised ultimate truth. If he hadn't found it, perhaps, he thought, it was not there to be found. And if he hadn't reached a solution for the sorrows about him, perhaps he had been looking the wrong way.

He continued living in the grove, walking to the town to beg alms in the morning, eating one moderate meal of whatever he was given before noon, making do with wild fruit when he received nothing, then meditating, often late into the night. His meditation was conscious now, with senses heightened instead of deadened, and its focus was sorrow, that of sickness, old age, death and rebirth, but most of all that of life. He thought and thought, till he was satisfied that he had some answers. Such was his enlightenment.

According to a few, that is. The accounts are actually many and contradictory, and most fall broadly into two opposing schools of thought, both equally far-fetched.

The first is alive with melodrama, colourful action-packed supernatural effects and larger-than-life villains. It describes the process as an actual fight between the forces of good, represented by the valiantly meditating Buddha-to-be, and those of evil, represented by the demon-god Mara. The entire world gears up for this cosmic battle, with even natural phenomena overcome – the earth quaking in terror, the rivers rushing back to their sources, the sun cloaking itself in blackness, and so on. Mara brings on his battalions, hordes of ghouls, monsters, goblins, thunderstorms and fire-breathing reptiles, then his fearsome family, and finally himself, the Prince of Evil or Darkness Incarnate. All are defeated. And then the entire world, right up to the gods in the heavens, rises up, dances with joy and showers benedictions on the victorious Buddha.

The other school is dry and sophisticated. It shows a man meditating again, but deeper than anyone had ever meditated before – penetrating right into his own consciousness, higher and higher, transcending joy, pain, reason, anger and ignorance, then remembering all his past existences, thousands of them, then rising higher to discover heaven and hell, and still further to dispel all the ills in himself including the worst of them all – the possibility of rebirth. The odyssey ends with the merging of inner consciousness with external eternality, and thus 'Nirvana', or no-wind, a state of pure emotionless clarity. And thus was he emancipated, enlightened, the Buddha. A little colour might be added to this, by describing the moment of Nirvana as a bolt of lightning, illuminating him as though he was enveloped in a divine fire. Or as a gentle tide, lapping at his feet and then lifting him up, higher and higher, till he floated on a vast blue sea, or a white one of milk. And thus became one with the Absolute.

The latter school is the more popular, with or without colour. And it suggests that the Buddha's enlightenment was not very different from what so many others were seeking at the time. He wasn't different, he was just successful.

But the Buddha *was* different. He didn't set up an ashram with a bunch of disciples and spend the rest of his life meditating and teaching others how to meditate. He didn't preach acceptance. He didn't meet with other sramanas three times every fortnight to lock horns over ultimate truths, nor did he retire to the jungle and seek ever-higher levels of mystical self-realization. He did become a teacher, but not of philosophy, personal salvation, or the achievement of no-wind. In fact, he is said to have dismissed the endless wrangles of the different schools of metaphysicians as 'the thicket of theorizing, the wilderness of theorizing, the tangle, the bondage and shackles of theorizing'.

He became a teacher of reason, tolerance, non-violence, compassion, belief in oneself and change, all real and practical matters. The only direction he offered in the spiritual sphere was of a negative and again typically practical nature, an end to blood-sacrifice. Besides that, he said, people's spiritual lives were their own. For the rest of his life, he travelled the land, seeking out people in cities, villages and jungles, preaching his ideas and teaching other teachers, not only along the highways but far off the beaten track as well, and that too in a time when roads were few and crude, and jungles vast and unfriendly.

The Buddha was really different as was his enlightenment – different but simple to grasp. Because it was simple, which was probably why it seemed so difficult, even 'profound, hard to perceive, hard to know, tranquil, transcendent, beyond the realm of reasoning, subtle, to be known by the wise', as one enthusiastic description goes. It was an awareness of mankind, without the spectacles of fear, awe, greed, myth, or xenophobia, an attempt to understand what was lacking, and a broad plan of action, which he called his Dharma, or Dhamma as they said in Magadhi, the commoners' tongue that was now his own. The same word would be used later in Pali and Ardhamagadhi. He also called it the Middle Way, for it rejected both the rampant violence, sensuality and ambition ruling the world and the extreme life-renunciation and philosophical contortions of the bulk of those who rejected the former.

His disciples would systemize his teaching as the Four Noble Truths and the Noble Eightfold Path. The world was a sorrowful place, this was the first Truth. The second Truth was that this sorrow was caused by ignorance, which was of two types. One was ignorance of the world's fundamentalities, its transience and ever-changing nature – birth, illness, death and loss were as inevitable as the seasons. One had to live with this and a little detachment in one's attitude would help. The second ignorance was within human society itself, in the values humans lived by. And this was different; this condition could be changed, reduced, even negated. That was the third Truth – that most sufferings can be cured or at least mitigated, if they are first understood. There had to be a way, there was a Way. This was the fourth Truth. The Way was explained as the Noble Eightfold Path – right views, right resolve, right speech, right conduct, right livelihood, right effort, right recollection and right meditation.

It was a strange Way, to say the least. First because it was not spiritual. Second because, instead of respecting the norms of orthodoxy as the brahmin ascetics did, Siddarth sought to actively challenge them. And instead of forgetting the outside world, which was the first thing all non-brahmin ascetics strived for, he preached understanding, even intervention. Even where his Way sounded just like the others, it managed to be irritatingly different. For example, it called for renunciation, as most everybody did, but not for any spiritual reward, or any compensation at all. For itself. And to ensure enough for everybody else. It renounced strong passions and attachments, but also indifference. Concern for all was the ideal, and active concern at that. It was non-violent, towards people and other creatures, but not because violence was polluting. Because violence was cruel.

It could be strongly individualistic too. As on the question of morality. Instead of a socially-enforced code of conduct – abiding by which again guaranteed rich rewards in the hereafter – morality was redefined to mean self-criticism. Intelligent self-criticism was every individual's responsibility; people had to use their reason instead of blindly following norms. And the responsibility for every action belonged to the actor. 'By oneself is wrong done, by oneself one suffers…. No one can pollute or purify anybody else.' The Way offered no absolution of guilt, no purifying bath, no uplifting hymn, no magical charm, nothing – nobody could escape the consequences of their actions. Arya meant noble, agreed Siddarth, but nobility was something that anybody could achieve. It was not something you were born into, but the way you lived your life.

His Way did not espouse ritual, magic, idolatry, altars, hymns or any meditational exercise that promised the Ultimate. Forget eternalities, live in the real world and try to understand it. It did insist on physical and mental discipline, but not for any mystic powers. Simply to function better, to be more intelligent, aware and efficient. It did not deny the existence of any god or Absolute or Infinite, nor did it affirm them, but it did express doubt as to their importance.

His Way was about how to live – light on the earth, mindful of one's fellow-beings, guided by reason – it said nothing about anything above or below, before or afterwards.

That was the whole problem. Most people, then and later, were not bothered about how to live – but worried sick about eternalities. His Way shocked them. How could an enlightened person care so little for the most fundamental issues of creation and the hereafter, they asked; he shocked them further. These issues were not fundamental, he said, they were irrelevant and intellectual luxuries. The world had always been there, it changed according to its own inherent laws, it would probably always be there. Mankind had to make the best of it, and was perfectly capable of doing so.

Even his followers had doubts. Many years later, one of them, Malunkya by name, would come to him and demand to be told, once and for all, whether the world was eternal or not, and what man's purpose in it was, or whether the Buddha did not himself know. Upon which the Buddha asked Malunkya whether he had ever promised to enlighten him on such abstruse issues when he had joined the Sangha. Malunkya unhappily responded in the negative. The Buddha then explained why, with his trademark dry though sometimes long-winded wit.

'You see, Malunkya, it's as if a man were to be shot by a poison-tipped arrow. His kinfolk rush and get the best physician they can – an expert in arrow wounds. The doctor is all ready to go to work, but the patient says he needs to know some things first. He wants to know, he says, whether the person who shot the arrow was an aristocrat, or a brahmin, or of a middle varna and jati, or a peasant; whether he was short or tall or of medium height; whether he was black in colour or brown or light-skinned; what particular village or township or city he hailed from; what kind of bow he had and whether his bow-string was made from bamboo or hemp or leaves; whether the arrowshaft was a wild reed or a planted shoot; whether the shaft was feathered with the plumage of a vulture or a heron or a falcon or a peacock or some other bird; whether the gut binding that shaft came from an ox or a buffalo or a hart or a monkey; whether the arrow was plain or barbed with horn, iron, a calf's tooth, or an oleander thorn. He insists on knowing all this, but before he learns even half, he's dead.

'I haven't taught that the world is eternal or not, that it is finite or not, that the breath and the body are identical or not, nor that a person after death will pass to a future existence, or not, or both, or neither. And do you know why Malunkya, I've never bothered to even touch on all this? Simply because these issues are pointless, unprofitable, a waste of time.'

Malunkya probably got the message.

PATALIPUTRA

'Have you finished, Thera Upali?'

Upali rose, lowered himself to the floor, pressed his nose into the softest silkiness he had ever touched, got to his feet again, joined his palms and bowed low. It was standard court etiquette, they had learnt, and tedious, to say the least. But something about the soldiers hovering all around this Great Hall of Audience did not inspire innovation. 'Yes, Thera, for the moment.'

Mogalliputta turned towards the throne above his head. Upali waited. He could not hear the conversation and he wondered whether the throne had heard his reading. And what of the rest of the congregation? He and Ananda had spoken loudly, but there seemed to be hundreds of people around them, monks and others.

He peered around and realized that the real question was whether anybody was interested. Most faces looked distracted, many quite grim. All thanks to the announcements of the previous day, the first day of the Congress. The Magadhe-Raja had declared that the Sangha had to be united; the Thera Mogalliputta had identified eighteen ideological factions within it, and declared eleven as henceforth banned. Banned. They were not to propagate their views any more. They were to 're-educate' themselves. And they comprised nearly one half of the current assembly, including some big monasteries like Mathura and Nalanda.

Upali's throat felt itchy. His scalp too. It always did when the stubble reached this far; he had forgotten again to ask Harsha to shave him. He probably clashed strongly with the polished pates on all sides. But who would notice? Too much had happened on the previous day....

It had begun with a rather austere welcome by Mogalliputta. The Magadhe-Raja wished to inform the monks that the Court of the Mauryas was honoured and delighted by their presence. Despite appearances, he might have added. Nothing, not the mansions of Tosali or Ujjayani, nor even his visit to the Prime Minister the first night here, could have prepared Upali for this grim fortress complex, actually another city within the city and barricaded against it by a huge moat and Cyclopean walls.

Outside the fortress, the monks had been greeted with smiles, waves and bows by people on the streets. Some had even touched their feet. Inside the fortress, via a gigantic swastika-shaped entrance and past a procession of armouries, barracks, stables and other military paraphernalia set off by ranks of soldiers standing at attention all along the way, they were treated more like criminals. Their carriages were emptied and searched twice, they themselves were patted down. The landscape softened after a while, flowering parks replaced parade grounds, the high blue-flagged turrets and silver barrel vaults last seen from mid-river appeared above the tree-tops, but the soldiers remained grimly suspicious. One last turreted timber portal – this encrusted with ivory and gold leaf along with the regulation iron spikes – admitted them to a court with a lotus pool in the centre, which fronted this Great Hall. Also called the Hall of Columns. Towering stone monoliths were arranged in four rows of about twenty each. Through this forest of colossi, exactly opposite the entrance doors and connected to them by a long central aisle ending in a flight of steps, could be seen a stone dais crowned with a glittering but empty throne.

Standing exactly below it, Mogalliputta had continued his welcome address. Every day of the Congress would begin with meditation, he announced, followed by the reciting of important passages of Dhamma. These passages were being compiled and written down by the Pataliputra monastery, and would be available to all others soon. They were to be discussed during the fortnightly uposatha by every monastery henceforth, and all would do well to ponder often on their significance for they contained the very essence of Dhamma and the responsibility on the shoulders of the Sangha.

'Essence and responsibility, according to whom?' muttered Harsha during lunch. 'The Buddha made no such distinction between his teachings. Essence according to the Pataliputra monastery, which means Mogalliputta, which means the Magadhe-Raja, and who is he to decide?'

Upali had not answered, for the answer was obvious – he was the Magadhe-Raja. Besides, it was foolish to grumble in Pataliputra, and that too at Court where every speck of dust was likely to be on the spymaster's payroll.

He had arrived suddenly in the middle of the day. A young monk of Pataliputra was reciting one of the 'essential' passages, when cymbals began to crash outside the door. Someone roared, 'Make way for the Beloved of the Gods, His Sacred Majesty the Magadhe-Raja!' Everybody in the Hall rose, but in some confusion, for they were expected to rise only to promptly fall flat on their faces and lie there motionless till he was seated on his throne.

'Rise,' said a low voice finally. They rose, seated themselves and stared, Upali especially – for this was not the tough soldier of Sanchi's Raja Vihara. This figure was cold, dazzling, almost unreal, quite a bit like all those excessive descriptions of Ram of Ayodhya, except for the swarthy skin and the swarthier eye-piece, the last of which clashed a little with the shimmering white dhoti, the broad gold bands about neck, arms and ankles, and the red silk shawl held in place by the snarling face of a gold tiger. His head was bare though, as at Sanchi, and the good eye just as piercing.

The monk who had been reciting disappeared. His position below the throne was taken by a soldier who announced a royal proclamation:

'The Beloved of the Gods wishes all in the land to celebrate the inauguration of the Congress of the Sangha, and hence announces the release of all detainees. All prisoners are free. Their misdeeds have caused the Magadhe-Raja much grief, but they too are his children and he bids them to forswear their wickedness on this auspicious day and rejoin their loved ones.'

Bhima was free! Upali could not believe it – he turned and gaped at Harsha and Ananda and then was almost deafened when the Court erupted in a roar: 'The Raja has spoken!' It turned out to be the normal way of greeting royal announcements.

It was a day of announcements. The afternoon session was launched by the Beloved of the Gods himself, slightly blurred now thanks to the thin reams of fragrant sandal smoke from many silver braziers, giving everybody a heavy head and a watery vision.

He welcomed them more effusively than Mogalliputta and in the same breath explained why they were there. 'I am,' he said, 'honoured beyond measure to welcome the monks and nuns of the Shakyamuni's Order. I welcome you as the Magadhe-Raja but also as a humble fellow-member of the Sangha, a seeker of enlightenment as all of you. But I have not called you here for my pleasure alone. There is another reason, a very serious one. It is this – the Sangha seems lost and moribund. Our numbers are stagnant, our message nearly unknown. Where are the new novices, the forces that will take Dhamma all across the land? Do we forget the thousands of miles walked by the Shakyamuni to spread his noble message? What are we doing to live up to that tremendous example?'

He paused to drink water. Nobody offered any answers.

'No, our Order cannot rest like this. We have to take up the responsibility that we accepted in word when we joined the Sangha. And I, as Magadhe-Raja, promise you that I will do my best. I have taken some decisions that I would like to announce in your august presence.

'I have resolved to spread Dhamma as best I can by way of amendments as necessary to the law of the land, as well as inscriptions and proclamations regarding these changes. I have resolved to create a new cadre of government officers, the Dhamma Mahamattas, who will oversee the spread of Dhamma. And punish its violation.' Upali felt tension in his stomach, neck, back, everywhere, and realized it was outside him too; hanging in the air all around like the sandal fog. 'I have resolved to create new monasteries as well as monuments to Dhamma, especially at sites made holy by the Shakyamuni's presence; and to endow all monasteries with enough aid that they may fulfil their responsibilities without difficulty.

'Finally, I have resolved to forswear war.'

He paused here and the Hall blinked uncertainly. What was that? Sidelong glances were required to restore his audience's confidence in its ears, before the Hall gasped, murmured, stared at the soldiers against the walls, and recalled the hundreds more they had seen in the morning. Thousands. The double row of ministerial types seated below the dais did not look surprised, just glum.

'Yes. My army will never go to war again. For war is anathema to Dhamma. Henceforth the army of Magadh, the greatest army in the world, greater today than even that of the mighty Chandragupta, will only defend our borders.

'But it is not easy for a king to give up war. For an emperor, almost impossible. Look at this realm. It is a huge jumble of nations, races and peoples, separated by vast jungle, mountain and marsh, even more by language, beliefs, gods, food, everything. Where former kings and chieftains are not only still alive, but looking for a chance to restore themselves to their old thrones. And the people too sometimes support their rulers, for they are the past and the past is tradition and security. But if these rulers come back, that past will come back, with all of them continuously trying to expand, to conquer, enslave and destroy! There is no end to that. So, we cannot let the empire crumble, it is not fair to our people. For it is a prosperous empire, with potential of even greater prosperity for all. And yet, how can one hold it in peace, without one campaign after another, against a revolt here and an uprising there, perforce leaving a broad trail of blood behind? That was the way of Magadh, of every kingdom in the world since time immemorial. Nobody had ever heard of any other way.

'But I have thought of another.

'It is the Middle Way. The way of Dhamma. The way of Law. A way of peace and tolerance in which every person in my realm will live fruitfully for the good of self and community, without fear of violence or turmoil....'

And so on. He needed the Sangha for his plans, he said. The Sangha had to become a teacher of tolerance, a bridge between those with centuries of civilization and high culture behind them, and those who were still savages and head-hunters, a guide and a refuge for all those who were frightened, pessimistic, paralysed, clinging to their old laws of clan, sangha, caste and country. There were some monasteries that had already taken up this civilizational role, who were teaching people to think positively, to be productive and peaceful. He was referring, he said, to the new monasteries of the south, also those of Sanchi, Mathura and Maheshwar.

Harsha was startled. As were others. Not Kalinga, Upali thought, but then the Kalinga monastery was dead. But Bhima would be free soon, free to try and talk sense into his people. Hopefully they would listen, hopefully they would spread the idea to the other villages of deportees, for the iron project had to be a collective effort. Some would call Bhima a coward. Perhaps a traitor. Perhaps even a madman, if he spoke of his own bizarre option. But they would call a secret meeting of their samiti, the general assembly, which was not supposed to exist any more. Finally they would vote. The majority decision would prevail. It was scary, because the majority was often the most conservative.

The Sangha would have to clean up its act, the Beloved of the Gods was saying, it would have to give up squabbling, over-theorizing, small-mindedness, indiscipline, and concentrate instead on transforming people's lives.

'Remember, Thera and Theris, there is a great responsibility on your shoulders. Both this world and the next are hard to achieve, except by love of the law, self-examination, obedience, respect, energy. This is my rule: government by the law, administration according to the law, gratification of my people under the law, protection through the law. And my law is Dhamma.'

He stopped. There was a pause before the explosive confirmation that the Raja had spoken.

The Magadhe-Raja nodded at Mogalliputta who leapt from his seat; he seemed to have become younger since Sanchi. He spoke curtly again, more like an armyman than a monk – but then the Murderer had appropriated the latter role for himself.

'Venerable Theras and Theriis, the task ahead is difficult. On the one hand is the need to preach Dhamma with the greatest vigour and dedication, on the other the importance of maintaining the purity of Dhamma. It is difficult to reconcile the two, but we have to. The only solution is stringent discipline. One issue is of appearance – it is important that the Sangha be recognized by the public, for recognition means both honour and responsibility. It has been decided that all monks and nuns will wear robes of saffron-coloured cloth, the colour being the one most common in the Shakyamuni's time, for it was one of the earliest dyes developed in Kashi. Two sets of robes will be handed over to each monk and nun tomorrow.

'The second change is more important. We have carried out a study of the differences currently within the Order and concluded that there are eighteen different ideological groups, different in their rules of self-discipline, membership, behaviour and practice, of understanding and preaching of the Middle Way. These eighteen can however be divided into two broad categories. The first, with seven sects, are those with very slight deviations or none at all from the Buddha's original teachings. I am happy to announce that most of our brethren belong to this group. Barely one-fifth belong to the remaining eleven sects, which have unfortunately lost their way quite irrevocably. On behalf of the Beloved of the

Gods, the Magadhe-Raja, I announce that these eleven sects are, as of now, banned. They include....'

How did the old man know what the Buddha's original teachings were, and what classified as slight deviations? He did not explain. The offensive was followed by another, yet another royal proclamation read out by a soldier.

'The Beloved of the Gods orders the officers of all cities thus:

"'No one is to cause dissension in the Sangha. The Shakyamuni's Order of monks and nuns is now united, and this unity should last for not only as long as my sons and grandsons, but for as long as the moon and the sun. Anybody who creates a schism in the Sangha, whether monk or nun, is to be defrocked of their venerable saffron robes and sent away from all monasteries and all monks or nuns. For it is my wish that the Sangha must remain united and endure for long. This is to be made known to the Order of monks and nuns. They are to keep one copy of this document in their meeting hall and give one copy to the local laity. The lay-people must come on every uposatha day to endorse it. The same applies to the Dhamma Mahamatas, the Ministers of Dhamma, who must also regularly attend the uposathas, endorse this order and make it publicly known. I want this text circulated exactly as it is throughout your district. You must also have it circulated in all the border districts and those under military control."'

Typical – to threaten to take away the robes even before they were put on!

That was the end of the first day of the Congress. The monks took time to recover. By nightfall however discussions had begun, some secretive, others loud and angry, as one between the Venerable Jeevana, who held that the bans were long overdue, and Thera Deepak from Kushinara, who questioned the Magadhe-Raja's authority in the matter.

'He has selected teachings,' Deepak was saying when Upali and Ananda came out for a break from their writing, 'though the Buddha himself only enumerated the Eightfold Path. He's giving us a uniform, when the Buddha wore rags from rubbish heaps! The Buddha said that four or five monks were free to formulate their own rules of living, but now it is to be set by Pataliputra!'

'The times have changed, Deepak,' said Jeevana. 'And the Buddha himself held that one had to change with the times. Why should we not select for ourselves the most important of his teachings, the most important for our own struggle – ?'

'It is not you doing the selecting.'

' – and is there any doubt that the Sangha needs to be cleaned up, that there are monks today who are not practising even elementary discipline?'

'That is precisely because the Magadhe-Raja now finances monasteries – monk-hood has become a comfortable life!' Deepak smiled around challengingly. 'There are really two issues. One is whether we need to unify our practice. The second issue is of who will judge the correctness of practice. The Buddha said that the Sangha was to have no leader. Dhamma was to be our guide. So where does the Magadhe-Raja come in? He is not the first Raja who talks of Dhamma, but surely the first who acts like its leader!'

'He is the first who is truly a follower, Deepak! Don't forget he has actually forsworn war.'

'Is that really possible – a king without war?'

'It's unheard of – it can't be done. It would be suicidal!' This was a monk from Brahmagiri, right at the southern border. 'If word gets out, every kingdom around will start polishing their armaments and preparing for battle!'

'Word *is* out,' said the Sanchi Thera softly. 'The Magadhe-Raja's speech was read out simultaneously in the city. It will soon be proclaimed all over the empire.'

He should go back to work, or continue walking, anything far away from these die-hard debaters, Upali had been thinking. Instead he joined in. 'Have you people actually fallen for that nonsense? He slaughters Kalinga one minute and preaches peace the next? Who is responsible for the lack of peace – us? Does he think we're fools?'

'Always Kalinga!' The Sanchi Thera raised his hands melodramatically. 'Upali, at this rate some might doubt your patriotism!'

'There is nothing to doubt. I'm a member of the Sangha, not of any nation!'

'Anyway,' Harsha laid a calming hand on Upali's arm – it was the first time he had spoken since the Magadhe-Raja's afternoon speech, Ananda realized; the first time in Pataliputra that his forehead was uncreased – 'Let it be.'

'Funding will be the end,' smiled Deepak, a happy prophet of doom. 'All kinds of riffraff will flock to the monasteries for the rich pickings.' It was exactly what Harsha had been saying for a long time, but he was silent now.

'What nonsense! Funding started long ago, without any ill-effects.' The boss of the most lavishly-funded one was firm. 'And the riffraff are out, as of today – nobody will dare to join the Sangha henceforth unless they are clear about its aims and ideas. All that superstitious Mahasanghika nonsense is over and done with, thank god! I really don't understand why we are worried. What is a grant after all, but alms again? If we can receive alms from the people, why can't we receive them from the Court?'

Upali couldn't believe his ears. 'Are you serious, Thera? So a king's grant, taken from the taxes he extracts from the people, handed over with instructions of what to do with it – and you can be sure of that, from all the instructions handed out today – is alms; but the production of food violates Dhamma?'

The Sanchi Thera was silent. Nobody else met his eye either. Except for the Takshashila monk Vipul, sitting at the back. When Upali's gaze reached him, he nodded quickly, rose and disappeared around the corner. Whatever was the young fool up to?

Upali leaned over to Ananda, 'I want to rest a while. We'll work later.' He got up and followed Vipul, and found him waiting on the other side of the vihara.

'Thera, can you come with me? I need to check up on something that Pradyota had arranged....'

'Arranged? What do you mean?'

Vipul looked pale, as if he had not eaten for a long time. 'A consignment of some goods for his cousin in Ujjayani. It was to reach Takshashila some three months back; a merchant there had agreed to take it to Ujjayani. But Pradyota had to leave before it arrived, so he asked me to check on it. It still hasn't reached. I'm going to find the man who he was in touch with, a factory supervisor named Shankardas in the iron and steel district.'

Upali glared at him. 'Listen Vipul, I understand your sorrow over Pradyota, but this is a political plot. About which the Court is already aware! They questioned me – and they asked about you. The consignment must be arms. They're planning something in Ujjayani. Take my advice and forget all this. Or you'll be in trouble.'

'I promised Pradyota.'

'Are you listening to me? They cannot defeat Magadh – '

'I thought you supported the cause of freedom!'

'Vipul, do you know the size of the Magadhan army? Avanti will be pulped. And everybody else in the vicinity.' Vipul was clearly not listening. He seemed to be communing instead with a large grey owl on a jack tree near by. 'You have to put it behind you. Pradyota is dead. He's probably dead because of all this – '

'I can't betray him.'

'He's gone, Vipul. You can't betray him even if you tried! Death is unbetrayable!' Vipul turned away. 'Where are you going?'

'My dormitory.'

'Good. Just forget it all.' Vipul walked off leaving Upali to the baleful contempt of the owl. Yes, I know it sounded like cowardice but that's how sanity sometimes sounds. And what difference did it really make whether Magadh or the Sungas ruled Avanti? None. For all the commoners, the peasants, jungle-folk and deportees, it was like a choice between a tiger and a pack of wild dogs! That's what he should have told Vipul, instead of talking of defeat. People who'd never known war were not frightened by defeat.

But the owl had transformed itself, and into Prime Minister, Radhagupta.

It was a nasty shock. He was back in the Great Hall facing the throne, with the Prime Minister seated in an untidy heap at its foot. But there was something in his stare. Enough to make Upali wish he was far away. He wished he had never started this story. He wished the ancient Mogalliputta would stop his jabbering to the throne. What were they speaking of for so long?

Finally, Mogalliputta turned his long length around. 'We are obliged to the Venerable Thera Upali. Questions and comments on his reading may follow after the meal.'

The Magadhe-Raja rose and the assembly fell to the floor. He swept out; it got up and rubbed knees and elbows. Ananda and Upali bound up their sheets and joined Harsha at the tail of the stream wending its way out of the Hall and down an infinite number of tall corridors, their walls inset with sculpted ivory or hung with embroidered silk, all immortalizing the exploits of Chandragupta – at war, at the hunt, receiving homage. His son and grandson were not very visible. Perhaps they did not want to disturb the ghost of that most aggressively successful of the Mauryas. What would he have said to this declaration of no war? It seemed a joke, a bad joke, as they walked past the grandfather charging, cutting, hacking his way to glory. On and on. There must be nearly a thousand rooms in the place, perhaps more, since Chandragupta was reputed to have never slept in the same room twice for fear of assassination.

Their destination was a long dining hall, laid with rows of seats of ivory-inlaid rosewood – how many elephants had to die for all the monks to sit on their teeth, Harsha had grumbled the previous morning. But he was grumbling less today. Now he seated himself on the teeth and said nothing, not even about the banana leaf plates, though they were trimmed to exactly the same size and rimmed delicately with gold thread, all to be disposed of after the meal.

'Thera, may I speak to you for a moment?' It was one of the senior Pataliputra monks, Brajesh by name. He squatted down in front of Upali.

'Yes?'

'I heard you speak yesterday evening of Kalinga. Then I remembered I had heard Mahesh speak so many times of an Upali – '

'You know Mahesh?' Finally, after four years, he had found one of his old comrades! 'Where is he?'

'He was with us....'

'Where's he now?'

'I'm sorry, Thera, but he died. A year ago.' He paused, Upali waited. 'It was an accident.'

Upali waited. The waiters contorted themselves elaborately around Brajesh to try and serve him rice, dal, vegetables and sweets, and looked disappointed when he refused everything.

'He was a little – unstable. He had arrived with a raging fever, which left him weak, I think. He used to see things, dreams, nightmares, whatever.

'It was at an uposatha with His Majesty – His Majesty began to attend our sessions two or three years ago. Not regularly of course, once in a while. This was the second time. A few of us spoke, about our work and so on, the others were too nervous. Mahesh was silent. Then His Majesty began to speak of Kalinga, he was talking of the lives lost, I think. We were seated in a large circle, His Majesty too but on a little seat. Behind us, all around, stood his soldiers. Suddenly Mahesh got up and rushed forwards, shouting something. It was very sudden. One moment we were all listening quietly, Mahesh too I suppose, the next minute he was in front of His Majesty, about to fall on him, it seemed. And one of the soldiers threw his spear. Straight at Mahesh.

'His Majesty was furious, he turned on the soldier with an oath and bent to Mahesh himself, but his ministers rushed forward too, so he rose and left. The others stayed behind, physicians arrived too, but... it was hopeless.'

Upali just stared at his plate.

'I wish he'd known you had survived. He was obsessed with the war. I tried to tell him to forget. These things are fated to happen.'

'What happened to the killer?'

'Who? Oh, the soldier? I don't know. Though I suppose he was just doing his job.' Brajesh waited for a while, finally added, 'I'm really sorry, Thera,' and moved off.

How many times had Upali himself thought of killing the Magadhe-Raja? Mahesh had actually tried. And now Mahesh was dead, like Narayan. That left Arjun and Nayana. The two other nuns had left earlier for their parents' homes, the novices too, before Upali left for Tosali. When he got back, there was only Narayan, an incoherent Narayan in a burning village.

He wished he had carried Loka's medicine with him. He began to inhale slowly, very slowly, feeling his stomach rise painfully, letting it out even slower; then noticed the Sanchi Thera. He was sitting opposite him and staring across quite irritably.

'Is something wrong, Thera?'

'No, nothing,' The Thera looked away and then back. 'You might as well know – your sculptor has been arrested in Ujjayani!'

It took a moment for Upali to understand. 'Devadina?'

'Who else?' Others turned; the Thera lowered his voice. 'He went to meet his girl apparently – the fool! It's all your fault, Upali. If you hadn't come and blabbed needlessly, the Viceroy would never have heard of him!'

This was probably true but Upali felt a bit confused by the sudden attack. 'Anyway, what will happen now?'

'Nothing, I hope. Execution luckily requires the sanction of the home ministry here. But he is being held in the Viceroy's palace itself. It's very irregular. The Viceroy is a strange man, Upali. You really should choose your friends more carefully!'

'It was you who introduced him to me! And Devadina's not in any danger, surely? What proof do they have?'

'Proof is easy to invent!'

The Thera got up and walked out before Upali could ask why the Viceroy would invent proof against Devadina. He felt like shaking his head, to clear it. It was good to see the usually complacent Thera worried about someone. But a little strange too.

'I'm sorry about your friend Mahesh,' he heard Harsha say.

Upali nodded and dismissed the Thera from his mind. 'Look at this.' He lifted his upper lip, revealing a gap in the top row of teeth.

'Your teeth?'

'The gap. A raja complained against us and we – Mahesh and I – were called to Tosali, by the Gana Sabha, to explain. The plaintiff spoke at length about how we were encouraging the youth towards blasphemy, disrespect, pollution, whatever. Then we replied. Then the Chief began to speak, and I thought of something I had forgotten. So I said, "One moment, lord – " and I think I passed out. One of the rajas had just smashed his sword into my face. Luckily the flat of it, or I wouldn't be here today. Luckily also a little lower down, or I would be blind. Anyway, my jaw broke and those teeth fell out. It took six months to heal. And Mahesh said at least you've learnt not to interrupt anybody at a royal assembly!'

'I again thank the Most Venerable Thera Upali,' announced Mogalliputta back in the Great Hall. 'Questions and comments can proceed now. All may speak by turn.'

There was a long silence. Everybody expected the first comment to come from the dais. But it remained silent. Finally a very old monk raised a hand and rose. 'Sire, with all respect, I must say that I was shocked by the description of the Shakyamuni's enlightenment. It was flippant and wishy-washy. The author has clearly not the slightest appreciation of the meaning of that great moment. The last chapter is impossible.'

He bowed and sat down. The Raja's eye was closed but the blunt condemnation seemed to inspire everybody. Another hand went up immediately. 'Sire, with your permission, I too am surprised by the enlightenment. The Thera has focused on the doing part – what the Buddha wanted his followers to do – and quite ignored the understanding part. There is not a word about the very core, which is the realization of the nothingness of the world. That all objects in the world are characterized by a suchness, which makes them unique, but also a sameness, which makes them all the same. The realization that this world is an illusion.'

Another followed. 'With all respect, sire, I was shocked by the description of the noble Shakyas – they have been vilified. The Buddha was always proud of being a Shakya. He even boasted that the kshatriyas could trace their lineage back through seven generations! But the worst is the human sacrifice in chapter one. Where in all the scriptures does the Most Venerable Thera find a confirmation of this?'

Mogalliputta nodded to Upali. He rose reluctantly. 'The practice was a well-known part of the rites of many orthodox communities. I've seen it with my own eyes.' The smoky air caught at his throat; he was glad to close his mouth.

'Where? At Kalinga? Surely the Thera is not equating the noble Shakyas with the savages of Kalinga!'

There were some titters. Kalinga was not only savages, you moron, said Upali but silently.

Jeevana's old bête noire Keshav Seshadri of Nalanda was next. 'While one must appreciate the hard work put in by the Thera, I am genuinely surprised by this interpretation of the Shakyamuni's sorrow. Surely it is clearly mentioned that his sorrow was over the inherent contradiction in human existence – which is very simply that birth is the cause of death. All who are born must age, take ill and die. That is the chilling sadness in life. And that is the problem to which the Buddha sought a solution. I also object strongly to the description of the enlightenment. The story of Mara is of course a fairy-tale, but the spiritual quest rather meanly described as the second school of ideas – that should be treated better, as my brother just now explained.'

So the 'suchness and sameness' describer was from Nalanda. Upali stayed seated. Keshava was followed by others, rising half-visibly through the forest of columns with mostly similar problems, as if it was the forest itself speaking. There were a few exceptions, like a monk from Topra, who said, 'I would like to express my gratitude. I feel that I understand Dhamma much better now, thanks to Thera Upali's efforts'; and Therii Vrinda of Ujjayani who said something similar; and one more who also complimented Ananda's reading. The Raja's eye stayed closed. Upali stayed seated, and avoided Mogalliputta's eye as well.

Till, 'Sire, I object to many things in the account just presented.' The speaker was hidden, but his sharpness was immediately familiar. 'Especially the pathetic depiction of the Buddha himself, weaker and more impressionable than he ever could have been. And also the description of his enlightenment. By denying the Buddha's enlightenment, by denying Nirvana, Upali is actually denying the efforts of the whole Sangha!'

It was old Mahanta. And Upali did not know why, but he stood up. 'Sire, Nirvana is an idea of great beauty and great merit.' He felt Harsha's surprised stare. 'Its merit is in its universality and its ethic – it promises improvement in every successive life, if one follows the Way. Irrespective of one's community and caste. And the ultimate reward it promises is nothingness. I never understood this before – I saw it as a negative position, a rejection of life, a defeat at the hands of worldly problems – but now I see it differently. Nirvana is indeed nothing, yet everything. It is the point of truth, of purity, of clarity, uncluttered by desire. Of no power and yet every power – for to have no desire at all is a powerful state. It is freedom from the world, a freedom that harks back, for every jungle-dweller and every peasant, perhaps for even the powerful bureaucrat and merchant, to the ancient and revered golden age, that time of purity, when man had little and yet enough. When there were no differences between men, and no competition. No money, no great godowns of rice, no gold ornaments or four-horse carriages, but also no war, no slave-owners, tax-collectors or prisons. But it remembers too the ignorance, the subservience to nature, the easy death. So it was the time when man was nothing, and yet everything. Nirvana is nostalgia for a time that is gone, a craving terribly painful for those who have just lost that life, a blissful dream even for those who never knew it. And the Sangha built this craving into the Way. Not deliberately or manipulatively, for the monks were and are people too, of the same mettle and the same memory. And they removed the narrowness, the ritualism, the limitation of tribe and race. A Chandala can be born a brahmin, and vice versa; and both can achieve Nirvana. I believe these beliefs began with the Mahasanghikas, though they are now common.' He listened for a moment to the low gasps. 'The Sangha's Nirvana is broad-minded, compassionate, beautiful. But I do not believe the Buddha bothered himself with any such thing. He was a profoundly rational person. Though not argumentative.'

The disembodied voice was not interested at all. 'Sire, I foresee dangerous confusion over the tasks of the Sangha. Are monks not to seek freedom from rebirth? Are they not to teach people salvation from the cycle of sorrow? Are they to merely carry out the compassionate deeds that the Sangha took up among its mundane tasks, and forget about the fundamental ones?'

This was becoming an argument, but Mogalliputta seemed unbothered. Upali was finding the process of rising, prostrating, that too towards an apparently sleeping object, and rising again to speak, exhausting to say the least. But if old Mahanta could do it, so could he.

'Thera Mahanta, what you call mundane tasks – compassion, peace, tolerance, ignoring birth and background – were hugely radical ideas for that time, and for today as well. They sound simple but are nearly impossible to do. Which is why the Buddha died a somewhat unsatisfied man. Which is why then you have a lot of his ideas simplified or even misunderstood. The legend can turn even elementary issues on their head. For example, it is impossible that he could have boasted of his kshatriya lineage, or have been pollution-conscious. He used to eat whatever was put in his alms-bowl. This was shocking at the time and later. So little adjustments came in. As when, according to one story, the monks refused Raja Pasenadi's alms because they regarded themselves as kshatriyas – so to improve his status among them, Pasenadi asked for the hand of a Shakya rajkumari!'

'Basically, Upali, you have used the scriptures selectively! What you do not like, you condemn as lies added later. You seem to believe that the Sangha deteriorated after the Buddha.'

'Changed, at least. We can all see the great differences in theories and practise between the monasteries gathered here today. And I do not say that these are deliberately introduced. These are interpretations, adjustments, understandings and misunderstandings. I believe the Sangha has done the best it could.'

'You are kind, Thera. But you do the Sangha an injury, especially in the matter of caste bias. The Sangha has always been a broad-minded organization, and you yourself are the proof.' Mahanta paused and coughed a little; Ananda hoped he would choke; everybody else waited. 'You are Chandala-born, Upali. But the Sangha took you in. Knowingly, from your mother. Can anything be more liberal than that?'

There was another pause, a long one in which Ananda thought he could hear every breath in the hall. Yet when Upali responded, he was louder than normal, as if he had to penetrate right through the cacophony of columns, as if he knew he could not get through. But he didn't answer the question. 'Thera, I was asked recently whether I was a brahmin and I replied that I am a monk. I am still a monk.'

People were staring at him, they looked confused, even shocked. Ananda glared at them but they ignored him, so he turned away to first the floor, then the ceiling, both of which were comfortingly noncommittal.

The Magadhe-Raja opened his eye and raised a hand as if to silence the dumbstruck hall. 'The issue is hardly relevant to the debate at hand.'

But he seemed to find it so himself, for he immediately rose and left. Everybody fell to the floor and got up in quiet chaos. The Sanchi Thera, Jeevana and others converged on Mahanta, others drifted hesitantly towards them. Ananda stared upwards and waited for Upali to do something. Upali slowly untied his folder, looked inside as though unaware of the contents, tied it up and rose.

But then Mogalliputta announced in a voice more guttural than usual, 'Theras, Theris, we will close today with an interval of meditation. Each of you please listen to your own inner voice.'

Jeevana looked as if he wanted the others to listen to his outer voice, but took his seat. Everybody settled down in padmasan; the Pataliputra monks began a low chant. The Sanchi one. *Budham saranam gachaami, dhammam saranam gachchaami, sangham saranam gachchaami....* Upali had always found the words evocative of passive helplessness, rather than the sturdy commitment one would expect from people with a mission. But today he surrendered to them completely. He felt himself dissolving, snuggling his way into their gentle throbbing embrace. I take refuge in the Buddha, I take refuge in the Dhamma, I take refuge in the Sangha... I take refuge... I take refuge.... Loka would have been pleased with him.

They went back to the monastery in a carriage of silent monks. Upali wanted to ask Harsha what he thought of Mahanta's revelation but he was not sure how. Besides, everybody was staring at him surreptitiously.

They reached, everybody alighted, and Harsha turned and asked, 'Are you two planning to work this evening? Otherwise I thought we could stroll around and see the city.'

Upali nodded in silence and Harsha went to ask the soldiers at the gates for advice about strolling around, when a young monk of Pataliputra, Shashank by name, came up to Upali and Ananda.

'Thera, there was something...' he began awkwardly.

'Yes?'

'About your story.'

Upali brightened. 'Oh. Yes, what is it, brother?'

'I didn't want to speak at Court, but I thought I'd tell you. It's a little – dull.'

Ananda was surprised, Upali a hundred times more. 'Dull?'

'Yes, slightly.'

'Whatever do you mean?'

'I mean, it's not as exciting as the suttas.'

'What exactly do you mean?'

Shashank looked worried. 'Nothing. I mean – well, especially the suttas about the Buddha's enlightenment...' Ananda nodded encouragingly and he perked up. 'Now those are exciting! There's that description of how the maid Sujatha makes the richest of all porridges for the Buddha – how she feeds the milk of a 1000 of her best cows to 500, and then the milk of the 500 cows to 250, and so on till she ends with the milk of 8 cows, the richest, sweetest, strongest milk imaginable! And then there's the sutta of Mara. How the God of Evil sends all kinds of monstrous forces – huge fire-breathing serpents, and then goblins and then a black reeking storm, monstrous thunder and lightning; then his beautiful daughters, as shapely and seductive as imaginable at first, then transformed into hideous witches... and how all of nature is terrified by this cosmic turmoil, day becoming night, the elements in chaos, but the Buddha is absolutely undisturbed! It's all so exciting!' Shashank suddenly noticed Upali's expression – 'I don't know much about all this, of course. It's just what I thought, I thought I'd tell you.'

'Listen,' said Upali a little grimly and Ananda felt sorry for Shashank. 'Have you ever seen a cow drinking milk?' He raised his hands, Sanchi-Thera-style. 'Have you ever seen a cow, damn it? I can't believe this! The battle with Mara! That's exactly the kind of childish superstitious nonsense that I'm trying to get rid of!'

Shashank shifted from one foot to the other and finally offered, 'Yes, I understand. It's just – it's composed well, that's all. Thank you, Thera.'

He shuffled off. Upali glared into the distance; Ananda adjusted his shoulder cloth over his head to hide a grin. Harsha finished his deliberations with the soldiers and led them out of the gates and straight into the path of a big figure on a bigger horse. It was the charioteer Chandra.

'I heard the Congress was over early today, so I wondered whether you'd like to see the city. I am free this evening.'

He was warmly received, so he left his horse at the monastery and the four of them set out on foot. 'We are now in the middle eastern quarter, not too far from the city centre.'

'Where's your sword, Chandra?' asked Ananda, the arms-loving monk.

'At the armoury. No one can move armed in the city, not even soldiers, unless they are on duty here. I'm off duty for a few days now.'

The locality about the monastery was quiet and shady. Many big merchants lived hereabouts, said Chandra, the estates behind the walls could be quite vast. They moved on into a more commercial district, where the buildings were fronted by shops and the busy streets became busier still, till they were walking single file and vehicular traffic slowed to a near standstill. The streets themselves remained broad and straight, intersecting always at right angles. Pataliputra was laid out according to a design, Chandra shouted for all to hear – Chandragupta's design. 'He tore down the whole city and started from scratch.'

'Where did people live in the meanwhile?' asked Harsha from somewhere.

'I don't know. Maybe it was done part by part.' Chandra was not too bothered. Like his namesake Maurya no doubt, thought Upali sourly. But he felt a little better.

The buildings hugged the roads, both resenting the pavements in between but providing thankful shade in the process. They passed government offices of various kinds, many large shopping establishments, guild-houses, schools, hospitals and alms-houses, most adorned again by quite a bit of fret-worked timber and paint. Boats stood at anchor near one entrance – the ship-builders' guild. Robust women, pots balanced on their heads and plump children dancing at their feet, greeted invalids at a hospital. Crowds of people pushed past scenes of crowded people. Pataliputrans liked art, Chandra explained sagely.

They were getting pushed apart regularly now and having to stop to wait for each other at every street corner. Grim soldiers stood there too, breaking up traffic jams efficiently while looking quite capable of breaking heads too.

'This is the most crowded city in the empire,' declared Chandra proudly. 'This road is known as the King's Way – you should see it when the Magadhe-Raja passes through. Absolute silence, except for one single drum and the swish of the gold brocade elephant quilts trailing behind each beast. The poise, the magnificence, the discipline is enough to make you cry.' Not a bad simile at all, thought Upali.

'Well,' Chandra added a moment later. 'This is more or less the centre.'

It was a vast crossroads, rimmed all around by tall sober buildings. In the centre, a timber railing enclosed a high stepped platform of black stone, from which rose a single column. Similar to the one at Sanchi, of the same dark buff sandstone that shone like steel. There, far up against the clouds, could be made out four elephants standing back-to-back, oblivious to the noise and crowd, staring straight out along the four roads to some distant horizon.

'Ahead is the palace complex,' pointed Chandra. 'This side, the police headquarters and courts. That side, the industries and then the docks. There the markets, then more residential areas, of the artisans and workers – '

His audience stared instead at the stambha. The one at Sanchi had lain on its side; who could have imagined it like this? This had to be the thunderbolt of the Shatterer of Cities, no, the axis mundi joining sky to earth, around which Harsha's Universal Cycles were reputed to revolve. It cast a long shadow in the evening light that shot straight across the junction and up the face of a building.

'It's – magnificent...' breathed Harsha slowly.

'But why does he build these, Chandra?' asked Ananda. 'I mean, they're a bit strange too.'

'Well, I see the height as divinity. The shadow is governance. The gaze of the four beasts is the reach of the empire, in every direction, to the horizon and beyond. And the actual column – the monolithic shaft, its size and burnish, the calmness and regality of the whole – all that is civilization. Law, discipline, technology, the order of Magadh.'

Harsha and Ananda were staring at the charioteer now; their gaze was awed and irritating. 'It's the ideal,' Chandra added. 'The reality is more difficult.'

'Aren't you a bit sentimental?' burst out Upali. 'What about power? Arrogance? Autocracy? Ambition? The desire for immortality? I think they explain this somewhat better!'

But every king had his fair share of all these, yet nobody built this way. Building was power, the power to create, to change the earth's surface, rival its beauty, challenge its majesty. But outside their own palaces, most rulers built only massive shrines, and images of the gods. That was how they saw themselves – as the representative and foremost servant of the supernatural. This was different. This was not for the gods, it was for the dialogue between the Magadhe-Raja and his 'children'. It was really a monument to the Magadhe-Raja himself.

Chandra broke the spell. 'Did you know that His Majesty is issuing a statement on Kalinga?'

'What do you mean?'

'Come on.' He marched off down a new road. 'It was read out this morning in the army quarters. An apology for the war. To the people of Kalinga, and to the army as well.'

Harsha's hand gripped Upali's shoulder. 'See?'

Upali shrugged it off. 'Don't you army people find it a bit strange?'

'It is strange, I suppose. But the Magadhe-Raja is a great commander, the best ever perhaps, after his grandfather. The army supports him totally.'

'But Magadh's whole past has been about conquest and annexation! Aren't you surprised?'

The charioteer shrugged. 'We were, at the start. Seriously. For a monarch to talk about giving up war – it's unheard of. And when you remember that he had already given up hunting and eating meat – ' He shook his head and marched on so that his followers had to dodge around passersby and nearly run to hear him – 'There were whispers about his mental state, even his manhood! But a few of us had faith – and we were justified. What he's doing is simple. Magadh has reached realistic limits. There's no place left to conquer. Worth it, I mean. I was part of this southern campaign and the place is complete jungle. It has rich gold mines, of course, and now they are ours. And the small republics there are friendly and pay tribute. So what more do we want? And if we invest in the enormous campaigns required to conquer the icy north west beyond Bactra, we may lose the south. We already have the largest empire in the world. We have to make the most of it. The army will still be vital, but its focus will be different. Even now if you see, it is mainly involved in defence, and internal law and order, especially in the jungle districts where the more stubborn of the jungle tribes have still to be tamed. Also developmental work, like the Sudarshan dam we built in Girnar. There is a lot more to be done.'

There was a small pause, then Harsha laughed. 'Chandra, you sound like a Maurya yourself!'

Upali did not. 'This is what it all is – not really Dhamma, or a love for peace, just realpolitic. Using Dhamma to hold on to empire….'

'Whatever the reason, Upali,' said Harsha, 'even if it is about politics, it is also about peace and tolerance. We should be grateful for that.'

'Not to mention the crumbs of praise thrown at us!'

The air was touched with an abrupt chill; the sun was beginning to dip. 'The wholesale markets,' Chandra announced at the head of another busy street. There, somewhere past the warehouses fronted by broad verandas displaying diverse types of products and even more diverse varieties of merchant, perhaps not far from the wholesale grocery markets where the air was alive with the pickling of spices and the cacophony of incarcerated fowl – though the meat market was seriously collapsing, according to Chandra, thanks to the royal proselytizing on vegetarianism – Upali saw a familiar figure. That walk, the slight leaning on the left hip, that dark thick braid of hair, the way she swung the basket slightly. Her shoulders were bare, the skin as dark and smooth as it had always been. It had to be! She vanished into the crowd and then reappeared, but still way ahead. It was her, this time there was no doubt at all. But no, he would not make a fool of himself again. He would follow her and make sure.

The others thought nothing when Upali stopped Chandra from turning right at the next junction. But they were slightly surprised when he insisted 'Straight, straight' at the one following, though Harsha wanted to examine the school to their left, and then they could hardly miss it when he said at the third, 'Listen, I'll meet you later at this shop, all right?'

'Where are you going?' asked Harsha.

'Nowhere. You go ahead. I'll meet you soon.'

'We'll come too,' said Ananda.

'I want to be alone!' Upali marched away, leaving the others staring after him.

'Let's follow him,' suggested Ananda, but Harsha had scruples. Upali, he said, would explain things when he returned.

Upali returned soon enough because he had lost Nayana at the beginning of the very next lane, if it was she; he explained nothing.

'What area is this?' he asked Chandra.

'The brothel quarter.'

'Are you all right, Upali?' asked Harsha. 'Do you want to sit?'

'No. Let's go back – I'm tired,' Upali mumbled. There was a rumble of thunder; a moist breeze drifted up and he shivered. Turning away to avoid Ananda's gaze, he walked straight into the horses of an open carriage. They reared and pawed the air, shimmering pearl-plaited manes flashing outrage. Chandra only just managed to yank him out of the way. The driver calmed the animals, then turned to berate the blasted fool of a pedestrian. Chandra joined issue, telling the driver that it was time for him to learn driving instead of jerking about like a drunkard looking for a gutter to fall into. The driver was just expressing serious doubt about the origins of Chandra, his mother, father, clan and nation, when a gentleman in the carriage hailed Upali.

It was Milindachanda, the merchant whose caravan had escorted them to Sanchi, except that he was unrecognizably swathed in an embroidered silk shawl of rich emerald hue, with heavy gold ornaments at wrists, throat and ears. He lived very near Ashokarama, he said, and insisted that they travel back with him and visit his house. Ashokarama? It was the name of the monastery – Ashoka's monastery.

To Ananda's surprise, Upali accepted. Harsha did not protest. Chandra quietly bade them farewell.

It started raining as they reached Milindachanda's mansion, but servants were waiting on the porch with warm scented water for their feet and napkins for their heads. Milindachanda led the way to a hall lit by porcelain lamps and crowded with ornamental vases, statuettes and a few people – his son, whom they had met earlier, a well-dressed couple and a large woman whose gold embellishments rivalled his own.

Milindachanda introduced the couple as Lalit, a metal engineer, and his wife; the gold exhibition was his own spouse. The fellow-occupant of his carriage was Samudraraja, a noble if the raja suffix was anything to go by.

The couple responded by touching the feet of the monks. Lalit was just back from a trip to Takshashila, explained Milindachanda, concerning a new metal testing centre.

The engineer nodded. 'For our iron exports. The demand is tremendous – from even China now. It is growing at a faster rate than we can supply, even with the new southern Deccan mines.'

'How are things in Takshashila?' asked Milindachanda's wife.

'All right. A bit more chaotic. Earlier the confusion used to be restricted to the outskirts, but now with the relaxation in the city laws, anybody can live anywhere. Not that I'm against it, it's doing wonders for business. But the Greeks are busy spreading chaos everywhere. Those people are incapable of following laws! If we didn't have a strong administration, the place would be a slum – like Susa or Miletus!'

Everybody settled down against silk bolsters, and servants appeared with water, wine, pastries and fruit. Three girls followed carrying large peacock feathered fans in ivory holders and stood fanning away behind the guests.

'What were you doing near the brothel quarter?' Milindachanda asked Upali. 'Not the place where one would expect to see monks!'

Upali smiled. 'We were just walking around, looking at your city. And you, what were you doing there?'

'Samudraraja needs dancers. We had heard that there were still some cheap Kalinga girls available at some places, but the prices were ridiculous.'

Upali hunched over a little and stared at his hands; anything to avoid looking at Harsha and Ananda. Samudraraja, who was popping savouries into his mouth in a steady stream, paused and spoke for the first time: 'Monstrous – especially considering the glut in the market since the war! But you cannot blame them, Milinda, it's the taxes. The Mauryas have made even brothel-keeping unprofitable! But I shall go back tomorrow. Remember that little wench with the long braid? I liked her. I'll pay their price.'

'None of you are eating anything,' said Milindachanda to the monks. He waved at some shiny red fruit. 'Those are apples from Takshashila – have you seen them before? Or have these savouries. Come on, everything is vegetarian.'

'Milindachanda has almost given up meat,' Samudraraja told Lalit. 'And he's supposed to be a brahmin!'

'Most people have cut down, except extreme conservatives!' retorted Milindachanda. 'And I feel healthier.'

'Naturally – imitating the Court is always healthier!'

Milindachanda's wife waved a placatory tray. 'Have a sweet. You also, boy – '

Ananda picked up a pastry, and found the steamed cover disintegrating halfway to his mouth. The whole thing collapsed in semi-liquid dollops of coconut, jaggery and milk.

'That's quite all right! Take another,' said Milindachanda's wife. A servant arrived almost immediately with a cloth and wiped the mess around a bit.

Upali turned to Lalit. 'Are you familiar with the iron and steel district in the city?'

'A little, why?'

'A friend of mine was looking for somebody there – an officer named Shankardas.'

Lalit seemed to pause before shaking his head. 'I'm sorry, I don't recall anybody by that name.'

'Eat something, Thera,' urged Milindachanda.

'No, thank you. I have a stomach ache.'

'What – after partaking of Court hospitality?' asked Samudraraja with a grin. 'And I thought that the only thing of guaranteed and unadulterated profit nowadays was to become a monk!'

Harsha raised his brows. 'Profit and monks? To compare our monks with rich lords like you is almost ridiculous.'

'That might be true, my friend, in the foreign provinces where you live. But it is far from ridiculous here in Magadh. Rich and poor – all that means nothing now! The real thing is power, and that is with the monks!'

'Wealth has always bought power without much difficulty – '

'With great difficulty, sir! I speak from experience.' He laughed. 'The government is squeezing us out of every area – we're being reduced to transporters of government goods! Even brahmins and rajas, the most ancient of blue-blooded lineages, all are treated like dirt. The best thing is to give up and work for them – become their slave – kiss their backside and receive a salary every full moon day!'

'Which incidentally is not ungenerous at all!' Lalit's smile was unoffended. 'Anyway, Samudra, if trade is so bad, you can always retire to your estates in the north!' He nodded at the monks. 'Your

Maheshwar is going to be a busy place soon. Magadh will need more and more of southern iron and copper in the days to come.'

Milindachanda frowned. 'Why, are the mines here exhausted or something?'

'Exhausted? Far from it!'

'I heard some rumours of water levels being reached in the copper mines south of Gaya.'

'Well, my dear fellow, you would have noticed a rise in the price then, wouldn't you? There is no problem here. It is just that the demand, internal and international, is insatiable – we can use all the metal we find!' He laughed, but awkwardly, and picked up a little grey-green statuette from a group of three on an ivory table. 'This is pretty.'

His host accepted the change in topic gloomily. 'It's jade, from Siam via Tosali. These used to come through Bhrgukacha before, all the way around the coast. Now they're really cheap.'

'Not cheap, Sethi,' said Upali. 'It was paid for in blood.' Ananda was relieved. This sounded like the normal Upali.

'See, this is the problem!' declared Samudra. 'Name one thing, Thera, that has not been paid for in blood! Do you think Magadh would be what it is today – able, for example, to support a huge community of idle monks – without conquest and violence? Wealth and progress need violence. Mark my words – this whole sentimental monkish nonsense will finish us!'

Upali was silent, staring at the statuette. But Harsha smiled. 'Violence is not unique to Magadh, my lord. Every little kingdom, every tiny republic and tribe has believed in war since time immemorial – right till the moment when they were conquered by Magadh! Magadhan success in fact is the victory of something more – a different politics, and attitude – '

'The attitude is the problem! Magadh is going to the dogs, Thera, and not surprisingly – under a mad king!' Samudra was amazing. Had he never heard of spies, leave alone those in the guise of monks? 'Do you know, Lalit, that the city administration now allows outcastes to shop at the city markets – nobody has dared to, of course, but the idea! I've even heard of a proposal to amend the criminal law, to consider all cases equally! This Dhamma business has got the Maurya behaving as though he needs votes – as though he's a republican chief, and that too of the outcastes!'

Ananda licked his fingertips and hoped it was time to leave, Milindachanda looked embarrassed, the ladies bored.

'If you want such a large empire, you have to think of how to unite it, how to reduce barriers – ' began Harsha but he was not allowed to finish.

'You should unite it with your oldest and best traditions, not some strange new rubbish! Removing barriers is what causes tension, Thera. Barriers help a man know his place, removing them will not give you a united society but a confused one. The tigers are braying and the donkeys roaring! And – '

'Samudra, sometimes you surprise me,' interrupted Lalit too, and firmly. 'The genius of Magadh has been in keeping war to a minimum, even while expanding. Do you think this would have been possible without Dhamma – the very ideas that you are complaining of? What else is teaching the jungle-folk to work quietly on the fields that feed our army, instead of plundering caravans and villages like they used to? What is teaching them to respect our wealth, but not to envy it? How come you employ so many bright young people today, educated, willing to work for anybody irrespective of background, to even travel the world and sell your goods? Dhamma has always been one of the strengths of Magadh, but today we have a brilliant monarch who really understands this. It is these monks whom you mock who actually ensure your wealth!' He ended with a smile at Harsha who did not smile back.

'So, how is your Congress coming along?' asked Milindachanda a little desperately.

His son perked up. 'A lot of excitement, I believe! I heard that a Thera was exposed as a Chandala today!'

'What! Really?' Milindachanda asked Upali.

'Quite....'

'Well, I'm not surprised,' said Samudra. 'The question is, what will the Sangha do with the creature now? Probably embrace him to their bosom!'

'I certainly hope so,' said Upali lightly. 'Since the monk in question is myself.' He rose, Milindachanda's jaw dropped, but before he could say anything, Samudra had jumped up.

'So this is the hospitality you extend nowadays, Milindachanda – to the scum of the world! But at least you could have warned me in advance!' With that he headed for the doors, then turned back and spat full in Upali's face. Upali raised his hands and the spittle distributed itself over them, his face and Harsha. 'Scum!' Samudra emphasized, and left.

Upali wiped his face with his dirty hands and nodded at Milindachanda. 'Good bye.'

'But – but – but how could you? You sat in my carriage, entered my house! Ate my food!' Milindachanda lost control of his voice, which went from loud to shrill, ending as a weak scream. Servants rushed in; Lalit and the women rose but said nothing; the fanning girls shrank into the background. 'We'll have to get the house purified! We'll have to call a – '

His son interrupted without rising. 'Father, control yourself!'

It was like a whiplash. The company stared at him in shock, except for the three monks who walked out. In silence they found the main doors, the compound gates, and the route down the wet roads to the monastery. In silence the trees dripped on them, in silence they passed the soldiers at the monastery entrance.

'I think we can manage a quick bath before meditation,' said Harsha.

They made for the well, though Upali asked Ananda, 'Why you? Nothing fell on you.'

'I want to wash off that place and those stupid people. I polluted myself by having that pastry!'

There were others at the well, but somehow, after the customary greetings, everybody fell into silence. He didn't care, Upali decided, let them not talk to him. They didn't. He washed thoroughly, feeling his chest thump under the icy water, soaped himself till his skin felt raw, and washed his clothes as well. Hardly anybody acknowledged him in the meditation hall either.

'I want to go for a walk,' he told Ananda later. 'You go to sleep. And don't follow me!'

He was stopped at the gates.

'Monks are not to wander around at night, lord,' the sentry said.

'Why, are we prisoners?'

'It is not safe. I have orders.'

Upali turned back but only to pause not far away behind a large tamarind tree. He wanted to find Nayana. He waited behind the tree for a long while, marching on the spot to keep warm. Finally one sentry went off somewhere, while the other turned his back on the gate to relieve his bladder into the bushes. It was enough. Upali slunk out behind him and crept along the road in the shadows till the crossroads, where he turned, straightened and looked about him.

It was clear that Pataliputra did not retire very readily. The night was full of noise – laughter from glamorous carriages, echoes of song and dance from brightly-lit taverns, drunken invitations from passing revellers, the monotonous tramp of the city patrols.

Upali ignored the invitations firmly, the tramps a little tremulously. He asked for directions, more than once, for the enthusiastic response was often erroneous. But it was a relief to be alone for a change. His mind went back to Mahanta's revelation. It made no difference to him. Nor could it for the Sangha. Milindachanda and his friend were fools, backward conservative idiots. No, that wasn't true. They were well-travelled merchants, about as cosmopolitan as you could get. For the world, Mahanta's declaration meant everything. He was a Chandala. His parents must have lived in those little hovels near the Sarnath cremation-ground, wearing clothes off the corpses, hiding away from the sight of 'good' people. Would they be alive now? Why had they given him up? Mahanta was probably the only person around who might know.

It was quite late by the time he found the brothel street and the house where he thought he had lost Nayana. That was the end of his search. The lady proprietor of the house politely refused to answer his queries and referred him to the inspector's office in the neighbouring road. Upali, now in a foul mood thanks to the long chilly walk, insisted that he knew Nayana was there, there was no need for prevarication and could he please see her a moment, again and again, till the lady got fed up and asked a servant to see him out. He had to be pushed out physically into the street where he stood and called, 'Nayana, Nayana!' many times to no avail. The neighbourhood seemed capable of tolerating this nuisance indefinitely, so he finally struggled to enter the house again with a couple of customers, upon which the servant, a big burly man, lost his cool, picked him up and threw him out.

He landed with a thump and had time to only think, 'Oh damn, now I've broken my neck,' before somebody began shining a huge lamp right into his eyes.

He tried to shout at them but they refused to budge, so finally he forced his lids open into the beam and found himself lying on a pallet in a large whitewashed hall, with sunshine flooding in through big windows along one side and Ananda seated next to him, but so keenly examining the rafters of the timber roof, apparently in an effort to ignore what some officious looking types were doing to somebody on a neighbouring pallet, that he jumped when Upali said, 'Water.'

'Master! How are you?' He lifted a clay tumbler above Upali's mouth and poured in a trickle of tepid tastelessness.

'My head hurts.'

'You hit the back of it on a stone, probably. What were you doing?' Upali said nothing. 'They brought you here and then contacted us. You were snoring when we arrived. They had already bandaged your head. Just look at this hospice – it's huge! I walked around a little while ago – there are four halls of patients, at least sixty beds, and an operation theatre as well. One of the doctors said that he is coming to Ujjayani in summer so I invited him to the monastery. What do you think?'

'I feel sick,' said Upali sourly and turned away.

Harsha came in soon afterwards, with Nagarjuna and Therii Vrinda. Ananda indicated that Upali was asleep.

'Now, Ananda, you go back and sleep too,' whispered Harsha. 'I'll remain here – I won't attend the Congress today.'

'I can't sleep now,' said Ananda. 'I'll finish copying out the next chapter and come back in the evening.'

'Will you bring it with you?' whispered Nagarjuna. 'I shall come back in the evening and I'd love to hear it. It's really amazing.'

Upali flipped over on his side. 'You don't find it dull, do you?'

SANGHA

Siddarth took a while to begin his teaching. The legend-makers would give credit to the god Brahma for convincing him to enlighten the world, or to save it as some put it, while the Buddha himself was inclined to spend the rest of his life in meditation since he had achieved his aim of freedom from rebirth. He had achieved oneness with the Eternal, said the legend; he had 'come and gone'.

But it is more probable that he simply needed time to decide how to go about what he planned to do. He finally decided to start with his old gurus, Alara Kalama and Udaka Ramaputa and actually set off towards Rajgir in their quest but on the way discovered from sramana passersby that both had passed away. Then he remembered his five former followers and decided to go to Sarnath, for that was where they had been headed when they left him. He walked north till he came to the broad expanse of the Ganga, so placidly majestic and beautiful that in a burst of high spirits he decided not to wait for the ferry, but plunged in and swam right across. The exhilaration remained all the way to Sarnath and its deer park, and affected his old friends too, for though they decided to snub him at first, remembering him only as a weak backslider, they somehow could not.

Siddarth told them what he had learnt, or as it is said, Set in Motion the Wheel of Dhamma. It took a while and as he spoke, other people came up to check out the new teacher. The deer park was almost like a philosophy exhibition for the people of Banaras, a place where the latest ideas were sooner or later on display. His friends listened and were convinced, either by his words or by his conviction. But they had questions. First, because his Dhamma had nothing to say about eternalities. He was not interested in eternalities, he explained. He had no knowledge of the existence of the gods; about their intervention in everyday life, he was sceptical. And besides, mankind was perfectly capable of organizing its own existence, of developing a moral and just social order without help from any supernatural authority. Most miseries in the world were not caused by the gods, nor by Time, Destiny, Chance, Soul, or any such abstruse concept, but by human action. If people wanted peace and happiness, there was no use praying and sacrificing, they had to be ready to change – their thoughts, their actions, their speech, their livelihood, and more. To what end? For themselves. For society. The Way was not a means, it was the goal.

The Way was the goal. How many times did Siddarth explain this in his long life? Thousands of times at least, and yet people could not understand. The Way had to lead to something else, some divine prize waiting at the end of the effort. Or abjuring it must lead to some doom. How could one live gently, bravely and intelligently just for the sake of it? Freedom from rebirth was the least the others promised and that's what his later followers began to promise too. Heaven is what some promise today. Eternally magnificent multiple heavens, opulently carved out of gold and diamonds, crawling with divine radiance and sensuous beauty, perhaps they will promise in the future.

For his first audience, however, the most surprising thing of all was that he wanted to set up a sangha. How could anyone set up a sangha? Sanghas were about blood, lineage, shared secret inheritances, ancient totems. They had originated at the beginning of all time, they remained mystical in their present-day relationships. Many of them were on their last legs, true – but how does a man, even the greatest of sramanas, *start* a sangha? There was a touch of blasphemy to it. And what was the purpose of it? The land was thick with teachers and disciples, but nobody else spoke about organization of any kind. Teachers harangued their disciples, disciples trailed their teachers, till each had had their fill of the other – that was the extent of the relationship. Each looked to his own salvation and a lifetime was normally not enough for the task. Besides, most people already belonged to some sangha or the other. Siddarth himself did, so what did he mean?

'I no longer belong to the Shakya sangha. My sangha will be like what the Shakyas used to be, in some ways. In the upholding of democracy, equality and co-operation. But it will not be based on blood kinship or ancestry or any mythical past, for all that has neither strength nor value. It will be based on the kinship of ideas and practice. It will be a sangha worthy of the name.'

Was it possible to leave one's past, his interrogators wondered. And why did he want another sangha, if he had rejected his own?

These present-day sanghas were really hollow shells, he declared, only the name remained. The original sanghas were like that of the renowned Uttara Kurus, the legendary ancestors of mankind. The Uttara Kurus had lived near Mount Meru in a paradise on earth, where all men were born kind and lived a pure life. No land was brought under the plough, people lived on wild rice from the untilled soil of the forests, they did not ride chariots, they knew neither plough nor horse nor war.

Siddarth's account of the Uttara Kurus was original to an extent, perhaps influenced by Tara's stories. The legend upheld by the Shakyas had been different, of a heroic, horse-riding Arya clan, organized democratically, who sacrificed devoutedly to their gods and were, as a result, always successful in their battles for land, water and cows, all of which were owned in common. Whose chronicle was more accurate, no one can say. Certainly neither Siddarth, nor Tara, nor the Shakyas had come across either type in their own lifetimes. The later legend, always trying to go one better, would call the land of the Uttara Kurus a Golden Land which shone day and night, was absolutely level and calm, and whose trees bore no thorns.

In any case, Siddarth made it clear that he was not talking about travelling backwards. The past was over, you had to live in the present. His Dhamma would show people that they could be householders, farmers, merchants and artisans, all professions of the modern world, and still live close to revered and long-lost ideals.

The details of how the new Sangha would be organized and how it would function took time to develop. But some things were forsworn right at the start, like private property, caste divides and autocracy. All members would participate in all decisions – this was to be the key to its strength. This would be achieved in practice by detailed rules concerning the meeting of the Sangha assembly, its membership, quorum, and voting system. The rules were not original for their time – most were the basic laws of the existing sanghas, though not always followed in practice. But the new Sangha had an aim – to teach Dhamma, to convert people to its practice, to grow. And anybody could join; the Sangha was like the Great Ocean, Siddarth said. Just as all rivers lose their identity on reaching the mahasamudda, a man who joins the Sangha automatically forsakes his former name, tribe, gotra, jati and varna. He becomes one with the Sangha and the same as all other members.

All of which sounded bizarre. People flocked to stare at the self-proclaimed Sangha-founder – a young man of clearly aristocratic military background – and listen to his anti-aristocratic, anti-military message. They stared, they listened and a few even joined. Among them was Siddarth's old friend Yasa, now a rising merchant, a married man, a father many times over, and yet dissatisfied with life. His father was guild-master of Banaras, but that did not stop Yasa from coming to hear the new teacher in the deer park. It was a happy reunion and Yasa immediately declared himself a disciple. Siddarth said that he had no disciples, only fellow-travellers. The next day the new fellow-traveller brought along his wife, mother and father, all of whom became lay-followers, vowing to abide by the Way, to never trade in slaves, slaughter, intoxicants, weapons and poisons, and to treat the whole world with respect. Yasa himself said he wished to be a monk. In the days that followed, more joined. And, despite Siddarth, the world continued to use the term 'disciple'.

After a while, he decided it was time to move on. They had a message to spread and no time to lose. They began to walk, along the roads and off them into the forest as well, stopping outside every town and hamlet, living off alms and sleeping wherever they found shelter. They crossed the great river and moved southwards, into the heart of Magadh. Everywhere people were intrigued by the sramanas who wanted to speak to the world rather than communing with their own souls. They came to stare; Siddarth spoke and spoke.

Their audiences grew steadily and a pinnacle seemed reached when, one evening on the outskirts of Rajgir, they were visited by the Magadhe-Raja himself. Seniya Bimbisara was passing by on one of his inspection tours and, as was his wont, decided to have a look at the new preacher. It was the first meeting in a long association, an association that some would call a deep friendship.

Perhaps it was so. Certainly there was no ruler of the time more suited to befriend strange new ideas than this king. He had more than a few himself. He had adopted the prefix Seniya, 'with an army', after creating a strange one that comprised people from all and diverse backgrounds, who, unbelievably, owed allegiance to nothing and no one but himself. Even Kosala, which had a heterogeneous army too, had organized it into battalions based on sanghas, each of which rallied around their sangha totem below the Kosalan flag, each of which had nothing to do with the other, many being old enemies who would hesitate to confer even human status on the other. But there was no sangha to be seen in the Magadhan army. Anybody willing to fight could apply to join; their origin was ignored as also their opinions about each other; they were simply tested, trained and arranged on the basis of ability and weapon. Nagas fought alongside Aryas; Aryas whose native sanghas were at bloody loggerheads fought side by side; people who would have cursed and fled at the sight of each other also fought together. Even stranger, they fought not for sangha pride, nor kshatriya dharma, nor their gods, for none of the venerated things that men have always fought and died for – no, these soldiers fought only for the bronze Magadhan karsapana. They were paid monthly wages! The whole business was ludicrous, said observers – just wait and watch, it will be no time before this freakish army dissolves into nothing.

They were still waiting, however, while the freaks swept over the lower Ganga valley and beyond on whirlwind campaigns that smashed all before them.

Really smashed. That was another innovation. Bimbisara wasn't a conqueror of the old school, creating vassals who continued to rule while paying tribute. He annexed. Old rulers simply disappeared. Some said that he was under the influence of ideas from across the seven seas, others that he was a devil, but whatever the reason, Magadhan frontiers were continually being pushed out. And within the frontiers the landscape was transformed. The forests were steadily replaced by fields – no small task, for these primeval jungles on the eastern Ganga were the densest ever seen, a solid impenetrable mass of wood, vines and malarial swamp, with great snakes and greater cats. But then Bimbisara's men were not wielding fire or bronze, the old weapons of the earliest settlers, but iron, and that too the best in the world.

Yet another of his new fads was on personal control. He set up a huge administrative apparatus, within which he trusted nobody and kept a very close watch on everything, personally and through spies, and through spies watching spies. For example, he claimed to remember, by name, face, personality and record, each and every one of the thousand-plus village-chiefs in Magadh, a claim that even if exaggerated was something that the chiefs found hard to forget.

His first meeting with Siddarth was unremarkable. He arrived without warning at the grove where the monks had settled, descended from his chariot and strode up to the tree under which Siddarth was addressing a small audience of locals. The monks followed Siddarth's example and remained seated; everybody else prostrated themselves fearfully on the ground, though nobody was sure who the hard-faced, bejewelled and soldier-surrounded dignitary was. The Raja just joined his palms respectfully and sat down on an ornate seat produced by his attendants. A large brocade umbrella appeared over his head, a peacock-feathered ivory fan started to operate behind him. Siddarth's audience recovered its composure and Siddarth continued to talk.

At the end, one of the monks asked a new question, unexpected but hardly untimely. 'What is the meaning of kingship, Gotama? What is its purpose?'

The royal retinue stiffened, but the monks remained calm and waited for Siddarth to reply. Despite his remonstrations they already had an almost superhuman faith in his ability to answer any question as well as to protect them from its consequences.

'The Raja was originally the Mahasammatta – the Great Chosen One. Long ago, among the Uttara Kurus and before, people used to live in harmony, without argument or violence, everything provided for by joint effort and sharing. You can see this sometimes in the people of the distant jungles, though not in its purest form. The change came after the rise of the modern family, for then each one became bothered only about his own children and their future. With these feelings came private property, and with it strife. A formal law was then required and a higher controlling authority – hence the Mahasammata, the Great Elect. The Mahasammata was the wisest and most experienced man who settled disputes and kept the peace. He was elected every few years and received a fixed share in the land as a salary.'

The expression of the Magadhe-Raja did not change. Nor did he challenge the Buddha's idea of kingship, though it clashed substantially with popular theories. Most rulers and their brahmins held that the king was divine in ancestry and invested with the sacred duty to govern by Indra, king of the gods. Another theory claimed that the common people asked the god Brahma for a protector, upon which he gave them a king. Years later, Kautilya would study all the options and advise the king to tell his soldiers on the eve of a battle that he was an employee of the nation just like them. All in all, kingship was clearly a matter of lively puzzlement.

Bimbisara however said nothing at all and left soon after.

They were good, those first few months. But they did not last. If Siddarth was surprised by the speed with which his Sangha grew in its early days, others were soon aghast. Families like Yasa's, who appreciated and followed their sons down the new Way, were rare. Most families were shocked at the diabolic new teacher, who did not retire to the densest of forests as all such should, leaving potential disciples to gather the courage, resolve and stamina to seek him out at their own cost. No, he came to their door and plucked them directly from their homes! And took them roaming all about with him, about every town and village, in the company of all sorts of riffraff, eating rubbish from every hand, to taunt their families and cut off their noses in shame!

Good families could not take this lying down. Alms were denied and dogs set on him; the local yakshas, the demons who guard the gates of every town, were importuned with lavish offerings to keep him out, and if they failed, for demons are not always amenable, local thugs were hired to do the job.

The brahmins took up the task of preaching against him with enthusiasm, although they hated all radicals without discrimination. And the issue they targeted was also their old one – celibacy. Not surprising when you remember the ethos of the land, which commanded every person to multiply as much as possible, and promised a variety of colourful dooms for parents with unmarried daughters, women who failed to bear children, and men without sons. Siddarth never actually preached celibacy; it was just part of the sramana baggage that he inherited, a part that he did not reject. But his critics were not bothered about such subtleties. He would unleash childlessness, they declared. He would destroy families. Other philosopher-teachers, who had seen their own flocks diminish thanks to the new Sangha, joined the chorus. Public antipathy grew.

The outcastes, slaves and jungle-folk were the only ones who did not fall for the propaganda, for they were not close to the brahmins. Thus it was that many of the earliest members of the Sangha were from the humblest of origins. But things became even worse around the upper-caste towns and villages, for the Sangha now looked like a frightening collection of the lowest of the low – there were Nagas in human form, as the expression went, there were field-hands, reed-workers, basket-makers, dog-catchers, sweepers and rat-eaters, people whose face was misfortune, people whom one had to take a bath after seeing, people whom one should never see at all; good people felt threatened the moment the quiet, ragged bunch appeared on the horizon. The monks – or bhiksus as they were taunted, for their begging for alms remained the most appalling aspect of their behaviour – were assaulted so frequently, along with their dwindling audiences, that finally Siddarth decided to take a break.

He decided to go north, to the republics, first to the Shakyas. Perhaps he was curious about his family. No doubt he also hoped to find at least a discriminating few who would know a true Sangha from a false one.

So the Sangha crossed the mother-of-all-rivers again, and took the uttarapatha north west, subsisting on alms or nuts and fruit gathered in the jungle, stopping to preach whenever they came across people. On the way Siddarth discovered that one of the bhiksus was limping. He immediately called a halt, examined the limper's feet, and insisted on cleaning and binding the bruises himself, with leaves held in place by a strip torn from his shoulder cloth. Job done, he sat back and advised all those with delicate or injured feet to wear sandals. They stared in surprise. He stared back critically. Some of them were dressed like him, in battered robes obtained in alms or extricated from rubbish dumps. A few who had been sramanas previously were naked or nearly so. Some carried alms-bowls, others nothing at all. Their legs were dusty, calloused and bleeding, their hair long, tangled and matted, their beards unshaven and untrimmed, their entire bodies unwashed. Some had not eaten for days, and not only because of the inhospitality of the populace. They had not bothered – that was the sramana way!

Sramanas were in fact also called Jatilas, or the Matted, for many of them held that the more matted the hair, the more spiritual the mind it covered – the ultimate being a single solid mud-encrusted mass that could not be budged by wind, rain or hammer.

That was the sramana way, but as it turned out, it was not Siddarth's. There was no virtue in dirt and bruises and sickness, he said. The Sangha had a purpose outside the monks and they had to be able to fulfil it. They were to take all simple means to protect themselves and look after their health. Nakedness was not permitted. They all had to wear clothes, of any simple material or even rags, but adequate to protect the entire body. Monks who were unwell were to be cared for by the others, carried in a litter if required. All were to carry needles, razors, nailcutters and dusters to keep themselves neat and tidy. They were to bathe everyday, with hot water in winter if available, and eat only one meal obtained by begging in the mornings. They should preferably not accept alms in their hands, but in clean alms-bowls of iron or clay. Any food offered as alms was to be eaten. The rest of the day they were to spend on their work. This was the personal discipline of the Sangha as laid down by its founder.

It was a strange discipline, felt his followers, a very soft discipline compared to the rigours practised by other sramanas. They suspected they would be accused of worldliness, and they were right. They were roundly accused, laughed at and condemned for wallowing in luxury. Especially by the Ajivikas, as the followers of Gosala were called – who renounced clothes, utensils and tools, and consumed only cold water, raw seeds and suchlike – and the Jinnas, the followers of Neelkanth Nataputha, who also went naked or wore only a single robe, and had even more severe restrictions on food. There were others who believed in eating decayed food, dressing in bark and bathing only on the coldest nights of the year. Hot baths and nailcutters for sramanas! The others did not know whether to laugh or cry. Siddarth asked his followers not to enter such pointless debate; he had never claimed that his was a Sangha of sramanas. But his disciples opted to charge into battle aggressively, with the accusation that to insist on complex restrictions and austerities was self-centred. Only those who concentrated on themselves and cared nothing for the world could indulge in such exertions. The debate of course did not end there. The accusations and counter-accusations continued for centuries.

They reached Kapilavastu at long last one evening and spent the night in the wood above the city. Siddarth had grown quiet. Years in the hot flat plains of the Ganga had driven the image of his homeland from his mind, but now the verdant hills with their sparkling streams and fine dense bamboo thickets, the air fragrant with oak except where it was touched by the pungency of rhino, the shadow of mighty Himavat above, all made him feel a little sentimental. His followers were unpleasantly startled more than once by the armoured beasts for which these valleys were famous, of elephantine proportions and given to lumbering abruptly on to the road and peering short-sightedly along a huge and nasty-looking horn. Their leader however beamed and once even stepped forward in a friendly manner; the beast luckily backed away and vanished into the tall grass. Siddarth's eyes actually misted when he stared down at the familiar valley of Kapilavastu. He recovered however on seeing that the outcaste settlement was much bigger than before.

Word of their approach had spread through the city. The Chief's long-absconding son was on his way home. People were intrigued and excited. Everybody – those who knew him and those who had never set eyes on him – recalled charm and good looks, any number of miracles and out-of-this-world moments. His family heard the news as well and steeled their hearts. They recalled no out-of-this-world moments, only how they had been really and painfully hurt. The aging Shudodhan remembered how he had loved, pampered and protected this son, only to see him betray almost every duty of Arya filialdom. Shudodhan's wife Prajapati remembered her sister who had died to beget this child, then her husband's grief and despair when he left them. Yashodhara remembered her long wait to marry him, his poor performance as a husband, and how he had abandoned her and their newborn infant in the dead of night without even a word of farewell. Now, after seven years of silence, he had remembered them. Each one decided that they would not go to meet him. Let him come and beg forgiveness. Let him apologize and weep. Then they would see.

But to their shock, the villain did not come to them at all. He entered the city with his followers early in the morning and went around scandalously begging for alms, beginning with the 'dung hills' of the outcastes outside the gates. A crowd gathered to gape at the former heir to the chieftainship in his new avatar, and he recognized many old acquaintances in it. They looked embarrassed and did not greet him. Siddarth and the others walked from door to door, silently displaying their clay bowls. The poor housewives were distraught – what was worse, to shut their door on the son of the Chief, or to feed him and support his astounding disdain of pollution laws? While they dithered, the monks waited; if not attended to for more than three or four minutes, they moved on. At noon they gathered at a park near the city market to eat what they had collected. Then Siddarth began to speak of Dhamma.

The Way was explained. The Sangha was explained. Siddarth was very deliberate in his condemnation of slavery. Slavery was cruel and detrimental to the slave, but even more so to the slave-owner, to his character, morals, spiritual growth, everything. Nobody had the right to own other human beings, however exalted the lineage they conferred on themselves. In any case, lineage was rubbish. The other point that made waves was his condemnation of the sacred yagnas. Stupid, wasteful, destructive, meritless, cruel, foolish – that was how he described them. Let people eat, instead of burning wealth! The audience looked shocked, a few furious.

It was actually only Siddarth's exalted lineage that protected him at that point.

News of his doings reached Shudodhan's ears. He had intended to stay at home that day but his friend Mahanaman paid a visit, to inform him that his son was not only a beggar, and of food, and from outcastes, but he was doing it all in the very heart of the sangha of which his father was Chief. The insult may not have been deliberate, or maybe it was, but there was no doubt that it had to be stopped. Shudodhan had to invite Siddarth home. Or throw him out of the city.

Shudodhan betook himself to the park. And found his son almost unrecognizable. Not just because he wore rags. He was still tall and straight, if thinner, darker, weather-beaten. But very confident and clearly happy as well. He was speaking to a group of visitors when the delegation of senior Shakyas arrived. He finished what he was saying and rose, palms joined.

'Father,' he said in the most affectionate voice Shudodhan had ever heard him use. 'It's good to see you. How are you?'

No apologies, no weeping, not a shadow of remorse. How do I look? Shudodhan wanted to rage in reply. Look at me! The laughing stock of my republic! I'm the man who loved, no, treasured and doted on his son, and received a kick in the face for his pains! I'm the Chief who raised and nurtured another, only to see him treat the honour like a piece of dirt! I'm a father who wept for weeks.... But what was the use?

'I'm well. I want to invite you to dine at home while you are in Kapilavastu.'

'We eat together and by the alms-bowl....'

'Siddarth, please give me this opportunity of serving you – and your companions. Don't deny me that!'

Siddarth gave in. 'Very well. We're discussing Dhamma at the moment. We'll come later.'

Dhamma? What's that – some Naga word? You're insulting your sacred mother tongue now? It's Dharma, for heaven's sake! But Shudodhan said nothing. There was no point. He just noted the motley crowd about his son and went home to announce the impending guests with very mixed feelings. Family, servants and priests were waiting to receive Siddarth when he arrived, among them Channa and his stepmother, both of whom began to weep on seeing him. His two half-brothers and the other slaves looked solemn. The priests gawked at his friends. His father's demeanour remained grimly unchanged through the visit. But Siddarth beamed, embraced everybody, and looked around with interest. The house was as beautiful, sumptuous and busy as he remembered. Only he was a stranger, a thought that pleased him, as also the consciousness, as he walked through the gilded halls and the scented courtyard gardens, of Tara's warm presence. He had recovered from her death, he realized, he could remember her now without that old biting pain.

Only Yashodhara was not to be seen and he finally asked about her. She is in her rooms, with your son, he was told. So Siddarth climbed the polished teak staircase with its delicately carved balustrade to his old apartments, where he found his wife waiting with the traditional lamps of welcome. She seemed at first sight to be exactly as he had left her, a little more subdued than usual. The truth was that she had been undecided about how to receive him. Should she berate him for his abandonment, accuse him of having been a good-for-nothing, who had tricked her into marriage when he had no interest in it from the start? Should she refuse to look at him until he asked for forgiveness? Should she weep? But she finally did nothing. She did not even perform the welcoming ritual. She seemed to go into shock when she saw the ragged ascetic with his smiling visage, and simply sank to the floor on the spot. Siddarth lifted her up gently, greeted her and then his son, a seven-year-old clinging to his mother's robes and staring at the sramana in fear. What was he doing in their rooms?

The visit was not a success. Siddarth's family felt only further betrayed by the revelation that the offender was happy and free of remorse. In fact, there was a new and cheerful innocence about him that irritated them all the more. Worse, his preaching was quite effective and he managed to attract a sizeable new contingent of followers, many of whom even opted to 'go forth' with him, among whom was his half-brother Nanda, some of his cousins, some lower-castes as well, like Upali, a young barber. As elsewhere, the families were unhappy.

Siddarth's own family was left doubly morose, for they lost not only a second son, but also Rahul, Shudodhan's grandson and present heir. Yashodhara was devastated, for she blamed herself. Every day of Siddarth's visit, she had sent the child to the park where the monks had put up. 'Your father has much treasure, my son. Go and ask him for your inheritance,' she urged; Rahul obeyed. Perhaps Yashodhara wanted to prove to both husband and son that Siddarth had nothing to offer his child. But that was not so. On the day before he left Kapilavastu, Siddarth did not respond to the boy's query with his customary smile, but sat down and said, 'Yes, Rahul, I will give you your inheritance...' proceeding to explain his Dhamma in the simplest possible terms. It was a simple enough philosophy – some critics even called it childish – and the boy seemed to grasp it immediately, or at any rate was attracted to its propounder and his adventurous life, for his only question at the end was, 'I too wish to go forth in the Sangha. May I join you?'

Shudodhan now soundly and publicly berated Siddarth. How could he poison the ears of an impressionable child? How could he wean babes away from their homes and families? It was unethical, no, it was worse, it was kidnapping. Siddarth just smiled sympathetically. He did not even point out that Shudodhan was wrong, in this case at least, for Siddarth was the father and legally the sole decision-maker for Rahul. Moreover, Rahul wanted to go with Siddarth. There was nothing anybody could do about it, though they said a lot.

But Siddarth did see the sense in his father's anger. Henceforth, he said, all those below the age of twenty would require their parents' permission to join the Sangha. Shudodhan was hardly comforted by this. He took leave of his sons and grandson with much bitterness, which only intensified through the elaborate and expensive ceremonies of purification that followed their departure, the variegated band of beggars having dined every day in his house.

More of his countrymen and even women joined Siddarth in the years that followed, enthusiastically abandoning families and worldly responsibilities, and keeping Shakya resentment against the Shakyamuni, as he was known by the others, sky-high.

The irony is that had the Shakyas been able to see the future, they might have been grateful. For it was only their 'going forth' that saved so many of their sons and daughters from death a few years later. But then, if people could see the future, everything would be different.

Siddarth and his disciples spent the monsoon in the jungle. This varshavaas, or monsoon retreat in a forest, became the norm henceforth, because the roads and rivers were impassable in the rains and Siddarth did not want to burden any one settlement with feeding the company for so long a period. Later on however, people would confuse this retreat with the Upanishadic renunciation of society for the forest. Siddarth had no romantic attachment to forest life.

Monsoon over, they returned to Magadh where they found the situation much improved. One reason could be because they had hardly arrived at the outskirts of Rajgir when the Magadhe-

Raja sent word, inviting 'the Buddha Shakyaraja' and all his Sangha to dinner. Siddarth pondered over this, discussed it with the others, and accepted. They were immediately escorted to Rajgir's palace fortress amidst the beating of drums and cymbals, and the sprinkling of sandal, kevda and jasmine essences. There, in an opulent audience hall, they found Seniya Bimbisara himself waiting at the head of a ceremonial banquet, along with his entire court.

There was not much conversation except at the very end when the king suddenly asked Siddarth for advice. 'As you know, the rains are late this year. My priest informs me that the only solution is to offer a hundred of my finest goats. But I am a little reluctant to kill the creatures. What do you think?'

Siddarth looked at the priest. 'How will the murder of goats affect the rains?'

'Aryaputra, with all respect, it is a little foolish to refer to the sacred yagna in the manner you do.' The brahmin turned to the Raja. 'Your sorrow for the beasts is quite unnecessary, sire. They will not suffer, no, they will rejoice. For they will attain heaven.'

'Is your father alive, sir?' asked Siddarth.

The priest frowned. 'Yes he is, as a matter of fact. But he will not dispute my – '

'Then why not sacrifice him instead? Can any offering be as rich as a brahmin? And he will attain heaven instead of the goats.'

The Court became very silent. The priest turned a little purple and began to splutter. 'Sire, you cannot allow this – sire – this is – '

'Yes?'

He gave up. 'Your Majesty, I would like to be excused.'

The brahmin left and Bimbisara abruptly changed the topic by inviting Siddarth to become the general of his armies.

It was Siddarth's turn to gape. 'General of your armies?'

'Yes. I need a sensible, forward-looking man, untrammelled by superstition and bigotry, but with sufficient military experience. I think, Aryaputra, you would be ideal.'

Siddarth paused to look around at the entire august company, then spoke very loud and clear. 'I am against war, Your Majesty.

In fact, I strongly deplore the dedication of my Shakya clansmen to arms and conquest. I think the days of petty wars and ambition are over and it is high time we realized it.'

'I see,' was the Magadhe-Raja's comment, but he was probably in agreement. The days of petty wars were indeed getting over; the petty were being put, by Bimbisara himself among others, into the garbage bin of history. He did not however mention this. 'You have forsaken your varna dharma then?'

'I have made my own dharma.'

The Raja looked surprised. 'Is it sensible to meddle in such otherworldly matters?'

'I think it is essential.'

Bimbisara was silent a while and then asked whether he could become a lay disciple. Siddarth gaped again, but couldn't think of any reason to refuse; that was the end of the evening.

Bimbisara turned out to be the first of many royal disciples, all of whom claimed to be deeply impressed by the Buddha. All across the valley of the Ganga in the years to come, large and small potentates would extol the ideas of compassion, tolerance, atheism and renunciation, the criticism of hereditary varnas and the condemnation of sacrifice. The Middle Way was their way, it would seem! This was not really surprising. Laughing at the varna hierarchy was great, because they were mostly low-born themselves. Atheism dispensed with the pesky brahmins. And criticism of the great yajnas was welcome, for their leading traders and tax-payers also loathed them and were willing to pay anyone to end them.

Hence, the admiration. What these potentates did, however, was another matter. They started off normally as opinionated, oppressive and violent personalities; often they did not change at all, sometimes they changed for the worse. Their kingdoms were full of poor people, people who had lost their ancestral lands, people who had lost livelihoods, families and freedom. The richer the realm, in fact, the more the poor and the greater the exploitation, Magadh being the richest and the worst. The Rajas however did not seem to see this as a challenge to their new creed.

Look at the issues of tolerance, peace and renunciation. They liked them, they said. Enough to encourage them among their subjects. Tolerance in the poor and dispossessed made for a more peaceful kingdom. And renunciation was a brilliant idea – if people scorned wealth, they would not notice the inequities in its availability. The matter was different for themselves. Their own tolerance, of their neighbours for example, remained low. Their avarice for greater land and revenues remained largely unabated. Nor did they forswear violence towards anybody – their neighbours, their subjects, even their own kinsmen who chanced to cast a covetous eye on their thrones.

The Buddha preached his Way, they went theirs.

Bimbisara's son and heir Ajatashatru is generally regarded as the worst offender in this regard. He was actually very like Bimbisara – a ruthless conqueror, efficient administrator and self-declared disciple of the Buddha – but history, which is largely Buddhist history, has never forgiven him for killing his father after falling in with the equally ambitious but never-successful Devdutta, cousin of the Buddha. Ajatashatru went on to attend the Buddha with great fidelity, and was extra considerate to the Sangha too, offering facilities and hospitality both during and after the Buddha's life, including the organization of the First Council. And he always regarded the Buddha as the fount of wisdom; for example, he asked him for the secret of the Licchavis' strength and used the answer to destroy the Licchavis. All this made some people wonder about the Way, not least its founder.

The reception by His Sacred Majesty Seniya Bimbisara created a new aura about the Sangha. Brahminical and upper caste derision remained, but it became covert. The Sangha did not need to try to attract audiences any more – people flocked to examine the Raja's new guru, a Shakyaraja first invited to lead the Magadhan armies. Among them were leading merchants from Kosala who always pressed Siddarth to visit their native land. So, many months later, the monks made the long journey north-west back through the realms of the Licchavis, the Mallas and the Shakyas, to Shravasti, the Kosalan capital. Everywhere Siddarth's fame as the teacher of Bimbisara preceded him, though if you asked him, he said that he was not exactly sure what the king was learning from him. But the crowds who attended him were impressed and impressive. At Shravasti, they included Pasenadi, the Raja of Kosala.

Siddarth remembered Pasenadi from long ago in Banaras, a youth who had looked sternly resolute. He had lost that look now. Pasenadi was only forty years old, in the prime of life and ruling the largest realm in Bharatvarsha, but a devotee of philosophy. He was interested in Siddarth as a philosopher, also in what Seniya Bimbisara, his brother-in-law and most formidable enemy, saw in him. No two monarchs could have been less alike. Pasenadi was as ignorant of the practical day-to-day matters of his realm as Bimbisara was engrossed in his own; Pasenadi's head was normally in the clouds while Bimbisara was a tough and pragmatic realist. Pasenadi was interested in eternalities, in the origin and the hereafter, in theories of the One, the Many and the Absolute. Few would have expected him to be impressed with the simple and practical Dhamma. None could have imagined him as a staunch, even blind, follower of the Buddha. But it happened.

The reason was a new disciple of Siddarth's – Angulimala, the feared and legendary dacoit. He belonged to a tribe in the forests between Kosala and the Shakyas, which had long ago taken to banditry to survive. They were nothing special at first, the usual crudely-armed characters who could be withstood with a few well-armed guards. But Angulimala had taken charge some years ago and transformed them into a bigger, better-armed and professionally-trained force. Now they practically controlled that stretch of highway, exacting heavy tolls which if unpaid had to be compensated by all the fingers possessed by the caravan. Merchants had begun arriving at Shravasti waving bandaged stumps and screaming for justice a decade ago. But the Kosalan army seemed helpless. Angulimala bestrode the forest like a small colossus, attired in the typical animal-skins of the jungle-folk, plus rather modern weaponry, plus multiple necklaces strung of the fingers of those who tried to evade his taxes. He was rumoured to have some high-ranking Kosalans in his pocket for he always seemed to know when an army patrol was on its way. There was certainly some network in operation for the loot was found to travel to markets on the other side of the country. It was difficult to prove, because it was difficult to join Angulimala's gang. One had to belong to his tribe and also pass a series of tests, which included killing a tiger and robbing Angulimala's own house.

Despite all this information, Pasenadi's army and intelligence system could neither find the bandit nor his rumoured collaborators. There were a few intrepid officers who reached close and returned dead, if they returned at all. The Kosalan merchants got used to carrying extra revenue for the brigand. Or they found other routes. It was terribly humiliating for Pasenadi. He had to make do with denying that there were any collaborators at all, and expanding Angulimala's image to supernatural and super-rakshasa proportions which, given the man's rather individual taste in ornament, was not difficult.

So Pasenadi was in for a shock when he visited the new teacher in a grove just outside Shravasti. He had no problems with the compassionate and peaceful Dhamma, with its opposition to ritual, superstition and sacrifice. It all seemed quite harmless and not very impressive. But when the discourse was over and the Raja got up to leave, Siddarth held up his hand.

'Wait, my friend.' Pasenadi could not think of anyone who had ever addressed him thus. 'My brother Angulimala wishes to speak to you.'

Pasenadi was struck by the name. Another Angulimala? How could anybody use that feared name, or, heaven forbid, give it to their child? He stared at the monk who had risen from his position next to the Shakyamuni, to prostrate himself at the king's feet. He was short, dark and stocky, shabbily robed like the others but with a sharply intelligent face. He wore no ornament at all.

'Angulimala?'

The man's voice was a little muffled by his position on the ground. 'Sire, I am a criminal. I have been a bandit on Your Majesty's eastern highway, robbing Your Majesty's caravans and cruelly torturing those who would thwart me. But I was fortunate to meet the Buddha recently. I surrender myself to you for punishment, sire.' Though muffled, the brigand's tone was confident, even proud. He was clearly enjoying the situation and his own central role. Everybody was. They were all, including the Buddha, smiling happily.

Pasenadi was struck dumb by a variety of emotions. The first was annoyance over the fact that, thanks to his dimwit cousin Prince Jeta, he had left his royal guards outside the grove. The second was disbelief that this short, ordinary-looking man was really the larger-than-life bloodsucking monster. But that was his own fable and, as everybody knows, propagandists are often the most susceptible to their creations. The third and strongest emotion was awe. Whatever had the Buddha said to make the brigand give up his ways?

'Whatever did the Buddha say to make you give up your ways?'

'Nothing much, sire, in one sense. Everything, in another.'

Pasenadi felt like having his head cut off there and then. But he had left his guards outside. 'What exactly do you mean?'

'Well, he explained the futility of my ways. I was strutting about, proud of being Chief of the strongest bandit tribe ever, proud that when children in Kosala troubled their mothers, they were told, "Be still, or I'll call Angulimala!" The Buddha showed me what I really am – one who does no creation, only destruction. Nothing except pillage, murder… and hiding in the jungles like an animal. And I was endangering my people, destroying their future. And far from being strong, we were really puppets! Who lived at great risk and always at the mercy of those great lords, Your Majesty's officers, who take two-thirds of my loot. One cannot be a great robber without government help! Whenever they decide, my head would roll. Well, I heard him out and decided that I had had enough of brigandry. My men are with me, they too surrender to you. And I will give you the names of your corrupt officers.'

Pasenadi sank down on the ground before Siddarth. 'It makes no sense to me, Shakyamuni. No, tell me really, what magic did you use?'

'It is as he says, my friend.'

Pasenadi decided to forgive Angulimala and his band. He waffled a while over the bandit's list of officers, which was long and frightening. Finally, he cut off the heads of the junior ones and exiled the senior, who promptly went to Magadh where they offered Bimbisara all they knew of Kosala. Bimbisara promised them high office, took their information and had them put to death. He did not mind traitors, he said, but these long-term, corrupt vermin were of no use to anybody.

Pasenadi meanwhile declared himself a disciple, though again in his own strange fashion. Siddarth explained his Dhamma but he listened with only half an ear. Here was clearly a magician of awesome power, he mused. It must be a combination of that ancient warrior-blood and all those sramana exertions. He felt himself lowly in comparison and spent many agitated days wondering how the situation could be corrected. Finally he realized – a blood tie! He immediately announced his decision. He wished to make a marriage alliance with his dear and loyal vassals, the Shakyas.

The Shakyas responded with shock, rage and vituperation. 'It is your son who is responsible for this!' Some shouted at the aged Shudodhan. He remained silent, ashamed and furious at once. How long would the godforsaken antics of his offspring continue to haunt him?

'But the gall of that dirty cur – how dare he even think of a Shakyakumari?'

'Vassalage is one thing, marriage quite another – we cannot pollute our blood!'

'I would like to answer him with my sword....'

And so on. But better judgment, or rather duplicity, prevailed. Not at the first discussion, but at the third, after a cold reminder of the royal proposal had just arrived from Shravasti. It was then that Mahanaman had his brainwave. A slave.

'A slave?'

'Yes. And I have a girl who will be perfect for the task. She is actually also my daughter. Her mother is a Pukusa woman in my kitchen. The girl has been brought up as a maid in my household, and she knows our customs. She is beautiful, extremely so, and clever too, I'm told. And she has just come of age.'

The others were dumbstruck by this panegyric, then doubtful. How would she manage the rituals, the sacraments, the ancient hymns? Not to mention the dress, the language, the tone, the walk! Hundreds of things! It was ridiculous.

'She can be trained,' insisted Mahanaman. 'We will ask for some time. What does that barbarian know of our traditions! He will never catch her mistakes.'

'You want to teach a Naga our holy rituals?'

'You'd prefer to give him your daughter?'

'We have to simply refuse...' but it was not long before the Gana Sabha was persuaded.

'If she really can be trained....'

'If she does resemble Mahanaman's family....'

'Is she a virgin?'

'Yes, I'd planned to gift her to my son-in-law. She is perfect, I tell you. We'll say she is my daughter and that is the truth.'

Vassabha's mother Nagamunda was terrified when she heard the news. After she had finished her duties for the day, she went to the chambers of Mahanaman. She had never been back after he had tired of her body many years ago. Now his attendant stopped her from entering. She waited outside for an entire night, then another and a third, before he called her in. She fell on the floor and wept, 'Please, Aryaputra, I beg of you. Do not do this. They will kill her....'

Mahanaman was cold. 'Don't be a fool. Your girl is going to be a queen. What more can you want for her?'

'But it is a terrible fraud. They will find out and kill her. Don't send her to her death, please have mercy, lord.'

'It is up to her not to get caught. And I warn you, both she and you will die if you try to interfere in our plans.'

Thus it was that the Shakyas carefully set the seal on their own doom. Vassabha was transformed into a rajkumari. Everything she had done so far, the whole life she had lived, was now to be forgotten or reversed. She had learnt as a child to always look at the floor, to come running when called, to be near but invisible. She was now to stand tall and dignified, to walk gracefully, to cow others with one haughty glance, to command. Earlier she would have paid with her life if found imitating her mistresses at their rituals, now they and the priests sat down to train her in the same. She was also taught how to oversee a huge household, to get work done, to discipline and punish servants, but these were things she already knew.

Her rags were stripped off, her body bathed and massaged with the best oils and unguents. Her hair was cut, shaped, oiled and washed, dried in the perfumed smoke of a sandalwood brazier, and dressed with flowers and jewels. Expensive cosmetics were applied to her pale gold skin, the skin that was the trademark and pride of Mahanaman's family. Her eyes, Nagamunda's huge almond-shaped eyes with their bristling black lashes, were edged with kohl and gold dust. A gathered cotton skirt was tied around her waist; over that was draped a translucent sari of the finest gold tussore. Ornaments circled, pierced or dangled from every conceivable part of her, all made of the best pearls set in heavy gold – a generous marriage portion provided by her father, who however did not come to meet her.

But at the end of it all, her work-roughened hands remained a dead give-away. They received the most attention, with emollients of turmeric, milk cream and various herbs, and oils of coconut, sandalwood, jasmine, eucalyptus from the far south, and almond from beyond Takshashila, but they just refused to be transformed into the soft, delicate, muscle-less appendages of a mistress of slaves. Mahanaman's maids had to be content with dabbing them with perfumes and weighing them down with rings and bangles.

Vassabha was watched constantly but she made no effort to escape. No one knew what she thought of the whole scheme for she said nothing to anyone after she left her mother. That last night mother and daughter wept together, but by morning the mother's words prevailed – forget everything, and live. Above all, live.

So the slave became a queen. The nuptials were performed in Shudodhan's mansion – the republic would bear the expenses of purification this time – and the ambience was notable for a strange bevy of barely-suppressed emotions. Condescending benevolence in the bearing of the groom, sly triumph in the obeisance of the vassals, pure terror in the eyes of the bride. Siddarth had been invited to grace the occasion by Pasenadi but remained absent without explanation. Mahanaman ended the ceremony with a curt blessing for the newly wedded pair – a silent namaste. That was all, but Pasenadi did not seem to expect more. He made no move to touch his father-in-law's feet, nor surprisingly did his bride. There was no mention of a banquet or any festivities by either side. Instead the bride and groom left for Shravasti immediately, surrounded by crack troops of the Kosalan army.

Nagamunda was wrong. Vassabha lived up to every one of her father's expectations. She was the perfect queen – beautiful, docile, mindful of all rituals, and fertile too. In no time at all she produced a son, who was named Virudhaka. As was the practice, her husband sent her to her father's home for her confinement, which vastly irritated the Shakyas. Mahanaman could not let a slave's birth pollute his house, nor could he let the retinue of a Queen of Kosala see her ensconced in the slave quarters. So he had to go to the trouble of an entirely new house for her on his estate, though he managed, after some arguments, to get the other rajas to pitch in with contributions.

Pasenadi was delighted to hear of a son and came in person to escort his wife and child home. He thanked the Shakyas warmly and pointed out that they were now represented in the crown of Kosala. The Shakyas quietly sneered at the fool who thought he had linked his foul blood with theirs.

Their secret seemed safe. There were only a few slaves of Mahanaman's household who knew the truth, but as luck would have had it, though perhaps it was not totally luck, all of them including Nagamunda died soon after. Vassabha learnt of her mother's death but did not return. She never set foot in Kapilavastu again, and all she would say in explanation was that Kosala was now her home. Pasenadi was not unhappy. Too many of his queens spent their time and powers conspiring to further the interests of their kinsmen. In any case he had his own interests, besides many other wives and concubines, to keep him from puzzling about her cold relations with her native land.

But when Siddarth next visited Shravasti, Pasenadi made it a point to reveal that he was now kin. Siddarth responded rather surprisingly with a hearty laugh. For someone who saw the world as sorrowful, Pasenadi thought irritably, he laughed quite frequently. What did the Shakyamuni find funny? Siddarth explained that for him at least, blood relationships meant little. The day of blood relationships was over. How much meaning remained in the relationship among fellow-rajas, or for that matter, between fathers and sons? The modern world demanded relationships between ideas, ideals, ambitions and professions. That was why the bhiksus were his true sangha and only kin. As for nobility, that was a personal achievement; it could not be born into or married.

Pasenadi was a little perplexed, but finally cheered up. Sages, everybody knew, like to be contrary.

ASHOKA

The sky outside the hospice window was lit by a warm yellow moon. But it was an icy evening. Ananda put the last sheet down, nodded at the Therii who were beaming at him in a congratulatory manner, and wrapped his hands around his throat to warm them.

'Well!' began Nagarjuna but then Ananda was distracted by a pair of soldiers who walked into the hospital ward and straight to them.

'Thera Upali?' one asked. Upali opened his eyes. 'His Eminence, the Lord Nagaraka, Minister for the City, wishes to see you.'

'Right now?'

'Right now.'

'Do your ministers only meet people at night?' Upali asked as he clambered out of bed. There was no reply.

This ministry turned out to be one of the sober buildings that rimmed the city centre with its great stambha. The Nagaraka was busy when Upali reached and he was asked to wait in the lobby, in the company of a life-size bust of Chandragupta. The artist had recreated him as a grim and balding man with an air of domineering overconfidence; Upali soon tired of his steely gaze and went out to stand on the veranda. The yellow lantern making its ascent through the night sky reminded him of Kalinga, but in front of it stood the great and equally steely stambha, as unlike Kalinga as could be. As unlike anything.

The minister was a tall aristocratic type, swathed in silk, who greeted him with a deep bow. 'Thera, do come in. And many thanks for coming here when you are still unwell.'

'I was given no choice.'

'My apologies. But I had no choice myself.'

He waited for Upali to settle down on a cushioned divan, before seating himself opposite. 'My dear Thera, I truly regret what happened last night. It is not just the matter of disturbing the peace. It is the prestige of the Sangha. Were you drunk? They reported that you were asking for a girl.'

'I was asking about a friend! A nun.'

'A nun? Are you serious?'

'From Kalinga, Nayana by name. I saw her yesterday on the road and I think she entered that building. That brothel.'

The minister was frowning. 'I really doubt, Thera, that there could be a nun anywhere there. The brothels are all closely monitored on a regular basis.'

'You know who's there?'

'Everybody. Each woman is interrogated. And I am a follower of Dhamma myself, my lord, I would never have tolerated even a rumour.'

Upali's smile was sour. 'Whose Dhamma, the Buddha's or the Magadhe-Raja's?'

'Surely both are the same!' The minister rose. 'Come, Thera. I shall have you reached back. And I'll check up on the whole street tomorrow.'

They walked out into the cold air and to a carriage waiting on the road.

'To the hospital or – ?' The Nagaraka broke off. Upali turned and followed his gaze; a small group was approaching down the dark pavement. The oil lamps on the compound walls flickered over four soldiers, then lower, to a covered object on a bier between two. Feet protruded on one side.

They marched up and saluted. One said, 'A body found in the harbour, lord.' He glanced at Upali and murmured, 'A monk.'

'What!' Upali pushed past and lifted the corner of the sheet. The face was bloated, cheesy, no longer beautiful, but still Vipul.

'Thera, are you all right?'

'Yes.'

The soldiers carried on into the compound with their load. But the minister looked at Upali worriedly. 'You're pale, Thera. Are you sure – '

'I'm quite all right, thank you.'

'Then I'll take you to my home first, Thera, where you can rest for a while.'

Upali got into the carriage silently. The inside was lined with tiger skin. It felt warm to the touch; he began to shiver. The Nagaraka asked, 'Did you know him well?'

'No.' Only enough to know that Vipul must have ignored his advice. He must have gone in search of that contact of Pradyota's, the factory supervisor in the iron and steel district. But how had he reached the harbour?

'Must have been an accident, poor chap.'

'Tell me, lord, since you are a follower of Dhamma, did you hear of the monk, Thera Mahesh, who was killed by the Raja's guard last year?'

'Yes, of course! It was a terrible accident. He was probably unwell.'

'So the Magadhe-Raja's Dhamma permits killing? Of monks, and others…' His stomach was churning. He unclenched his teeth and slowed his breath, in and out, in and out.

'I feel terrible about it myself, Thera. But it is best forgot now.' The minister peered at him in the gloom. 'This is terrible too, but it was obviously – '

'I know. Another accident,' said Upali slowly. 'I'm worried actually for a man imprisoned in Ujjayani, falsely accused of murder – because of me…. If a monk can die so easily….'

'What do you mean?' The Nagaraka's voice was sharp but Upali did not answer the question.

'My lord, I need to meet the Prime Minister.'

The carriage halted. The air was full of fragrance and light music. Servant-like figures bobbed around with lamps. But the Nagaraka just stared at Upali. 'The Prime Minister?'

'Yes. Urgently.'

'The Prime Minister doesn't meet anybody, Thera!'

'I've met him before, just three days ago, on the same matter. He will meet me.'

'You met the Prime Minister?' The minister realized he was gaping and closed his mouth. 'Well – I can request an appointment, I suppose, tomorrow. You'll have to wait for a reply. Come now, welcome to my house.'

'Lord, I'd like to return to the hospice. My colleagues will be waiting there.'

'But – '

'Don't worry, I'll walk.'

'Just a minute, please!' He got off, spoke to the driver, then unwound the thick silk shawl from his own shoulders, and bowed to Upali. 'Take this, Thera. It is a cold night, and I would be honoured.'

Upali stared at a very intricate design of fire-breathing monsters with great waving tails, gold threads gleaming in the servant-proffered lamplight, then at the minister, and blurted, 'Thank you very much, my lord, for all your kindness. Do you know I am Chandala by birth?'

The minister's face was as yellow as the moon. Then he bowed again, turned and walked into his house, the shawl still on his own arm.

Harsha was fast asleep next to Upali's empty pallet. Upali curled up fearfully, expecting to see a bloated face the minute he closed his eyes. Or perhaps Devadina's honest eyes, racked by torture. Perhaps Bhima as well, just for good measure. No, Bhima was free.

He fell immediately into a dreamless sleep and woke three hours later to bright sunlight.

And Harsha's stare. 'What happened? What did they want you for? And why did you go back to that brothel lane?'

Upali told him everything on the long walk back to the monastery. It was easier. About Vipul, the Viceroy, the ex-Raja, everything. Even Nayana. The morning mist seemed intent on freezing him alive at first, but he felt better as he walked and spoke. The only thing he did not mention was Bhima's furnaces. But that problem must have sorted itself out by now.

Harsha was shocked by the news of Vipul and even more by Upali's hypothesis.

'Murdered? But who would murder him?'

'Isn't it obvious? I'm just worried about Devadina now. Vipul's death was so quick, so casual. As if you kill first, and think later…. The Viceroy and his friend might feel the need of a trophy murderer who's Magadhan.'

'Vipul might be a suicide, Upali. He really looked so strange. Besides, the Raja's against violence. He would never allow this.'

Upali sighed. 'Well, he should protect Devadina then.'

Harsha took Nayana's story calmly. Only asking, why the secrecy? Upali had no answer and Harsha said nothing more, but Upali knew what he meant. If it was just concern about a comrade, there was nothing to hide.

It was more. And no doubt Nayana had known it too, for she was very sharp. But she had never indicated it, she was always respectful, friendly, correct. It was Upali who was in the wrong. And he was the Thera of the monastery – it was inexcusable. His old teacher had been understanding in such matters, as when he'd come across an attachment between a novice and a village girl – the others had wanted to expel the offender but he had refused. It was a natural thing, he said, something that could happen any time, that should happen at least once in a life. He advised the boy to fight it if he wished to remain a monk, or to leave and marry the girl. But there was no way her family would let her marry an outsider, and she would not disobey them; the novice had perforce to 'fight it'. The Thera had not believed in the mystic powers ascribed to celibacy, but the tremendous public respect for the celibate was worth maintaining. He was a gentle person and very cynical at times. But he would have been surprised at Upali now.

Not the Buddha though – he would have probably been unfazed by even Vipul and Pradyota, the bereaved monk and the monk who-had-prayed-for-us. Upali pushed Vipul out of his mind hurriedly. Why did he feel guilty, as if he was responsible for the boy's death?

They reached the monastery just in time to collect Ananda and get into the last carriage heading to Court. There they found Mogalliputta Tissa waiting for Upali.

'Thera Upali, I hope you are well now. I have a message for you from the Magadhe-Raja. He wishes you to remain in Pataliputra for a while, to help in the compilation of the suttas. At least six months.' Upali was a little nonplussed, but the old man did not wait for him to respond. 'And he has decided that it would be better to keep this project of yours, the Buddha's life-story, aside for the moment. It is throwing up too many controversies – as we all saw the other day. Perhaps we can continue it later. For the moment he conveys his immense thanks and asks you to submit it to the Court. Via me, that is. I can take it now.'

Upali stared at the opaque wrinkled greyish visage, and had to resist a sudden urge to hit it, to destroy the cool disinterest permanently. Instead he turned away. Behind him Mogalliputta continued, 'Thera, I hope you understand. His Majesty is highly impressed by your work, we all are....'

Who were they to stop his work? They had not started it! Upali did not realize that he was trembling as he sat down. He felt Harsha's hand on his shoulder and shrugged it off.

The Magadhe-Raja did not join them that morning. Mogalliputta began the session by announcing mourning for 'our dear brother Vipul of Takshashila, who passed away in a sad accident yesterday'. The funeral would be in the evening. The usual reciting of important passages followed, but preceded by a statement by Nagarjuna. A monk had just taken his place below the empty throne, when he rose and asked, 'May I speak, Brother?'

The monk looked to Mogalliputta who looked distinctly irritated. 'Yes, Thera Nagarjuna?'

'I wish to comment on Thera Mahanta's statement of the day before yesterday. He informed us of Thera Upali's origin. I did not give it any importance, for we all know the varied backgrounds of our monks, of ourselves. The Buddha himself ordained the Venerable Sopaka, who went on to become a universally revered Thera, and he was of the same Chandala jati. There were others who were slaves, basket-weavers, sweepers, leather-workers, every origin possible.

'As I said, I felt nothing. But then I noticed a distinct tension among many monks, which I believe was connected to the revelation. It made me wonder, will we be able to teach the Way to the world when we feel such divides? Brothers and sisters, we must fight such weakness. We must develop in us the compassion of the Buddha, for the Buddha is in all of us, every one, quite irrespective of our origin. He loves us as much as we love him.'

Nagarjuna smiled at Upali who looked away; with friends like this, did he need enemies? Mogalliputta looked a bit baffled too.

Jeevana rose, but Mogalliputta shook his head and said, 'Thera Nagarjuna, your manner of expression is strange, in fact, almost – anyway. We appreciate your concern. And I think I can speak for all this assembly when I say that we are not biased in the matters you mention. Let us proceed.'

The day wore on, notable only for an argument by Harsha over one small discourse, from the Vinaya, according to the Pataliputra monk reciting it. It was about membership of the Sangha.

'The Buddha, while being the most compassionate and generous of men, had in his infinite wisdom realized that there are social norms, duties and laws which should not be transgressed if a society is to function responsibly. Hence he had ordained that there are some who are NOT to be admitted into the Sangha under any circumstances. They include anyone under the age of twenty years; any son or unmarried daughter without consent of the parents, any married woman without the consent of her husband's family; all those in royal service; those suffering from diseases and deformities, from leprosy, boils, fits, and such unpleasantness; those slaves not first released from slavery by their owners; jail-breakers; those who have been castigated by whips or branded; all thieves, debtors, murderers, violators of nuns and monks; all hermaphrodites, schismatics and animals in human form.'

It was simply ridiculous, but Upali did not care. What was there to be surprised about? Let them re-invent the Buddha!

Harsha raised his hand. 'With all respect, I do not think this can be considered a vital teaching. Or even a teaching at all. It clearly belongs to a period after the Buddha. Many of these groups were probably banned on the basis of the secular law later prevailing.'

'It is in the Vinaya.'

'No doubt, Brother. I think it is an obvious example of what Thera Upali spoke about – the incorporation of later ideas. There were so many slaves, people under twenty, women who ran away from home, thieves, debtors, even murderers and parricides admitted to the Sangha by the Buddha himself – does anyone doubt this? What of Angulimala – a thief and murderer, Ajatashatru – a murderer, Jivaka – a physician in royal service, so many monks with all kinds of diseases? And what is this "animals in human form" but ignorant superstition, or an insult to Nagas – the Buddha would have ridiculed such ideas!'

Ananda was impressed. Deepak of Kushinara raised his hand. 'Thera Harsha is correct, I think. This passage is clearly marked by later conservatism.'

'The point is well made, Theras,' said Mogalliputta. 'But is it not possible that these were the ideals of the Shakyamuni, though realities forced the Sangha to be less stringent?' Harsha, Deepak, as well as a third monk raised their hands simultaneously, but he hurried on, 'And it does fit in with our own manner of functioning today. So there is hardly any harm in including it.'

Harsha did not give in. Even Upali raised his drooping head to better appreciate his, 'No, Thera, it sets a dangerous precedent. People should know that the original Sangha was not the cream of society – that it abounded in social misfits and rejects! Let us not pretend that what we do today is what the Buddha did, or we will lose the Buddha!'

'The Thera is right.' Jeevana rose and spoke in one movement, without anybody getting a chance to refuse him permission and without making it clear which Thera he meant.

But Mogalliputta gave up. 'Very well then, we will not include it in the important sermons.'

A soldier came up to Upali at the end of the session. 'Thera, His Eminence the Nagaraka sends word that the Prime Minister will receive you this evening. Be at the Nagaraka's office at sunset.'

The minister had not failed him, despite his Chandala-ness. It was a relief in many ways, except that the tall coldness of Mogalliputta was standing behind.

'Upali, you didn't give me the story.'

'I don't have it now,' snapped Upali.

Mogalliputta's icy glance swept over the red folder in Upali's arms. 'Please do submit it soon.' he said, and walked off.

'I'm damned if I will,' whispered Upali to Harsha.

'Listen, Upali – ' began Harsha but Upali turned away too.

The Magadhe-Raja joined them in the afternoon, for another royal proclamation. It was about Kalinga.

When he had been consecrated eight years (read the reader),
the Beloved of the Gods, the Magadhe-Raja Piyadassi,
conquered the Kalingas. A hundred and fifty thousand
people were deported, a hundred thousand were killed and
many times that number perished. Afterwards, after the
land of the Kalingas was annexed, the Beloved of the Gods

began to practise Dhamma in earnest, he began to yearn
for Dhamma and to teach Dhamma. And he felt remorse
for the conquest of the independent country of the
Kalingas, for the terrible slaughter, death and deportation
of the people there. The memory of all this continues to
grieve him even today. What is most painful is that even
the righteous who dwelt in those lands – whether sramanas,
brahmins or those of other sects, or honest householders,
or all those who respect their superiors, their parents and
their teachers, who behave well and devotedly to their
friends, acquaintances, colleagues, relatives, slaves and
servants – all have suffered violence, murder or separation
from their loved ones. Even those who are fortunate to
have escaped all this themselves, suffer from the brutal
misfortunes of their friends, acquaintances, colleagues and
relatives. This mass suffering weighs very heavily on the
mind of the Beloved of the Gods. Today, if a hundredth or
a thousandth part of those people who died or were deported
when Kalinga was annexed were to suffer similarly, it
would be very painful for him.

Today the Beloved of the Gods considers victory by
Dhamma to be the foremost victory. And he has won this
victory on all his frontiers to a distance of one thousand
miles where the Greek king named Antiochus reigns, and
even beyond the realm of Antiochus to the lands of the
four kings named Ptolemy, Antigonus, Magas and
Alexander, and in the south over the Cholas and Pandyas,
as far as Lanka. Likewise, here, within the imperial
territories, those who follow the Beloved of the Gods'
instructions in Dhamma include the foreign Kambojas
and the Greeks, the Nabhakas and Nabhakpanktis, Bhojas
and Pitinikas, Andhras and Parindas. Even where his
envoys are yet to visit, people have heard of his conduct,
his laws and his instructions in Dhamma, and they too
have begun to follow Dhamma.

Victory has been won in all these lands, and victory is always delightful. But this time the delight is more, because the victory is of Dhamma, a victory in both this world and the next.

But the Beloved of the Gods has power even in his remorse. He believes that wrong-doers should be forgiven as far as is possible and so he conciliates the forest tribes of his empire, but he also warns them to repent and stop their evil ways. Lest they force him to take action. For the Beloved of the Gods wishes that all beings should be unharmed, self-controlled, calm in mind and gentle.

This inscription of Dhamma has been engraved so that my sons, grandsons and great-grandsons should not think of new conquests, and in whatever victories they may gain should be satisfied with patience and light punishment. They should consider conquest by Dhamma as the only true conquest, and delight in Dhamma as their whole delight, for this is of value in this world and the next.

What of those who did not want to be part of your world, or your next? Upali was suddenly deeply, humbly, all-pervasively thankful that he had not told Harsha of Bhima's furnaces back at Maheshwar, even if they were cold and broken to bits and lost in the jungle darkness. He glanced at him and met his eyes – Harsha had a beaming I-told-you-so all over his face.

The Beloved of the Gods himself took over again. The royal proclamation came to an end. 'I am having this message put up across the empire. Let no one forget the sorrow of Kalinga. Let it be remembered and never repeated....'

As if an apology could erase the past.

Covered carriages were waiting to take them to Vipul's funeral in the afternoon, big and powerful like Nigrodha's, drawn by four steeds each, all of it useless in the crowded streets. It took nearly an hour to reach the southern gates and the huge moat, really a full-fledged river, but the city was still not over. It poured out of the walls, southwards along the valley of the Sone, even beyond the quiet riverside terrace that was the crematorium. Shady trees dotted the terrace; a cluster on one side contained a few huts. Chandalas.

Upali got off the carriage and slowly followed the others to the neat stack of logs – sal with just a couple of sandal. Next to it, on a bier and fanned by two loin-cloth-clad squatting men, lay Vipul. Suicide, Harsha thought. But why wait till Pataliputra, when you had so much opportunity to drown on the boat journey?

The monks shuffled up and the two Chandalas lifted Vipul, placed him gently on the pyre and backed away out of view, apparently expecting the rites to begin. Jeevana, who seemed in charge again, had to ask them to continue. They immediately began stacking the remaining logs around and over the body till it disappeared. There was a smaller log burning in a clay pot to the side. Jeevana picked it up and walked around the pyre, setting it alight at the four corners. It caught slowly.

'He genuinely mourned Pradyota, I think,' murmured a voice next to Upali. The Sanchi Thera's face was rosy from the fire. 'I'm surprised how many did, even people in Vidisha and the villages around have been making pilgrimages to his vihara. He seems to have inspired them.'

To what? A corner had caught well; the wind from the river made for a flickering vision. Jeevana signalled for meditation. Once again the chant – *I take refuge in the Buddha, I take...* but Upali watched the river this time, a wide windswept turbulence, great waves lashing the edge of the terraces. It was rushing, eager to meet the Ganga just a little way ahead. The Buddha had swum across these rivers, right up to the last year of his life. Though that was not why he had been known as a Tirthankar, a ford maker. It was the common title given to sages of his day by people who likened the great rivers to the great divide between man and god, between ignorance and enlightenment, between samsara and Moksha. Probably because so many met their end on the rickety ferry-boats that plied them.

The Buddha could have taught people to swim across actual rivers, here and now, but all they wanted was guidance to heaven.

'Pradyota was really a very talented person,' continued the Thera. 'He had a great capacity for communication, for making friends and followers. And a mystic calling too. He could have really strengthened our work, if only....'

If only he did not have to be killed? 'He sounded very strange to me – he used to pray for the monks, someone said.'

'Well, I suppose each of us has our own method of practising Dhamma,' smiled the Thera. Then hurriedly, 'Of course, now things will be simpler, with these clarifications from Pataliputra.'

After half an hour, everybody rose and turned to walk back to the royal carriages.

But Upali moved towards the two Chandalas, trying to ignore the waves of heat flicking at him over them, and said, 'Greetings, brothers. I am Upali, from Maheshwar.'

Both jumped up staring and backed away in the same movement, till he said, 'Stop!' and reached out to pull them away from the pyre.

But they jerked away and squatted down, before one asked, in a surprisingly firm voice, 'Your orders, lord?'

'I just wanted to talk to you. You see – I am Chandala too, originally of Banaras. We're visiting the capital... for a Congress.'

He paused. They waited, staring at the ground. 'We have to go now. Farewell. And thank you.' The man who had spoken nodded. Upali turned away, feeling a fool.

Harsha again wanted to accompany him to the Prime Minister's office and again could not. A long chariot ride back into the fortress later, Upali was once again in the same over-warm den where the fat old man lay sprawled on a silk-uphostered divan, his legs stretched out this time and being pressed by a boy.

'Well, Thera? You have been leading an exciting life of late, I hear.'

'Lord Prime Minister, I have to speak to you about that sculptor Devadina in Ujjayani – you know of course that he has been arrested?'

'And so?'

'He is falsely accused of murder, of the monk Pradyota! What will happen now? Is it possible that they could... execute him?'

'They have to send us the case history first.' The Prime Minister picked up a gold glass off a little table and drank something.

'But they might torture him, mightn't they? During interrogation? Can't you order him freed, my lord?'

The Prime Minister watched him over the glass for a minute. 'No. Not at the moment. We have no proof of his innocence. Do you?'

'I know he's innocent! And isn't it a crime to hurt a royal employee?'

'Not if they hurt you first! And how can you be sure he's innocent? He might have got into an argument with Pradyota – over his temple dancer. These passionate lover types can be very hot-headed! Or do you suspect someone else?'

There was no other possibility, nobody who wanted Pradyota dead, but Magadh. Devadina was convenient for Magadh too. 'It could have something to do with the ex-Raja's ambitions, you know....'

'It could,' agreed the old man coolly. 'We're investigating that business, checking all links. We haven't finished as yet.'

Vipul had been a link. Now checked. Upali stared at the pale sagging face, the eyes like dead black stones. It belonged to the earlier Kautilyan tradition of Magadhan politics. The real tradition. Not the Dhamma preached by the Magadhe-Raja today, but that practised by Magadh for centuries, the dharma of dandaniti – the law of punishment, or more accurately, the cult of power, in which a king was morally obliged to do everything within his power, everything, to secure victory. 'When wishing to smite, he should speak gently; after smiting he should speak gentler still; after striking off a head with his sword, he should grieve and weep.' So said the Mahabharat of the king.

'I only hope you have learnt a lesson, Thera, to stay out of politics, out of all matters that do not concern the Sangha.'

But Devadina's love story had hardly seemed political. And the Magadhe-Raja had said that everything concerned the Sangha.

But Upali was tired. 'Lord, I wish to leave for Ujjayani this evening. I may be able to help Devadina myself.'

'How? By breaking open the prison gates? No, I forgot – you would stand on the road outside shouting his name, right?' Many chins jiggled violently as the Prime Minister laughed. His eyes however stayed cold. 'No, Thera. You will complete the duties for which you are here. Good bye.'

'But – ' a soldier appeared at Upali's side.

'Escort the Thera out,' said the Prime Minister.

Upali felt a firm grip on his arm, which turned him without much effort toward the doors and out. They were crossing the anteroom when there was a distant thumping. Like light palms on a drum at first, but softer. The soldiers around Upali were immediately alert, one reached for him again just as the thumps became the sound of leather marching on stone.

There was a roar: 'Make way for the Beloved of the Gods, His Sacred Majesty, the Magadhe-Raja!' Upali saw a column of soldiers marching towards them – just before he was propelled to the wall and pushed downwards till his nose touched the polished tiles of the floor. He could see thick-soled leather sandals, also a bit of the Prime Minister kneeling at his office doorway. The marching leather was close, it started to pass by, and on the spur of a mad moment, he suddenly shouted, 'Sire!'

And remembered Mahesh. He waited to die. But though the blunt end of a spear was immediately and excruciatingly pushed into his back, it was still only the blunt end. And the marching had stopped.

'Yes, Thera, what is it?' asked a familiar voice.

The spear was removed discreetly but his throat was dry. Spears were instead crossed in front of his head to prevent any more surprises. Beyond them, he could just see a different pair of sandals, embroidered in silk thread and gold. The tasselled end of a purple silk shawl trailed on the ground behind.

'Speak, Thera!'

'Your permission, sire, to leave for Ujjayani!' he finally managed. 'There is a sculptor, Your Majesty's sculptor, implicated in a crime there. Because of me.'

'But you'll miss the Congress.'

'With all respect, I feel it might be to the best. I don't think either me or my writings have found favour with the Congress.'

The shawl twitched impatiently. 'What d'you mean? Oh, it's you, Upali!' The tone became distinctly friendlier. 'But I require you to help in the work of compilation, weren't you informed? And I want to hear the rest of the story.'

'But, sire, you ordered me to stop writing....'

'Get up – I can't see your face.'

Upali tried, felt a pain in his back and had to pause. The voice ordered, 'Help him up, you!' A hand was immediately placed beneath each arm; he was raised like a doll and placed firmly upright. But his eyes remained stuck to the floor.

'Listen, Upali. First of all, I'm happy with your work. The only question is – is the Sangha ready for this? And I think, from what we saw the other day, the answer is no.'

'You mean because of what Mahanta said?' asked Upali of the sandals. 'About me?'

'About you? Is that what you believe of me, Thera, that I would call myself a follower of Dhamma, yet stoop to all those superstitions? See here – ' The sandals stepped forward, someone pushed away the spears, grasped Upali by the upper arms, and swept him again like a doll into a crushing embrace. Upali was stunned, not least because his shorter height led to him being lifted off his feet and nearly suffocated against a hard musk-scented chest. His mind went blank; his chest felt like it would burst. Finally he was released, and would have collapsed but for the discreet support of the soldiers. He gasped for breath, but would have suffered double to see the expression on Radhagupta's face.

'See, Upali – you're no untouchable to me! I've no patience for all that nonsense, nor for the opinions of priests. But I am interested in strengthening the Sangha. Listen, Upali – come to the palace tonight, with your story, the whole account. You can read the remaining chapters, then we can talk about what to do.'

Upali looked up then. At the quizzical eye beneath its heavy eyelid, the diagonal slash of black silk, the thick black brows, the fleshy mouth. The thick grey-flecked hair looked a little tousled, as if he had just risen from sleep. He wore no ornament at all. Upali stared and stared, he was just unable to shift his gaze. Radhagupta and the soldiers were motionless, they might have been statues.

'Upali?' The eye was suddenly sharp.

'Sire! Yes, sire... but there is only one more chapter ready at the moment. I thought I'd read it out to the assembly....'

The Magadhe-Raja seemed to notice the kneeling Radhagupta for the first time. He waved him upright. 'Read it to me first.'

Later that night, as Upali hurriedly checked, rechecked and packed his sheets into the red folder, Harsha and Ananda were amazed and disbelieving.

'He hugged you?' repeated Ananda.

'Why, were you weeping or something?' asked Harsha rather perspicaciously, and to Upali's irritation.

'Of course not! That Chandala thing happened to come up, that's all....'

'Happened to! Upali, please stop this nonsense. You're not a Chandala.'

'What do you mean? Of course I am! Mahanta may be many things but he's not a liar!'

Harsha's eyes bulged in exasperation. 'I mean, you've never experienced what Chandalas go through! You're a monk, from babyhood and for much longer than me, and in fact, that really makes you a kind of brahmin in today's world, if anything. But without all their fears of pollution. Monks are an elite in a way – that creepy Samudra was not completely wrong. And you were raised in this elite, you didn't even have to struggle to come here. So don't pity yourself. It is insulting to Chandalas.'

Upali sat stumped for a moment.

'The Magadhe-Raja is really impressed with the story, isn't he?' asked Ananda happily.

'Impressed enough to want to stop it!'

'For a while,' corrected Harsha. 'That's what Mogalliputta said. And going by the reactions that day, it makes sense to me. It could result in more confusion – just when he's trying to unite the Sangha!'

'Harsha, what's more important – the Maurya's aims or the truth?'

'Upali, be reasonable!' Harsha's eyes were ready to fall out. 'This king is different – can't you see that? Look at his laws, his statements, his actions! Has any king ever talked of judging crimes without seeing the caste of the criminals? Has anyone tried to ban violence, including that by the government? Or apologized for war? The most admired kings so far have been victors, conquerors, glorified destroyers! That's all and everything that kingship has ever meant! But this one will be remembered differently. I know it.'

Upali saw his breath standing in the air in front of him when he put the sheets down. The different king was leaning forward on his divan, chin on a clenched fist, eye closed. Mogalliputta's eyes were shut too. Upali turned away from them to the windows and the moon hovering outside.

They were in a private audience hall right at the top of the Raja's new palace, more than seven storeys tall, through which Upali had risen in a teakwood box drawn up, so his escort informed him, like a bucket in a well with the help of servants and pulleys on the roof. What if they let go, Upali asked, remembering how many times he himself got distracted at the Maheshwar well, and was brought back to earth by a distant splash. The soldier just smiled. Mauryan servants could not afford to get distracted, probably; it was one of the luxuries of what Mahanta had called ivory tower intellectualism.

The room was small by Upali's now palatial standards, and simple too, panelled in plain polished teak, and furnished with very low divans, on which were sitting Mogalliputta, Radhagupta and a few personages to whom Upali had not been introduced. What was amazing were the walls. Two of them, opposite sides of the room, on Upali's right and left, were completely open except for timber fretwork cut in all the familiar motifs from the royal stambhas – bells, lotuses and regal beasts. Nowhere was the wood more than a hand in width, and from where Upali sat, on a little divan, he could see on one side the shimmering reflections in the great blackness of the river, on the other the sharper street- lamps of the city, laid out in the grid pattern that Chandra had boasted of. He wondered how it would be in the daytime, when the harbour and the city were rumbling with activity. Or at dawn when the sunlight crept in over the horizon to the vast sweep of water below. It was dizzying. It was like being in the heavens. Or being an emperor, over a realm so vast that all this was really nothing but a dot. A dot that was power, nothing and everything. Upali shook himself, for the Magadhe-Raja had asked him a question.

'How much more is there?'

'Sire. Two chapters on his ministry, the issues that came up, the opposition and how he faced it, the development and expansion of the Sangha including the Order of Nuns. The way his legend grew. And finally one last chapter on the end, of his life and to an extent, his hopes.'

'His hopes? You mentioned this before – that he died a dissatisfied man. What do you mean? When he died the Sangha had a membership of thousands – '

'That's an obvious exaggeration!' interrupted Upali before he could help himself. Would he never learn? 'I'm sorry, I mean – '

'It was an exaggeration, you say – but even if it was only 500, or 200, or whatever, it was a Sangha that would take his message ahead, wasn't it? Even if they were only fifty, they succeeded in keeping it going, in the midst of tremendous opposition, backwardness, hatred, fear! When I think of those monks and how they must have suffered and struggled after their leader was dead – I can only bow my head in respect, and shame for my own pathetic contribution!' Contribution? In burning down the Kalinga monastery? But the single eye was on him, holding him so tight that he could not even blink. 'Of course, the Buddha's own life is even more humbling. I had never imagined how he had to struggle, till I heard your story. It was difficult to separate him from the legend, or maybe one never really tried.'

'Sire, Thera Mogalliputta said that you wanted me to stop....'

'That has nothing to do with the story, or you. It is for the Sangha. Will your story help the monks? I myself found it both informative and inspiring, but from what I could see yesterday, many seemed confused. You see, Upali, most of our monks are burdened by quite a different legacy, of endless and pointless speculation on the metaphysical. The Sangha has to be a social transformer – that, I think, was the Buddha's idea – but for that the monks have to break out of their limited perspective and think about the real world. They have to become one strong united force, with clear ideas and practices that will attract the masses. It is a big enough challenge. After yesterday, I feel your story must wait a while.'

'But it is hardly encouraging of metaphysics.'

'It's far too dismissive! Even the monks are not ready for it, forget the common people!' But the eye softened. 'Upali, I want to make Dhamma a reality – for everybody including the lowest slave and the worst savage, all those who used to die like flies, of hunger and war, who still die of sickness, overwork, superstition. This is a rich land, the richest in the world, so I've been told. There is more than enough here for all of us – if only we look ahead, if only we stop our foolish bigotries. And yet, that is the greatest danger. I am not scared of any outside force – I mean it, Upali. Nobody threatens us, except ourselves. We desperately need a new thinking, among peasants, nobles, forest tribes, everybody. We need schools in every district of the realm, and not to teach the scriptures! But the biggest challenge is the state. When the government is harsh, unseeing, unfair, the people follow, they react with selfishness and chicanery. We need a strong government – for people respect strength – but a fair one. A government who, as the Buddha said, will provide seed to the farmer and capital to the trader, who will care for the weak and diseased, and provide every opportunity to every citizen to better themselves.'

'Sire, we need the Buddha too. The real Buddha. But he is already becoming unrecognizable....'

'If I had my way, Upali, we would spread your story across the length and breadth of the realm. It is high time we began to separate reality from myth, and science from magic! But I can't afford disharmony within the Sangha. You yourself said that the most difficult thing for people to understand, even monks, even those who actually heard the Buddha himself, was that the Way was not a means but the goal. If he could not convince them, how will we? And their practice is more important than whether they hope for heaven at the end of it, or whether they believe the Buddha was a man or a god!'

Upali noticed something in the king's hand; the latter noticed his gaze. 'Here.' He held out his hand.

Upali stumbled to his feet but kept a wary eye on the soldier behind the royal divan while walking up to the royal palm and taking the little figurine out of it. He bowed and backed away before examining it. It was a wooden statuette, barely six inches high. A man seated in padmasan. A mass of curly hair was pulled up into a beautiful knot on top of his head; his dhoti lay in perfect folds on his crossed legs. His eyes were closed; a tiny smile played about his lips.

'Isn't it beautiful?' asked the Magadhe-Raja. Upali stepped forward and handed it back. 'It is the Buddha. It was carved and presented to me in Takshashila years ago.'

'The Buddha, sire? So carefully coiffured?' Upali tried to back to his seat, missed it by nearly three feet, tried to move sideways, nearly fell and then turned firmly to face it, walked to it and sat down. There was another moon in the river, he noticed; it seemed bigger than the original.

'That's the Greek style. And Takshashila's ignorance. But it is beautiful, isn't it?'

Upali stared at the two moons for a moment and tried to slow his breathing, to fool his stomach that he was meditating. 'My old teacher believed that the first man-made shrines were to the Buddha. Before that, mankind worshipped the elements – fire, water, rain, the moon, the sun, animals – and their shrines were great trees, cliffs, rivers, remains of their own ancestors. They did build cairns over their ancestors, so that was a man-made shrine, I suppose. But it was their own. Raja Ajatashatru's stupas to the Buddha were the first to one who was not an ancestor, the first shrine to be worshipped by all – I don't know how many actually did, but still. My old Thera was almost proud of it.' He looked up. 'But it's strange. One of the Buddha's ideas was of the oneness of mankind – so it makes sense, in a strange way, that he should receive a universal worship. But all his other ideas....'

'His ideas were just too radical. They could belong to either a mad man, in which case people would laugh at them, or a god – '

' – in which case they accept them whole-heartedly, blindly, mindlessly!' He had interrupted again, but he didn't care. 'Either way, they will forget him.'

'Posterity will never forget the Buddha, Thera,' said Mogalliputta suddenly and coldly.

'It might the man.'

'Upali!' The Magadhe-Raja sounded impatient. 'Look at it this way, there is surely no harm in people worshipping him – a man of peace, tolerance, compassion, intelligence – what better god can there ever be?'

'To make him a god is to make him ordinary. He will be one of thousands – this is a land of gods! He will be swallowed up by myth and ritual. He might even become a sacrifice-demander and a slavery-patron tomorrow, one who needs blood and flowers and incense and servants!'

It was Mogalliputta who barked, 'The Buddha will never be one of thousands. He is far above all the others!'

The Raja was silent, staring out at the harbour.

'Sire, to make him a god is to lose his message. His message was against myth. It was for people to believe in themselves, to use their reason.'

'This land is not ready for that message.' He seemed to speak to the moon floating in the water. 'No land is. I don't know whether people anywhere ever will be.'

'Sire.' Upali's stomach was tired of the discussion. 'Sire, I – I feel it is important to complete the story. I must. I'm sorry, but I must.'

The Magadhe-Raja turned then. His eye was cool but he nodded. 'Fine. Finish it then. It will be a valued addition to my library – and we will decide later when to propagate it. You can work in the Pataliputra monastery if you like, or here in the palace. We can easily make room for you – can't we?' He addressed one of the silent men, who nodded too. Next to him was Mogalliputta, with both mouth and eyes closed now. 'You have a tremendous contribution to make to the Sangha, Upali. Not only in writing. You must think of what you would like to do later. I can offer you a high position here in the Pataliputra monastery. Or at Takshashila, if you wish, for that is a cosmopolitan province too, less bothered about stupidities like caste. And I have decided to send missions to spread Dhamma beyond our borders – it will be a huge project and I expect all senior Theras to participate.'

'Sire, right now I only wish to leave. For Ujjayani. There is a sculptor there in trouble because of me.'

'Don't worry about him,' interrupted Prime Minister Radhagupta. 'We will solve that problem very soon.'

Upali looked at him and back at the king. 'And there is also....'

'Yes?'

'Sire – we – we had a problem in Maheshwar. Some peasants – deportees actually – had been arrested; now, thanks to Your Majesty's order, they have been released. But I think it would be good if I went back. They don't interact much with others....'

'The Thera's dedication is admirable,' murmured Mogalliputta.

'All right,' said the Magadhe-Raja. 'But you must come back soon, Upali. We need you here. And leave your story here. I'd like to go through it.'

Upali held up his red folder. 'This is a copy of all the completed chapters.' A soldier came up from behind, took the folder and handed it to the king.

'I'd like to have everything, rough drafts as well as fair. My palace is probably safer for it than the jungles of Maheshwar! Send it through someone at the monastery.' He got up abruptly. 'I must get back to my work now.'

And he was gone, through a doorway behind his divan, much before Upali could scramble up and prostrate himself. The lights had gone out over the harbour; there were only the two moons. But the reflection was closer, brighter. Victorious.

So they took their leave of the greatest city in the world. All three of them, for Harsha would not hear of Upali leaving alone. Ananda was unhappy. It was good to be getting away from the somewhat disapproving mien of the Pataliputra monks, but had he seen everything there was to see? No, if even a fraction of Nigrodha's stories were true.

Nobody asked the reason for the sudden departure; Upali was sure that it was put down to Mahanta's revelation. The two nuns from Ujjayani decided to leave with them, and obtained permission from Mogalliputta for the same. 'We're not considered worthy of compilation work, or anything important – being mere women!' declared Therii Vrinda. 'And there is plenty of work back home, so we might as well leave when we have company.'

Prince Nigrodha did not leave with them. He did not know what his uncle had in store for him, and he always felt it better not to ask, he said, when he came to see them off.

'But it was he who told me you were leaving. He asked me to bid you farewell and to ask about your story, Thera Upali – you were supposed to submit all the drafts to him, he said. I can take them if you like.'

'Don't worry,' said Upali. 'I'll send it later.'

'He's quite impressed by it. With your Buddha, with his stubborn sensibleness, as he put it. And with you, Thera. He found your story very moving, he said. Sometimes when he speaks like that, you can't believe he's the Magadhe-Raja.'

'That's really true!' beamed Harsha. 'He has changed, hasn't he? Since he became a follower of Dhamma, I mean. It's a complete about-turn, from one extreme to – '

Nigrodha smiled too, but grimly. 'The monks like to think so; sometimes I think they'd like to demonize his early life, so that it contrasts the better! While others wonder whether he's crazy. Even Radhagupta, who loves him like a son, was a little unsure at first. But I wasn't. I know Ashoka and I don't think he's changed at all. He was never a demon and he's not a saint. He's just intelligent, far-sighted and very, very tough – '

Harsha's smile had vanished. 'Prince, please! Someone might overhear and – '

'Inform the authorities? I've been talking like this for years, Thera – my uncle seems to be used to it!'

They left Pataliputra with a caravan on the southern route, up the rich valley of the Sone, to the head of the Narmada. They passed Vipul's cremation-ground, beyond which the city continued for a long while, but shabbily, clearly a secondary city of people with only a precarious toe-hold on urban acceptance, even in the rule of Dhamma. The straggle finally blended into a rural vista of farms, not the tiny little peasant-holds of Maheshwar, but great estates laid out on a clear grid of grain, cane and orchard, dotted by mansions and slave shacks. Like a quilt, the Buddha had said. The quilt was much bigger now.

They travelled seated in a bullock-cart; the merchants would not hear otherwise. The rocking of the hard planks was rather taxing on the posterior, but the hooped bamboo roof was a welcome barrier to the midday sun. Ten days passed before forests began to defy the quilt and little hills the horizon, many more before they reached the city of Rupnath on the edge of the high wild plateau simply called the Dakshina, the south.

This was the frontier of old Magadh, one of the mounted guards informed them. Henceforth were the Mauryan conquests. About half the journey was over.

Half remained. 'I just hope Devadina is all right,' said Upali for the umpteenth time, as they rumbled past the city walls. Outside the gates was a towering grey rock. The front surface had been smoothed and inscribed with all the old edicts as well as the new ones against schisms in the Sangha and about Kalinga, the whole finished in gold-coloured paint. That was fast.

'I won't be able to forgive myself if....' But he looked relaxed really, thought Ananda, except when he looked at Harsha. 'It's a bit ridiculous, though, to travel almost halfway across the world for only five days.'

'But really quite amazing that we could. And quite comfortably too,' said the Therii, wincing a little as the cart jerked over a pot-hole.

Harsha was silent, his face averted, the rest of him rocking stiffly with the cart. He had said very little during the trip so far, and almost nothing to Upali.

'Is something wrong, Harsha?' asked the Therii.

There was no response. Upali took a deep breath. 'Harsha, listen – I'm sorry for the other day. I was upset with that Brajesh.'

It was the night before they had left. Thera Brajesh had come up to ask Upali for his remaining sheets; Upali said he had already handed them over. Brajesh hesitated, nodded and left.

'Why did you lie to him?' Harsha had asked.

'Because I've already given the Magadhe-Raja one copy. He can read that as much as he wants, but he wants everything! It's safer here, he says, as though the leopards in Maheshwar are waiting to finish it! Those who don't like it are here, so I want a copy with me.'

But Brajesh asked again, the next dawn, as they were leaving. A message had come again from the Court, he said. Good bye, said Upali. Ananda had felt embarrassed; Harsha had said nothing.

He said nothing now too, though his eyes bulged.

'Are you feeling all right, Harsha?' asked Upali. 'Harsha?'

He finally looked up. 'I'm just worried about your stubbornness.'

'Don't be scared. Nothing will happen.'

'I'm not scared!' snapped Harsha. 'I think you're being childish. And short-sighted.'

'You don't mind then, if the Buddha becomes a myth?'

Harsha shook his head in irritation. 'It's not a question of whether I mind or not, Upali! The Buddha is already a god – one story can't stop it!'

'It can at least show another point of view. It can show the real Buddha. It can preserve his message in the future, before all the knowledge we have today is lost and only the myth remains – what's the matter?'

Harsha was suddenly smiling. 'Thera Mogalliputta was right – it's a personal crusade! Are you looking for immortality through your story, Upali?'

'Mogalliputta? Did he speak about this to you?'

'Well, he mentioned it, yes.' Harsha combed his pate. 'We happened to meet….'

'Happened to? Where? When? He didn't speak to me, but he spoke to you about me? Or did he come to meet you specially?'

'Whatever – I don't know! How does it matter?'

'It doesn't,' Upali turned away to watch a troupe of monkeys shinning lightly up an almost vertical rock-face abutting the road. 'It's just ironic, when you remember that Magadh has broken many of the old myths – that is one of their positive achievements, except that they did it so cold-bloodedly that the result was cynicism, which is another myth. But this Raja is smarter; after Kalinga, he's now annexed the Dhamma as well!'

'He's trying to strengthen the Sangha, Upali. I think we should appreciate that.'

'You're just thrilled that he banned the Mahasanghikas and those others! But banning a few falsehoods isn't enough – even if you had the right to, even if it ever worked! You have to stand for the truth.'

The journey wore on, hot, sticky, aching, till finally they reached the first valley of the Narmada, where a stream came from the south to tumble into a vast, cold and transparent lake. The highway circled the lake at a safe distance from a gathering of elephants and buffalo wallowing companionably in the shallows, to where the stream emerged, bigger now as it turned west and poured through the first of many gorges and out into another lake, a beautiful one fringed by tall marbled pillars standing in the water, silk, cotton and acacia on the banks. The water downstream was wider and smoother, though still in a great hurry. There was a tiny town on the bank – Tripuri. From here they would take boats.

The caravan entered the town and came to a halt outside the docks, where a flotilla of some twenty flat-bottomed boats waited at anchor. The carts trundled into a queue to begin the process of unloading and loading; everyone else milled around confusedly. Two day halt, announced a merchant. The monks could rest at the local post-house inn. Or visit the monastery. Monastery? Somewhere there, he said, pointing vaguely to a nearby mountain ridge where a waterfall glinted in the afternoon sun. Or there, pointing to another. A porter on the jetty proved more informative.

'Yes, in that hill.'

'On that hill?'

'In.'

'In?'

'They are caves.'

'Caves?'

'Yes.' The porter was a patient man. 'Given by His Sacred Majesty, the Magadhe-Raja himself.'

'Why caves?' asked Upali. 'Monks are not bats!'

'It's a foreign custom. From Egypt, I think.' Harsha finally looked a little excited. 'We must see them.'

The porter offered to get them a guide, and appeared some time later with a handsome young man wearing an antelope skin around his hips and a couple of large teeth on a thong around his neck. His name was Sampan.

'It's very close,' he said.

'How much time exactly?' asked Upali. Very close in the jungle could mean a two day walk. Or two weeks.

'Back by nightfall. Before.'

So they set off the next day at dawn, out of the town gates and civilization, for their guide led them off the highway into the forest, onto a barely visible mud track, at the start of which he disappeared behind some trees and came back with a bamboo bow and a leather bag of arrows, which he adjusted behind one shoulder.

'We're not allowed to carry weapons into the town.'

The path led them into the hills, through dark thickets of bamboo, asparagus and amla, in the shade of towering teak trees and giant jacks; then it vanished abruptly and completely, leaving Sampan's footfalls to do the job. Ananda began to chant a spell to ward off forest spirits. Under his breath, to avoid being heard by Upali.

'Place your feet carefully,' said their guide. 'This is a great serpent mountain.'

Great, thought Ananda. It was difficult to be careful in the half-dark, and the route soon became so steep that they had to use both hands and feet to climb. The ground was in any case blanketed with enough leaves to hide any number of anything. It was delicious though to be walking on leaves and mud again, after days of hard timber paving. But he did not want to step on a snake. Luckily Sampan managed to spot many, picking up two and flinging them to the side casually, and organizing a detour around a king cobra whom he did not feel like tackling.

They reached a small settlement perched on the hillside – some ten thatch huts – where a man called out to Sampan. They spoke in an unfamiliar tongue, though with enough passion in the man's voice and surprise in Sampan's to excite interest.

'Is something wrong?' asked Upali the minute they could get a word in.

'Bad news, lord! A tiger's in the area. It was seen with a kill yesterday, a neelgai.' These hills were leopard country, he added in an aggrieved manner, no tiger had climbed so high in years.

The friend threw a spear to Sampan in farewell, a bamboo sharpened into a long tapering spike at one end. It looked scarily frail.

They went on, and Sampan began to sing, a loud and lively song in his native tongue, to scare off the tiger in case it was still around, he said. Chital and langurs looked taken aback; birds and rabbits fled away. Ananda dumped his spell and tried to assist the effort but he found it difficult to curl his tongue around the words even for the chorus.

Hours later, after many halts to regain breath and assurances of 'very close' by Sampan, they reached a local sacred spot – a huge old ficus, standing amidst the fawning roots of its children and grandchildren, with a fresh goat head at its foot. Behind it was an almost sheer rock face, not very high, but their sweaty hands were slippery and it was with difficulty that they finally managed to pull themselves up to a narrow little ledge against another higher near-perpendicular cliff face. They sat there, getting their breath back, when Sampan disappeared around the corner and reappeared with Arjun.

Arjun from Kalinga. Arjun, whom Upali had last seen three days before the last battle outside Tosali, when he had left to check up on his parents in their village some miles away. Upali was too tired to say anything. Arjun was deeply affected; his jaw dropped, he stuttered, hugged Upali and called to others.

Three more monks appeared. Arjun fetched a clay pitcher to wash the visitors' feet, then water to drink and a big bunch of wild bananas, talking all the while.

He had found his village burnt down, he explained, but could not return in the pandemonium that ripped through the region the next day. When he returned to the monastery, it was deserted. He drifted around then, till he was arrested by the army and brought north, to the Sasaram monastery. Then a year ago, he came here.

The pictures he painted were difficult to imagine. Sitting on the ledge and staring down at the rich dark greens of the valley, interrupted only by the sparkling river, next to it the smooth brown rope of the highway, the little township strung like a bead on a double-stranded necklace, the world was peaceful, paradisiacal.

Arjun got up. 'Come, you must see the viharas.'

He led the way up the ledge to the entrance of a tall cavern cut into the vertical cliff face. Ananda hung behind, expecting some dark fungus-encrusted chamber, with suspicious spots of wetness at the edges and even more suspicious coiled heaps in the corners, the whole thing reeking of bat. He couldn't have been more wrong. The visitors were all struck dumb by a long apsidal hall edged by a row of pillars on either side, pillars that were astounding miniatures of the Magadhe-Raja's stambhas, right down to the beasts on the capitals. The two rows divided the hall into a central nave flanked by narrow aisles which met each other behind a stupa at the far end. The walls were full of colour, painted with scenes from the suttas that glowed amazingly in the light filtering in from the entrance.

'It's – unbelievable!' breathed Therii Vrinda finally.

'Did you create this yourself?' demanded Harsha.

'No, of course not! We have a royal grant – so we were able to employ some masons from Sasaram.'

'But how did they do it?'

'You start from the top, instead of the bottom like other buildings.'

The visitors looked up at the inside of a barrel vault, its arched wooden planks intersected by more delicate purlins running longitudinally, just like any vihara, except that above this simple wooden truss were tonnes and tonnes of rock. The idea, or perhaps the cool air, made the sweaty gapers shiver a bit.

'They placed ladders on the ledge, climbed up on the face of the cliff to the level of the ceiling and started cutting in. Then they crawled in and continued chipping away till they reached the length we wanted. After that they sculpted the ceiling and fitted in the wooden members, then cut steadily downwards, to the level of the floor, one step above the ledge outside. Blocks were left standing in the middle for the stupa and the columns and their capitals. Everything had to be thought of in advance – nothing could be redone afterwards!'

Everything inverted, turned on its head. Upali walked slowly around the stupa, feeling its smooth cold surface, and then down the aisle between the columns and the wall of the cave. He could hear his chest thumping. Then he heard an echo, as if the mountain was thumping with him. Or he with the mountain. It was an uncomfortable feeling. He joined the others in the centre of the nave.

'It's really regal,' said Harsha. 'And out here in the middle of the wilderness!' He had apparently quite recovered.

'Why the stupa within?' asked the Therii. 'That's a little strange.'

'Why the columns for that matter?' asked Upali. 'They are not actually doing anything, are they? Not holding up anything, I mean. The whole thing is scooped out of the mountain.'

'Yes. The pillars are the mountain too. But it's a vihara. It should feel like one.'

'Then why not build one? This is a cave disguised as a building!'

Arjun looked almost hurt. 'This is more permanent than a building. This will last and last, it can be used by many generations of monks.'

Like the Dhamma stambhas – everything designed for immortality. But Upali calmed down. 'It's really beautiful, of course, but strange. It's almost like challenging the mountain.'

'Or becoming part of it,' said one of Arjun's colleagues, clearly their leader, a stocky man whose gleaming and unlined dark skin clashed a little strangely with the tufts of white hair coming out of his ears. 'It is a combination of powers, Thera. The familiarity of the vihara, the tradition of the stupa within its forest grove – which are the pillars here – all sheltered within mother earth. It's like the womb, with the power to create. It is easy to forget the world when you are inside, to forget everything and soar high into your own consciousness.'

'Do you spend all your time in meditation?' asked the Therii.

'This has actually been started as a teaching monastery for the jungle-folk around,' said Arjun.

'By whom?'

'Pataliputra. But the locals are still wary of us, though less than before. A few do visit nowadays, after worshipping at the tree-shrine just below. Most come just to see the viharas – they are our biggest magnet!'

'They were very hostile at first, and not surprisingly,' said the old monk. 'This place is changing very rapidly. Forest clearing is going on all along the river. A new branch of the highway is to head south from here to Paithan and further. When we first arrived, there were those terrible punishments displayed all the way to Sasaram and beyond. But now the situation is more peaceful.'

'It must have been scary at the start,' said the Therii.

'Not really. You see, we came after the cantonment below. Some amount of peace had already been ensured, and the soldiers kept an eye on us for a while.'

Upali shook his head. 'A monastery and an army, hand in hand. Magadh is really amazing!'

'A civilizer, that's the truth!' smiled the old man. 'It's taking time, of course. But our attempt is really to bring people to civilization before they are flung into it.'

'To enslave their minds, before their bodies. That's what we all do, I suppose. Even in Kalinga, we were really getting people to fit into Magadh.'

The monk was unruffled. 'Civilization need not enslave, it can be a boon. Especially nowadays. Those old columns of slaves, bound like beasts, headed for the mines or the markets, are all things of the past. Magadh has many positive strengths – it is cosmopolitan, cultured, educated, with the best technology in the world and now the enlightened policies of this Magadhe-Raja. And the forest tribes have their strengths too – they are honest, brave, fair, hugely knowledgeable about the forests. Now they will have the best of both worlds.'

'But no choice in the matter! They will have to fit into the Maurya's Dhamma. And who's to say that the best will prevail? What if the worst aspects of both cultures triumph? What if only avarice, crookedness and selfish ambition trickle down, and superstition, atavism and xenophobia rise up?'

'You can't have it both ways, Upali – no war, and no peace either!' burst out Harsha. 'The only option then is for everybody to stay apart, and that is not possible. The Buddha realized that in his day itself – physical distance was vanishing, the mental distance had to go too.'

'Actually some still manage to remain apart,' interjected Arjun. 'By pushing further away into the jungles. There is always that option.'

Upali looked at him for a moment. 'Is it really an option? After all, Magadh is really a huge forest-clearing agency....'

'Even so, look about you! It is days from here to the next army command post, weeks to any farmlands. The jungle is vast, unimaginably vast. It doesn't even notice Magadh!'

'So, how did the Magadhe-Raja's Congress go?' asked the old monk suddenly.

'Why didn't you attend?' asked Harsha.

'Oh, I'm uncomfortable with that crowd. I'm from Nalanda originally, but I found the monastery there completely engrossed in fancy philosophical debate. I left it for Pataliputra, but I didn't fit in there either – they had even less contact with the people. The Mahasanghikas at least hold mass meditation sessions and so on. The Pataliputrans are courtiers! Anyway, when the Magadhe-Raja announced that he wanted monks to start work in completely new areas, I volunteered. And I've never felt like going back.'

'I can understand,' nodded Harsha. 'This place is truly inspiring. And if the Magadhe-Raja's vision is fulfilled it will be mindboggling. A peaceful transition to civilization everywhere, new cities coming up, connected by safe roads, surrounded by peasant hamlets, with laws that are humane, administrations that are responsible....'

'And monasteries to preside over the whole business!'

It was soon time to leave.

Arjun hugged Upali tight. 'When shall we meet again?'

'Soon,' said Upali firmly. 'I have work in Ujjayani now. But I'll be back and then we must return to Kalinga.'

'Upali – ' began Harsha.

'Yes. There is work there – and we can't spend all our lives in foreign lands!'

It was much easier to travel downhill, they discovered. More exciting too. They were about halfway to the little hamlet on the mountainside, when they came across a herd of spotted antelope browsing in a glen. Sampan made a sign with his hand for silence and began to move slowly but firmly along the edge of the herd. Ananda felt a little sorry; the animals looked so innocent and Sampan so inevitable. He was heading towards the stag, a tall red-brown patriarch feeding calmly on the other side of the glen, when there was a sudden urgent '*hoon-hoon-hoon*'. A flock of pink doves rose as one from a tangle of castor and raced away over his head. Monkeys started screeching. The antelope looked up, got the message and bounded off. Before anybody else could react, there was a rumble. A low one, then it came again, a little stronger.

'Was that thunder?' said Ananda, pale but hopeful.

Nobody bothered to answer, or to look at the sky. Sampan rejoined them and led the way on, but lightening his hold on his little spear the meanwhile, bouncing it a little in his hand, as if testing the weight. Ananda felt his heart sink like a stone into his stomach. The rumble came again, closer. Sampan motioned them to slow down. What was the point, Ananda wondered. They crept along quietly, straight towards the sound-maker apparently, for the next rumble was so close, so loud, that it was not a rumble at all but a roar, so that they were deafened and came to a shuddering stop. It felt as though something physical had hit them in the face. It was on their immediate left now, within an opaque thicket of bamboo and mahua. Or behind it. Ananda felt his knees wobble; Upali was the left-most, he stared at him in horror and waited for the thicket to explode. But he felt his head explode instead, apparently right inside another roar which burst out over the hillside and into the valley, an unimaginable force of sound that seemed to ricochet off the hills in the distance, to return in dizzying waves.

When Ananda finally recovered, he was amazed to find himself still in one piece. But his teeth were chattering and his hands were on his ears. He peered around slowly without lowering them, fearfully, not wanting to see, not wanting to know who was missing, lost to the roarer in the thicket – and discovered that their number had instead gone up by one. For the tiger had joined them, it was right there, just in front of Upali and gazing at the statues around with some interest. It was huge, its head almost as high as Upali's, its girth more than three Upalis, its body pale gleaming gold striped with black, shining like liquid. Ananda's mind was blank, he could remember no prayer at all.

Upali meanwhile could feel every hair on his body, he tried to control them and convince them not to move, but it was hopeless. Their shivers made him shiver, teeter and then fall backwards, hitting some stones quite painfully. It was the end, but when nothing happened and he looked up, it was straight into the biggest yawn he had ever seen, a gigantic cavernous invitation that could have swallowed his head whole, full of great curved white teeth to tear off chunks if it preferred to eat small, full of bad breath that was really, awfully, unspeakably, bad. The beast shut his mouth with a grunt and a snuffle, glanced briefly at Upali, then padded across into the neighbouring greenness.

It was a long time before Upali could unlock his gaze from the greenness and look around. Had that really happened? Or was it his imagination? But his skin felt blistered by that golden-yellow glance. And Ananda's face was wet, the Theriis were white, Harsha a little green. He wondered what he looked like. He could not rise and nobody else seemed able to move either, except for Sampan. He was bent on one knee, his spear poised above a shoulder; now he prostrated himself face-down in the direction of the vanished passerby. Upali felt his stomach rumble threateningly and leaned over just in time to bring up Arjun's bananas.

'A neelgai makes a very filling meal,' explained Sampan as he rose.

The loaders finished their job the next day and the flotilla set off at dawn through the many valleys of the river. The guards relaxed, for the most dangerous part of the journey was over.

Days passed before villages appeared on one bank, along with fields of barley, wheat and tall yellowing sugarcane, all enclosed by the steep gorges and wooded walls of the plateau. This was the old Chedi kingdom, swallowed by Chandragupta many years ago. The water was still frothy here and very fast, cutting its way impatiently between overhanging cliffs, which the boatmen navigated standing on the prow with their stout poles. Then that danger too was past as the stream widened and slowed down. They were back in jungle, broken here and there by the odd hamlet. At one time this river had flowed through many nations and peoples, when those lower down had no idea at all who lived upriver and vice-versa. Now the entire thousand-kilometre span began and ended under Magadh. And most everybody knew it.

But Upali was conscious of a tremendous relief, mixed however with indecision. They would go to Ujjayani, explain away the nonsense of Devadina, then leave for Maheshwar and Bhima. He prayed that the furnaces were dead, broken, scattered, gone for good. But supposed they weren't? No, he decided, he would check on Bhima first and then go to Ujjayani. But Devadina was in prison – suppose they decided to rush through to execution? He had to go to Ujjayani first.

The Therii Vrinda interrupted his reverie one morning, to ask, 'Upali, why did you say, in Court that day, that the Buddha died an unsatisfied man?'

He smiled sourly at Harsha. 'Yes, it doesn't make sense, does it? That a god should die unhappy?'

Harsha ignored him.

'Well, why did you say it?' repeated the Therii.

'Are you sure you want to know? After visiting the latest temple to him? At this rate he'll soon overshadow – '

Harsha sighed. 'Men need gods, Upali. And the gods they have are cruel, narrow, distrustful. They cannot tolerate peace. Or Dhamma.'

'So we give them a new one? What will you have us become – Kautilya?'

'Upali, don't pretend that you still suspect the Raja's intentions! Your problem is not with what he is doing, but who he is!' Harsha paused and calmed down. 'Be honest now – do you really think he is just another follower of Kautilya?'

Upali glared at a great basalt boulder on the crest of a cliff above the river; it seemed undecided about whether to crash down on them or not. 'No,' he admitted finally. 'I think he does intend to rule according to his version of Dhamma. And that's better for the people than earlier. Definitely. But Harsha – he can't be the leader of the Sangha! Can't you see? Dhamma is also about each of us, every man and woman, becoming a thinking, reasoning, reasonable person. We can't be led by a king, even if he is the best ruler that this land has had – even the best it will ever have! We can't be funded and dictated to. It will kill us.' The others just stared at him. 'It will kill us,' he repeated. 'From reformers of society – successful or not – we will become paid servants. An arm of the state. We will be cut off from the people, even when we live among them. Do you think any organization, any individual, can remain immune to such changes? And what of the future? What will happen under another kind of Raja? Who is even more generous, gives us lavish grants and opulent monasteries – and worships the Buddha too – but wars and rapes and plunders in between?'

'This is needless pessimism,' said Harsha quietly. 'Who knows what the future will bring? The Magadhe-Raja's ideas of peace might spread, his successors will surely follow him.'

'I'm not very knowledgeable in these matters,' intervened the Therii. 'But I think that the Magadhe-Raja is trying for a real unity of this realm, beyond the physical unity which is a forced one – which you justly condemn, Upali. Like with the monastery at Tripuri. He is trying to give everybody a stake in the future – '

'Exactly!' said Harsha.

' – but he needs a new focus – something which unites and holds everyone – which is the Buddha. Or perhaps, himself.'

Harsha looked at her for a moment before nodding. 'Unity as well as prosperity. And it's not an easy task. As it is, conservatives are calling him a mad king, they are condemning his ideas of social harmony as crazed weakness. We at least should give him the benefit of doubt!' He turned to Upali. 'Don't you see – he can do it. If he were a sage, or a monk like us, nobody would listen to him. Even the Buddha died dissatisfied, you said. But the Raja has power! Tremendous undisputed power, and huge resources, which he wants to use in the cause of Dhamma. And he has the following of the most ruthless brains and bloodstained hands in the empire – because he was the greatest at that game! They respected him then, and now that he's doing something else, they can't dismiss it.' His voice was suddenly a plea. 'He could change things, Upali. I really think he could.'

Even Ananda couldn't read Upali's expression. Was it resignation, or was it pity? Or was it just his stomach? In any case, he said nothing for so long that when he did, it almost didn't matter. 'If change could be brought by a king, why did the Buddha become a beggar?'

DHAMMA

He spent his life tramping across the land for eight months of every year, cutting across national boundaries without bias, speaking to whomever he met. He learnt to speak many tongues and he became known even among the jungle-folk as the sramana who actively sought out company, often lying in wait at the most sacred sites of ritual to launch forth on his irritating ideas about peace and tolerance and non-violence. He spoke especially against blood sacrifice, not hesitating even when he chanced on one in progress. The sacrificers looked askance, even more his disciples who were sure that he and they were destined for the altar themselves. But, though this was indeed the fate of some of his greatest disciples who took Dhamma far and wide later on, he remained unscathed and even won the following of many a staunch sacrificer.

There were rejections aplenty, of course, in the jungle, in cities and villages too. In which case he just walked on. And there were quite a few attacks as well. The legend is full of these attempts and how they were miraculously foiled. Like when a maddened tusker was sent charging towards him and the Buddha apparently just raised a hand, enough to bring it not only skidding to a stop but actually prostrate at his feet. Or when a huge boulder, big enough to crush a house, was sent rolling down a hill at the bottom of which he sat with his followers. Here there was not even a raised hand – the boulder exploded into fragments by itself before it reached him, and the fragments too disposed of themselves quietly with nary a scratch on the monks. The legend likes drama.

The real incidents were quieter. Like when a rich brahmin came across the Buddha, begging bowl in hand, at his door.

'Do some work, you!' he shouted. 'Are your limbs broken or something? Or go to the jungle and live off wild berries like proper sramanas!' And so on. Passersby halted in interest and he appealed to them. 'Look at this character – a healthy young man expecting all the people of the world to feed him for free! Why should we patronize such feeble-minded idlers?'

The Buddha waited patiently for a pause in the vituperation. And perhaps, being now a practised speaker, for a crowd to collect. Then he held out his clay bowl. 'Here, my strong-minded friend, do you have the character to eat this free food?'

A few handfuls of cooked rice could be seen in the bowl. Clearly of varied parentage, some fresh-looking, most a little yellowed, some stained with gravy, all smelling a little sour.

The brahmin leapt back. 'Don't bring that near me!'

'What's the matter? You look scared, brother. Scared to touch food cooked by another, scared to even look at it. And forget food – you're scared to touch most people as well, to catch sight of some, to stand on the leeward side of others! How do you manage to live in the city, my friend, when you carry with you all the courage and character of a frightened jungle beast?'

A proper sramana would live in the jungle and eat wild berries broken by his own hand – he would maintain all the pollution taboos even miles away from civilization. Easily. Because that was really where pollution taboos belonged – to the jungle. It took character to live with people, character that people had to build for themselves if they wanted to be truly civilized.

The brahmin slammed his door shut.

Some tried to use women. Women sramanas were unheard of then, or indeed women in the public eye in any way. There were some who claimed that this exclusion was a recent phenomenon; in ancient times, they said, Arya women had worsted men at public debate. But those days were long gone, if they ever had existed. Now outspoken women were reminiscent of the jungle where old crones lorded it over the tribes and gods cringed under the fearsome and arbitrary dictat of goddesses.

Siddarth did not start his Order of Nuns himself till much later, after much thought according to some, but he was concerned about women right from the start, insisting that they were perfectly capable of living by Dhamma. His preaching was also different from the rest – he spoke not only about the duties of wives, mothers, daughters and daughters-in-law, on which the brahmins could also hold forth at great length, but also and in greater detail of their rights.

Not surprisingly, few liked this. He was accused of destroying womanhood, of making women loose, free and careless about their responsibilities. Of launching a tidal wave of illegitimate offspring! When this propaganda did not work, when it in fact brought many more women to his talks, the attacks became personal. He was accused of sleeping with women followers, of putting some in the family way, once even of murdering one. The woman was a Kosalan lady and a frequent visitor to the Buddha's sermons at Shravasti; her dead body was found one day in the grove occupied by the Sangha. The city was shocked, doors were slammed on the monks, they were stoned and abused. The Buddha did not respond, nor did he change his daily routine. When his disciples were hurt, he bandaged their wounds. When they asked him what was to be done, he asked them to just concentrate on their work. Then a drunken brawl in a city tavern exposed two men as the hired assassins. They were arrested and Pasenadi announced an apology to the Sangha. His enemies persevered nonetheless, whispering that the exposure was all a fraud to save the Buddha.

Some of the attacks came from the sramana world, for many there felt that the Sangha was as worldly as could be, destructive of spirituality in fact, an insult to sramanahood. They taunted the disciples and challenged the teacher. The Buddha responded with his usual politeness. As once, when a sage of great name and fame challenged him to display his magical powers. And boasted of what he himself had achieved. 'As a result of twenty years of rigorous austerities,' he declared, 'I can walk over the Ganga without getting wet. Do you want to see me do it?'

'No my friend, but you have my sympathy,' said the Buddha gently. 'All that time and trouble, when there are good boatmen willing to take you across for half a copper!'

All of this was not surprising. He expected opposition, attacks, even violence against his person; they could even be seen as confirmation that his ideas were not ignorable. The real worry was elsewhere – with those who honoured, even eulogized, him. People would later speak reams about the Buddha's friendship with the rich and the powerful, and indeed, as we already know, there were many such who called themselves his disciples. Some offered hot water, robes and banquets, others parks, groves and palaces, few any commitment to the Way. Except perhaps for Pasenadi of Kosala, but his understanding was mystical, even superstitious; he was unable to implement anything worthwhile in kingship. The more he followed the Way, the more his government seemed to lose its; with his people battered from all sides by corrupt bureaucrats, avaricious nobles, organized bandits and the like.

The Licchavis were disciples too. Their city of Vaishali in fact came to be very beloved of the Buddha, not for its renowned grace and beauty but for its Moat Hall where the Gana Sabha discussions were as intense as among the Shakyas, but far more frequent and less afflicted by vicious factionalization and personal ambitions. This was a sangha that still treasured the essence of the republic – the open debates, the common table, the conduct of business by the full assembly, the genuine elections. The Buddha praised the Licchavis greatly, but suffered some disappointment here as well when he spoke of broadening citizenship to include resident non-Licchavis.

Then there were individual problems too, like that created by Magandaya, an opulent brahmin of Kosambi, who first declared himself a lay-follower, then determined to marry his daughter to the Shakyamuni. It took a long while to convince him that the Buddha had absolutely no intention of marrying anybody ever again, by which time the daughter felt humiliated. She should actually have been grateful, for she finally married not an itinerant sage but the Raja of Kosambi. But she never forgot the perceived insult; years later when she happened to encounter another follower of the Buddha, a new wife of her husband, she had the lady murdered.

His own Sangha worried him the most. For it was supposed to practise the highest ideals of Dhamma, while many monks seemed incapable of even understanding them. It was not really surprising for most had joined the Sangha not to change the world but for themselves. This is not to imply that they were greedy or ambitious – the life of the Sangha was difficult, even impossible at times, for all that its leader was admired by kings. A king might feed the monks for a day, but the next day might find them eating rotten grain, the third day smelly leftovers, the fourth day nothing. No, the driving force of new discipleship was not a search for personal comfort, but escape from personal distress. Loneliness, poverty, disease, the death of loved ones, ill-treatment at home or at work, the loss of homes or livelihood – these were the common reasons. There were widows and widowers, runaway slaves and bankrupt businessmen, lepers, invalids and disabled people, destitute women, debtors in flight, natives of nations that no longer existed. They were people who felt that life had nothing to offer them and wanted to get away – for themselves, not for Dhamma.

This was natural; the society they were living in was creating misfits and marginalized by the hundreds every day. But far from being models of rectitude and dedicated practitioners of the Way, they were often depressed, surly, insensitive, hypersensitive, noisy, rude, dirty, narrow-minded, quarrelsome, promiscuous and everything else under the sun. They respected and admired the Buddha devotedly, but their treatment of each other and the rest of the world left much to be desired.

Siddarth tried to set a personal example. His manner was always dispassionate but kindly. He was the first to tend to the ill, homeless and weary – whether monks or lay-people who came to hear his sermons, or the destitute by the road – greeting them with respect, washing and drying their feet, feeding them, all with his own hands, even as his disciples watched. He is said to have been deeply upset once when he came across a monk, ill with an offensive skin disease and lying in his own excreta with none of the others willing to go near him. The Buddha picked him up, carried him indoors, heated water for his bath, bathed him, clothed him in fresh robes and dry clothes and fed him, before speaking to the rest.

'At least for yourself, monks, if not the world, rethink your behaviour. None of you have either parent or family. If you don't look after each other, if you don't care for the sick and the needy amongst you, who is going to bother about you? Those of you who would like to attend to me should first attend to the sick.'

Many of them liked to attend to him, he knew to his irritation, less for his ideas and more because they believed in magic and miracles. He sternly admonished them against such beliefs; it had little effect. He urged people to visit doctors instead of magicians. He declared time and again that he himself had no supernatural powers, no way to bring back the dead or tell the future, nor to cure the sick or wounded beyond the simple humane help that all people could and should render one another. They didn't believe him.

Once, it is reported, when he had finished a discourse, an old woman got up from a small group of solemn people at the back of the crowd. She carried a sleeping boy in her arms. When she came close, it became clear that the boy was not sleeping, he was dead. And she was not old but young, though her skin was faded, her hair withered, her frame wizened way beyond her years – all the handiwork of poverty and overwork, and now also grief. Dry-eyed grief.

'Shakyamuni! Please give my child back to me. Please do something!'

He got up and took her burden from her. A monk spread a mat and they laid the body gently on it. The lady meanwhile fell at the Buddha's feet and held them fiercely. 'Get him back, Shakyamuni! I will give you anything, anything!' She was a widow; the child was all she had and now he was dead.

He tried to raise her but without success. 'Sister, please....'

'You have the power. You can bring him back. Please do your magic. I'll give you anything in return – I'll slave all my life to pay you back. Don't refuse me! Please – '

'She won't let us cremate him...' said a man accompanying her.

She was asking for a ritual, a formula, a do this, that, and the other in the correct order and you can move the heavens. Siddarth had said time and again that he had no faith in magic.

But he sounded different now. 'Rise, sister. I know a way of bringing him back. Rise and I will tell you.'

She got up immediately.

'Listen carefully, sister. Only one thing can bring him back. A small thing. A handful of special mustard seed. Special in that it should come only from a household that has never seen death. Never, you understand? Bring me this, and I will get your son back.'

She left the boy with the Sangha and went off, smiling a little, followed by her bemused friends, from house to house, first among her community, then among others, even the outcastes outside the gates. But she found no house that had not seen death. A thousand times she heard of death, met the grieving and the recovered and those who remembered it only in distant memory, and somewhere along the way she understood – it was inevitable. At night she came back, exhausted, weeping and resigned, and took her child for cremation.

Others insisted on believing in previous births, later births and in various fates after death, though the Buddha remonstrated against this too. But he pandered again sometimes to special cases, like an old miserable couple at the town of Sumsumaragiri, who had lost their only son and who attended the Buddha's sermon only to insist at the end that the Buddha was he, their dead son. The Buddha tried in vain to convince them otherwise; he finally accepted the position, though he refused to obey their command to accompany them home and take up his filial responsibilities.

But sometimes he wearied of it all, especially when such ideas came from his closest companions. Once, the legend goes, his disciple Ananda came to him with a lot of questions. 'Lord, I just heard that the monk named Salha has died at Nadika. Where has he been reborn, and what is his destiny now? And a sister named Nanda has also died. What about her – '

The Buddha is reported to have been irritated. 'It isn't strange, Ananda, that one person should die here, another there, and so on. But when each does so, that you should come to me to enquire about his or her future – this is really amazing!'

It is said that he sometimes wondered in his last years why he had been cursed with such a long life, for he could not see any positive result of it. It was not just that most of his contemporaries were dead, including Sariputta, Malunkya and many disciples, his friends Jeta and Jivaka, his patrons Pasenadi and Bimbisara. That was to be expected, since he himself passed on only at the very substantial age of eighty years. His long life and the relatively good health he enjoyed through most of it – he is said to have swum across the Ganga in his seventies – is a bit of a certificate for the Sangha way of life.

But the Sangha itself was not doing so well. The first schism had already taken place, a warning of the confusion within, of what would happen later. It was the legend's arch-villain Devdutta who is credited with the business, by demanding a more austere and sramanaic code of conduct. The monks should live only in the forests and never approach any settlement, he said, they should not accept gifts of robes or meals, they should reside only in the open, they should be strictly vegetarian. Siddarth said that anyone who wished to follow such rules was free to, but he would not make them compulsory. And he did not seem surprised when quite a few monks followed Devdutta out of the Sangha.

By the time he died, it was obvious that the republics were dying as well. His own, that of the Shakyas, had already vanished from the face of the earth, the Licchavis were on the point of defeat, others would follow. The past was vanishing, the future looked terrifying, inexorable, more and more like Ajatashatru of Magadh. One of Siddarth's last journeys was to Vaishali, to warn the Licchavis of the new king of Magadh. The hatred of all monarchs for the old republics was implacable, he warned. Stay together, hold your Samiti and Sabha meetings frequently, be wary of outsiders. They vowed to follow his advice.

But Ajatashatru learnt of this advice too and better than them. He sent his trusted minister Vassakara to the Licchavis, posing as a refugee whose nose and ears had been cut off for disappointing his king. The Licchavis received the mutilated exile with sympathy, first snubbed his offers of help against Magadh, then slowly relented, began giving him importance and finally even allowed him into Sabha meetings. It took time but Vassakara slowly set one raja against another, encouraged each to claim more than his fair share of everything, advised slighted ones to boycott assemblies and army drills, and urged all others to punish such claims and boycotts. The Licchavis came to blows with one another, though all contending sides continued to regard Vassakara as their friend, right up till the moment when he opened the city gates to Ajatashatru. But then they recovered and put up a tremendous fight – it took more than a decade for Ajatashatru to smash them completely.

Siddarth was luckily not around to see their end. But he did have to suffer that of his own Shakyas. And the cause was illustrative of one of the weakest aspects of the old republicanism – the rabid belief in exclusivity. It came about at the hands of Virudhaka, crown prince of Kosala and the Shakyas' own grandson. The first-born of Pasenadi's marriage to a half-breed slave passed off as a Shakya rajkumari, Virudhaka had always been intrigued by his celebrated maternal ancestry. When he reached the age of fifteen, he went to his father and informed him that he would like to visit his Shakya grandparents. The only Shakyas he had ever met were their representatives at court, who were always cold and formal. Pasenadi did not object, so Virudhaka informed his mother, who objected strongly. His grandfather, she said, was an unpleasant and cantankerous old man.

'But he has never met me before. Won't he be happy to see his grandson? And what of you? Doesn't he want to see his daughter?'

'I am too old to travel so far.'

'Too old – !'

But the queen silenced him with a look, and then almost to concede his opinion, pushed away the maid pressing her feet, rose and strolled to the window. A bright green parakeet emerged from a silver cage hanging there, to perch on her hand. Her son watched her, he was among many who enjoyed just watching her. For time had been more than generous to Vassabha, or Vassabha-Khatiya as she was now known, for she was Pasenadi's only kshatriya queen; he called her the most precious jewel in the world's most glittering court. Her golden skin was still flawless, her figure plump but voluptuously so, her long hair thick and glossy, bright streaks of auburn and purple hiding the white and launching a craze for the colours among men as well as women. She had reduced the gold and diamonds in her raiment – she found them too heavy now, she explained, though others said it was more to do with the problems of the Kosalan treasury – but if anything her regality was the greater. It was that aristocratic blood, that pure Arya heritage, believed her proud son, it needed no embellishment at all.

She stood at the window, staring out at her private garden with its thickly perfumed planting. 'Yes, it is too far for me. And for him. And he does not really appreciate such ties.'

'But I want to see him and all my relatives. Surely they are interested in their royal cousin? After all, I am also their future King.'

'I do not know. I have not met them for long.'

'But why, Mother?'

'They are different, Virudhaka – of noble blood perhaps, but with a provincial small town mentality, hardly cultured – '

'Hardly cultured! But I have always heard the opposite, that the Shakyas have the most exquisite sensibilities among all the Arya peoples.'

' – And they are republicans, which is hardly a modern outlook. You know what your father's ministers say – the republics are the biggest challenge to a kingdom like ours. As long as they exist, people everywhere will always hanker for the days when they too lived in that confused system of endless discussions, arguments, elections and votes. Without any monarch. The republics are a remnant of the past – there is nothing you can learn there!'

'Still, Mother....'

'This discussion tires me, Virudhaka. Do what you will. All I can say is that you are wasting your time. I think you will be bored and offended by your Shakya relatives. Concentrate on your studies instead.' Her voice was cold. Her son rarely disobeyed when she sounded like this.

But Virudhaka went. He rode up to Kapilavastu in a cavalcade of chariots, many loaded with costly presents, causing the soldiers at the city gates no small panic. The prince was favourably impressed by the town, by its old world decorum and grace and genuflecting passersby, which couldn't contrast more with bustling cosmopolitan Shravasti. This was clearly a land of ancient and courtly tradition, where everyone knew his place, unlike loose and easy Kosala. He felt exalted and also humbled.

Mahanaman's compound pleased him too, though the mansion was not half as big as those of the merchants of Shravasti, leave aside his father's palace. But it seemed built of only the best teak, the facade lightened by numerous balconies, window shades and delicate sculpture. The red and gold paint of the balcony balusters and the fretted cornices was fresh, the polish blinding. Virudhaka marched happily up onto the veranda. One of his slaves lifted the bell-pull and rang. That was where the prince's happiness ended.

The slave who opened the doors looked surprised at the visitor, uneasy when he heard the introduction, and then simply vanished. A long and irritating wait followed, but finally another servant arrived, who was followed by an old man, tall and stern and very straight. It was his grandfather and Virudhaka was pleasantly surprised to see that he resembled him quite a lot. He forgot his irritation, stepped forward and without a word touched his feet. Mahanaman moved slightly backward. 'Yes?'

'Raja Mahanaman, I am Virudhaka, Rajkumar of Kosala, son of Pasenadi and Vassabha, your grandson. Did the servant not inform you? I have come for your blessings.'

'I bless you,' said Mahanaman coldly, his palms joined.

Virudhaka had expected something more effusive and wondered what to do.

'May I come in?' he asked finally.

'Do.' Mahanaman motioned him into an anteroom. Silence again. Virudhaka stared at his grandfather, Mahanaman examined the floor. The prince started a struggle for conversation.

'I have wanted to meet my mother's family for a long time. But somehow, thanks to my studies… and Mother wanted to come too, but the distance is great….'

Mahanaman said nothing.

'Is my grandmother, your respected wife, able to receive me?'

'I am afraid my wife is unwell.'

Another long silence. Virudhaka felt deeply uncomfortable but could not give up. 'I have travelled a long way, Grandfather. I am tired and hungry.'

'Yes, of course. Wait. ' Mahanaman disappeared inside and was gone a long while. Finally, when Virudhaka thought he had been forgotten, he returned and said, 'Come.'

He led the way to a small but beautiful dining room panelled in carved ebony, the darkness relieved by brass lamps set in little wall-niches. One place had been laid with silver plate, bowls, and glass. There was an array of dishes and two slaves waiting to serve.

'Only one plate? Won't you eat with me, my lord?'

Mahanaman suddenly looked grey and tired, and colder than ever. His mother had been right, thought Virudhaka. This had to be the iciest grandfather who ever lived. And monosyllabic too.

'I eat very little in my old age....'

'No, this won't do, Grandfather. You must taste a little of the sweets I have brought. Mother and Father have sent many gifts, along with their apologies for not being able to come. My father has many duties of state, as you will understand – today is the bimonthly meeting of....'

But Mahanaman was not listening. He was looking out of the window instead, towards the midday sun, though it glared blindingly white. For a moment he seemed to speak to it silently. Then he turned back. 'Very well. I will have my bath and come. Please do not wait for me.'

He left. The maids arranged another set of seat, plate and bowls. Virudhaka waited and waited, and was finally tempted by the aroma of the food. He ate some, then more and in no time had eaten an entire meal. The maid was pouring a pitcher of warm scented water over his hands when they heard loud wails. Virudhaka hurried out to the entrance hall, just in time to see a man being carried into the house. It was Mahanaman. He was soaking wet and quite dead.

The body was carried by servants. A few men, who had apparently brought it, sank to the ground outside the door. Two of them were as wet as the body. One was speaking to all who would listen. 'He walked into the river in front of me. He was a good swimmer, you know... but he went right in, without swimming at all and then I saw him floating....'

Virudhaka was stunned. He watched as the body was placed in the anteroom. Other people hurried in, all of whom completely ignored him. When he saw an old lady sit on the floor and take Mahanaman's head on her lap, he managed to get a grip on himself and walked towards her. But a brahmin standing near the door barred his way. Virudhaka was shocked. 'I am the Prince of Kosala, brahmin!'

The brahmin bowed and said, 'Please, sire. Please wait outside. Do not approach the body.'

The prince left the room in a daze and walked up and down the hall. Others were entering the anteroom, speaking to the widow, touching the body; the brahmin made no objection. He felt anger and confusion. Why had this visit gone so wrong?

His strides took him past the dining room where he had lunched earlier, but now the sour stink of urine assailed his nose. He peered in to see an old slave-woman washing the room with liberal amounts of reeking liquid.

'What are you doing?' he barked. She nearly jumped out of her skin and stared at him in fear. 'What are you doing, I asked. Answer me!'

'It is holy cow's urine, lord. I was instructed to wash the place. To purify it after the lowborn dined here – '

Without another word, Virudhaka swept out, into his chariot and homewards. He rode hard through the evening and night, driving his horse mercilessly, ignoring the attendants who desperately tried to keep pace, spoke to no one at all till he reached Shravasti and the palace, where he went straight to his father's bedchamber and woke him up. 'They insulted you, Father.'

'What?'

'The Shakyas. They called me a lowborn! They insulted us terribly. They must be punished!'

Pasenadi rubbed his eyes and stared at his son. 'Well, I am lower born than them.'

Virudhaka turned away furiously and went to his mother. She was seated at her window, wide awake and expecting him.

'I've sad news for you, Mother. Your father is dead.' His mother's expression did not change. Her lips did not even tremble, the long-lashed gaze she bestowed on him was, if anything, steely. 'But I feel no sorrow. They insulted me! Your father was very rude to me, and then he died and they wouldn't let me pay my respects. And then – then they tried to purify the house because of me, while I was still there! How dare they treat the Crown Prince of Kosala like that? And I am half a Shakyaraja myself!'

His mother's mouth started to tremble then and she raised a jewelled hand to cover it. But she was not crying, Virudhaka realized with horror, she was smiling, no, actually laughing.

'Mother, did you hear me? Your father's dead! He insisted on bathing before eating with me and drowned in the river!'

Vassabha stopped laughing, to glare at him in the coldest manner he had ever seen, not unlike her late father. 'He drowned himself, Virudhaka. To avoid eating with you. Because you are not half a Shakyaraja.' She turned to the window. 'I am the daughter of Mahanaman, yes, and a slave-woman. My mother was a Naga. The whole thing was a fraud on your father. The Shakyas did not want to link their blood to his.'

Virudhaka stood frozen for a few moments, then lifted his arm as if to protect himself from a blow and stumbled from the room. He went to his apartments and lay there almost comatose. Meanwhile Pasenadi was in a towering rage, for he had heard of Vassabha's explanation too, thanks to his harem spies. He decided to discard his wife and son with immediate effect, and announced so in his audience hall first thing in the morning. His Prime Minister was deputed to escort the two to the gates of the city. His wife however had already left, for the Jetavana grove where the Buddha was camped. She told him the entire story and begged for his help till he agreed to intervene. Pasenadi did not want to even look at him at first, but finally cooled down and listened quietly as the Buddha urged him to take back his wife and son, who were victims of the fraud as much as him.

'The Shakyas have nothing but these foolish ideas of birth to cling to. Why should you, an enlightened man, a beloved monarch and father of a worthy son, be bothered by them?'

Pasenadi sincerely admired the Buddha and did not take long to change his mind. He called back his wife and son, calmed down about the Shakyas, even came to a point where he could laugh about the whole incident.

Unlike his son. Virudhaka came out of the first shock, he too listened to the Buddha, but he never could forget the insult, and he nursed the hatred for many years, till he became king. In the meantime he developed into a strong and powerful prince, excelling at the art and science of war in a manner ironically true to his Shakya heritage, in a manner that the Buddha had never been able to. He became as shrewd and focused at governance as his father was wishy-washy and undecided. He was so proficient at fighting and, more importantly, at guiding and building the army, that when he was a little over thirty, his impressed father bestowed upon him a new and amazing title – Senapati, Lord of the Army.

Virudhaka Senapati was thence the absolute dictator of the Kosalan army and he concentrated on building it up into a force that could match the greatest of the time, that of Magadh. He studied all of Bimbisara's innovations and developed his own. His father did not interfere. In fact, as Virudhaka increased his influence, Pasenadi seemed to withdraw deeper into philosophy and metaphysical ponderings. The Buddha could see what was going on, he was possibly also conscious that his own influence on the Senapati was slim, so he hinted more than once at the duties of a Raja towards his people. But Pasenadi refused to take the hint. Nor would he consider abdicating in favour of his son, though this was hinted at too, by some of his ministers who were also not blind to the developments. From a power behind the throne, Virudhaka soon became the ruler in all but name, an ambitious and ruthless one at that; fatherly pride finally changed to unease. Pasenadi then tried to bring the Senapati to heel, but it was too late and his efforts only created a chasm between them.

It is possible, to give Virudhaka the benefit of doubt, that his violent rise to the throne was conditioned by Ajatashatru's just before. The throne had changed occupants in Magadh, and unconventionally. Seniya Bimbisara was arrested by his son, imprisoned and starved. One day, it is said, Ajatashatru felt remorse and went to see his parent. But when the cell door swung open revealing the visitor, Bimbisara misunderstood his purpose. Apparently deciding to save his son from the crime of patricide, he picked up a dagger and slew himself.

Ajatashatru, it is said, waxed grief-stricken. He even had the cheek to visit the Buddha and beat his breast in remorse.

'Evil overcame me, Lord Shakyamuni, in that, in my folly, stupidity and wickedness, for the sake of kingship, I deprived my dear father, the righteous Magadhe-Raja, of life,' he said with tears running down his face. 'I beg of you, lord, to accept my remorse, to punish and instruct me that I may be restrained in the future.'

The Buddha was sympathetic. 'It is truly sad. Your Majesty had all the makings of a saint, if only you had not killed that excellent man, your father.'

Ajatashatru – unrelenting student of Dhamma and founder of the first shrines to the Buddha – was notorious even in his youth, at least to all neighbours with any semblance of a secret service, as a man who was intelligently, ruthlessly and completely devoted to power, a general who had increased the strength of the formidable Magadhan army to astounding proportions, a prince who dreamt of empire. It was not an empty dream. Magadh was now trading iron on a regular basis with far away Persia, where a dynasty called the Achaemenids and a king named Cyrus had created a gigantic empire of many different peoples, races and languages. Their realm included several ancient and independent kingdoms which were now tribute-paying and slave-supplying provinces. Such accounts had seriously whetted royal appetites this side of the Sindhu, not least because a big stretch of the Sindhu itself had recently fallen to the Persians. They were at the doorstep of the subcontinent. Ajatashatru was preparing to match them. There seemed little doubt that Kosala and its philosopher-king would be simply crushed by one or the other.

Pasenadi's response to the death of his chief enemy and brother-in-law had been to rescind the Kashi villages that had been gifted to Magadh many years before. It was apparently just what Ajatashatru wanted. He sent a chunk of his vast army to occupy the villages. Then he waited.

Virudhaka too waited, for his father to respond, and waited in vain. Finally he decided to take matters in his own hands. He asked Pasenadi to abdicate; Pasenadi asked the Kosalan army to arrest his son; it arrested him instead. Most accounts say that Pasenadi was then murdered at the behest of the Senapati. According to a few however, the deposed king managed to escape with the help of a slave-woman and head towards Rajgir, where both he and she died of exposure outside the closed city gates.

So the Buddha's greatest royal fans were both done to death by their sons. And the fashion was to catch on. The next five kings of Magadh were also patricides. What is amazing is how it did not apparently occur to any of them to strangle their sons at birth.

'Princes are like crabs,' Kautilya would note later. 'They are father-eaters.' He went on to instruct the king at length about how to watch, control and restrain his sons from attempting a short-cut to the throne; and in the very next chapter, advised the prince on how to circumvent his father's precautions.

In any case, Virudhaka became king. And his first action, even before the appropriate period of mourning for his father was over, was to lead his army to the Shakya republic and destroy it. Cities and villages were torn down to rubble, fields set ablaze, people massacred. More than ten thousand rajas died impaled on stakes that lined the better part of the highway to the charred and smoking ruin that used to be the beautiful little city of Siddarth's childhood. The city itself, its double walls, elegant mansions, market, shops, and the ancient Moat Hall all struggled to withstand the efforts of elephants and battering rams, and managed for a while for they were among the best built buildings of the time. But Virudhaka was relentless, more elephants were put to the task, the Moat Hall was brought crashing down, other buildings followed. The wells were filled with rubble and dirt. Everything, with many dead still inside and some living too, was then burnt. More than fifty thousand people were killed in all.

'Be very clear about this,' Virudhaka had instructed his officers. 'I am not looking for tribute or plunder or even annexation. I don't want slaves. I want all traces of the Shakyas wiped off this land. I want them wiped off everybody's memory.'

He was successful. They say that the land was left as one mortally wounded, not a leaf or a breath moving for months after he left. Paddy fields, orchards, gardens, pastures, all were charred; predators scrounged around puzzled and fearful among the hot fallen timbers and crumbly bones that marked the sites of towns. Those Shakyas who had happened to be elsewhere at the time returned, stared at the vast charnel-grounds and stumbled away. Many took refuge in the Buddha's Sangha, multiplying the problems in that quarter. Nobody ever had the courage or the emotional stamina to try to restore the ruins, not even long after the death of the conqueror. It was left to nature to gently and firmly take them back to her bosom. Bamboo sprouted where the proud rajas had once argued, tigers raised their young near Shudodhan's family altar, thick creepers of wild jasmine blanketed the wall where Tara had died. Rhinos tasted the muddy grass on the old highway critically, while sal trees, the totem of the Shakyas, raised a lofty canopy of mourning over everything. It was as if the Shakyas had never been.

More than a hundred years would pass, the entire realm would go under the sceptre of Magadh, before people would return here. They would come over the hills and begin the laborious task of clearing what looked like virgin jungle; they would plant and build with all the dedicated back-breaking toil of new settlers; they would be easterners who had never heard of the dead republic. Not a trace would be found of Kapilavastu ever again, not even by the Magadhe-Raja who developed an awesome passion for the sage of the Shakyas. His men searched and searched, but the only link they found was a little grove of a goddess, without an edifice of any kind, but a name – Lumbini – that was familiar to the legend and sacred then and for centuries afterwards to jungle-folk who had never heard of the Shakyamuni. There he left a stupa.

That was much later. The first and immediate effect of the end of the Shakyas was to catapult Virudhaka of Kosala into the international limelight, as a monarch and a general who had shown enormous capacity to use an army to the most savage extent imaginable. All across Aryavarta and beyond, potentates took note. He looked colossal, ferocious, unstoppable. Ajatashatru paled in comparison. What did the future bode for all of them, with such ruthless ambition at the helm of the biggest kingdom in the land? Ideas of alliance came to mind, defence was discussed, plans of war put on hold. But a more permanent solution was provided almost immediately, and by divine intervention as it were. Virudhaka was hardly able to celebrate his revenge. He and a large part of his army put up camp one night on the dry bed of the Rapti not far from the ruins of Kapilavastu, whence they were all swept away by a flash flood. His body was never found.

It was punishment for what he had done to the Shakyas, said the few cowering far away. It was retribution for his treatment of his father, shuddered old ministers of Pasenadi. It was vindication of the magnificent destiny of Magadh, declared Ajatashatru.

And of all of them, he was right.

END

'Would you say, Upali, that the Buddha was defeated by Magadh?' mused Therii Vrinda as their boat was being expertly guided across the fast moving current to the small jetty that was the landing for Ujjayani. The journey was over.

'Or did the Buddha make Magadh?' asked her friend Lila.

'Definitely, if you mean today's Magadh,' answered Harsha. 'This is the first king who's really trying to implement the Way.'

'Both are probably true, aren't they, Upali?' asked Vrinda.

But Upali's mind was elsewhere, his stomach feeling exactly like the dark bottle-green water churning against the boat. Because Harsha had decided not to accompany them to Ujjayani; he was going straight on to Maheshwar and the monastery. Upali felt like racing ahead of him, to Bhima and the furnaces in the jungle, but the memory of Vipul's bloated face haunted him; he had to check on the imprisoned sculptor first. Besides, Bhima was free, he must have already spoken to his people. The furnaces project was surely long abandoned. If only Harsha would stay away from their village....

'Don't worry about Bhima, Upali,' said Harsha. 'I'll check on them, the moment I get there.' They hit the mossy planks of the jetty hard. The boat shuddered but before it could retreat, men had leapt to the jetty with ropes in their hands and fastened it. 'And listen, give me your folder. I'll take it to the monastery.'

Upali looked at him. 'No, I'll keep it with me.'

It was a small but awkward moment that cast gloom on the parting. The feeling lasted all the way to the city for it was a gloomy day even otherwise, thanks to a bank of clouds that was growing darker by the minute. But Ujjayani looked cheerful. People were hurrying through the gates, laughing, shouting excitedly, laying loud bets.

'The coals test,' explained a soldier, staring at the dusty monks and nuns. 'At the market square. A suspect is being tried.'

'The coals test?' asked Therii Vrinda. 'You mean walking on live coals?'

'Come on, we must stop it!' said Upali.

They followed the excitement into the city, pausing only to stare at a couple of buildings in the outermost quarter that seemed to have been burnt – only some blackened walls and fallen timbers remained, smoke rising from it all. The market square was unrecognizable, with the usual hawkers absent, shops closed and a huge crowd gathered around something at the centre. Everybody was trying to push through, so after much pleading Therii Vrinda gave up and led the way into one of the tall buildings edging the square. The first floor was packed but they managed to squeeze themselves onto a second floor balcony, and looked down at an enormous black box, about fifty feet long, edged by thick wooden planks and filled with coals, most glowing redly.

Upali had seen such exercises before, in villages where they were organized by sramanas to show off their magical powers, and in cities like Tosali and Banaras where they had always been a most respected test of guilt, one of a host which were actually just tests of confidence and certain other skills. If the walker walked fast enough, if the coals were covered by enough ash, if the surface was uneven enough so that only a few coals touched the foot at every moment, if the feet were little moist or sweaty, if one managed to control fear, since fear apparently increased the sensation of pain, and of course if the bed was small enough – passing the coals test was not difficult. But this bed was huge and too many of the coals looked live.

'Look at the sky. It will rain any moment – thank god!' said Vrinda. The clouds had indeed become heavier, barely held aloft by a few motionless columns of smoke, apparently from the burnt buildings. Smoke, the sign of a devout city.

A company of soldiers marched into the square. They wore the yellow uniform of the Viceroy's personal guard. Between them was a bound man in just a loin-cloth.

'We must stop them!' said Upali and tried to charge down the stairs, but there were many more people rushing to the top, so that by the time they finally reached the square, the soldiers had pushed the convict through the throng and it had sealed itself behind them.

A clatter of hooves announced a small troop of four men, led by an officer who looked familiar. It was the Commandant of the city garrison whom Upali had last met when Bhima was sentenced. He had been unhappy then and he looked unhappy now, frowning so fiercely that most people hurriedly backed out of his path.

'Listen here, my lord!' shouted Upali from behind. 'What do you mean by all this? Public spectacles like this are not allowed! Do you hear me – ?'

Nobody did. The crowd closed up behind the horse too and Upali discovered he was alone; his friends had opted to try their own methods of subverting the proceedings.

Ananda was the first who reached the pit, by crawling between the legs of the crowd most of the way. He felt a glow of success when he touched an edge of the knee-high box and immediately another one, a much more uncomfortable glow of red-hot heat from the coals. The inky red-black layers looked at least three or four deep, they crackled and winked at him, inviting him to pick one up. He did not succumb but began to sweatily wish he had been less zealous. He could hear Upali's voice politely asking to be excused somewhere way behind and then he saw the

Commandant not far away along the edge. He was staring across the width of the pit, over the rowdy crowd on the other side as well, to two men on horses at the back. One was the Viceroy. The other was a regal looking man in white robes on a white horse; people were bowing to him. The Commandant bowed slightly too, before they all turned towards the head of the box where a group of soldiers stood around the prisoner. Ananda looked too. It was Devadina.

He looked thin. There were streaks of dried blood on his chest, he seemed a little unsteady. But his gaze was intent and searching the mob.

Ananda tried to circumnavigate towards him but the crowd was too dense. The people nearest the box had become quiet, sobered perhaps by the grim heat and the rather fragile look of the prisoner. But those at the back were excited, pushing around wildly and shouting abuse. 'Foreign scum', 'Magadhan spy' and 'murderer' seemed the most popular. Some of them carried children on their shoulders, some were munching away thanks to the hawkers of roasted gram and nuts traversing the outer edges of the crowd. There were quite a few mounted observers and some aristocratic chariots lined up behind as well, though the occupants were content to watch from within. The ambience was festive; Ananda wanted to slap everybody.

A soldier untied Devadina's hands and prodded him towards the coals. Devadina's response was to shout, 'Sutanuka!' before sinking to his knees. The soldiers tried to kick him upright. That was when the audience started to pelt him with stones and vegetables.

'Stop this!' came Upali's voice. 'Stop at once!'

Ananda saw Therii Vrinda on the other side of the box, she seemed to be pleading with a pelter. The man sneered and raised an onion; she promptly boxed his ear, so hard that the onion fell to the ground and he followed. Meanwhile, the missiles luckily hit some soldiers who bellowed and cracked their whips. The pelting stopped. Devadina was propelled to the edge of the box. The crowd was suddenly grave, faces gleaming in the heat, waiting.

The silence was broken by the nun Lila, who startled everybody by falling on her knees and shouting in a piercing loud voice, 'May the lord Buddha punish those who torture a fellow being! May he douse these evil embers! Drown them and all who cheer them!'

Everybody gawked at her, then up at the dark sky. Upali managed to push through to the edge of the pit in the distraction. The sky glowered mildly, the crowd waited, then began to shuffle around awkwardly. Lila stopped cursing and was apparently meditating now, eyes still closed. The soldiers looked at the Viceroy who made a sign against the evil eye and nodded. The next moment Devadina was on the coals. For a minute he swayed, then he started stumbling along, almost running. His face was a shining wet grimace of pain and sweat and perhaps tears. His feet were clearly burning. The crowd was silent now, many looked again and again at the meditating nun and the embarrassed sky. Devadina persevered, and at great speed, and somehow reached an edge of the pit very near her, where he shouted, 'Sutanuka, don't worry. I'm all right!'

The only response was from a soldier who reached out and pushed him back so strongly that he fell, crashing down on the embers.

There was a roar of horror, followed by surprise as a boy suddenly jumped into the pit. A soldier thrust his spear in the way, but the boy dodged and simply ran through the coals towards the floundering sculptor, though tears started to stream down his face before he was halfway there. He was followed by Ananda from the other side; he seemed to be shouting some abuse that probably only the coals could hear. Upali was inspired to follow, but his first step was too heavy and he promptly lost his balance, for it went right in, like stepping into a hot hole. He would have fallen right there into the coals if the nearest soldier had not stepped up, caught hold of his arm and jerked him out sharply. 'Stay here!' he barked. Upali collapsed on the ground.

The two boys reached Devadina, who seemed to be in a daze. They had to drag him to the edge, where some watchers reached forward to help them out. The soldiers stepped forward too, but were halted by the Commandant's bark: 'Enough! Pull them out.'

The soldiers looked at the Viceroy. 'He has failed the test,' he said and rode off.

The Commandant waited while the three were pulled out, then got off his horse, walked to the meditating Lila, got right down and touched her feet with his head, before remounting and riding away. His gesture electrified the crowd. Nobody bothered to watch as the soldiers lifted the giddy Devadina to his feet, arranged themselves about him and marched off. Almost everybody headed for Lila instead, to touch her feet and hang around, waiting impatiently for her to get or do something – rise in the air perhaps, thought Upali, explode into fragments and then reunite, or bring general calamity. But she just sat there, a thin bald figure murmuring a little under her breath. He felt like shaking her.

But he could not rise. His foot really hurt. He crawled his way around the rectangle to where Ananda sat amidst dust and nutshells. The other boy was not to be seen. Ananda was furious. 'I wish I could kill them! If I had a sword – '

'Calm down, Ananda. What you did was the best possible thing.'

Ananda looked at him. 'Sutanuka saw me, didn't she?'

Upali sighed. 'Everybody saw you. For those with any sense, you're a hero. And that other boy. He was amazing!'

Therii Vrinda nodded. 'Yes. There are many good people in this city – '

'Good people!' spluttered Ananda. 'They are cowards – complete cowards! They are – '

'Ananda,' the Therii was gentle but firm, 'you were very brave; I couldn't have done it myself. But you have to admit that it's easier for us – we have only to steel ourselves – if you have children, parents, a family, it's more difficult to be a hero.'

She sat by her colleague; finally Lila opened her eyes. The people hanging around moved off. Nobody said anything about the Buddha's failure to respond.

The nuns at the Ujjayani convent-hospice exclaimed in horror on seeing the travellers back from the Congress, so tired, bruised, even burnt. They rushed around arranging a pallet for Ananda and bandages for his feet, while explaining that the city had been tense for the past few weeks, thanks to Devadina's arrest. He was said to be a Magadhan spy; the ex-Raja had taken to making public announcements to the effect that Avanti would not take such assaults lying down. The result was that some Magadhan-owned establishments and workers had been attacked. There was some incident or the other almost every night.

'Do they think they can throw Magadh out?' wondered Upali. 'If they really revolt, they will be flattened out of existence.'

'Our job is to prevent such a time coming,' declared the Therii Vrinda. 'A war will destroy ordinary people. The Magadhe-Raja has charged us with great responsibility, sisters. We are not to sit quiet when madness rages all around!' Her colleagues looked worried, but she ignored them and turned to Upali. 'Thera, I think we should meet the Viceroy.' Upali nodded, though he would have preferred to go alone.

The nuns served up a cummin-flavoured khichdi of rice and chickpeas, after which Upali and the Therii set out, down roads that were quiet and past people who looked nervously rushed. Shops seemed to be closing down. Is there something wrong, Upali asked a soldier; the reply was negative. A crowd of supplicants was waiting outside the heavily guarded flag-flying gates of the Viceregal palace. But one look at the bald and saffron-clad duo and the soldiers saluted and made way. Monks were the elite, Upali remembered. But it hadn't helped in the morning.

They were led into a large anteroom adorned with swords, shields and ivory panels depicting the battlefield heroics of some conqueror.

'Is that Chandragupta?' asked Upali, examining one. 'But what is a Maurya doing in the Ujjayani palace? Or did they alter the palace after they conquered Avanti?'

'They altered it – by burning it down to the ground!' said the Therii. 'This palace is barely twenty years old. No ruler will live in another's palace after Chandragupta's experience with the Nandas!'

That had been one colourful experience, another chapter in the great Kautilya legend. The Nandas were the rulers of Magadh before Chandragupta. His forces had just defeated the last Nanda, taken over the imperial capital and occupied the palace, when, on the very second day, Prime Minister Kautilya noticed ants carrying grain out of a crack in the floor. He had the crack examined and discovered hordes of Nanda soldiers in a basement below, preparing for a surprise attack. The palace was promptly emptied of the Maurya entourage and burnt to the ground. Kautilya was emotionless about such matters. In fact, the only time he was known to show emotion was when the Nanda was killed. He went to see the body before tying up his hair, for he had vowed a decade before, after being insulted at the Magadhan court, that he would leave his topknot untied as long as the insult was unavenged. His famed discovery and training of the young Chandragupta, and the rise of the latter to wipe out the entire Nanda dynasty, was all part of that vengeance. But apparently Kautilya still felt something lacking, for he now demanded that the king's body be left uncremated. He wanted it simply discarded, to become carrion. Chandragupta coolly acquiesced; his officers quietly shuddered – did even the Nanda deserve such a barbaric end? And wouldn't a price have to be paid for such an insult to a man's immortal soul? Not by the insulters apparently, for though many of the new court later reported sightings of the Nanda's unhappy ghost, it seemed to avoid the Maurya and his Prime Minister. Wisely, no doubt.

The Viceroy greeted them warmly. 'Upali! How was the – '

'My lord,' interrupted Vrinda. 'We were shocked by that display in the morning. Surely torture of criminals has been banned?'

The Viceroy raised his eyebrows. 'That was not torture. It was a test.'

'What nonsense! It's just a way of finding a scapegoat! And you could be in great trouble now. Devadina is an employee of the Magadhe-Raja himself.'

'I am quite aware of that, Therii. But if he was innocent, nothing would have happened to him.'

'Are you mad? Anybody's feet will burn if they walk on live coals! This is simply superstition!'

The Viceroy was frowning. 'Madam, this is an old and highly respected practice of the Magadhan judicial system. You are close to being in contempt of the State!'

'Not as close as you!' Her glare was fiercer. 'Anyway, you have to send your case to Pataliputra, don't you?'

'Ordinarily. But this is not an ordinary case. The public is very angry. They're demanding immediate punishment. In fact, there have been riots in parts of the city against foreigners. The situation is – '

'Out of control? Perhaps you should resign if you can't manage things – '

'You're really planning – what? An execution?' interrupted Upali. It was the first thing he had said and the Viceroy turned to him almost gratefully.

'I have no option, Upali – '

'But where's the proof? Except for – '

'You'll be in big trouble, lord, really big!' The Therii rose. 'We'd like to meet Devadina now.'

'He isn't here. He was shifted to the main prison this morning.'

Therii Vrinda stalked out without a word. Upali was about to follow when the Viceroy added, 'Upali, one moment.' He waited till the doors closed behind the Therii. 'Did you meet Vipul of Takshashila?'

'Lord, this is a complete travesty of justice. You're ready to kill an innocent, just to hit at Magadh!'

'Upali, you don't understand these things! Anyway – didn't you meet Vipul?'

'He's dead! Magadh has a spy in your household – '

'He's dead too. What else did you learn?'

Upali stared open-mouthed for a moment, then walked out.

'What did he want?' asked the Therii.

Upali shook his head. 'Let's go meet Devadina. I want to speak to that Commandant as well.'

Devadina lay on a dirty straw mat, wrapped in a cotton blanket, looking feverish but cheerful. How was he? The burns? Was he in great pain? Was he being fed? Why was he so thin? He shrugged away the questions. Vrinda gave him an ointment for his burns; he accepted it absent-mindedly and asked, 'How is Sutanuka?'

Upali realized that they had not met her. 'I don't know. I'll find out and tell you. Don't worry. And keep your spirits up,' he added gloomily. 'We'll get you out soon.'

Devadina nodded. 'Yes. But take care of Sutanuka. She has been very depressed with all this.'

But first they had to meet a far more depressed personage, the city Commandant, who greeted them sourly. 'Well, Thera? Once again with friends behind bars?'

Upali opened his mouth but the Therii was quicker. 'How could you permit that spectacle in the morning, my lord? It amounts to fanning the worst kind of superstition – '

'It had nothing to do with me. The whole investigation has been taken over by the Viceroy. With his friend, the ex-Raja. I don't subscribe to those tests either – they're nonsense! I've sent my report to Pataliputra.'

'Are you aware, my lord,' asked Upali, 'that the Viceroy is planning a quick hanging? And besides, why do you suspect Devadina at all? You have no proof, no reason to suspect him! Isn't anybody interested in finding the real killer?'

The Chief stared at him silently.

'And what are you doing about all these attacks on foreigners?' continued the Therii. 'Writing more reports?'

The Chief drummed his fingers on the table. 'The truth is the Viceroy ordered a reduction in the regular patrols in this last month. He is my superior – I could not do anything – '

'Even after miscreants started running wild? I would advise you to start acting quickly, my lord, to at least restore peace. As for the Viceroy, I suspect he's going to find himself in trouble soon.'

The Chief looked at her and away. 'Yes, well, I'm trying, Therii.'

But not hard enough, apparently, for by the time they reached the market square, flickering light and new smoke could be seen wafting up into the dark sky. They could hear crackling and small explosions, familiar sounds that made Upali shiver for they were the stuff of his nightmares. He had never seen the market so dark and absolutely deserted. A couple of the shops had been broken into; he stepped into a large puddle of something very thick and sticky, and smelled a strong smell. Sandal oil, worth a fortune probably.

His sticky foot slowed him down while the Therii had speeded up. She was almost running, out of the square and down quiet lanes, past a few people hurrying in the opposite direction. Some trouble, was all they said before disappearing. A building was burning in the next lane; Upali lagged behind even more. Yet another was burning just ahead, with a lot of crashing and bursting sounds from within. The lane was otherwise dark and shut up and as desolate as a cemetery, the other buildings standing around like grim-faced mourners. And here I am, a Chandala to tend the pyres. And I've done this before too, watched a settlement become a cemetery, waited while timbers cracked and thatch dissolved and all the digging, hauling, carpentering, plastering, and painting struggle of creating a building vanished like it had no value at all. But the Therii had peered around and about one pyre and was now running to the next, looking for something, and he forced himself to run too. She found a body, of a man, stabbed in the chest and quite dead, and she felt him and spoke to him and closed his terrified eyes, and then ran on saying things that Upali could not hear, to the next lane, and the next, and more pyres, and around them and behind them, till she found something else that made her stop. It was a small boy squatting next to a pile of goods on a smoky road. A closer look revealed a man doubled up and unconscious among them. His grandfather, muttered the boy.

Upali hefted the man up over his shoulder and they went on, heading for the convent, the boy scampering quietly in between, the Therii still making her detours. But they found nobody more, only empty streets lit up by flares in the sky and stinking acridly of burnt wood, cloth, food, metal. And sandal oil.

The convent looked beautiful, so beautiful that it took a moment to realize that it was burning too. Just a corner of the thatch, and the scene was completely different. Nuns and others were running about on the road with buckets of water, handing them up into the neighbouring building, from where they thrown across to the flames. Two nuns rushed forward and took the injured man from Upali, the child hurried in behind them.

Upali felt a tear fall on his arm. Then another; the drizzle soon became a downpour. Lila's prayers had worked, hours later. Steam rose from the thatch and the flames died out meekly.

It was a long night, for the police apparently did get into some kind of action after a while, perhaps inspired by the rains. They brought some more injured people to the convent, mostly with burns, a few with stab wounds. The violence was over, they reported, though they hadn't been able to arrest even a single suspect. And they insisted they had no idea who was responsible.

It was past midnight and still pouring when Upali went to check on Ananda and found Sutanuka sitting with him. She looked as tired as he felt but rose immediately to touch his feet. Do you really want a Chandala's blessing, he thought as he touched her head lightly. 'How are you, sister?'

She looked quiet, younger, less confident than before. It was probably just her simple outfit, for when she spoke she sounded the same. 'Thera, what will happen now?'

He took a moment to understand. 'To Devadina? I'm not sure....' What was one more death in so many? He was ashamed of himself. It was everything. 'Nothing for the moment, I think. The law says they must get the permission of Magadh for capital punishment.'

'But the law does not permit what they did in the morning, does it? Public torture is banned now, Devadina said. Yet they did it.'

Upali was a little surprised. 'Yes, that's true actually. Well, we met the Viceroy and the Commandant and the Therii warned them quite substantially. I don't know what else to do – '

'You've done the best you can, lord. Now it is up to the gods.'

He smiled despite himself. 'Lila tried to get the Buddha in, but he took his time.' A flash of lightning lit up the room for a second. Ananda jumped and glared at Upali. Why did he have to talk like that?

'Yes,' said Sutanuka. 'That was surprising – a nun appealing to the heavens.' But her smile was without humour. She was stunningly beautiful, he suddenly realized. Or perhaps it was just that she was the first un-bald woman he was speaking to in quite a while. 'If only he had gone away! I told to him to leave long ago, before all this began, but he kept on about my going with him....'

Upali was again surprised. 'But why? Why did you want him to leave? Did you expect this?'

She looked at him a moment, then away. 'We have no future. Only evil will come of all this.' Of all what? But she got up. 'Sleep well, Ananda.'

Upali was lying wide awake on the veranda outside Ananda's ward, listening to the dripping eaves, when a shadow slipped up to him.

'Devadina! What – How did you – '

'I escaped. One of the guards helped me.'

'Who? Why?'

'They are going to hang me tomorrow.'

'What?'

'How is Sutanuka?' The bandages around his legs were torn. His feet were swollen and black, and oozing pus in places. There were burns on his arms as well.

'Do you want to speak to her?'

'No, not now, I need to get out of the city fast. Can you help me?'

'Yes, of course! You can wear Ananda's robes. But cover your hair. Nobody will question you in the robes of a monk.'

'The soldiers at the gates question everybody at night. We will have to leave by the moat. Can you come with me? Do you swim?'

'The moat? What of the walls in between? And how will you manage with these wounds? I can carry you, I suppose.' Upali was nearly a third shorter than Devadina.

'Let us see. I don't know how to thank you, Thera.'

Ananda was fast asleep. There were others sleeping nearby so Upali first gently touched him on the shoulder, to no response, then a little harder and finally had to shake him.

'Wha – ?'

'Shhh! Listen, Ananda, I'm leaving now – I'll explain later. If I'm not back tomorrow, go to Maheshwar. Here, keep this with you.' He thrust a saffron folder into Ananda's hands. 'It's the story. Guard it with your life! No – I don't mean that, of course. Just look after it. Don't let it get wet.'

'But where are you going?'

'No questions. But don't worry. And don't follow me! You'll infect the burns and your feet will have to be cut off, do you understand?'

'All right, all right. But take care, Master.' Ananda was clearly irritated.

Upali followed Devadina through the gates, down the lane and into the next. The rain had stopped and the air smelt of wet ash and mud. Nothing disturbed Upali's sense of stillness, though his ears were straining for the faintest thump of leather sandals. But even the crickets seemed to have wound up for the night. Devadina however stiffened suddenly, signalled silence and started to run, as lightly as possible. They turned a corner and he whispered, 'Come on, hurry up!' but Upali grabbed his arm.

'Wait!'

They pressed against a wall and waited. The whisper of steps became louder, then a figure rushed stealthily round the corner, wrapped in the same kind of sheet they wore.

'Ananda, why don't you ever listen to me?'

Ananda nearly collapsed in fright, but recovered fast. 'Devadina! Did you escape?' The sculptor just glared at him, though with relief, so he turned back to Upali. 'Let me come with you, Master, please!'

'No, and I really mean it. You will be responsible for us being caught, do you understand? Don't be childish, please!'

Ananda looked stubborn but then Devadina whispered, 'Will you give a message to Sutanuka for me, Ananda?'

'Yes, of course!'

'Tell her that I'll come for her when things are quiet.'

'I'll tell her,' said Ananda and turned back happily.

Upali shook his head and followed Devadina off the main road and into a narrow and muddy passage between two building compounds, then into another, and another, all the routes of servants and sweepers whom good people did not like to set eyes upon. It was amazing how Devadina was able to move through them confidently; he himself lost his sense of direction after a couple of turns. Finally they reached the first city wall, where the sculptor squelched around, stopping and examining the ground many times, before he apparently found whatever he was looking for, and started to shift mud and grass with his hands. Upali joined him with a small rock and after digging about a hand's depth into the ground, they reached a metal lid with a handle attached. Devadina heaved it up and Upali looked down into darkness.

'I'll go first.' Devadina placed his hands on either side of the hole and lowered himself in slowly, till only a bit of his head poked out. 'We'll have to bend and walk. Come, don't be scared. It's very short.'

'I'm not scared,' said Upali indignantly and lowered himself in quickly. His shorter height went all the way in before he hit a soft muddy floor.

'Move ahead slightly,' said Devadina. 'I'll close the lid.'

The moonless night had still been quite bright; without it Upali did feel a little nervous.

'Here, I'll walk ahead,' Devadina's voice echoed slightly as he pushed past Upali. 'Hold my shoulder, all right? You can hold on with both hands if you like, or use one to feel the wall.'

'I'll do that,' said Upali a little confusedly, and put one hand out in the direction of the wall, which turned out to be rocky and slightly moist. But it was good to talk, and not think about the darkness, the stuffiness and the fact that they were underground. He could smell wet earth and vague rot. Devadina started to move ahead slowly and Upali followed, one hand on his shoulder, the other feeling the wall. This was a different Devadina, not the lovelorn sculptor he had known. 'You seem very knowledgeable about all this, Devadina?'

'The guard told me.'

'But why – ' Just then his hand on the wall brushed something very dry, cool and silky smooth which moved away silently. Upali thought he would faint. 'I think I touched a snake! There may be many here!'

'Just hold on to me. We'll be out soon.'

Upali shifted his other hand to Devadina's waist; and felt like a fool. But it was better than feeling snakes.

'How are your burns?'

'Fine. See, I think we've passed under the first wall, we should be under the middle area now. I'm going to walk very slowly because at some point this tunnel steps downward and joins the moat. We have to swim under the second wall.' Devadina suddenly stopped in his tracks; Upali bumped into him. 'Here we are. There are steps ahead. Can you feel the coldness in the air? That's the water below. Come along now, slowly. Feel for the edge of the steps.'

The steps were steep and a little slippery. Upali kept his hand on Devadina's shoulder. About ten steps down, the sculptor stopped. 'Water at the next one. Are you ready? Come on!'

His shoulder dropped out of Upali's grasp into the darkness with a mild splash. 'It's cold!'

Upali stepped forth hurriedly, less with enthusiasm than aversion to being left behind. The water was not so much cold as freezing. He heard his heart thump in his ears and started to shiver.

'Follow me. When we reach the wall, we have to dive down through a tunnel that goes below and connects to the moat outside. You can swim underwater, can't you?'

What a great time to ask. 'I used to, a bit.'

'Okay, come on!'

Upali's teeth were chattering and he was beginning to feel a little useless and grumpy. Devadina didn't seem to need his help, so why had he got him along? But there was no opportunity to ask. He splashed along behind and discovered that the water stank quite strongly. Then he remembered that the city's sewers emptied into the moat, which then drained out into the river. They were swimming in the city sewage.

Devadina stopped suddenly. 'Here's the wall.'

Upali came up next to him and felt the wet rocky surface himself. His teeth were chattering steadily.

'Now we have to dive to the tunnel that runs through the wall. I'll go down and look for it, okay? Wait here and keep paddling. That way you'll stay warm.'

There was a little invisible splash and Devadina was gone. Upali was alone in the dark stillness, surrounded by freezing sewage. He thought he heard a light swishing behind him; he turned quickly but could not make anything out. It must be a snake, a huge poisonous snake, perhaps more than one, like the knot of cobras that he had once come across in a corner of the garden at Kalinga long ago, one of whom had been thicker than his leg. Fresh-water snakes were not poisonous, he told himself sternly, yet he could feel panic rising in him, slowly choking his throat. He struggled to control it and himself. He remembered the tortures undergone by sramanas of the past. The Buddha too. They used to do this kind of thing without a tremor and some still did – spending days and months in the dark all alone, among all kinds of noxious creatures. If they managed to tolerate any kind of horror on the ground, they believed, they would be able to concentrate on issues that were higher, more sublime. But then, they really believed in a higher truth. They believed that this world, however painful, happy or frightening, was all a sham, a temporary existence, a prelude. A nothing. They lived for the future. The Buddha had believed differently. He held that self-torture was itself a form of indulgence. And he believed in this world. So did Upali. One could not ignore this world, one had to try and face it. Because there was nothing higher or lower, this world was all and everything. And right now this world was the knot of poisonous snakes just behind....

But there was a splash and Devadina's shout echoed in the darkness, 'I found it!'

'Is it far?'

'No, very close. I went in and swam all the way to the moat and back. Feel the wall as you go down and you'll feel the opening. Or just follow me, but be careful of my legs. It's not far at all – come on!' The water rippled and he was gone.

Come on, come on, come on – Upali felt as though he had been following Devadina all his life. He took a deep breath and plunged in obediently. The hole was not difficult to find, for there was a dim light emerging at that point. The shadow that was Devadina disappeared inside and Upali followed, his lungs just beginning to complain. The tunnel was comfortably wide, but very long, city walls not being known for slenderness. Twenty feet, he thought first, then forty. His chest started to panic half way through, though he tried to reassure it – relax, we've nearly reached, it's very close. But it was not. Why did they need such thick walls any more, anyway?

This is the end, his lungs were screaming, when the light reappeared. The tunnel was over, he was in warmer water and kicking desperately upwards. But it felt as though a tremendous weight was crushing his chest. A blackness fell over his eyes again, like a shroud, then he crashed through the surface of the water, and started to gulp in air in huge gasps and heaves. It was a little while before he thought of looking around, and yes, he was indeed out and under a sky beautifully filled by thousands of twinkling stars! He wanted to weep with gratitude, to kiss the earth, the sky, everything in sight, even the soldier staring down from the bank just above.

'What is a monk doing swimming in the moat at this time?'

I was busy at my normal time, thought Upali, but the soldier was frowning sternly. 'The thing is….' He looked at the water for ideas, and also for Devadina. But the surface was still.

'Yes?'

'I-I mean, I don't really know. I think I was sleep-walking, soldier. I don't remember how I got here.'

More soldiers ran up. They pulled him out and escorted him to the police compound. Upali steeled himself for more questions, tough questions. But he was just taken to a well at the back to wash up, then to a cell where he was given clothes – the prisoner's uniform of white loin-cloth and white tunic, both dirtied to grey. But they were dry and he was grateful.

He changed and sat down on a pile of straw. Where was Devadina? He must have escaped out of the moat. Or gone back in through the tunnel into the city. Or did he get stuck somewhere? Should Upali ask the soldiers to search the moat? On the other hand, he could not imagine Devadina stuck anywhere. He had handled the whole business in a very competent manner. Really amazingly competent, when you consider the injuries on his feet and legs.

Grey whispers of light appeared at last around the crack of the window, followed shortly by a guard at the door, with a glass of water, a large bajra chapati and Upali's robes folded over his arm. It was mid-morning before the Commandant arrived. Beaming.

'What's up?' asked Upali.

'I hope you are fine, Thera.' The man looked positively jaunty. 'I had to hold you – because of the situation. But you're free to leave now.'

'Why are you smiling so much?'

The Commandant turned the beam down a bit and left, leaving the cell door open, without asking why Upali had been in the moat or saying a word about Devadina. Upali slowly changed his clothes and left. The roads outside were full of mud and wariness, shopkeepers and hawkers opening up their businesses but peering constantly over the shoulders of their equally jumpy customers, everybody trying to act normal but prepared to run at a moment's notice.

Upali was halfway to the convent when he heard thunder. Everybody looked at the clear grey-blue above; the road emptied. But he just moved to the side and waited, though his stomach began to ache, for this was a familiar thunder. It became louder, deafening, and then a great military band, at least a hundred strong, turned the corner of the street and bore down upon him. Behind were elephants in silver-studded leather armour, some thirty pairs, soldiers carrying flags on top and completely ignoring the world below, then infantry-men, armoured, helmeted, weapons at the ready…. Upali felt like throwing stones at the whole lot, as he had seen children do in occupied Tosali. But he couldn't run as fast as they did afterwards.

The convent was agog with news. The first was that the ex-Raja Pururavas was dead.

'He toppled over at dinner last night. Suddenly, just like that. Some mischief is suspected.' Therii Vrinda ran a hand unhappily over her slightly dented pate. It remained uneven, in strong contrast to her smooth face and calm eyes. 'It's nasty, of course, but better than war.'

'Better for us that they finish one another at the top.'

'Yes,' said Upali. 'That's more or less what Kautilya said.'

And the Viceroy had been recalled; he was to leave for Pataliputra immediately. The Commandant was now Acting-Viceroy. A new company of the army had arrived from Kosambi and was patrolling the city, along with the old.

In all this excitement Therii Vrinda almost forgot to react to Upali's return. Almost, but not quite. 'Thera, were you crazy? What if the police discover what you did? You may put the convent and all our work in jeopardy!'

'They already know. I spent the night in prison. The Commandant himself freed me just now – with apologies. Either he does not know that Devadina's gone. Or he does not care.' For once she seemed at a loss for words. 'Anyway, I think we can leave for Maheshwar tomorrow, if Ananda's all right.'

'I'm fine. But Sutanuka's gone to her temple, Master,' said Ananda. 'She was gone when I awoke.'

'Her temple?'

'Yes. To check out whether people there are okay, she said. We should check if she's all right, before we leave.'

'Tell her not to be scared. We can look after her, and her family too if they're in any trouble,' urged the Therii, apparently forgetting how nervous she had been when Sutanuka had first arrived.

Upali didn't remind her. 'We'll tell her.'

They set out in the afternoon, Ananda limping slightly, though it was unclear whether this was because of his injuries or the unfamiliar wooden clogs the nuns had insisted he wear. He towered over Upali as they pushed their way through the market square where Devadina had been tortured just the previous morning, and which had looked a ghost town the previous evening. Now the place bustled with shopkeepers haggling on their verandas, peasants calling out their wares next to big cane baskets of vegetables, and crowds of customers. The cloth lanes were overflowing with cottons and silks; the timber ones were stacked precipitously with all the rich dark Vindhya woods. There were oils safely in their bottles, perfumes, precious stones, arguments, music, animal cries, absolute normalcy. The previous day seemed like a bad dream.

Sutanuka did not seem surprised by their visit. She smiled when Upali explained, 'We just wanted to check up on you before we left. How are things?'

'Thera. It's my fault. It is wrong to break one's commitment like I did. That is why Devadina is being punished.'

'Devadina has escaped. He's left the city.'

'What!'

'Yes. And he asked you to wait for him. He'll come for you.'

'This is madness!' Sutanuka suddenly shuddered. 'I cannot go with him. I will stay here – '

Upali said sharply, ' – And hope for better next time? Sister, you can't lead this life planning for the next!' She was silent, and he sighed exasperatedly. 'You may not agree with my opinion of these matters, Sutanuka. But this faith in rebirth is really a sad thing. It's like admitting that you have some unfinished business in this life, which you don't have the guts to do. It's an acceptance that one's life was futile, that one did nothing beyond the ordinary and the expected. That it was a waste, and that given again it will be wasted again! It's a terrible idea, really. I think one should make the most of each life and each moment of each life.'

'I know.' Her voice was suddenly firm. 'I'm trying to do that. And I think – I do not want to wait for Devadina. Please do not be angry, Thera.'

'What do you mean?'

'I can't explain. But I don't want to marry Devadina.' It was Upali's turn for silence, and for such a long time that she smiled.

'What is it, Thera, am I to be so grateful that someone wants to wed me, that I must agree?'

'No, no, Sutanuka,' he managed. 'But you seemed to want to marry him.' He paused but she just fidgeted with the edge of her shawl. 'Well, that's fine, I suppose. The real issue is not whether you marry Devadina or not, but that you think of your own future. That you don't just accept your life quietly – because there are opportunities today, for change, for freedom. You know, of course, that you can join the convent. They will welcome you.'

'Thank you, Thera. I will think about it. Only – he will come back – '

'Sister, what is wrong? Don't you owe him an explanation?' Upali controlled himself with difficulty. 'Anyway, you can still go to the convent. The nuns will protect you, they will not force you to marry anybody. Or even meet anybody!'

'I will visit the convent, definitely.' She looked at Ananda's wide eyes and back at Upali, and smiled. 'But it's not really a place of protection, is it? More of conviction – which I don't have at the moment. What I have is a position, in this temple. I am respected here – not as much as in earlier times, I know, but still.' They just stared at her and she looked away and nodded at bowing passersby. 'It's not the brave choice, perhaps. Following tradition is easy, it tells you about right and wrong, what to do every step of the way. When you free yourself from tradition, you have to think for yourself. All my life, I've gone to the river every dawn, not just for a bath but to wash away the past, to start afresh. While you people face your past everyday. I'm not that brave, not as yet. So it's better I do what I can, as well as possible.'

'I respect your choice, Sutanuka,' said Upali finally. 'Though I can't say I understand it. Take care of yourself.'

Her eyes filled suddenly; she mumbled, 'You too. And you, Ananda,' and vanished through the gate.

'I'm confused too,' Upali said to Ananda, before the latter could open his mouth.

They returned to the convent to find a cavalcade of five great chariots waiting outside. A row of mounted soldiers stood like equestrian statues on both sides of the gate. One statue unbent enough to order them to the side.

A group came out, really a halo of nuns and army-types around the Commandant. He nodded farewell to the nuns and strode to one of the chariots. The cavalcade took off slowly.

Therii Vrinda explained that the Commandant, now Acting-Viceroy, had come to pay his respects. He had touched the feet of Lila again. The Therii had asked him about Devadina, all he said was that there was no need to worry. He had urged them to approach his office directly with any problem; they were to remember that the well-being of the convent was important for the Magadhe-Raja. It was amazing. But pleasant.

They were not the only ones impressed. Everything returned to normal the very next day, perhaps a little more exuberantly than normal. The Magadhe-Raja had declared a tax holiday for his beloved city of Ujjayani for three months, announced the Acting-Viceroy, along with a generous endowment for the Sangha hospice, another for the Shiva temple, more for new hostelries, parks and fountains. Be benevolent after victory, Kautilya had said.

Merchants and shopkeepers distributed sweets, flowers and incense in the market square. The Magadhe-Raja's edicts – all of them, of remorse for Kalinga, love for Dhamma, against torture, violence, killing, war and festivities – were read out amid cheers and without mentioning the torture, violence and killing of the previous day.

The friends and supporters of the late ex-Raja were absolutely quiet. Perhaps they were scared of their food.

Upali and Ananda left for home, back to their monastery in Maheshwar the next morning at dawn, with a caravan of cloth. The merchant was a local and very relieved with the developments. 'All this anti-foreigner nonsense – these people belong to a village, I say, not a city! Every few years they pop up with the same old ideas, and then, after huge losses of business, they realize that we just cannot prosper alone – so they come to their senses!'

'Not to mention that you cannot defeat Magadh,' said Upali. Rather rudely, thought Ananda.

T he winter forest was dry and crunchy under its browsing herds, the air touched by the heady sweetness of early mango blossoms, the sky filled with hawks and eagles swooping lower than normal and screaming more shrilly – their nesting season was on. But nothing did as much for the ambience as the absence of the old highway gallows and their dead. Somebody had removed them cleanly and completely. The caravan stopped at the inn where the animal doctor had offered them lunch a long time ago he and found him even warmer. He had just visited Sanchi to offer thanks, he said, after his son had been admitted to the new government school in Vidisha. It was managed by the Sanchi monks; his son's future was made.

They walked the last stretch from the highway to the monastery, reaching at nearly noon, a bright dry winter noon, the next day. To be greeted by a surprise. Mohan's shout on seeing them brought out almost all the monks, followed last of all by a limping Devadina. He leaned on a staff, looking tired but happy.

Loka appeared on the veranda. 'Devadina! I told you to rest!'

Devadina smiled at Upali and hobbled off. Ananda charged behind him and Harsha began, 'He showed up just a few hours ago – '

'He escaped.'

'Yes, he told me. Are they looking for him?'

Upali had expected some comment on his own role in the business. 'They didn't seem to be, actually. Anyway, how're Bhima and all?'

Harsha's face became red, his eyes bulged. Loka had told him all about the furnaces, he said; he was shocked, outraged. How could Upali have kept this a secret? It was subterfuge, a breach of monastery discipline, an offence against Sangha Vinaya, a crime against the State, a –

'We haven't had an uposatha since then, Harsha. When we have one, I'll report everything. And Bhima promised to end it.'

'And you believed him? Good god! Anyway, I went to their village yesterday, but nobody would speak to me. They are in mourning – for their Chief – '

'What?'

'Yes. It seems his body was found floating downstream of their river some weeks ago. It looks like suicide, though the villagers won't say anything, as usual. They seem okay though; they were busy with the last funeral rites yesterday. I'd decided to go to Ujjayani today and report the whole thing, but then Devadina arrived at dawn and I thought you would too, soon.'

'I'm glad you waited.'

Harsha combed his pate with nervous fingers. 'At one level, the whole thing is too impossible to believe. I mean, can they really make enough iron for enough swords? And where has the ore come from?'

'Yes, it didn't make much sense.' He didn't mention the dark brown incrustations on the rocks that Bhima had shown him many times on walks through the forest. The mother stone, Bhima called it. Or that Bhima's people, like most of the native people of the eastern coast, were the best iron-smelters in the world. After Magadh. 'Anyway, I'll go right now and check on them.'

'I'll come with you. But eat something first. You look exhausted.'

It was his stomach. But it felt better after he drank one of Loka's potions. He ignored the latter's suggestion of rest and they set out immediately through the dappled light of the afternoon jungle, listening to harsh calls of aquiline courtship, poking the heaps of leaves with their staffs before venturing over them, all in awkward silence till Harsha noticed the lump around Upali's middle.

'What's that? A bandage?'

'My story.'

'What? Why are you still carrying it with you?' Harsha was suddenly angry. 'Do you think somebody's going to steal it or something?'

'No, of course not! I think I'll read it to Bhima,' said Upali on the spur of the moment. 'So that he might appreciate what we're trying to do.'

'But you're not supposed to read it to anybody, right?'

'Is that what Mogalliputta said? He would prefer we talk about miracles, I suppose – or maybe start sacrificing to the Buddha?'

'Upali, be reasonable. The Magadhe-Raja admires you – you have a bright future in Pataliputra! And he liked the story. When he feels things are right, he will definitely ask you to finish it.'

'It's my story – it has nothing to do with him! In any case, he said I could finish it. Who told you that I can't? Mogalliputta?'

'You're just going to create enemies by this attitude, problems for yourself and all of us!'

Upali said nothing and they walked in silence till they reached the rim of Bhima's valley. Then Harsha reached out and gripped his arm.

'Upali, listen. Have you forgotten everything we've struggled to achieve for so long, at this monastery and yours too, back east? You're jeopardizing it all if you defy the Court – and this was the Magadhe-Raja's own personal request! Do you want to see our work come to a halt? When so many opportunities have opened up, so many avenues to prove ourselves – '

'To the Magadhe-Raja. Yes, I suppose he is worth forgetting the Buddha for!'

'Why are you so stubborn?'

'Why are you so scared?'

They found Bhima's village busy in preparations for the tax-collector. Grain was being measured and poured into sacks, pots were being churned out, dried, fired, and stacked up. It was an industrious scene and a peaceful one. The villagers nodded at the monks, and pointed to Bhima who was sitting at the potter's wheel.

'Bhima! How are you? I heard about your Chief – what happened?'

He seemed thinner, there were hollows under his eyes, but he looked a hundred times more cheerful than when they had seen him last, in jail. 'How was your visit to the great city?'

'Interesting. I'll tell you in detail. But I was thrilled when the Magadhe-Raja announced the release of prisoners!'

Bhima nodded and turned back to watch his hands as they brought the final smoothness to the surface of a spinning pot. Upali looked around. Harsha was talking to Kali. He dropped his voice. 'Bhima, the furnaces? Are they – ?'

'They're over. We argued for days, but finally the majority supported me.'

'I'm really glad.' Upali sat back and relaxed. He watched a pair of red-headed cranes picking their way elegantly around the mud banks of the little river, before asking, 'How long had the furnaces been working?'

Bhima paused and thought. 'About a year.'

A year? How many swords did that mean? Where were they? Did the majority support Bhima because the job was done? But Upali did not ask all this. 'And your Chief?'

Bhima set the pot on the ground next to the others and stared at them. 'He killed himself. For us. It was an offering to the gods, because some were scared about the failure of the other earlier one. It was also a demonstration, that death is not something to be scared of.' He looked at Upali. 'And it was a sneer, at me. I have given up, he said to me, I have become like the others, like you.' He shook his head and threw the next lump, his eyes angry but his fingers gentling it into a holed lump, then a tall cylinder, finally a curved jar. 'See, look at these pots. They're all alike! The machine trains your hand fast, and every pot you make is the same, exactly the same. I have made more than sixty pots today, each identical, without character, without heart. We used to make only one or two pots at a time at home, as many as we needed.'

The monastery was aglow with the sunset when they got back, neat fields waiting to be weeded, novices chatting at the well, others in the orchard and dairy, everywhere laughter and light. But Upali's stomach was hurting. He dozed through meditation and then slept as though he hadn't slept in a month, waking up at mid-morning to another potion, only to go back to sleep. He rose in the afternoon to join the others on the fields, weeding, raking, cleaning, feeling the crisp new saffron folder – given by a Pataliputra monk to replace the one he had given the Raja – crackle as he bent. Finally he went back to the dormitory, opened the folder, separated the final chapters from the rough work, placed the former in an old piece of shawl under his waistband and the rest back in the folder and under his pallet.

In the evening, he reported the happenings in Ujjayani, then retired to sleep instead of attending meditation. But when Ananda came to check on him later, he was awake, listening to the crickets in the thatch. Harsha followed.

'Master, are you unwell?'

'Is it your stomach, Upali?'

Upali sat up. 'No, I'm just tired. But it's great that the furnaces are broken, isn't it?'

'But wasn't the atmosphere in their village strange? Is it possible that they are lying?'

'I believe Bhima. But why don't you go and check out that valley, with Loka?'

'Which valley? Do you know how huge the jungle is? And Loka has only the vaguest memory of where he was before he got lost.'

'Yes, it is huge, isn't it?' Upali lay back and stared at the ceiling.

'Have you spoken to Devadina?'

'No.'

'After worrying about him for over a month? Well, anyway, go to sleep.'

Upali knew he was avoiding Devadina. But he couldn't do it indefinitely, especially after Ananda, then Loka, then Mohan, kept on reminding him the next day that the sculptor was asking for him. Finally he went to the small infirmary shack in the evening. Devadina was sitting up on his pallet, his legs and feet covered with some greenish-black ointment, new pink skin shining through here and there. He looked a little feverish. 'Greetings, Upali!'

'Greetings.' When had he started calling Upali Upali? It had been lord at first, then Thera. But all that was a long time ago. 'Tell me, Devadina, was it the Commandant who released you that night?'

Devadina nodded. 'But secretly, without a single soldier knowing. He didn't know which of them might be in the pay of the Viceroy. That's why your presence could have made all the difference, if we were caught.'

Upali just stared around the little room before settling his gaze on a medium-sized yellow gecko on the wall opposite.

'How is Sutanuka?'

'All right,' said Upali to the reptile.

'She has given up on me, I think.' Upali looked up at that; Devadina's face was dark with something, far away. But then he seemed to shake himself and smiled at Upali, a gentle smile, a smile of such benevolence that Upali suddenly felt like weeping. Or slapping him. 'Upali, I owe you more than I can say. But there is something I must tell you.'

Upali suddenly noticed Ananda sitting at the foot of the pallet. 'Aren't you supposed to be out on the fields?'

Ananda disappeared. Upali got up too. 'I have some work too. I'll come later...' but Devadina caught hold of his arm.

'It was me, Upali. I killed that monk. Yes,' for Upali had slumped back to the ground, 'I'm a soldier, Upali, an assassin by specialization. I was sent to Sanchi because there were rumours of an uprising brewing here. Magadh believes in stopping these things before they really start, you know. Anyway, I don't know the details – it's not my business to ask – but the Viceroy himself was involved. He was under watch too, but my charge was the monk Pradyota, the one keeping the links between all the old nobles of Avanti. And attracting new support. I followed him to the Ujjayani temple once, and saw Sutanuka. I met her later, and I knew that she was the only thing I wanted in life. But then I received my orders and I went to his room that night.'

He paused but his audience was silent.

'He was awake, so I said I wanted to speak about Sutanuka. I did, actually, I wanted to talk to anybody who could help – I'd been trying to speak to the Sanchi Thera for days. And I think that if Pradyota had spoken differently, I really might have disobeyed my orders. But he threatened Sutanuka. Her behaviour was evil, he said; he would see that she was punished. He spoke a lot of bullshit about how he had strange powers, nobody could hurt him, even death was impossible till he himself had decided. Anyway, at some point I hit him. He hit me back and then I – well, I had gone prepared.'

His audience sat looking at the floor for a moment, then got up and walked out. And passed Ananda, slumped just outside the door, without either noticing the other.

Upali took a while to recover. Ananda watched him avoiding Devadina for days, getting up and leaving even the meditation hall if his eyes fell on him. His face looked a little grey. And he was not interested in working out the last chapters.

Devadina, on the other hand, seemed more comfortable with each passing day. It was as if a great burden had lifted off his shoulders. He smiled more often, even began to laugh. By the time his legs were fully recovered, he was part of the monastery rhythm. He found a place for himself in the forge where, since he knew something about ironsmithing, he spent the whole day repairing old and broken knives, axes, hammers and plough shares. He also fashioned crude sculpting tools, which he demonstrated to the novices at night – it was almost a new class. They were enthralled by his mastery of the pick and stone, confidently talking away, even laughing, but with his eyes always on his job and his hands able to hit the hammer exactly where he wanted, to get the stone to split exactly where planned. When they tried, tongues hanging outside their mouths in grim concentration, the stone would break in the most unexpected of directions, or simply explode. It was practice and patience, Devadina said. It was magic, the novices knew. Even Ananda was slowly pulled into his orbit; so that he almost forgot the conversation in the infirmary, almost but not quite.

Upali meanwhile wondered how to tell Harsha, and then whether he needed to. An easy friendship seemed to have sprung up between Harsha and Devadina. But the fortnightly uposatha came around and everything came out. Harsha and Loka reported actually finding the valley of the furnaces and also finding nothing there but the remnants of some old sacrifices. Upali wondered where the iron was, but silently; he spoke aloud of Devadina's confession. Nobody looked very surprised.

'Anyway,' he concluded, 'I made a fool of myself. He never actually lied to me. It was I who gave him more credit, more nobility than he deserved. Purely because he was willing to marry a priestess, because he was not bothered about caste or virginity. But then that is Magadh – she has tossed out the old myths, but is ruthless about what she wants. The ends count, not the means.'

'That's what's changed now. Under this Raja, the means also count,' said Harsha.

'Yes,' said Upali. 'Long live this Raja. By the way, don't tell Devadina of the furnaces, okay? If it reaches the authorities – '

'I already did, and he said he won't tell anybody.'

Upali was silent a moment. 'When is he leaving?'

'He wants to stay awhile – he says he feels at peace here. I don't see any problem.'

Nobody seemed to. The local patrol visited the next day, but the usual grimness was missing as they conveyed the greetings of the former Commandant, present Acting-Viceroy of Avanti, to all the monks. And Devadina as well.

Bhima visited once, when Upali was away in the jungle with Loka, but left no message. Upali decided to go see him the next day. Ananda accompanied him. They found him hard at work again, seated in front of the village shrine and repairing a drum, a tall vertical one now lying on its side, made of leather bound on a wood frame and stretched very taut thanks to many thin leather strips fastened around the side. He was undoing the strips and replacing them with new ones lying next to him in a bowl of grease. He looked very pleased to see them.

'This is one of your war drums, isn't it, Bhima?' asked Upali. 'Why – ?'

'It needed repair,' said Bhima and looked at him for a moment. 'That's all.'

Upali nodded. They watched him and the drum for a while. The frame could be seen shining brightly between the transverse strips that he was inserting, for it was made of polished black wood coloured vividly with dabs of yellow and sapphire blue. Before a battle, Upali knew, it would be further adorned with bright peacock plumes and various flowers.

'Bhima, I have to tell you,' he began after a while, 'I'm a Chandala. I didn't know it myself – I was adopted by the monks when a child. But we met an old monk recently who knew me as a child; he told me.'

Bhima yanked a leather strip hard. It expanded to nearly double its length. 'Is it so bad?'

Perhaps only better than being a Bhuirya. 'It's considered so by people in these parts, in Magadh too. The lowest. I don't know why. I think they were forest-folk once – but now it seems a general term of abuse by the so-called upper castes. Like Naga earlier. I'm not sure. I don't know what their history is…' Upali's voice faltered and stopped. You know everybody's history but that of your own people. 'I must find out – I'll ask them on the cremation-ground outside Brghukacha, or outside Ujjayani….'

'Why does it matter?' asked Ananda suddenly.

It was Bhima who answered as he knotted the strand fluidly. 'Origin is everything, Ananda. Everything. If you don't know who you are, how will you understand your destiny?'

'You make your own destiny nowadays,' answered Ananda belligerently. 'A peasant we met from near Vidisha has become an animal doctor, his son will become something else. The Mauryas were shudras but look at them now – Chandragupta made his own future!' He turned to Upali. 'And you used to say that, from the stories people tell, we must have all come from the forests at some time or the other, the Mauryas, the Buddha, me, Bhima, you, so our origin is the same. It's just that some remember and some have forgotten.'

'Everything in the forest is not the same,' said Bhima slowly. 'Nothing is the same. Magadh has this way of demeaning the forests – using them, plundering them, destroying them, and ignoring the richness, the layers, the differences, the thousands of thousands of differences.'

'They are better forgotten! The Buddha said that we are all rivers who together make up the ocean – the rivers have different origins, but the ocean forgets them. Like those different waterfalls there, all coming down to your river!'

Bhima just shrugged, a little sadly. 'Sometimes I'm not sure, to be honest. I used to never doubt these things earlier. But now I've become confused, living here, away from our roots….'

'Or perhaps you've changed,' suggested Upali gently.

'That's what my Chief said.' He stared at the ridge of a distant hill, where elephants stood outlined against the evening sun. 'And he was right in a way, I think. I have changed. If I were to stay here I'd probably have no option but to join your Sangha.'

He smiled again. But all Upali heard was, *if* I were to stay here.

'It's a band of misfits, isn't it?' added Bhima. 'People who have no origin, and no destiny, but their own.'

'That's really true!' beamed Ananda.

Upali recovered a little, but gloomily. 'That's how it was. Now it seems to have an imperial destiny. The Magadhe-Raja has adopted us, and his aims seem to have become ours.'

'Oop-oop-oop-oop!'

Bhima looked up with a smile. At a big yellow-haired monkey sitting on a mango tree not far away. It was staring straight back, and whooping away. 'He's been coming every day for a month. He's a macaque – there was one like him back home, who I had trained to bring down beehives after I'd smoked the the bees out. Fruits too. He would carry great jackfruit all the way down carefully, against his chest. His tail was a little smaller than this chap's, that's all.' He glanced at Upali. 'I think it's a sign.'

This monkey had a tail like a lion. He stopped whooping and began to scratch his black-topped head, staring at the others now. Bhima went into his hut and returned with a banana. Ananda took it from him and offered it to the visitor, who looked bored.

Bhima came back and sat down. 'The Chief said my suggestion of leaving quietly – you know, moving silently through the forests – into the forests – was cowardice.'

That was probably the best thing about it. 'Your people are not cowards, Bhima. You have fought many times, using Magadh's methods, and in that fight, the biggest brute wins.' Upali paused a moment before asking, 'Through the forests – homewards?'

Bhima stared at the macaque. 'Perhaps.'

'What do the others feel? Kali?'

'That we won't reach.'

'She's probably right.' Upali pointed and the shadow of his hand was an emphasis. 'Your home is there, towards the morning sun. More than eight hundred miles away. Walking that means months, years.'

'But we still might reach.'

'And there are great obstacles in between. Mountains, rivers, wild beasts, disease. Jungle-folk. Magadh. You're really likely not to. It's nearly impossible!'

'We can try. Even if we fail, we'll reach somewhere far away, where we can live in peace. Magadh is the cities and the roads. Not the jungle. The jungle is vast, there's more than enough space for us.'

Upali was silent.

'And rich. Great herds of game, streams thick with fish, thickets of fruit, nuts, herbs. The jungle will feed us. And hide us, completely.'

'Yes….' But for how long? With Magadh's insatiable appetite for farmland? At some time or the other, Bhima or his children would have to come to terms with the ravenous plough.

He felt Bhima's hand on his arm. 'Don't worry, Upali.'

The monkey was waving its tail irritably now. Then it gave up, climbed down to Ananda for the banana, and made off through the trees, revealing a startlingly red bottom.

Ananda returned triumphant. Upali changed the subject.

'Things are not very good at the monastery,' he said and then corrected himself. 'No, actually things are very good. I'm the only problem. My story. One of the new orders was to stop my story. I refused. Harsha is really upset.'

'Why are you writing the story?'

Upali stared at him for a moment. 'Well – I mean….'

'Especially when you say that origin does not matter?'

Bhima's drum looked small as compared to those in his memory. 'It was after the war. My life seemed over. Dhamma seemed a joke. But I began to think of the Buddha – he had seen terrible things too. The experience didn't shatter him. He became stronger, in fact. Strong enough to think of changing the world, sane enough to realize that he couldn't. But he tried – and managed to push away some of the fog. I suppose I thought I could too.'

Bhima was silent. Upali shook his head. 'You know, Bhima, you're only the second person to ask. The first was a foreigner too, a yellow-haired man from the west. Nobody in the Sangha is interested. They're almost scared, and not only because of the Magadhe-Raja. They're scared of the Buddha, of his aims and his failure to achieve them. Because they're hoping to be successful. The legend will make the Buddha successful too. By changing his aims, making them spiritual – and commonplace.'

They waited for Bhima to finish his drum. He placed it upright to dry and then accompanied them through the fields to the edge of the forest, and raised a silent hand in farewell. His face was stern but he blinked his eyes hard once and Upali felt his heart sink, but Ananda was with them, so he merely raised a hand too. He turned to look back after a few steps, but the forest was already in the way; he couldn't see Bhima.

They walked half the way in silence, Upali's stomach aching again, then saw smoke rising in the distance. It was early for forest fires. Was somebody burning something? When they climbed the next hill, they realized it was the monastery. But when they reached, at a run and panting, the fire was out. Just one vihara was affected – the dormitory – and just one side of it. Harsha and Devadina were staring at the blackened thatch, buckets in their hands.

'I don't know how it began,' said Harsha. 'We tried to get everything out.' There was a heap of bedclothes on the ground in the mud, a wooden shelf, mats, clay tumblers.

'Did you get my pallet?' asked Upali.

'No, that got burnt, I'm afraid.'

'Well, I'm glad that I'm carrying my story with me,' said Upali quietly. 'My pallet contained only the rough work.'

Harsha stared at him in silence, eyes bulging. Devadina however beamed. 'That's good, Thera!'

'Harsha, how could you?' Upali suddenly shouted, to Ananda's surprise; after all, this was not the first time a shack had gone up in flames, a stray spark was all that was needed sometimes in summer. But Upali was pale with rage. 'How low are you going to stoop? And you're taking the help of this – this – !'

'Upali, stop talking rubbish – ' began Harsha.

But Upali marched away to the fields, where he began weeding furiously, finishing the entire remaining half of the last field before Ananda and Loka came to call him for meditation. He refused to come, and almost drove Loka away when he kept on saying that it would make him feel better. By then his stomach was just a wave of pain. He tried pressing it in, breathing very slowly, holding his breath, even chanting Sanchi's meditation mantra, but it was a long time and he was completely exhausted by the time it subsided, unable to even turn and acknowledge Ananda who had come back after meditation and settled down quietly some distance behind. They watched the moon as it crept up over the rim of the next valley; they listened to the cacophony of the night, the frogs, crickets and lizards close at hand, the wild dogs howling in their unpleasant high-pitched way somewhere in the distance, indeterminate others hunting, eating, fleeing, courting. An owl screeched just above their heads, making both jump. Upali watched it swoop after something and jumped again to find a large shadow right next to him.

'Upali?' It was Devadina. He sat down without waiting to be asked. 'I'm leaving tomorrow, Upali. I just want to say I'm sorry for deceiving you. I was just doing my job.'

Which only made it worse. But Upali couldn't help glancing at him, straight into his gaze – honest, he had once called it – and he saw that it was still honest. He almost shuddered. But at least he was leaving.

'Harsha is a good man, Upali. Like you. Please try to understand his problems.'

He had, thought Upali; that was the problem. He stared at the moon weaving its way up through streamers of purple clouds, and waited for Devadina to go away. But he seemed content to admire the sky too, so Upali finally got up and walked back, to find the others laying mats and blankets under the peepal tree. Devadina followed him and went back to a new mortar and pestle he was fashioning for Loka. Harsha and Loka were cleaning out the last of the burnt mess from the dormitory.

'I'll burn it all tomorrow, along with that heap of weeds,' said Loka. 'We can scatter the ash over the fields.'

'Keep some buckets of water handy,' said Devadina. 'I'll help if you do it early. I must leave before noon.'

'What of the case against you – of Pradyota's murder?' asked Harsha.

'I believe the Viceroy is suspected now,' Devadina polished his mortar serenely. 'Pradyota was not a traitor; he was going to expose the plot – so the Viceroy must have had him killed.'

Upali couldn't help himself. 'What a pity, Devadina! After all you've done for Magadh, you won't even get credit – at least not publicly!'

'That's life,' said Devadina, calmer than ever. 'Sometimes one does things, even really worthwhile things, which are not credited to you.'

Upali collected a mat and curled up with his back to everybody else.

Meditation was just over the next morning when Mohan came panting in. He had stayed overnight at one of the villages, to help them prepare a petition for a reduction in the coming quarter's tax, a portion of the harvest having disappeared into some elephants who had passed by the previous month.

'What's wrong?' Loka was stoking a big fire near the track, far from any shack. He left it to Devadina and ran to the pot on the kitchen veranda, to get a tumblerful for the panter.

'What's up?' called Upali from the shade of the peepal where he and his students were arranging themselves for the morning class.

Mohan talked through gulps of water. 'Bhima's village – they've disappeared. I passed by there just now and saw it myself. They're gone, completely. Not a soul….'

'What do you mean?' Harsha had come out of the kitchen.

'They're not there. Nobody. The huts are empty. Completely. Could they be arrested, or something – ?'

'Or on the war path?' breathed Harsha in a low voice. He turned to Upali. 'Come on, we must stop them!'

'Wait,' said Upali but Harsha was already running. 'Wait, listen!'

But Harsha did not stop; there was no option but to follow. Mohan and Loka looked at one another and followed too, the novices were right behind. All of them sprinted through the forest madly, bumping into trees, pushing through bushes, scraping, tripping, falling. Ananda flew through the air after his foot stubbed a root, Santosh waited for him while the others crashed on. Upali came to within grabbing distance of Harsha more than a few times, but he had changed his mind and decided not to stop him after all.

At last they reached the little jewel-like bowl of a valley. Ananda paused to catch his breath at the top. The waterfalls had shrunk, two had vanished. Below him, the saffron-clad troop was still in motion, Harsha still comfortably in the lead, his tubby legs making short jumps that seemed to dither every time between carrying him ahead or to the ground. The village looked as usual, the thatched huts grouped quietly around the central court with its little shrine. Except that there was no plume of smoke. And no idols in their shrine. No person either.

'Where could they have gone?' panted Loka.

'Do you think they have attacked somebody? The next village?' Harsha spoke in heaves. 'I knew something strange was up! We must go and report this immediately. My god, there might be a blood bath!'

'Wait,' said Upali again but again Harsha had turned away to start climbing back up the hill. 'Harsha, wait! They have not gone to war. They have just left.'

Harsha stopped. 'Left? What do you mean?'

'Just left. Gone into the jungle. Peacefully.'

'Gone into the jungle?'

'Yes. But they are not going to fight, they just had to go back – '

'Back? They're trying to get back? You can't be serious!'

'Not back – that's a dream. They've gone away, that's all. They'll probably settle down when they get far enough away.'

'Upali, don't be silly! Where did you get this absolutely ridiculous notion?'

'From Bhima. It was his idea. As an option to all these continuous revolts, and killings and madness. I think it makes sense.'

'But – but Upali – is that what you told him – that it made sense? Are you mad? Kalinga is hundreds of miles away! They can die a hundred times before they reach there! In fact, they'll be caught immediately. And then it's back to jail – '

Upali's hand was on his stomach. 'They need not be caught. They just have to reach deep enough into the jungle. It won't be easy of course, but they're jungle-folk. See, Harsha. It's not really about reaching Kalinga – it's about being free. I'm not saying it's the best option – the best is probably to settle down here and send their children to the monastery school – but it's better than making swords! They have a good chance of making a lot of distance, if the patrols don't go after them immediately....'

'You're not proposing that we keep quiet about this?'

'Why not? They aren't going to hurt anybody – there's nothing to worry about. And who will know that we knew?'

'Devadina,' said Ananda.

The others jumped, as if an invisible body had spoken.

'Just don't tell anybody, Harsha,' said Upali quietly. 'At least for a day or two. Let's tell Devadina that we found them, doing something – anything – in the forest. That way they'll get some time and they might be safe. They're just going away – '

'Upali, they made iron, they probably have weapons with them! What if they attack a village? Do you forget how they tried to kill that man? Or did they tell you about that plan beforehand as well? I can't keep quiet. I have a responsibility! You're different – you just do whatever you want – always! It doesn't matter to you whether we survive, whether our work survives....'

And so on. They reached the monastery to find Devadina seated near Loka's fire. Ananda saw him see them and get up; he saw Harsha see him; he saw Harsha's expression. Fear, helplessness, panic. Harsha turned to Upali for a moment, there was apology too.

'Well, I'm off,' said Devadina. 'I want to reach Ujjayani by nightfall. What happened? Did you find them?'

'Harsha, don't!' whispered Upali. He caught hold of Harsha's arm, but Harsha shook him off and walked determinedly past Loka's fire towards the sculptor.

'It's not worth it, Upali. I can't take this as well.'

'Just wait a moment, will you – my stomach is hurting!'

'Tell Loka! I'm sorry, Upali, but I can't wait!'

Devadina looked at the two of them, at the tense group around and in between. His face remained expressionless. 'What's up?'

Everybody scattered themselves awkwardly back to their work. Loka squatted next to his fire and began to stoke it though it didn't really need any attention; it was burning well. Upali stopped next to him and stared at it.

'Devadina – ' began Harsha.

Upali's face was stiff and suddenly a little yellow, Ananda noticed, perhaps from the flames. 'Listen, Harsha. You were right, it isn't worth it.' He reached underneath his shawl, pulled out the cloth bundle tucked into his dhoti, and waved it. 'Look! I've decided – the story's over. You'll feel better, won't you?'

Harsha turned then. 'What do you mean?'

Ananda realized what Upali meant and jumped up, but Upali was next to the fire and it needed only a flick of the most ungainly of wrists to send the bundle flying in.

'Master!'

A fountain of sparks flew out, sending Loka jerking backwards. The cloth cover looked stubborn for a moment, then melted off. The parched palm sheets vanished without a murmur, Ananda's beautiful writing with them, the flames roaring up a little to check whether there was any more.

Upali turned to Devadina, who was staring at him open-mouthed. 'Good bye, Devadina. And congratulations. Perhaps you can get credit for this.'

Devadina remained frozen.

'Good bye, I said! Go – now!'

Devadina looked at the others but they were all staring at the fire. Finally he turned and walked off down the track into the trees.

Only Upali watched him go. Ananda was kneeling at the flames, trying to dig into them with a stick, shouting something about water and then mud, while his tears made little nearly-invisible splutters in the blaze and Loka's hand on his shoulder stopped him from joining them. Harsha was standing behind, watching them like a statue. Upali waited till Devadina vanished, then sat down slowly in the dust and crunched his knees up against his chest.

'My stomach is on fire, I think, Ananda.' He keeled over completely, into silence.

Glossary

sangha: tribe; tribe-based republic

Sangha: the organization created by the Buddha

Shakyas, Licchavis, Koliyas, Mallas, Videhas: tribe-based republics in the Buddha's time

Kalingas: tribe-based republic in Ashoka's time, conquered by him about 260 BCE

Kosala, Magadha, Avanti: territorial kingdoms in the Buddha's time

Arya: 'Noble', term of self-identity for communities who practised Vedic rites in the Buddha's time

Naga: an Arya term for forest-dwellers

Chandala, Pukusa, Nisada: originally perhaps tribes, later on low status or outcaste groups according to self-identified Aryas

Maurya: the dynasty that ruled almost the whole Indian sub-continent 321-185 BCE; Chandragupta Maurya was its founder, Ashoka the third king

Jina, Ajivika, Lokayat, Sankya: philosophical sects

dharma: the inherent order of the world; an individual's sacred duty in that order

Dhamma: dharma in the commoner's language; the Sangha's description of the Buddha's teachings

raja: title of each male member of the tribal republics; later on it came to mean king

varna: 4 tier system of caste hierarchy

jati: caste or endogamous group; a jati's varna position was often contested

brahmins kshatriyas, vaishyas, shudras: priests, warriors, farmers/

artisans/traders, servants/slaves; the 4 tiers of the varna system
dvija: 'twice-born', a person who has undergone the thread
  ceremony, traditionally reserved for male members of the
  brahmin, kshatriya and vaishya varnas.

sramana: ascetic

yajna: sacrifice

yajman: patron of the yajna

stupa, chaitya, dagaba: terms for the tumuli that became the signature
  shrine of Buddhism

ghat: step, including the steps built on the banks of a river for
  bathing, cremations, etc

puskara: tank or lake, especially one attached to a temple

thera, therii: monk and nun of the Sangha

bhiksu: beggar; the early mendicant members of the Sangha

uposatha: fortnightly confessional for the members of the Sangha

Devanampiya Piyadassi: Emperor Ashoka's titles, the 'Beloved of
  the Gods' and 'Of Gracious Mien'